D0722312

Murder Most Delectable

THE

Murder Most Delectable

Savory Tales of Culinary Crimes

Edited by Martin H. Greenberg

Cumberland House
Nashville, Tennessee

Copyright © 2000 by Tekno Books

Published by Cumberland House Publishing, Inc., 431 Harding Industrial Drive, Nashville, Tennessee 37211

Cover design by Gore Studio, Inc.
Page design by Mike Towle

Library of Congress Cataloging-in-Publication Data
Murder most delectable : savory tales of culinary crimes / edited by Martin H. Greenberg.
    p. cm.
    Includes a selection of recipes for dishes or ingredients mentioned in individual stories.
    ISBN 1-58182-119-0 (alk. paper)
    1. Detective and mystery stories, American. 2. Detective and mystery stories, English. 3. Cookery–Fiction. 4 Food–Fiction. 5. Cookery. I. Greenberg, Martin Harry.

    PS374.D4 M855 2000
    813'.087208355–dc21

                                                                00-031800

Printed in the United States of America
1 2 3 4 5 6 7 8 9 — 05 04 03 02 01 00

Contents

Introduction   vii
John Helfers

The Last Bottle in the World   1
Stanley Ellin

Takeout   23
Joyce Christmas

The Case of the Shaggy Caps   39
Ruth Rendell

The Cassoulet   67
Walter Satterthwait

Tea for Two   81
M. D. Lake

The Second-Oldest Profession   91
Linda Grant

Connoisseur   105
Bill Pronzini

Gored   115
Bill Crider

Day for a Picnic   131
Edward D. Hoch

Guardian Angel   143
Caroline Benton

The Main Event   151
Peter Crowther

The Deadly Egg   163
Janwillem van de Wetering

Dead and Breakfast   181
Barbara Collins

Recipe for a Happy Marriage   197
Nedra Tyre

Death Cup   215
Joyce Carol Oates

Poison Peach   245
Gillian Linscott

Of Course You Know that Chocolate Is a Vegetable   265
Barbara D'Amato

Poison à la Carte   277
Rex Stout

Authors' Biographies   333

Copyrights and Permissions   339

Introduction

"Let the stoics say what they please, we do not eat for the good of living, but because the meat is savory and the appetite is keen."

Ralph Waldo Emerson

"When the wine goes in, the murder comes out."

The Talmud

Of all the various kinds of romance throughout the world, there is one that cultures and peoples from America to Europe to Asia indulge in freely and, for the most part, without remorse. Ever since the first man speared a chunk of mammoth or bison and held it over a roaring fire, we have indulged in our passion for food.

And what a grand love affair it is, for food is the only thing that can delight all five of our senses at once. The sound of a porterhouse steak as it sears on the grill . . . the sight of a golden brown turkey roasting in the oven . . . the cool feel of watermelon on a hot day . . . the smell of an apple pie as it bakes to perfection . . . I'm sorry, I think I lost my train of thought for a moment.

When all is said and done, the final, most glorious sense is sated with that first delectable bite . . . taste. For no matter how beautifully it is prepared or how mouthwatering it smells, that first bite will reveal if the chef has created a triumph or a tragedy. From a simple backyard barbecue to the most elegant seven-course meal, there are as many ways to prepare a meal as there are people on this planet. Each person has his or her own favorite dish and a method for preparing it that they consider to be the best, for when it all comes down to it, the ideal meal is truly a matter of personal taste.

Of course, some peoples' appetite for food is exceeded only by their appetite for crime. As our demand for most flavorful and intricate dishes has increased, so has the opportunity for these evil epicureans to combine their talent for wickedness and their love for good food in one fell swoop to lay another low, the device for the crime nothing more than a well-cooked meal. With that in mind, we've collected these eighteen stories of culinary crimes and deaths by dinner party. Joyce Carol Oates explores a relationship between two brothers that leaves a sour taste in one's mouth. Peter Crowther invites us to a gourmet dinner party where murder is a crucial ingredient in every course. Gillian Linscott visits a nineteenth-century manor house where the fruit flies aren't the only pests exterminated in the orchard. And Rex Stout's incomparable gourmand and sleuth, Nero Wolfe, turns his talents to his own dining club, where one member gives up his membership permanently after a meal prepared by Wolfe's own private chef.

Make sure all your hunger pangs have been quieted before turning the page, for even though many of these crimes involve food, the meals described are often worth dying for. As an extra bonus, we've added recipes for many of the dishes or ingredients mentioned here, with special thanks going to Denise Little for providing the majority of these recipes. So tuck in your napkin, pick up your knife and fork, and dive into this eighteen-course feast of *Murder Most Delectable.*

Murder Most Delectable

The Last Bottle in the World

Stanley Ellin

It was a bad moment. The café on the rue de Rivoli near the Meurice had looked tempting. I had taken a chair at one of its sidewalk tables, and then, glancing casually across at the next table, had found myself staring into the eyes of a young woman who was looking at me with startled recognition. It was Madame Sophia Kassoulas. Suddenly, the past towered over me like a monstrous genie released from a bottle. The shock was so great that I could actually feel the blood draining from my face.

Madame Kassoulas was instantly at my side.

"Monsieur Drummond, what is it? You look so ill. Is there anything I can do?"

"No, no. A drink, that's all. Cognac, please."

She ordered me one, then sat down to solicitously undo the buttons of my jacket. "Oh, you men. The way you dress in this summer heat."

This might have been pleasant under other conditions, but I realized with embarrassment that the picture we offered the other patrons of the café must certainly be that of a pitiful, white-haired old grandpa being attended to by his softhearted granddaughter.

1

"Madame, I assure you—"

She pressed a finger firmly against my lips. "Please. Not another word until you've had your cognac and feel like yourself again. Not one little word."

I yielded the point. Besides, turnabout was fair play. During that nightmarish scene six months before when we were last in each other's company, she had been the one to show weakness and I had been the one to apply the restoratives. Meeting me now, the woman must have been as hard hit by cruel memory as I was. I had to admire her for bearing up so well under the blow.

My cognac was brought to me, and even *in extremis*, so to speak, I automatically held it up to the sunlight to see its color. Madame Kassoulas's lips quirked in a faint smile.

"Dear Monsieur Drummond," she murmured. "Always the connoisseur."

Which, indeed, I was. And which, I saw on grim reflection, was how the whole thing had started on a sunny Parisian day like this the year before. . . .

THAT WAS THE DAY a man named Max de Marechal sought me out in the offices of my company, Broulet and Drummond, wine merchants, on the rue de Berri. I vaguely knew of de Marechal as the editor of a glossy little magazine, *La Cave*, published solely for the enlightenment of wine connoisseurs. Not a trade publication, but a sort of house organ for *La Société de la Cave*, a select little circle of amateur wine fanciers. Since I generally approved of the magazine's judgments, I was pleased to meet its editor.

Face to face with him, however, I found myself disliking him intensely. In his middle forties, he was one of those dapper, florid types who resemble superannuated leading men. And there was a feverish volatility about him which put me on edge. I tend to be low-geared and phlegmatic myself. People who are always bouncing about on top of their emotions like a Ping-Pong ball on a jet of water make me acutely uncomfortable.

The purpose of his visit, he said, was to obtain an interview from me. In preparation for a series of articles to be run in his magazine, he was asking various authorities on wine to express their opinions about the greatest vintage they had ever sampled. This way, perhaps, a consensus could be made and placed on record. If—

"If," I cut in, "you ever get agreement on the greatest vintage. Ask a dozen experts about it and you'll get a dozen different opinions."

"It did look like that at the start. By now, however, I have found some small agreement on the supremacy of two vintages."

"Which two?"

"Both are Burgundies. One is the Richebourg 1923. The other is the Romanée-Conti 1934. And both, of course, indisputably rank among the noblest wines."

"Indisputably."

"Would one of these be your own choice as the vintage without peer?"

"I refuse to make any choice, Monsieur de Marechal. When it comes to wines like these, comparisons are not merely odious, they are impossible."

"Then you do not believe any one vintage stands by itself beyond comparison?"

"No, it's possible there is one. I've never tasted it, but the descriptions written of it praise it without restraint. A Burgundy, of course, from an estate which never again produced anything like it. A very small estate. Have you any idea which vintage I'm referring to?"

"I believe I do." De Marechal's eyes gleamed with fervor. "The glorious Nuits Saint-Oen 1929. Am I right?"

"You are."

He shrugged helplessly "But what good is knowing about it when I've never yet met anyone who has actually tasted it? I want my series of articles to be backed by living authorities. Those I've questioned all know about this legendary Saint-Oen, but not one has even seen a bottle of it. What a disaster when all that remains of such a vintage—possibly the greatest of all—should only be a legend. If there were only one wretched bottle left on the face of the earth—"

"Why are you so sure there isn't?" I said.

"Why?" De Marechal gave me a pitying smile. "Because, my dear Drummond, there can't be. I was at the Saint-Oen estate myself not long ago. The *vigneron*'s records there attest that only forty dozen cases of the 1929 were produced altogether. Consider. A scant forty dozen cases spread over all the years from then to now, and with thousands of connoisseurs thirsting for them. I assure you, the last bottle was emptied a generation ago."

I had not intended to come off with it, but that superior smile of his got under my skin.

"I'm afraid your calculations are a bit off, my dear de Marechal." It was going to be a pleasure setting him back on his heels. "You see, a bottle of Nuits Saint-Oen 1929 is, at this very moment, resting in my company's cellars."

The revelation jarred him as hard as I thought it would. His jaw fell. He gaped at me in speechless wonderment. Then his face darkened with suspicion.

"You're joking," he said. "You must be. You just told me you've never tasted the vintage. Now you tell me—"

"Only the truth. After my partner's death last year I found the bottle among his private stock."

"And you haven't been tempted to open it?"

"I resist the temptation. The wine is dangerously old. It would be extremely painful to open it and find it has already died."

"Ah, no!" De Marechal clapped a hand to his brow. "You're an American, monsieur, that's your trouble. Only an American could talk this way, someone who's inherited the obscene Puritan pleasure in self-denial. And for the last existing bottle of Nuits Saint-Oen 1929 to have such an owner! It won't do. It absolutely will not do. Monsieur Drummond, we must come to terms. What price do you ask for this Saint-Oen?"

"None. It is not for sale."

"It must be for sale!" de Marechal said explosively. With an effort he got himself under control. "Look, I'll be frank with you. I am not a rich man. You could get at least a thousand francs—possibly as much as two thousand—for that bottle of wine, and I'm in no position to lay out that kind of money. But I am close to someone who can meet any terms you set. Monsieur Kyros Kassoulas. Perhaps you know of him?"

Since Kyros Kassoulas was one of the richest men on the Continent, someone other magnates approached with their hats off, it would be hard not to know of him despite his well-publicized efforts to live in close seclusion.

"Of course," I said.

"And do you know of the one great interest in his life?"

"I can't say I do. According to the newspapers, he seems to be quite the man of mystery."

"A phrase concocted by journalists to describe anyone of such wealth who chooses to be reticent about his private affairs. Not that there is anything scandalous about them. You see, Monsieur Kassoulas is a fanatic connoisseur of wines." De Marechal gave me a meaningful wink. "That's how I interested him in founding our *Société de la Cave* and in establishing its magazine."

"And in making you its editor."

"So he did," said de Marechal calmly. "Naturally, I'm grateful to him for that. He, in turn, is grateful to me for giving him sound instruction on the great vintages. Strictly between us, he was a sad case when I first met him. A man without any appetite for vice, without any capacity to enjoy literature or music or art, he was being driven to distraction by the emptiness of his life. I filled that emptiness the day I pointed out to him that he must cultivate his extraordinarily true palate for fine wine. The exploration of the worthier vintages since then has been for him a journey through a wonderland. By now, as I have said, he is a fanatic connoisseur. He would know without being told that your bottle of Nuits Saint-Oen 1929 is to other wines what the Mona Lisa is to other paintings. Do you see what that means to you in a business way? He's a tough man to bargain with, but in the end he'll pay two thousand francs for that bottle. You have my word on it."

I shook my head. "I can only repeat, Monsieur de Marechal, the wine is not for sale. There is no price on it."

"And I insist you set a price on it!"

That was too much.

"All right," I said, "then the price is one hundred thousand francs. And without any guarantee the wine isn't dead. One hundred thousand francs exactly."

"Ah," de Marechal said furiously, "so you really don't intend to sell it! But to play dog in the manger—!"

Suddenly, he went rigid. His features contorted, his hands clutched convulsively at his chest. As crimson with passion as his face had been the moment before, it was now ghastly pale and bloodless. He lowered himself heavily into a chair.

"My heart," he gasped in agonized explanation. "It's all right. I have pills—"

The pill he slipped under his tongue was nitroglycerine, I was sure. I had once seen my late partner Broulet undergo a seizure like this.

"I'll call a doctor," I said, but when I went to the phone de Marechal made a violent gesture of protest.

"No, don't bother. I'm used to this. It's an old story with me."

He was, in fact, looking better now.

"If it's an old story you should know better," I told him. "For a man with a heart condition you allow yourself to become much too emotional."

"Do I? And how would you feel, my friend, if you saw a legendary vintage suddenly appear before you and then found it remained just out of reach? No, forgive me for that. It's your privilege not to sell your goods if you don't choose to."

"It is."

"But one small favor. Would you, at least, allow me to see the bottle of Saint-Oen? I'm not questioning its existence. It's only that the pleasure of viewing it, of holding it in my hands—"

It was a small enough favor to grant him. The cellars of Broulet and Drummond were near the Halles au Vin, a short trip by car from the office. There I conducted him through the cool, stony labyrinth bordering the Seine, led him to the Nuits Saint-Oen racks where, apart from all the lesser vintages of later years, the one remaining bottle of 1929 rested in solitary grandeur. I carefully took it down and handed it to de Marechal, who received it with reverence.

He examined the label with an expert eye, delicately ran a fingertip over the cork. "The cork is in good condition."

"What of it? That can't save the wine if its time has already come."

"Naturally. But it's an encouraging sign." He held the bottle up to peer through it. "And there seems to be only a normal sediment. Bear in mind, Monsieur Drummond, that some great Burgundies have lived for fifty years. Some even longer."

He surrendered the bottle to me with reluctance. His eyes remained fixed on it so intensely as I replaced it in the rack that he looked like a man under hypnosis. I had to nudge him out of the spell before I could lead him upstairs to the sunlit outer world.

We parted there.

"I'll keep in touch with you," he said as we shook hands. "Perhaps we can get together for lunch later this week."

"I'm sorry," I said without regret, "but later this week I'm leaving for New York to look in on my office there."

"Too bad. But of course you'll let me know as soon as you return to Paris."

"Of course," I lied.

HOWEVER, THERE WAS NO putting off Max de Marechal now that he had that vision of the Nuits Saint-Oen 1929 before his eyes. He must have bribed one of the help in my Paris office to tell him when I was back from the States, because no sooner was I again at my desk on the rue de Berri than he was on the phone. He greeted me with fervor. What luck he had timed his call so perfectly! My luck, as well as his. Why? Because *La Société de la Cave* was to have a dinner the coming weekend, a positive orgy of wine sampling, and its presiding officer, Kyros Kassoulas himself, had requested my presence at it!

My first impulse was to refuse the invitation. For one thing, I knew its motive. Kassoulas had been told about the Nuits Saint-Oen 1929 and wanted to get me where he could personally bargain for it without losing face. For another thing, these wine-tasting sessions held by various societies of connoisseurs were not for me. Sampling a rare and excellent vintage is certainly among life's most rewarding experiences, but, for some reason I could never fathom, doing it in the company of one's fellow *aficionados* seems to bring out all the fakery hidden away in the soul of even the most honest citizen. And to sit there, watching ordinarily sensible men vie with each other in their portrayals of ecstasy over a glass of wine, rolling their eyes, flaring their nostrils, straining to find the most incongruous adjectives with which to describe it, has always been a trial to me.

Weighed against all this was simple curiosity. Kyros Kassoulas was a remote and awesome figure, and here I was being handed the chance to actually meet him. In the end, curiosity won. I attended the dinner. I met Kassoulas there and I quickly realized, with gratification, that we were striking it off perfectly.

It was easy to understand why. As de Marechal had put it, Kyros Kassoulas was a fanatic on wines, a man with a single-minded interest in their qualities, their history, and their lore; and I could offer him more information on the subject than anyone else he knew. More, he pointed out to me, than even the knowledgeable Max de Marechal.

As the dinner progressed, it intrigued me to observe that where everyone else in the room deferred to Kassoulas—especially de Marechal, a shameless sycophant—Kassoulas himself deferred to me. I enjoyed that. Before long I found myself really liking the man instead of merely being impressed by him.

He was impressive, of course. About fifty, short, and barrel-chested, with a swarthy, deeply lined face and almost simian ears, he was ugly in a way that some clever women would find fascinating. Somehow, he suggested an ancient idol rough-hewn out of a block of mahogany. His habitual expression was a granite impassivity, relieved at times by a light of interest in those veiled, ever-watchful eyes. That light became intense when he finally touched on the matter of my bottle of Saint-Oen.

He had been told its price, he remarked with wry humor, and felt that a hundred thousand francs—twenty thousand hard American dollars—was, perhaps, a little excessive. Now if I would settle for two thousand francs—

I smilingly shook my head.

"It's a handsome offer," Kassoulas said. "It happens to be more than I've paid for any half dozen bottles of wine in my cellar."

"I won't dispute that, Monsieur Kassoulas."

"But you won't sell, either. What are the chances of the wine's being fit to drink?"

"Who can tell? The 1929 vintage at Saint-Oen was late to mature, so it may live longer than most. Or it may already be dead. That's why I won't open the bottle myself or sell anyone else the privilege of opening it. This way, it's a unique and magnificent treasure. Once its secret is out, it may simply be another bottle of wine gone bad."

To his credit, he understood that. And, when he invited me to be a guest at his estate near Saint-Cloud the next weekend, it was with the blunt assurance that it was only my company he sought, not the opportunity to further dicker for the bottle of Saint-Oen. In fact, said he, he would never again broach the matter. All he wanted was my word that if I ever decided to sell the bottle, he would be given first chance to make an offer for it. And to that I cheerfully agreed.

The weekend at his estate was a pleasant time for me, the first of many I spent there. It was an enormous place but smoothly run by a host of efficient help under the authority of a burly, grizzled majordomo named Joseph. Joseph was evidently Kassoulas's devoted slave. It came as no surprise to learn he had been a sergeant in the Foreign Legion. He responded to orders as if his master was the colonel of his regiment.

What did come as a surprise was the lady of the house, Sophia Kassoulas. I don't know exactly what I expected Kassoulas's wife to be like, but certainly not a girl young enough to be his daughter, a gentle, timid creature whose voice was hardly more than a whisper. By today's standards which require a young woman to be a lank-haired rack of bones she was, perhaps, a little too voluptuous, a little too ripely curved, but I am an old-fashioned sort of man who believes women should be ripely curved. And if, like Sophia Kassoulas, they are pale, dark-eyed, blushing beauties, so much the better.

As time passed and I became more and more a friend of the family, I was able to draw from her the story of her marriage, now approaching its fifth anniversary. Sophia Kassoulas was a distant cousin of her husband. Born to poor parents in a mountain village of Greece, convent bred, she had met Kassoulas for the first time at a gathering of the family in Athens, and, hardly out of her girlhood, had married him soon afterward. She was, she assured me in that soft little voice, the most fortunate of women. Yes, to have been chosen by a man like Kyros to be his wife, surely the most fortunate of women—

But she said it as if she were desperately trying to convince herself of it. In fact, she seemed frightened to death of Kassoulas. When he addressed the most commonplace remark to her she shrank away from him. It became a familiar scene, watching this happen, and watching him respond to it by then treating her with an icily polite disregard that only intimidated her the more.

It made an unhealthy situation in that household because, as I saw from the corner of my eye, the engaging Max de Marechal was always right there to soothe Madame's fears away. It struck me after a while how very often an evening at Saint-Cloud wound up with Kassoulas and myself holding a discussion over our brandy at one end of the room while Madame Kassoulas and Max de Marechal were head to head in conversation at the other end. There was nothing indecorous about those *tête-à-têtes*, but still I didn't like the look of them. The girl appeared to be as wide-eyed and ingenuous as a doe, and de Marechal bore all the earmarks of the trained predator.

Kassoulas himself was either unaware of this or remarkably indifferent to it. Certainly, his regard for de Marechal was genuine. He mentioned it to me several times, and once, when de Marechal got himself dangerously heated up in an argument with me over the merits of some vintage or other, Kassoulas said to him with real concern, "Gently, Max, gently. Remember your heart. How many times has the doctor warned you against becoming overexcited?"—which, for Kassoulas, was an unusual show of feeling. Generally, like so many men of his type, he seemed wholly incapable of expressing any depth of emotion.

Indeed, the only time he ever let slip any show of his feelings about his troublesome marriage was once when I was inspecting his wine cellar with him and pointed out that a dozen Volnay-Caillerets 1955 he had just laid in were likely to prove extremely uneven. It had been a mistake to buy it. One never knew, in uncorking a bottle, whether or not he would find it sound.

Kassoulas shook his head.

"It was a calculated risk, Monsieur Drummond, not a mistake. I don't make mistakes." Then he gave an almost imperceptible little shrug. "Well, one perhaps. When a man marries a mere child—"

He cut it short at that. It was the first and last time he ever touched on the subject. What he wanted to talk about was wine, although sometimes under my prodding and because I was a good listener, he would recount stories about his past. My own life has been humdrum. It fascinated me to learn, in bits and pieces, about the life of Kyros Kassoulas, a Piraeus wharf rat who was a thief in his childhood, a smuggler in his youth, and a multimillionaire before he was thirty. It gave me the same sense of drama Kassoulas appeared to feel when I would recount to him stories about some of the great vintages which, like the Nuits Saint-Oen 1929, had been cranky and uncertain in the barrel until, by some miracle of nature, they had suddenly blossomed into their full greatness.

It was at such times that Max de Marechal himself was at his best. Watching him grow emotional in such discussions, I had to smile inwardly at the way he had once condescendingly described Kassoulas as a fanatic about wines. It was a description which fitted him even better. Whatever else might be false about Max de Marechal, his feelings about any great vintage were genuine.

During the months that passed, Kassoulas proved to be as good as his word. He had said he wouldn't again bargain with me for the precious bottle of Saint-Oen, and he didn't. We discussed the Saint-Oen often enough—it was an obsession with de Marechal—but no matter how much Kassoulas was tempted to renew the effort to buy it, he kept his word.

Then, one dismally cold and rainy day in early December, my secretary opened my office door to announce in awestruck tones that Monsieur Kyros Kassoulas was outside waiting to see me. This was a surprise. Although Sophia Kassoulas, who seemed to have no friends in the world apart from de Marechal and myself, had several times been persuaded to have lunch with me when she was in town to do shopping, her husband had never before deigned to visit me in my domain, and I was not expecting him now.

He came in accompanied by the ever dapper de Marechal who, I saw with increased mystification, was in a state of feverish excitement.

We had barely exchanged greetings when de Marechal leaped directly to the point.

"The bottle of Nuits Saint-Oen 1929, Monsieur Drummond," he said. "You'll remember you once set a price on it. One hundred thousand francs."

"Only because it won't be bought at any such price."

"Would you sell it for less?"

"I've already made clear I wouldn't."

"You drive a hard bargain, Monsieur Drummond. But you'll be pleased to know that Monsieur Kassoulas is now prepared to pay your price."

I turned incredulously to Kassoulas. Before I could recover my voice, he drew a check from his pocket and, impassive as ever, handed it to me. Involuntarily, I glanced at it. It was for one hundred thousand francs. It was worth, by the going rate of exchange, twenty thousand dollars.

"This is ridiculous," I finally managed to say. "I can't take it."

"But you must!" de Marechal said in alarm.

"I'm sorry. No wine is worth a fraction of this. Especially a wine that may be dead in the bottle."

"Ah," said Kassoulas, lightly, "then perhaps that's what I'm paying for—the chance to see whether it is or not."

"If that's your reason—" I protested, and Kassoulas shook his head.

"It isn't. The truth is, my friend, this wine solves a difficult problem for me. A great occasion is coming soon, the fifth anniversary of my marriage, and I've been wondering how Madame and I could properly celebrate it. Then inspiration struck me. What better way of celebrating it than to open the Saint-Oen and discover it is still in the flush of perfect health, still in its flawless maturity? What could be more deeply moving and significant on such an occasion?"

"That makes it all the worse if the wine is dead," I pointed out. The check was growing warm in my hand. I wanted to tear it up but couldn't bring myself to do it.

"No matter. The risk is all mine," said Kassoulas. "Of course, you'll be there to judge the wine for yourself. I insist on that. It will be a memorable experience, no matter how it goes. A small dinner with just the four of us at the table, and the Saint-Oen as climax to the occasion."

"The *pièce de résistance* must be an *entrecôte*," breathed de Marechal. "Beef, of course. It will suit the wine perfectly."

I had somehow been pushed past the point of no return. Slowly, I folded the check for the hundred thousand francs and placed it in my wallet. After all, I was in the business of selling wine for a profit.

"When is this dinner to be held?" I asked. "Remember that the wine must stand a few days before it's decanted."

"Naturally, I'm allowing for that," said Kassoulas. "Today is Monday; the dinner will be held Saturday. That means more than enough time to prepare every detail perfectly. On Wednesday I'll see that the temperature of the dining room is properly adjusted, the table set, and the bottle of Saint-Oen placed upright on it for the sediment to clear properly. The room will then be locked to avoid any mishap. By Saturday the last of the sediment should have settled completely. But I don't plan to decant the wine. I intend to serve it directly from the bottle."

"Risky," I said.

"Not if it's poured with a steady hand. One like this." Kassoulas held out a stubby-fingered, powerful-looking hand which showed not a sign of tremor. "Yes, this supreme vintage deserves the honor of being poured from its own bottle, risky as that may be. Surely you now have evidence, Monsieur Drummond, that I'm a man to take any risk if it's worthwhile to me."

I HAD GOOD CAUSE to remember those concluding words at a meeting I had with Sophia Kassoulas later in the week. That day she phoned early in the morning to ask if I could meet her for lunch at an hour when we might have privacy in the restaurant, and, thinking this had something to do with her own plans for the anniversary dinner, I cheerfully accepted the invitation. All the cheerfulness was washed out of me as soon as I joined her at our table in a far corner of the dimly lit, almost deserted room. She was obviously terrified.

"Something is very wrong," I said to her. "What is it?"

"Everything," she said piteously. "And you're the only one I can turn to for help, Monsieur Drummond. You've always been so kind to me. Will you help me now?"

"Gladly. If you tell me what's wrong and what I can do about it."

"Yes, there's no way around that. You must be told everything." Madame Kassoulas drew a shuddering breath. "It can be told very simply. I had an affair with Max de Marechal. Now Kyros has found out about it."

My heart sank. The last thing in the world I wanted was to get involved in anything like this.

"Madame," I said unhappily, "this is a matter to be settled between you and your husband. You must see that it's not my business at all."

"Oh, please! If you only understood—"

"I don't see what there is to understand."

"A great deal. About Kyros, about me, about my marriage. I didn't want to marry Kyros, I didn't want to marry anybody. But my family arranged it, so what could I do? And it's been dreadful from the start. All I am to Kyros is a pretty little decoration for his house. He has no feeling for me. He cares more about that bottle of wine he bought from you than he does for me. Where I'm concerned, he's like stone. But Max—"

"I know," I said wearily. "You found that Max was different. Max cared very much for you. Or, at least, he told you he did."

"Yes, he told me he did," Madame Kassoulas said with defiance. "And whether he meant it or not, I needed that. A woman must have some man to tell her he cares for her or she has nothing. But it was wicked of me to put Max in danger. And now that Kyros knows about us, Max is in terrible danger."

"What makes you think so? Has your husband made any threats?"

"No, he hasn't even said he knows about the affair. But he does. I can swear he does. It's in the way he's been behaving toward me these past few days, in the remarks he makes to me, as if he were enjoying a joke that only he understood. And it all seems to have something to do with that bottle of Saint-Oen locked up in the dining room. That's why I came to you for help. You know about these things."

"Madame, all I know is that the Saint-Oen is being made ready for your dinner party Saturday."

"Yes, that's what Kyros said. But the way he said it—" Madame Kassoulas leaned toward me intently. "Tell me one thing. Is it possible for a bottle of wine to be poisoned without its cork being drawn? Is there any way of doing that?"

"Oh, come now. Do you seriously believe for a moment that your husband intends to poison Max?"

"You don't know Kyros the way I do. You don't know what he's capable of."

"Even murder?"

"Even murder, if he was sure he could get away with it. They tell a story in my family about how, when he was very young, he killed a man who had cheated him out of a little money. Only it was done so cleverly that the police never found out who the murderer was."

That was when I suddenly recalled Kassoulas's words about taking any risk if it were worthwhile to him and felt a chill go through me. All too vividly, I had a mental picture of a hypodermic needle sliding through the cork in that bottle of Saint-Oen, of drops of deadly poison trickling into the wine. Then it struck me how wildly preposterous the picture was.

"Madame," I said, "I'll answer your question this way. Your husband does not intend to poison anyone at your dinner party unless he intends to poison us all, which I am sure he does not. Remember that I've also been invited to enjoy my share of the Saint-Oen."

"What if something were put into Max's glass alone?"

"It won't be. Your husband has too much respect for Max's palate for any such clumsy trick. If the wine is dead, Max will know it at once and won't drink it. If it's still good, he'd detect anything foreign in it with the first sip and not touch the rest. Anyhow, why not discuss it with Max? He's the one most concerned."

"I did try to talk to him about it, but he only laughed at me. He said it was all in my imagination. I know why. He's so insanely eager to try that wine that he won't let anything stop him from doing it."

"I can appreciate his feelings about that." Even with my equanimity restored I was anxious to get away from this unpleasant topic. "And he's right about your imagination. If you really want my advice, the best thing you can do is to behave with your husband as if nothing has happened and to steer clear of Monsieur de Marechal after this."

It was the only advice I could give her under the circumstances. I only hoped she wasn't too panic-stricken to follow it. Or too infatuated with Max de Marechal.

Knowing too much for my own comfort, I was ill at ease the evening of the party, so when I joined the company it was a relief to see that Madame Kassoulas had herself well in hand. As for Kassoulas, I could detect no change at all in his manner toward her or de Marechal. It was convincing evidence that Madame's guilty conscience had indeed been working overtime on her imagination, and that Kassoulas knew nothing at all about her *affaire*. He was hardly the man to take being cuckolded with composure, and he was wholly composed. As we sat down to dinner, it was plain that his only concern was about its menu, and, above all, about the bottle of Nuits Saint-Oen 1929 standing before him.

The bottle had been standing there three days, and everything that could be done to ensure the condition of its contents had been done. The temperature of the room was moderate; it had not been allowed to vary once the bottle was brought into the room, and, as Max de Marechal assured me, he had checked this at regular intervals every day. And, I was sure, had taken time to stare rapturously at the bottle, marking off the hours until it would be opened.

Furthermore, since the table at which our little company sat down was of a size to seat eighteen or twenty, it meant long distances between our places, but it provided room for the bottle to stand in lonely splendor clear of any careless hand that might upset it. It was noticeable that the servants waiting on us all gave it a wide berth. Joseph, the burly, hard-bitten majordomo who was supervising them with a dangerous look in his eye, must have put them in fear of death if they laid a hand near it.

Now, Kassoulas had to undertake two dangerous procedures as preludes to the wine-tasting ritual. Ordinarily, a great vintage like the Nuits Saint-Oen 1929 stands until all its sediment has collected in the base of the bottle, and is then decanted. This business of transferring it from bottle to decanter not only ensures that sediment and cork crumbs are left behind, but it also means that the wine is being properly aired. The older a wine, the more it needs to breathe the open air to rid itself of mustiness accumulated in the bottle.

But Kassoulas, in his determination to honor the Saint-Oen by serving it directly from its original bottle, had imposed on himself the delicate task of uncorking it at the table so skillfully that no bits of cork would filter into the liquid. Then, after the wine had stood open until the entrée was served, he would have to pour it with such control that none of the sediment in its base would roil up. It had taken three days for that sediment to settle. The least slip in uncorking the bottle or pouring from it, and it would be another three days before it was again fit to drink.

As soon as we were at the table, Kassoulas set to work on the first task. We all watched with bated breath as he grasped the neck of the bottle firmly and centered the point of the corkscrew in the cork. Then, with the concentration of a demolitions expert defusing a live bomb, he slowly, very slowly, turned the corkscrew, bearing down so lightly that the corkscrew almost had to take hold by itself. His object was to penetrate deep enough to get a grip on the cork so that it could be drawn, yet not to pierce the cork through; it was the one sure way of keeping specks of cork from filtering into the wine.

It takes enormous strength to draw a cork which has not been pierced through from a bottle of wine which it has sealed for decades. The bottle must be kept upright and immobile, the pull must be straight up and steady without any of the twisting and turning that will tear a cork apart. The old-fashioned corkscrew which exerts no artificial leverage is the instrument for this because it allows one to feel the exact working of the cork in the bottleneck.

The hand Kassoulas had around the bottle clamped it so hard that his knuckles gleamed white. His shoulders hunched, the muscles of his neck grew taut. Strong as he appeared to be, it seemed impossible for him to start the cork. But he would not give way, and in the end it was the cork that gave way. Slowly and smoothly it was pulled clear of the bottle-mouth, and for the first time since the wine had been drawn from its barrel long years before, it was now free to breathe the open air.

Kassoulas waved the cork back and forth under his nose, sampling its bouquet. He shrugged as he handed it to me.

"Impossible to tell anything this way," he said, and of course he was right. The fumes of fine Burgundy emanating from the cork meant nothing, since even dead wine may have a good bouquet.

De Marechal would not even bother to look at the cork.

"It's only the wine that matters," he said fervently. "Only the wine. And in an hour we'll know its secret for better or worse. It will seem like a long hour, I'm afraid."

I didn't agree with that at first. The dinner we were served was more than sufficient distraction for me. Its menu, in tribute to the Nuits Saint-Oen 1929, had been arranged the way a symphony conductor might arrange a short program of lighter composers in preparation for the playing of a Beethoven masterwork. Artichoke hearts in a butter sauce, *langouste* in mushrooms, and, to clear the palate, a lemon ice unusually tart. Simple dishes flawlessly prepared.

And the wines Kassoulas had selected to go with them were, I was intrigued to note, obviously chosen as settings for his diamond. A sound Chablis, a respectable Muscadet. Both were good, neither was calculated to do more than draw a small nod of approval from the connoisseur. It was Kassoulas's way of telling us that nothing would be allowed to dim the glorious promise of that open bottle of Nuits Saint-Oen standing before us.

Then my nerves began to get the better of me. Old as I was at the game, I found myself more and more filled with tension and as the dinner progressed I found the bottle of Saint-Oen a magnet for my eyes. It soon became an agony, waiting until the entrée would be served and the Saint-Oen poured.

Who, I wondered, would be given the honor of testing the first few drops? Kassoulas, the host, was entitled to that honor, but as a mark of respect he could assign it to anyone he chose. I wasn't sure whether or not I wanted to be chosen. I was braced for the worst, but I knew that being the first at the table to discover the wine was dead would be like stepping from an airplane above the clouds without a parachute. Yet, to be the first to discover that this greatest of vintages had survived the years—! Watching Max de Marechal, crimson with mounting excitement, sweating so that he had to constantly mop his brow, I suspected he was sharing my every thought.

The entrée was brought in at last, the *entrecôte* of beef that de Marechal had suggested. Only a salver of *petits pois* accompanied it. The *entrecôte* and peas were served. Then Kassoulas gestured at Joseph, and the majordomo cleared the room of the help. There must be no chance of disturbance while the wine was being poured, no possible distraction.

When the servants were gone and the massive doors of the dining room were closed behind them, Joseph returned to the table and took up his position near Kassoulas, ready for anything that might be required of him.

The time had come.

Kassoulas took hold of the bottle of Nuits Saint-Oen 1929. He lifted it slowly, with infinite care, making sure not to disturb the treacherous sediment. A ruby light flickered from it as he held it at arm's length, staring at it with brooding eyes.

"Monsieur Drummond, you were right," he said abruptly.

"I was?" I said, taken aback. "About what?"

"About your refusal to unlock the secret of this bottle. You once said that as long as the bottle kept its secret it was an extraordinary treasure, but that once it was opened it might prove to be nothing but another bottle of bad wine. A disaster. Worse than a disaster, a joke. That was the truth. And in the face of it I now find I haven't the courage to learn whether or not what I am holding here is a treasure or a joke."

De Marechal almost writhed with impatience.

"It's too late for that!" he protested violently. "The bottle is already open!"

"But there's a solution to my dilemma," Kassoulas said to him. "Now watch it. Watch it very closely."

His arm moved, carrying the bottle clear of the table. The bottle slowly tilted. Stupefied, I saw wine spurt from it, pour over the polished boards of the floor. Drops of wine spattered Kassoulas's shoes, stained the cuffs of his trousers. The puddle on the floor grew larger. Trickles of it crept out in thin red strings between the boards.

It was an unearthly choking sound from de Marechal which tore me free of the spell I was in. A wild cry of anguish from Sophia Kassoulas.

"Max!" she screamed. "Kyros, stop! For God's sake, stop! Don't you see what you're doing to him?"

She had reason to be terrified. I was terrified myself when I saw de Marechal's condition. His face was ashen, his mouth gaped wide open, his eyes, fixed on the stream of wine relentlessly gushing out of the bottle in Kassoulas's unwavering hand, were starting out of his head with horror.

Sophia Kassoulas ran to his side but he feebly thrust her away and tried to struggle to his feet. His hands reached out in supplication to the fast-emptying bottle of Nuits Saint-Oen 1929.

"Joseph," Kassoulas said dispassionately, "see to Monsieur de Marechal. The doctor warned that he must not move during these attacks."

The iron grasp Joseph clamped on de Marechal's shoulder prevented him from moving, but I saw his pallid hand fumbling into a pocket, and at last regained my wits.

"In his pocket!" I pleaded. "He has pills!"

It was too late. De Marechal suddenly clutched at his chest in that familiar gesture of unbearable pain, then his entire body went limp, his head lolling back against the chair, his eyes turning up in his head to glare sightlessly at the ceiling. The last thing they must have seen was the stream of Nuits Saint-Oen 1929 become a trickle, the trickle become an ooze of sediment clotting on the floor in the middle of the vast puddle there.

Too late to do anything for de Marechal, but Sophia Kassoulas stood swaying on her feet ready to faint. Weak-kneed myself, I helped her to her chair, saw to it that she downed the remains of the Chablis in her glass.

The wine penetrated her stupor. She sat there breathing hard, staring at her husband until she found the strength to utter words.

"You knew it would kill him," she whispered. "That's why you bought the wine. That's why you wasted it all."

"Enough, madame," Kassoulas said frigidly. "You don't know what you're saying. And you're embarrassing our guest with this emotionalism." He turned to me. "It's sad that our little party had to end this way, monsieur, but these things do happen. Poor Max. He invited disaster with his temperament. Now I think you had better go. The doctor must be called in to make an examination and fill out the necessary papers, and these medical matters can be distressing to witness. There's no need for you to be put out by them. I'll see you to the door."

I got away from there without knowing how. All I knew was that I had seen a murder committed and there was nothing I could do about it. Absolutely nothing. Merely to say aloud that what I had seen take place was murder would be enough to convict me of slander in any court. Kyros Kassoulas had planned and executed his revenge flawlessly, and all it would cost him, by my bitter calculations, were one hundred thousand francs and the loss of a faithless wife. It was unlikely that Sophia Kassoulas would spend another night in his house even if she had to leave it with only the clothes on her back.

I never heard from Kassoulas again after that night. For that much, at least, I was grateful . . .

Now, six months later, here I was at a café table on the rue de Rivoli with Sophia Kassoulas, a second witness to the murder and as helplessly bound to silence about it as I was. Considering the shock given me by our meeting, I had to admire her own composure as she hovered over me solicitously, saw to it that I took down a cognac and then another, chattered brightly about inconsequential things as if that could blot the recollection of the past from our minds.

She had changed since I had last seen her. Changed all for the better. The timid girl had become a lovely woman who glowed with self-assurance. The signs were easy to read. Somewhere, I was sure, she had found the right man for her and this time not a brute like Kassoulas or a shoddy Casanova like Max de Marechal.

The second cognac made me feel almost myself again, and when I saw my Samaritan glance at the small, brilliantly jeweled watch on her wrist I apologized for keeping her and thanked her for her kindness.

"Small kindness for such a friend," she said reproachfully. She rose and gathered up her gloves and purse. "But I did tell Kyros I would meet him at—"

"Kyros!"

"But of course. Kyros. My husband." Madame Kassoulas looked at me with puzzlement.

"Then you're still living with him?"

"Very happily." Then her face cleared. "You must forgive me for being so slow-witted. It took a moment to realize why you should ask such a question."

"Madame, I'm the one who should apologize. After all—"

"No, no, you had every right to ask it." Madame Kassoulas smiled at me. "But it's sometimes hard to remember I was ever unhappy with Kyros, the way everything changed so completely for me that night—

"But you were there, Monsieur Drummond. You saw for your-self how Kyros emptied the bottle of Saint-Oen on the floor, all because of me. What a revelation that was! What an awakening! And when it dawned on me that I really did mean more to him than even the last bottle of Nuits Saint-Oen 1929 in the whole world, when I found the courage to go to his room that night and tell him how this made me feel—oh, my dear Monsieur Drummond, it's been heaven for us ever since!"

Roast of Beef in Burgundy Wine Sauce with Roasted Garlic

3- to 4-lb. beef shoulder, chuck, blade, strip, or rump
   roast
1 head of garlic, peeled, separated into cloves, and
   sliced into thin slices
½ cup flour
3 Tbsp. olive oil
2 cups beef stock, canned or homemade
2 cups Burgundy wine
1 cup water
2 Tbsp. cornstarch

PREHEAT OVEN TO 300 degrees F.

DREDGE ROAST IN flour on all sides. Place olive oil in a big skillet.
Heat. Sauté garlic slices in the olive oil until soft and slightly clear.
Brown roast on all sides in the hot skillet. Place roast and garlic and
oil in a roasting pan. Add beef stock, wine, and water to the roasting pan. Place in oven and bake at 300 degrees F. for two to three
hours, turning roast over in pan every 30 minutes. Add additional
water to the roasting pan, if needed, to keep it from drying out.

REMOVE ROAST FROM oven when the meat is done to your satisfaction. Pull meat from roasting pan and set on platter. Place roasting
pan on stove burner set for low to medium heat, or, if this is not
possible, transfer contents of roast pan to a saucepan. Place cornstarch in an empty cup or bowl. Add hot liquid from the roast pan,
one tablespoon at a time, to the cornstarch, stirring carefully to
prevent lumps from forming. Continue adding liquid into cornstarch until it is fully dissolved. Add the liquid in the cup to contents of roasting pan, adding water if necessary to bring total
volume of liquid to a cup and a half. Cook, stirring constantly,
until the liquid takes on a glossy sheen and thickens. Remove
sauce from stove. Slice roast. Serve with warm sauce drizzled over
the slices or on the side.

Takeout

Joyce Christmas

Lady Margaret Priam, in spite of a fine aristocratic upbringing in England at the hands of her mother, the Countess of Brayfield, and her father, the earl, plus a select group of proper nannies, still harbored a dark secret that was allowed to surface now that she lived in Manhattan, rather than in London or at Priam's Priory, the family estate in England.

The secret—well, it was more of a shameful quirk—was that Margaret Priam, a woman of the upper classes, now in her mid-thirties and welcomed out and about in Manhattan society, possessed, indeed treasured, an extensive and wide-ranging collection of Chinese takeout menus for restaurants in her part of the fashionable Upper East Side of New York City.

Margaret was accustomed to being served, and she liked Chinese food, preferably eaten at home in the comfort of her well-appointed apartment on the twentieth floor of a fairly expensive high rise. Takeout food represented a workable solution, and the menus were the medium that made it possible.

She assumed, perhaps incorrectly, that deliverymen from New York City's Chinese restaurants received large bonuses based on the number of menus they were able to stuff under apartment doors when making deliveries. In any case, Margaret acquired every one she saw, and delighted in the grand names and flowery descriptions: "Three Kings of the Sea—shrimp, lobster meat, and scallops fit only for the connoisseur" . . . "Crispy Whole Fish

23

Hunan Style—fresh whole fish lightly battered and seared until golden brown, then smothered in a hot, pungent, homemade rice wine sauce. Delightful!" . . . "Special Garden—splendiferous array of vegetables enhanced by a bed of lotus stems, tasty wood-ear mushrooms, shredded dried bean curd, bamboo shoots, baby corn, snow pea pods, broccoli, and tomatoes in chef's special hot sauce." Tomatoes? Perhaps, although their wide distribution in China was somewhat doubtful.

She liked reading about the "delicious gentle sauces" and the creations "originally served to royal families, now brought to you." And, of course, there were the many "Triple Delights," "Lover's Nests," and General Tso dishes, and, finally, "Happy Family," which she remembered dining on long ago on first meeting her gentleman friend, Sam De Vere of the New York police. De Vere especially liked the many variations of Happy Family.

Mr. Davidson, the strict concierge on the ground floor, who was one step up in the building's hierarchy from the pleasant young man who actually opened the door, had strictly forbidden delivery-men to leave piles of menus in the semi-ornate lobby. They were also discouraged from shoving menus under the doors on the upper floors as they made their deliveries. Mr. Davidson, at his discretion and with tenant permission, did allow deliverymen he recognized to ascend alone with their plastic shopping bags of takeout food up to the tenants' floors and doors. If, however, they were found scattering menus about (and sometimes they did), he banned them from the upper floors, causing them and those who ordered food no end of inconvenience. Those of whom Mr. Davidson disapproved were required to be accompanied by a member of the building's staff. Since such a person was not always readily available, food got cold, and the restaurant lost future business.

She wasn't sure the other tenants were as dedicated to the concept of dinner packed in cardboard containers and rushed on bicycles or in little vans through the streets of New York to fill empty stomachs.

For herself, she was never happier than when she was leafing through her pile of Chinese menus, pencil in hand, deciding which restaurant to call and devising just the right combination of dishes to order in. Who had the best pan-fried noodles, the best orange-flavored beef, the puffiest roast pork buns, the crispiest spring roll? Whose shrimp was not old and recently unfrozen?

Whose fortune cookies not only gave fortunes but lucky numbers—enough to fill out one game of Lotto, surely leading to win-
nings in the millions of dollars?

She had many places to choose from, but she usually called
Pearl of the Orient, only a couple of blocks away, and she never
hesitated to call when a trip to the grocery store or deli was more
than she could handle in the rain, snow, sleet, or simply the cold of
a New York night.

Mr. Arrigo, whose apartment was two doors from hers, apparently had a taste for pizza, since she had several times seen a
handsome youth with a large padded pizza delivery box standing
at Mr. Arrigo's door and then be admitted.

Indeed, once or twice in the elevator she'd been engaged in conversation by Mr. Arrigo, who actually discussed the pleasures of a
large pie with pepperoni, and a big order of hot mussels with good
Italian bread to soak up the sauce. She did not admit that she was
unfamiliar with hot mussels, nor did she comment that it seemed a
great deal of food for one man to consume. Maybe Mr. Arrigo liked
leftovers. It seemed that he rather liked her, but she had long ago
learned that men of any age—Mr. Arrigo was perhaps in his fifties—
found it hard to resist a well-put-together blonde with an English
accent. Italian blood seemed to be especially stirred by blonde hair
and blue eyes. Her young friend Prince Paul Castrocani was similarly
bowled over by blondes, although he preferred to have an idea of
the woman's financial status before proceeding. Paul was undeniably nice, but he was also something of a gold digger. He had never,
however, to the best of her knowledge, used hot mussels to open a
conversation with a pretty wench.

As genial as Mr. Arrigo appeared to be in the close confines of
the elevator, she was wary of him. He had cold eyes, and the aura
of a man always keeping control of his temper. She remembered
times when that control slipped. The elevator door did not close
quickly enough to suit him, and he jabbed furiously at the buttons, purpling slightly, his mouth tight with anger. She'd heard
angry shouts as she passed his apartment door; and she'd seen
him become enraged when the doorman was not quick to open
the door—and the door of his long black town car purring at the
curb. She'd prefer not to be the object of Mr. Arrigo's anger.

Tonight—rainy and blustery—was perfect for ordering takeout,
and she had additional justification. Sam De Vere, when released

from his duties as a police detective, had half promised to make his way later to her place. On that expectation, she'd turned down an invitation to dine at the showplace apartment of a prominent woman Realtor to the well known and well heeled. Her legendary dinner parties drew the celebrated and the social from both coasts, as well as Washington's seats of power. Margaret preferred a quiet evening at home with De Vere, and she'd have something for him to eat when he arrived.

Margaret phoned Pearl of the Orient with her order, with the total cost precalculated from the menu prices, including the tax and, of course, the tip for Mr. Feng, the regular deliveryman.

Within fifteen minutes Mr. Davidson rang her intercom to announce the arrival of Mr. Feng, who was already on his way up. The concierge knew him well, and Mr. Feng knew his way around the corner from the elevators, along the corridor to her apartment.

The doorbell buzzed. Mr. Feng was outside the door, grinning and offering with a polite bob of his head a shopping bag crammed with brown paper bags holding white cardboard containers and aluminum foil dishes with cardboard covers, which were invariably splashed with soy and sweet and sour sauce from someone else's order.

No matter how horrid the weather, Mr. Feng was always cheerful, as though he had personally cooked Margaret's meal (perhaps he had) prior to delivering it on his beat-up bicycle through the inclemencies outside. He worked long hours. Margaret had seen him from time to time during the day careening through traffic on his rounds to deliver lunches to offices in the area, the bag of takeout food hooked over the handlebars. He did not seem to take particular heed of the traffic, but then, not many people did.

"Bad night," Mr. Feng said as he handed her a double order of wonton soup, stir-fried spinach with garlic, and prawns with black bean sauce.

A large drop of water made its way slowly down his nose. After a moment's suspension at the tip, it dropped to the carpet outside her apartment door. "You always calling on a bad night." He spoke it not as a complaint, but as a simple truth.

"Yes," Margaret said, "I do." She really didn't mind a bit that it was Mr. Feng rather than she out on a night like this.

She handed Mr. Feng the exact amount she'd calculated, a modest enough sum for her evening meal, with leftovers for De Vere or even breakfast. She stepped into the hall to take the bag from Mr. Feng and saw from the corner of her eye that the pizza delivery boy was entering Mr. Arrigo's apartment, laden with bags and a big white pizza box.

Mr. Feng looked at the money she'd handed him. "Ah, miss," he said, "is not enough. Look . . . lobster . . . eleven dollar, fifty cents . . ." He showed her the bill, with three items neatly printed in Chinese characters. "Lobster very expensive."

"Lobster! Then there's been a mistake! I ordered shrimp. I cannot eat lobster. I am allergic. It makes me very ill."

Mr. Feng looked concerned, and then suddenly alarmed, as though she might topple over from her doorway into his arms.

"You'll have to go back and bring me the right thing," Margaret said. "I simply can't eat lobster. I'll call the Pearl right away and have them fix the shrimp, so it will be waiting when you get there. You can bring it right back to me." The aroma of the dishes in the white bag seeped into the hall. She was hungry, but she handed the bag back to him.

"Ah," Mr. Feng said again, and brushed away another enormous drop of rain from the end of his nose. He looked so disconcerted that she felt sorry for him, since it couldn't have been his fault but rather that of the abrupt woman who took telephone orders. Mr. Feng was a nice, gentle man, shorter than she by several inches, with smooth, tannish skin and floppy, black hair, very badly cut. Tonight it was plastered down damply because of the rain. The poor man was wearing nothing in the way of rain gear, and he had a large white bandage affixed to the side of his head.

"Did you have an accident?" Margaret indicated the bandage with her chin.

Mr. Feng thought for a moment. "Car hit bicycle," he said. "Happens all the time. Is nothing."

"I'm so sorry," she said. "You must be more careful. Now let me just call the restaurant and tell them about the mistake."

She left him at the door and called the Pearl of the Orient. She had the number on speed dial. The explanation took some time, and then she agreed to examine the dish to be sure it was lobster.

She fetched the bag from Mr. Feng, who was lounging against the wall in the hallway. He seemed distracted as he peered down the corridor. She looked at the food he'd brought her. It was definitely lobster and not shrimp.

As she spoke to the restaurant again, she could hear the rain lashing the window that overlooked Third Avenue. The woman at the Pearl of the Orient sounded quite put-out, but finally agreed to correct the error. In the competitive takeout business, it paid to humor a good customer.

"All right," she said to Mr. Feng. "If you go back to the restaurant, they'll have the shrimp ready for you to bring back to me. I'll just keep the other things, so you don't have to carry them back and forth."

Mr. Feng appeared to be thinking hard, and seemed not even to be listening to her. She wondered if he understood, since she wasn't sure how strong his English was.

"Have to hurry, miss," he said. "Very bad night." He seemed anxious to depart. Then she wondered if she ought to tip him again when he returned. She probably should, since he was the one braving the bad weather, when it could so easily have been her.

"I'll be seeing you in just a few minutes," she said. As she closed the door, she remembered that De Vere loved fried dumplings. Mr. Feng could bring some back with the shrimp. She opened the door again. "Mr. Feng—"

She stopped abruptly. Mr. Feng was edging along the corridor, close to the wall, and was now opposite Mr. Arrigo's apartment door. He stopped and stared, with that look of alarm she recognized. The door was certainly open, because she heard it being slammed shut. Mr. Feng hesitated, and suddenly he ran—toward the branching hallway that led to the bank of elevators.

Mr. Arrigo, an impressive figure in a finely tailored charcoal business suit, stepped from his apartment and shouted after Mr. Feng, "Hey, you!"

Mr. Feng had disappeared around the corner. Mr. Arrigo sighed heavily and muttered to himself. Then he noticed Margaret. "Well, Lady Margaret . . ." He took a step in her direction. She was surprised to note that he was wearing a witty Nicole Miller necktie. "Who was that fellow? Know him? I saw him hanging around outside your door."

"Oh, it's only Mr. Feng, the deliveryman."

"Delivery?" Mr. Arrigo's tone was not warm.

"You know, Chinese takeout. Like your pizza boy."

Mr. Arrigo looked quickly back at his apartment door. "Izzat right? Like Tony? I don't think so. Tony knows to mind his own business. Where's your guy from?"

"I don't think . . ." She didn't like the look on Mr. Arrigo's face. "Pearl of the Orient," she said quickly. "The restaurant just up the avenue a few blocks. They made a mistake with my order, so he's gone off to bring back the right thing."

"Yeah, well, you can't get reliable service nowadays," Mr. Arrigo said. "Say, I'd have you over tonight for some of those hot mussels Tony just brought, but I got business associates in. You know how it is. We'll do it sometime, though, one of these days. Tony'll deliver 'em to us right off the stove, practically right out of the ocean."

"Lovely," Margaret said. "I'd like that. Sometime." She wasn't terribly keen on a *tête-à-tête* with Mr. Arrigo, since as far as she knew there was no Mrs. Arrigo, although any number of times she'd noticed sexy, well-dressed women coming and going from his place. Professionals, perhaps, who for a fee would agree to enjoy hot mussels and pizza with pepperoni.

"It's a deal," he said, and in an instant he had disappeared back into his apartment, calling, "Hey, Tony! On your feet!"

Margaret pondered Mr. Feng's hasty departure as she took from a cabinet a beautiful antique Chinese bowl of considerable value that her former employer, Bedros Kasparian, the Oriental art dealer, had given her when he closed his shop. He would be horrified—or maybe not—to know that she used it for the purpose for which it had been created. She dumped the wonton soup into the bowl and delicately placed some spinach on top, using her prized ebony chopsticks with tops of Baccarat crystal banded in gold.

She ate a little, but slowly, watching the news and the weather on television. The bad weather was due to continue all week.

It was quite a long time after Mr. Feng had left that Mr. Davidson rang to announce, "Delivery."

Poor Mr. Feng, she thought, *wet through again*. She found a few more dollars for a bigger tip.

"Oh!" She was startled when she opened the door at the doorbell's ring. It wasn't Mr. Feng at all but a different Chinese man she didn't recognize. He held out the white plastic bag to her.

"Shrimp, black bean sauce," he said. "No charge."

"Where is Mr. Feng?"

The deliveryman looked serious, shook his head. "Gone home," he said quickly. "Sick."

"Well, yes. He was soaked." She gave him a couple of dollars, not the whole amount she'd planned to tip Mr. Feng for his second trip.

"Bad sick," the man said. "Hit by car on Third Avenue." He started back in the direction of the elevators.

"Wait!" He stopped. "Tell me what happened. Please."

The deliveryman shrugged. "Little van from . . ." He gestured, making a wide circle with his arms.

"Pizza!"

The man smiled and nodded agreement. "Mr. Feng coming back with your order, van goes right at him. Don't worry, chef cooks more shrimp for you." He hurried back toward the elevator.

She found she was no longer very hungry.

Margaret put the shrimp aside in the kitchen, along with the spinach and the remains of the wonton soup. She was restless, remembering Mr. Feng's widened eyes as he looked into Mr. Arrigo's apartment, Mr. Arrigo's questions about Feng and the restaurant, and his shout for Tony.

Then Mr. Feng had been hit by a pizza delivery van as he bicycled back to her.

Ridiculous. There could be no possible connection, but she couldn't stop imagining things. What could Mr. Feng have seen through the open door or while he stood in the corridor? Something that would have caused him to be silenced on Mr. Arrigo's orders?

Which pizza restaurant did Tony deliver for? She couldn't, under the circumstances, ask Mr. Arrigo, even if she confessed an irresistible longing for her own order of hot mussels.

She remained as uncertain as ever as to the exact nature of hot mussels. She glanced at her shelf of cookbooks, but instead of leafing through an index or two, she suddenly remembered *moules marinere*, mussels cooked in white wine, vegetables, and herbs. That was a French dish, of course, but then she realized that it was an easy step linguistically from French *marinere* to Italian *marinara*. Aha! Hot mussels were certainly mussels cooked in marinara sauce, spiced with red pepper. She was rather proud of herself for figuring it out.

Again she thought how difficult it would be for one man to eat a large pizza and a large order of hot mussels—with bread to dip up the spicy red sauce—but Mr. Arrigo had said he had business associates visiting. No doubt all hearty eaters.

She didn't enjoy harboring suspicions about Mr. Arrigo. True, he was invariably polite, well dressed, quite distinguished-looking, but she had no idea what he did for a living, and certainly no idea what he might have been doing in his apartment—with the door open—that had alarmed Mr. Feng, and perhaps had led to his "accident." Or maybe it was something his "business associates" were doing. What was the worst thing she could imagine seeing? She made a mental list:

. . . The expression on Princess Margaret's face when she was told that she was not allowed to smoke.

. . . Getting off a subway train late at night at an empty station and seeing that the exit was at the far end.

She also imagined the look on people's faces if she showed up at the Metropolitan Museum of Art's Costume Institute Winter Gala in old jeans and a plaid man's shirt—without having had her hair or nails done.

. . . Finding a dead body, possibly murdered. A terrible sight.

The choice was easy. She'd found bodies, and the sight had been quite unnerving.

Now she was convinced that Mr. Feng must have seen something awful, like a body. What could be worse? Well, she'd once cautioned Princess Margaret about smoking, and that had been pretty awful, too.

She pushed the speed dial button for Pearl of the Orient.

"I . . . this is Lady Margaret Priam," she said to the woman who answered. It sounded like the woman who usually took phone orders.

"Boy is on the way," the woman said with some irritation. "No more trouble. Food is right this time."

"Yes, yes, it is," Margaret said hastily. "The deliveryman has been here. I wanted to ask about Mr. Feng."

The silence was so long she eventually said, "Hello? Are you there?"

"You want to order?"

"No. I mean, I wanted to know how Mr. Feng is. The deliveryman said he was hit by a car."

"No," the woman said firmly. "Everything is good. Mr. Feng fall off bicycle. Gone home. No car."

"But the deliveryman said—"

"No car," the woman said even more firmly, and hung up. Surely, if the substitute deliveryman saw what happened, someone else must have. The temptation to call De Vere was very strong. If a man had been hit by a car, even a lowly deliveryman who paid little heed to traffic, the police would know about it. But then she would have to explain why she wanted to know, and she had repeatedly promised De Vere that she wouldn't involve herself with mysterious deaths. She had encountered murders once or twice too often for De Vere's taste. Maybe Mr. Feng wasn't dead, but she was now certain that someone was, in Mr. Arrigo's apartment.

There were always the hospital emergency rooms, but she suspected that if Mr. Feng were able to make his way from such an accident, he would indeed have gone home.

By the time the local ten o'clock television news came on, De Vere had not yet appeared at her apartment. Margaret was still wondering what to do about Mr. Feng, when she heard a brief report of a hit-and-run accident on a street corner on the east side of Third Avenue. A victim, dead at the scene. A small van seen by witnesses speeding from the accident. The name was not given, but Margaret felt a sudden pang of sorrow for Mr. Feng, whose smiling face and punctilious courtesy had often softened the harsh realities of New York life. He was a kind of friend, the way the old servants at Priam's Priory were her friends. And her responsibility. She had to know the truth.

But what could she do tonight? Advancing on Mr. Arrigo to demand an explanation was considered. Very briefly. Affable, distinguished Mr. Arrigo might chat easily about trivialities in the elevator, he might find her attractive, but he did not appear to be a man who could be manipulated by a proper Brit lady into confessing a crime against his will. Given what she now suspected, crime could very well be his business, and murder—either of a "business associate" or a harmless deliveryman—only a minor blip on his screen of life.

She remembered with sadness the huge raindrops plopping from Mr. Feng's nose.

Then she remembered Tony. She got out the classified pages of the phone book and turned to the section on restaurants. On the page listing restaurants by type and location, there were lots of Italian restaurants, lots of pizzerias. And lots of them were in her general neighborhood. She picked up the phone.

"Hello? Do you have hot mussels and a delivery boy named Tony?"

"Lady, everybody's got a delivery boy named Tony." This was the fifth place she'd called. "Yeah, we got mussels . . ." The man sounded wary.

"Aren't you the place that delivers to Mr. Arrigo at . . . ?" She gave the building's address.

"Hey, yeah. Enzo Arrigo. You know him?" The man sounded impressed, and wavered between truculence and a desire to ingratiate himself with someone who was a friend of Enzo Arrigo's.

"My neighbor," Margaret said brightly. "He's so terribly enthusiastic about your food."

"Arrigo said that? Hey, it's only pizza and calzone, some pretty good lasagne, the usual stuff . . ."

"And Tony."

"Lady, Tony's only a kid, you know? Give him a break."

"I have no . . . no designs on Tony," Margaret said primly. "I just want . . ."

"So, what *do* you want?"

"Mussels. Hot mussels. Umm . . . Do you have a car for deliveries? I'll need them fast, I have a guest coming."

"Tony's just gone off," the man said quickly. "You'll like Sal just as good. He's a little older, you know? More of a man of the world. Yeah, we got a delivery truck for bad nights like this. I'll put your order in now. Fifteen, twenty, maybe twenty-five minutes at the outside, it'll be there. Apartment?"

Margaret was too impatient to wait quietly for Sal's arrival. If she took a stroll down the hall, past Mr. Arrigo's apartment, she might get an idea. . . .

Outside Mr. Arrigo's door, she looked down and froze.

On the deep-pile hall carpet was a splotch of red. Several splotches.

It can't be blood, she thought. *It can't. Things involving blood don't happen in my apartment building.*

Hesitantly, she touched one of the splotches with her finger, and retreated rapidly to her apartment. Inside, she looked at her finger, then sniffed it, but refused to taste it. It didn't look like blood, but still . . . There was a very faint scent of garlic and fennel, Italian herbs and spices.

Margaret relaxed with a sigh. Marinara sauce. It had to be. Not that it explained anything, unless some of the other splotches were not marinara, but something else.

Where was De Vere? He'd know what to do. She wiped the red substance from her finger, then wondered if she should collect more samples, just in case.

What if Mr. Feng had seen a body covered in blood in Mr. Arrigo's apartment? Or even one covered in marinara sauce? Something must have happened in or just outside of Mr. Arrigo's apartment that put Mr. Feng in danger. Someone had taken note of Mr. Feng.

The sharp ring of her doorbell startled her. Mr. Davidson rarely failed to advise her from downstairs of a delivery.

She took a deep breath and prepared to meet Sal, the man with the hot mussels.

Sal was outside her door, all right, but so was Mr. Arrigo, looking as grim as she'd ever seen him. He entered her apartment without waiting to be asked. "Come on in, kid," he said to Sal. "This here's a real lady, even if no lady I know pokes her nose into other people's private business."

Margaret heard herself babbling, "How nice of you to drop by. I kept thinking of how good those mussels you like sounded, so I ordered some. Have you eaten? Well, you must have, since Tony brought in all that food. What do I owe you, Sal?"

Mr. Arrigo cut her off. "It's been taken care of. So, you didn't like the Chinese takeout you got before?"

"I . . . I rather lost my appetite for it," Margaret said, and took a deep breath, "after what happened to the deliveryman."

"Yeah? So what did happen? Put that stuff down, Sal, and get lost." Sal obeyed promptly, closing the apartment door behind him.

"He was killed in a hit-and-run accident. Silly man, he paid no attention to traffic. I liked him."

"Did you, now? He's another one who poked his nose into things he shouldn't. It can be dangerous."

"Look, Mr. Arrigo . . . Enzo . . ." Margaret attempted wide-eyed winsomeness, but it didn't seem to work with Mr. Arrigo.

"No problem," Mr. Arrigo said. "He's dead." He stood in front of Margaret. "Now, what do I do about you?"

"Me?" Margaret said. "Whatever do you mean?"

"Hey, if that little Chinese guy saw my . . . associate, who was . . . seriously indisposed, he mighta told you, since you're such big pals." Arrigo ignored her vigorous denying headshake. "Anyhow, next I hear you're calling around about Tony and then I see you prowling around outside my door . . ."

"Someone was terribly careless," Margaret said. "The building people will be very cross about the marinara stains on the carpeting."

Mr. Arrigo stared at her. Then he laughed a loud, rumbling laugh. "Marinara! Geez! I bet you thought it was, like, blood. Well, so did I. We took this guy away. I was going to clean it up later. Hey, the joke's on me."

"Mr. Feng is dead," Margaret said. "That's no joke."

Mr. Arrigo grinned. "He was taken out by Tony, with his dinky delivery van." He rumbled again. "Taken out by the takeout guy! Now *that's* a joke. Get it?"

Margaret looked away. Yes, she got it, but she was rather more worried about herself, now that Mr. Arrigo had confirmed her suspicions.

"Sweetheart, you know a little too much." Mr. Arrigo frowned.

"I don't know anything," Margaret said firmly, "except that you spilled sauce from the hot mussels on the carpet when you were taking the trash to the trash room."

Mr. Arrigo chuckled. He seemed to be in high spirits. "Yeah, the trash. Right. Still . . ."

The buzzer from the concierge in the lobby sounded.

"What's that?"

"More takeout," Margaret said, and hoped he would believe her. "I've got to answer, or Mr. Davidson will send someone up to check."

"Okay, then. Just say, 'Yes.' No yelling for somebody. I mean it."

Margaret was sure he did. She said into the intercom phone, "Yes?"

Mr. Davidson said, "Your boyfriend's here. He's on his way up."

"That's good," Margaret said evenly. "Thank you." She hated the idea of being rescued by De Vere, but consider the alternative. She faced Mr. Arrigo. "Could I put the mussels away? I'll heat them up later." Was she being optimistic about there being a "later" for her?

"Go ahead." Arrigo followed her into the kitchen and watched her remove the aluminum container from the bag. The metal was very hot. Sal must have raced to the apartment.

The doorbell rang. De Vere at last.

"Could you get the door, please? My hands are full." She was busy dumping the container of mussels and sauce into the big cast-iron pot she always used for simmering pasta sauce.

Surprisingly, Mr. Arrigo went obediently to the door. He opened it to reveal Sam De Vere, who was definitely startled to be

facing Mr. Arrigo and not Lady Margaret Priam. Margaret edged
out of the kitchen, carrying the heavy pot full of mussels. Raising it
to her shoulder, she hurled it at Mr. Arrigo's back.

Her aim was perfect. A spray of shiny blue-black mussels and
bright red sauce exploded over Mr. Arrigo's handsome charcoal
jacket, the iron pot striking the back of his head. He staggered,
and was perhaps too stunned by the blow to think to reach for the
gun she imagined he carried.

Nevertheless, she shouted, "He has a gun!"

De Vere merely endured the surprise of his life and a few
splashes of marinara sauce on his sport jacket and jeans. But
then, he was not what one would call a cutting-edge dresser. As
Mr. Arrigo, awash in red marinara, lurched against the doorjamb,
De Vere managed to gain control of him. No gun was drawn,
although there was in fact a gun, which De Vere managed to lib-
erate from Mr. Arrigo's person.

"Margaret," De Vere said sternly, "exactly what is the meaning
of this?"

"It's about ordering takeout," Margaret said. "Come on in, and
I'll explain."

"Yes," DeVere said, "you will." Mussel shells crunched under the
men's shoes as De Vere prodded Mr. Arrigo into the apartment.

"For heaven's sake, put him in the leather chair, I don't need
marinara all over my chintz cushions," Margaret said.

De Vere said, "Now, how did you know that this gentleman
would have a gun?" Mr. Arrigo looked a little the worse for wear as
he sat heavily in the leather chair and rubbed the back of his
head.

Margaret shrugged. "The thought just occurred to me. Because
he arranged to have a friend of mine killed tonight. He's my
neighbor, Enzo Arrigo. He might have had someone else killed,
too." She gestured at the sauce and mussels on her floor. "He likes
Italian stuff, like hot mussels, so I called for takeout. Not that I was
planning on entertaining him . . . Sam, I'm so glad you came in
time, even if the mussels are gone."

"Margaret." De Vere was stern again, but he reached out and
squeezed her shoulder. "You know I prefer Chinese."

Chinese Takeout

CONSULT YELLOW PAGES under "Restaurants." Pick a Chinese restaurant that delivers in your neighborhood. If you already have a favorite Chinese restaurant, consult the wrinkled menu you've got stashed by the phone. Remove money from wallet. Call restaurant. Order what you like, ask for total with tax, and set aside appropriate money to pay the delivery person. Wait until delivery person arrives, and pay up. If food is hot, tip profusely. Close door, open cardboard containers. Break apart the chopsticks, and make sure all splinters are gone from them by rubbing the rough bits together. Dig in and enjoy!

The Case of the Shaggy Caps

Ruth Rendell

B lewits," said Inspector Burden, "Parasols, Horns of Plenty, Morels, and Boletus. Mean anything to you?"
Chief Inspector Wexford shrugged. "Sounds like one of those magazine quizzes. What have these in common? I'll make a guess and say they're crustacea. Or sea anemones. How about that?"

"They are edible fungi," said Burden.

"Are they now? And what have edible fungi to do with Mrs. Hannah Kingman's throwing herself off, or being pushed off, a balcony?"

The two men were sitting in Wexford's office at the police station, Kingsmarkham, in the County of Sussex. The month was November, but Wexford had only just returned from his holiday. And while he had been away, enjoying two weeks of Italian autumn, Hannah Kingman had committed suicide. Or so Burden had thought at first. Now he was in a dilemma, and as soon as Wexford had walked in that Monday morning, Burden had begun to tell the whole story to his chief.

Wexford, getting on for sixty, was a tall, ungainly, rather ugly man who had once been fat to the point of obesity but had slimmed to gauntness for reasons of health. Nearly twenty years his junior, Burden had the slenderness of a man who has always been thin. His face was ascetic, handsome in a frosty way. The older man, who had a good wife who looked after him devotedly, nevertheless always looked as if his clothes came off the peg from the War on Want shop, while the younger, a widower, was sartorially immaculate. A tramp and a Beau Brummell, they seemed to be, but the dandy relied on the tramp, trusted him, understood his powers and his perception. In secret he almost worshiped him.

Without his chief he had felt a little at sea in this case. Everything had pointed at first to Hannah Kingman's having killed herself. She had been a manic-depressive, with a strong sense of her own inadequacy; apparently her marriage, though not of long duration, had been unhappy, and her previous marriage had failed. Even in the absence of a suicide note or suicide threats, Burden would have taken her death for self-destruction—if her brother hadn't come along and told him about the edible fungi. And Wexford hadn't been there to do what he always could do—sort out sheep from goats and wheat from chaff.

"The thing is," Burden said across the desk, "we're not looking for proof of murder so much as proof of *attempted* murder. Axel Kingman could have pushed his wife off that balcony—he has no alibi for the time in question—but I had no reason to think he had done so until I was told of an attempt to murder her some two weeks before."

"Which attempt has something to do with edible fungi?"

Burden nodded. "Say with administering to her some noxious substance in a stew made from edible fungi. Though if he did it, God knows how he did it, because three other people, including himself, ate the stew without ill effects. I think I'd better tell you about it from the beginning."

"I think you had," said Wexford.

"The facts," Burden began, very like a prosecuting counsel, "are as follows. Axel Kingman is thirty-five years old and he keeps a health-food shop here in the High Street called Harvest Home. Know it?" When Wexford signified by a nod that he did, Burden went on, "He used to be a teacher in Myringham, and for about seven years before he came here he'd been living with a woman named Corinne Last. He left her, gave up his job, put all the capital he had into his shop, and married a Mrs. Hannah Nicholson."

"He's some sort of food freak, I take it," said Wexford.

Burden wrinkled his nose. "Lot of affected nonsense," he said. "Have you ever noticed what thin pale weeds these health-food people are? While the folks who live on roast beef and suet and whiskey and plum cake are full of beans and rarin' to go."

"Is Kingman a thin pale weed?"

"A feeble—what's the word?—aesthete, if you ask me. Anyway, he and Hannah opened this shop and took a flat in the high-rise tower our planning geniuses have been pleased to raise over the top of it. The fifth floor. Corinne Last, according to her and according to Kingman, accepted it after a while and they all remained friends."

"Tell me about them," Wexford said. "Leave the facts for a bit and tell me about them."

Burden never found this easy. He was inclined to describe people as "just ordinary" or "just like anyone else," a negative attitude, which exasperated Wexford. So he made an effort. "Kingman looks the sort who wouldn't hurt a fly. The fact is, I'd apply the word *gentle* to him if I wasn't coming round to thinking he's a cold-blooded wife killer. He's a total abstainer with a bee in his bonnet about drink. His father went bankrupt and finally died of a coronary as a result of alcoholism, and our Kingman is an anti-booze fanatic.

"The dead woman was twenty-nine. Her first husband left her after six months of marriage and went off with some girlfriend of hers. Hannah went back to live with her parents and had a part-time job helping out with the meals at the school where Kingman was a teacher. That was where they met."

"And the other woman?" said Wexford.

Burden's face took on a repressive expression. Sex outside marriage, however sanctioned by custom and general approval, was always distasteful to him. That, in the course of his work, he almost daily came across illicit sex had done nothing to mitigate his disapproval. As Wexford sometimes derisively put it, you would think that in Burden's eyes all the suffering in the world, and certainly all the crime, somehow derived from men and women going to bed together outside the bonds of wedlock. "God knows why he didn't marry her," Burden now said. "Personally, I think things were a lot better in the days when education authorities put their foot down about immorality among teachers."

"Let's not have your views on that now, Mike," said Wexford. "Presumably, Hannah Kingman didn't die because her husband didn't come to her a pure virgin."

Burden flushed slightly. "I'll tell you about this Corinne Last. She's very good-looking, if you like the dark sort of intense type. Her father left her some money and the house where she and Kingman lived, and she still lives in it. She's one of those women who seem to be good at everything they put their hands to. She paints and sells her paintings. She makes her own clothes, she's more or less the star in the local dramatic society, she's a violinist and plays in some string trio. Also she writes for health magazines and she's the author of a cookbook."

"It would look then," Wexford put in, "as if Kingman split up with her because all this was more than he could take. And hence he took up with the dull little schoolmeals lady. No competition from her, I fancy."

"I daresay you're right. As a matter of fact, that theory has already been put to me."

"By whom?" said Wexford. "Just where did you get all this information, Mike?"

"From an angry young man, the fourth member of the quartet, who happens to be Hannah's brother. His name is John Hood, and I think he's got a lot more to tell. But it's time I left off describing the people and got on with the story.

"No one saw Hannah fall from the balcony. It happened last Thursday afternoon at about four. According to her husband, he was in a sort of office behind the shop doing what he always did on early closing day—stock-taking and sticking labels on various bottles and packets.

"She fell onto a hard-top parking area at the back of the flats, and her body was found by a neighbor a couple of hours later between two parked cars. We were sent for, and Kingman seemed to be distraught. I asked him if he had had any idea that his wife would have wished to take her own life, and he said she had never threatened to do so but had lately been very depressed and there had been quarrels, principally about money. Her doctor had put her on tranquilizers—of which, by the way, Kingman disapproved—and the doctor himself, old Dr. Castle, told me Mrs. Kingman had been to him for depression and because she felt her life wasn't worth living and she was a drag on her husband. He wasn't surprised that she had killed herself and neither, by that time, was I. We were all set for an inquest verdict of suicide while the balance of the mind was disturbed when John Hood walked in here and told me Kingman had attempted to murder his wife on a previous occasion."

"He told you just like that?"

"Pretty well. It's plain he doesn't like Kingman, and no doubt he was fond of his sister. He also seems to like and admire Corinne Last. He told me that on a Saturday night at the end of October the four of them had a meal together in the Kingmans' flat. It was a lot of vegetarian stuff cooked by Kingman—he always did the cooking—and one of the dishes was made out of what I'm old-fashioned enough, or maybe narrow-minded enough, to call toadstools. They all ate it and they were all okay but for Hannah, who got up from the table, vomited for hours, and apparently was quite seriously ill."

Wexford's eyebrows went up. "Elucidate, please," he said.

Burden sat back, put his elbows on the arms of the chair, and pressed the tips of his fingers together. "A few days before this meal was eaten, Kingman and Hood met at the squash club of which they are both members. Kingman told Hood that Corinne Last had promised to get him some edible fungi called Shaggy Caps from her own garden, the garden of the house which they had at one time shared. A crop of these things show themselves every autumn under a tree in this garden. I've seen them myself, but we'll come to that in a minute.

"Kingman's got a thing about using weeds and whatnot for cooking, makes salads out of dandelions and sorrel, and he swears by this fungi rubbish, says they've got far more flavor than mushrooms. Give me something that comes in a plastic bag from the supermarket every time, but no doubt it takes all sorts to make a world. By the way, this cookbook of Corinne Last's is called *Cooking for Nothing*, and all the recipes are for making dishes out of stuff you pull up by the wayside or pluck from the hedgerow."

"These Warty Blobs or Spotted Puffets or whatever, had he cooked them before?"

"Shaggy Caps," said Burden, grinning, "or *Coprinus comatus*. Oh, yes, every year, and every year he and Corinne had eaten the resulting stew. He told Hood he was going to cook them again this time, and Hood says he seemed very grateful to Corinne for being so—well, magnanimous."

"Yes, I can see it would have been a wrench for her. Like hearing 'our tune' in the company of your ex-lover and your supplanter."

Wexford put on a vibrant growl. " 'Can you bear the sight of me eating our toadstools with another'?"

"As a matter of fact," said Burden seriously, "it could have been just like that. Anyway, the upshot of it was that Hood was invited round for the following Saturday to taste these delicacies and was told that Corinne would be there. Perhaps it was that fact which made him accept. Well, the day came. Hood looked in on his sister at lunchtime. She showed him the pot containing the stew, which Kingman had already made, and she said *she had tasted it* and it was delicious. She also showed Hood half a dozen specimens of Shaggy Caps, which she said Kingman hadn't needed and which they would fry for their breakfast. This is what she showed him."

Burden opened a drawer in the desk and produced one of those plastic bags which he had said so inspired him with confidence. But the contents of this one hadn't come from a supermarket. He removed the wire fastener and tipped out four whitish, scaly objects. They were egg-shaped, or rather elongated ovals, each with a short fleshy stalk.

"I picked them myself this morning," he said, "from Corinne Last's garden. When they get bigger, the egg-shaped bit opens like an umbrella, or a pagoda really, and there are sort of black gills underneath. You're supposed to eat them when they're in the stage these are."

"I suppose you've got a book on fungi?" said Wexford.

"Here." This also was produced from the drawer. *British Fungi, Edible and Poisonous.* "And here we are—Shaggy Caps."

Burden opened it at the "Edible" section and at a line and wash drawing of the species he held in his hand. He handed it to the chief inspector.

"'*Coprinus comatus,*'" Wexford read aloud. "'A common species, attaining when full grown a height of nine inches. The fungus is frequently to be found, during late summer and autumn, growing in fields, hedgerows, and often in gardens. It should be eaten before the cap opens and disgorges its inky fluid, but is at all times quite harmless.'" He put the book down but didn't close it. "Go on, please, Mike," he said.

"Hood called for Corinne and they arrived together. They got there just after eight. At about eight fifteen they all sat down to table and began the meal with avocado *vinaigrette*. The next course was to be the stew, followed by nut cutlets with a salad and then an applecake. Very obviously, there was no wine or any liquor on account of Kingman's prejudices. They drank grape juice from the shop.

"The kitchen opens directly out of the living-dining room. Kingman brought in the stew in a large tureen and served it himself at the table, beginning, of course, with Corinne. Each one of those Shaggy Caps had been sliced in half lengthwise, and the pieces were floating in a thickish gravy to which carrots, onions, and other vegetables had been added. Now, ever since he had been invited to this meal, Hood had been feeling uneasy about eating fungi, but Corinne had reassured him, and once he began to eat it and saw the others were eating it quite happily, he stopped worrying for the time being. In fact, he had a second helping.

"Kingman took the plates out and the empty tureen and immediately *rinsed them under the tap*. Both Hood and Corinne Last have told me this, though Kingman says it was something he always did, being fastidious about things of that sort."

"Surely his ex-girlfriend could confirm or deny that," Wexford put in, "since they lived together for so long."

"We must ask her. All traces of the stew were rinsed away. Kingman then brought in the nut concoction and the salad, but before he could begin to serve them, Hannah jumped up, covered her mouth with her napkin, and rushed to the bathroom.

"After a while Corinne went to her. Hood could hear a violent vomiting from the bathroom. He remained in the living room while Kingman and Corinne were both in the bathroom with Hannah. No one ate any more. Kingman eventually came back, said that Hannah must have picked up some 'bug' and that he had put her to bed. Hood went into the bedroom where Hannah was lying on the bed with Corinne sitting beside her. Her face was greenish and covered with sweat and she was evidently in great pain, because while he was there she doubled up and groaned. She had to go to the bathroom again and that time Kingman had to carry her back.

"Hood suggested Dr. Castle should be sent for, but this was strenuously opposed by Kingman, who dislikes doctors and is one of those people who go in for herbal remedies—raspberry-leaf tablets and camomile tea and that sort of thing. Also he told Hood, rather absurdly, that Hannah had had quite enough to do with doctors and that if this wasn't some gastric germ it was the result of her taking 'dangerous' tranquilizers.

"Hood thought Hannah was seriously ill and the argument got heated, with Hood trying to make Kingman either call a doctor or take her to a hospital. Kingman wouldn't do it, and Corinne took his part. Hood is one of those angry but weak people who are all bluster, and although he might have called a doctor himself, he didn't. The effect on him of Corinne again, I suppose. What he did do was tell Kingman he was a fool to mess about cooking things everyone knew weren't safe, to which Kingman replied that if the Shaggy Caps were dangerous, how was it they weren't all ill? Eventually, at about midnight, Hannah stopped retching, seemed to have no more pain, and fell asleep. Hood drove Corinne home, returned to the Kingmans', and remained there for the rest of the night, sleeping on their sofa.

"In the morning Hannah seemed perfectly well, though weak, which rather upset Kingman's theory about the gastric bug. Relations between the brothers-in-law were strained. Kingman said he hadn't liked Hood's suggestions and that when he wanted to see his sister he, Kingman, would rather he came there when he was out or in the shop. Hood went off home, and since that day he hasn't seen Kingman.

"The day after his sister's death he stormed in here, told me what I've told you, and accused Kingman of trying to poison Hannah. He was wild and nearly hysterical, but I felt I couldn't dismiss this allegation as—well, the ravings of a bereaved person. There were too many peculiar circumstances—the unhappiness of the marriage, the fact of Kingman's rinsing those plates, his refusal to call a doctor. Was I right?"

Burden stopped and sat waiting for approval. It came in the form of a not very enthusiastic nod.

After a moment Wexford spoke. "Could Kingman have pushed her off that balcony, Mike?"

"She was a small, fragile woman. It was physically possible. The back of the flats isn't overlooked. There's nothing behind but the parking area and then open fields. Kingman could have gone up by the stairs instead of using the lift and come down by the stairs. Two of the flats on the lower floors are empty. Below the Kingmans lives a bedridden woman whose husband was at work. Below that the tenant, a young married woman, was in but she saw and heard nothing. The invalid says she thinks she heard a scream during the afternoon but she did nothing about it, and if she did hear it, so what? It seems to me that a suicide, in those circumstances, is as likely to cry out as a murder victim."

"Okay," said Wexford. "Now to return to the curious business of this meal. The idea would presumably be that Kingman intended to kill her that night but that his plan misfired because whatever he gave her wasn't toxic enough. She was very ill but she didn't die. He chose those means and that company so that he would have witnesses to his innocence. They all ate the stew out of the same tureen, but only Hannah was affected by it. How then are you suggesting he gave her whatever poison he did give her?"

"I'm not," said Burden, frankly, "but others are making suggestions. Hood's a bit of a fool, and first of all he would only keep on about all fungi being dangerous and the whole dish being poisonous. When I pointed out that this was obviously not so, he said Kingman must have slipped something into Hannah's plate, or else it was the salt."

"What salt?"

"He remembered that no one but Hannah took salt with the stew. But that's absurd because Kingman couldn't have known that would happen. He wouldn't have dared put, say, arsenic in the saltcellar on the thin chance that only she would take salt. Besides, she recovered far too quickly for it to have been arsenic. Corinne Last, however, has a more feasible suggestion.

"Not that she goes along with Hood. She refuses to consider the possibility that Kingman might be guilty. But when I pressed her she said she was not actually sitting at the table while the stew was served. She had got up and gone into the hall to fetch her handbag. So she didn't see Kingman serve Hannah." Burden reached across and picked up the book Wexford had left open at the description and drawing of the Shaggy Caps. He flicked over to the "Poisonous" section and pushed the book back to the chief inspector. "Have a look at some of these."

"Ah, yes," said Wexford. "Our old friend, the Fly Agaric. A nice-looking little red job with white spots, much favored by illustrators of children's books. They usually stick a frog on top of it and a gnome underneath. I see that when ingested it causes nausea, vomiting, tetanic convulsions, coma, and death. Lots of these Agarics, aren't there? Purple, Crested, Warty, Verdigris—all more or less lethal. Aha! The Death Cap, *Amanita phalloides*. How very unpleasant. The most dangerous fungus known, it says here. Very

2

small quantities will cause intense suffering and often death. So where does all that get us?"

"Corinne Last says that the Death Cap is quite common round here. What she doesn't say, but what I infer, is that Kingman could have got hold of it easily. Now, suppose he cooked just one specimen separately and dropped it into the stew just before he brought it in from the kitchen? When he comes to serve Hannah he spoons up for her this specimen, or the pieces of it, in the same way as someone might select a special piece of chicken for someone out of a casserole. The gravy was thick, it wasn't like a thin soup."

Wexford looked dubious. "Well, we won't dismiss it as a theory. If he had contaminated the rest of the stew and others had been ill, that would have made it look even more like an accident, which was presumably what he wanted. But there's one drawback to that, Mike. If he meant Hannah to die, and was unscrupulous enough not to mind about Corinne and Hood being made ill, why did he rinse the plates? To *prove* that it was an accident, he would have wanted above all to keep some of that stew for analysis when the time came, for analysis would have shown the presence of poisonous as well as nonpoisonous fungi, and it would have seemed that he had merely been careless.

"But let's go and talk to these people, shall we?"

THE SHOP CALLED HARVEST Home was closed. Wexford and Burden went down an alley at the side of the block, passed the glass-doored main entrance, and went to the back to a door that was labeled "Stairs and Emergency Exit." They entered a small tiled vestibule and began to mount a steepish flight of stairs.

On each floor was a front door and a door to the lift. There was no one about. If there had been and they had had no wish to be seen, it would only have been necessary to wait behind the bend in the stairs until whoever it was had got into the lift. The bell by the front door on the fifth floor was marked "A. and H. Kingman." Wexford rang it.

The man who admitted them was smallish and mild-looking, and he looked sad. He showed Wexford the balcony from which his wife had fallen. It was one of two in the flat, the other being larger and extending outside the living-room windows. This one was outside a glazed kitchen door, a place for hanging washing and for gardening of the window-box variety. Herbs grew in pots, and in a long trough there still remained frostbitten tomato vines. The wall surrounding the balcony was about three feet high, the drop sheer to the hard-top below.

"Were you surprised that your wife committed suicide, Mr. Kingman?" said Wexford.

Kingman didn't answer directly "My wife set a very low valuation on herself. When we got married, I thought she was like me, a simple sort of person who doesn't ask much from life but has quite a capacity for contentment. It wasn't like that. She expected more support and more comfort and encouragement than I could give. That was especially so for the first three months of our marriage. Then she seemed to turn against me. She was very moody, always up and down. My business isn't doing very well, and she was spending more money than we could afford. I don't know where all the money was going, and we quarreled about it. Then she'd become depressed and say she was no use to me, she'd be better dead."

He had given, Wexford thought, rather a long explanation, for which he hadn't been asked. But it could be that these thoughts, defensive yet self-reproachful, were at the moment uppermost in his mind. "Mr. Kingman," he said, "we have reason to believe, as you know, that foul play may have been involved here. I should like to ask you a few questions about a meal you cooked on October 29, after which your wife was ill."

"I can guess who's been telling you about that."

Wexford took no notice. "When did Miss Last bring you these—er, Shaggy Caps?"

"On the evening of the twenty-eighth. I made the stew from them in the morning, according to Miss Last's own recipe."

"Was there any other type of fungus in the flat at the time?"

"Mushrooms, probably."

"Did you at any time add any noxious object or substance to that stew, Mr. Kingman?"

Kingman said quietly, wearily, "Of course not. My brother-in-law has a lot of ignorant prejudices. He refused to understand that that stew, which I have made dozens of times before in exactly the same way, was as wholesome as, say, a chicken casserole. More wholesome, in my view."

"Very well. Nevertheless, your wife was very ill. Why didn't you call a doctor?"

"Because my wife was not 'very' ill. She had pains and diarrhea, that's all. Perhaps you aren't aware of what the symptoms of fungus poisoning are. The victim doesn't just have pain and sickness. His vision is impaired, he very likely blacks out, or has convulsions of the kind associated with tetanus. There was nothing like that with Hannah."

"It was unfortunate that you rinsed those plates. Had you not done so and called a doctor, the remains of that stew would almost certainly have been sent for analysis, and if it was as harmless as you say, all this investigation could have been avoided."

"It was harmless," Kingman said stonily.

Out in the car Wexford said, "I'm inclined to believe him, Mike. And unless Hood or Corinne Last has something really positive to tell us, I'd let it rest. Shall we go and see her next?"

THE COTTAGE SHE HAD shared with Axel Kingman was on a lonely stretch of road outside the village of Myfleet. It was a stone cottage with a slate roof, surrounded by a well-tended pretty garden. A green Ford Escort stood on the drive in front of a weatherboard garage. Under a big old apple tree, from which the yellow leaves were falling, the Shaggy Caps, immediately recognizable, grew in three thick clumps.

She was a tall woman, the owner of this house, with a beautiful square-jawed, high-cheekboned face and a mass of dark hair. Wexford was at once reminded of the Klimt painting of a languorous red-lipped woman, gold-neckleted, half covered in gold draperies, though Corinne Last wore a sweater and a denim smock. Her voice was low and measured. He had the impression she could never be flustered or caught off her guard.

"You're the author of a cookbook, I believe?" he said.

She made no answer but handed him a paperback which she took down from a bookshelf. *Cooking for Nothing: Dishes from Hedgerow and Pasture* by Corinne Last. He looked through the index and found the recipe he wanted. Opposite it was a colored photograph of six people eating what looked like brown soup. The recipe included carrots, onions, herbs, cream, and a number of other harmless ingredients. The last lines read: "Stewed Shaggy Caps are best served piping hot with whole-wheat bread. For drinkables, see page 171." He glanced at page 171, then handed the book to Burden.

"This was the dish Mr. Kingman made that night?"

"Yes." She had a way of leaning back when she spoke and of half lowering her heavy, glossy eyelids. It was serpentine and a little repellent. "I picked the Shaggy Caps myself out of this garden. I don't understand how they could have made Hannah ill, but they must have, because she was fine when we first arrived. She hadn't got any sort of gastric infection, that's nonsense. And there was nothing wrong with the avocados or the dressing."

Burden put the book aside. "But you were all served stew out of the same tureen."

"I didn't see Axel actually serve Hannah. I was out of the room." The eyelids flickered and almost closed.

"Was it usual for Mr. Kingman to rinse plates as soon as they were removed?"

"Don't ask me." She moved her shoulders. "I don't know. I do know that Hannah was very ill just after eating that stew. Axel doesn't like doctors, of course, and perhaps it would have—well, embarrassed him to call Dr. Castle in the circumstances. Hannah had black spots in front of her eyes, she was getting double vision. I was extremely concerned for her."

"But you didn't take it on yourself to get a doctor, Miss Last? Or even support Mr. Hood in his allegations?"

"Whatever John Hood said, I knew it couldn't be the Shaggy Caps." There was a note of scorn when she spoke Hood's name. "And I was rather frightened. I couldn't help thinking it would be terrible if Axel got into some sort of trouble, if there was an inquiry or something."

"There's an inquiry now, Miss Last."

"Well, it's different now, isn't it? Hannah's dead. I mean, it's not just suspicion or conjecture anymore."

She saw them out and closed the front door before they had reached the garden gate. Farther along the roadside and under the hedges more Shaggy Caps could be seen as well as other kinds of fungi that Wexford couldn't identify—little mushroom-like things with pinkish gills, a cluster of small yellow umbrellas, and from the trunk of an oak tree, bulbous smoke-colored swellings that Burden said were Oyster Mushrooms.

"That woman," said Wexford, "is a mistress of the artless insinuation. She damned Kingman with almost every word, but she never came out with a direct insinuation." He shook his head. "I suppose Hood will be at work?"

"Presumably," said Burden, but Hood was not at work. He was waiting for them at the police station, fuming at the delay, and threatening "if something wasn't done at once" to take his grievances to the chief constable, even to the Home Office.

"Something is being done," said Wexford quietly. "I'm glad you've come here, Mr. Hood. But try to keep calm, will you, please?"

It was apparent to Wexford from the first that John Hood was in a different category of intelligence from that of Kingman and Corinne Last. He was a thickset man of perhaps no more than twenty-seven or twenty-eight, with bewildered, resentful blue eyes in a puffy, flushed face. *A man,* Wexford thought, *who would fling out rash accusations he couldn't substantiate, who would be driven to bombast and bluster in the company of the ex-teacher and that clever, subtle woman.*

He began to talk now, not wildly, but still without restraint, repeating what he had said to Burden, reiterating, without putting forward any real evidence, that his brother-in-law had meant to kill his sister that night. It was only by luck that she had survived. Kingman was a ruthless man who would have stopped at nothing to be rid of her. He, Hood, would never forgive himself that he hadn't made a stand and called the doctor.

"Yes, yes, Mr. Hood, but what exactly were your sister's symptoms?"

"Vomiting and stomach pains, violent pains," said Hood.

"She complained of nothing else?"

"Wasn't that enough? That's what you get when someone feeds you poisonous rubbish."

Wexford merely raised his eyebrows. Abruptly, he left the events of that evening and said, "What had gone wrong with your sister's marriage?"

Before Hood replied, Wexford could sense he was keeping something back. A wariness came into his eyes and then was gone. "Axel wasn't the right person for her," he began. "She had problems, she needed understanding, she wasn't . . ." His voice trailed away.

"Wasn't what, Mr. Hood? What problems?"

"It's got nothing to do with all this," Hood muttered.

"I'll be the judge of that. You made this accusation, you started this business off. It's not for you now to keep anything back." On a sudden inspiration Wexford said, "Had these problems anything to do with the money she was spending?"

Hood was silent and sullen. Wexford thought rapidly over the things he had been told—Axel Kingman's fanaticism on one particular subject, Hannah's desperate need of an unspecified kind of support during the early days of her marriage, and later on, her alternating moods, then the money, the weekly sums of money spent and unaccounted for.

He looked up and said baldly, "Was your sister an alcoholic, Mr. Hood?"

Hood hadn't liked his directness. He flushed and looked affronted. He skirted round a frank answer. Well, yes, she drank. She was at pains to conceal her drinking. It had been going on more or less consistently since her first marriage broke up.

"In fact, she was an alcoholic," said Wexford.

"I suppose so."

"Your brother-in-law didn't know?"

"Good God, no. Axel would have killed her!" He realized what he had said. "Maybe that's why, maybe he found out."

"I don't think so, Mr. Hood. Now, I imagine that in the first few months of her marriage she made an effort to give up drinking. She needed a good deal of support during this time, but she couldn't or wouldn't tell Mr. Kingman why she needed it. Her efforts failed, and slowly, because she couldn't manage without it, she began drinking again."

"She wasn't as bad as she used to be," Hood said with pathetic eagerness. "And only in the evenings. She told me she never had a drink before six, and then she'd have a few more, gulping them down on the quiet so Axel wouldn't know."

Burden said suddenly, "Had your sister been drinking that evening?"

"I expect so. She wouldn't have been able to face company, not even just Corinne and me, without a drink."

"Did anyone besides yourself know that your sister drank?"

"My mother did. My mother and I had a sort of pact to keep it dark from everyone so that Axel wouldn't find out." He hesitated, then said rather defiantly, "I did tell Corinne. She's a wonderful person, she's very clever. I was worried about it and I didn't know what I ought to do. She promised she wouldn't tell Axel."

"I see." Wexford had his own reasons for thinking that hadn't happened. Deep in thought, he got up and walked to the other end of the room, where he stood gazing out the window. Burden's continuing questions, Hood's answers, reached him only as a confused murmur of voices. Then he heard Burden say more loudly, "That's all for now, Mr. Hood, unless the chief inspector has anything more to ask you."

"No, no," said Wexford abstractedly, and when Hood had somewhat truculently departed, "Time for lunch. It's past two. Personally, I shall avoid any dishes containing fungi, even *Psalliota campestris*."

After Burden had looked that one up and identified it as the Common Mushroom, they lunched and then made a round of such wineshops in Kingsmarkham as were open at that hour. At the Wine Basket they drew a blank, but the assistant in the Vineyard told them that a woman answering Hannah Kingman's description had been a regular customer, and that on the previous Wednesday, the day before her death, she had called in and bought a bottle of Courvoisier cognac.

"There was no liquor of any kind in Kingman's flat," said Burden. "Might have been an empty bottle in the rubbish, I suppose." He made a rueful face. "We didn't look, didn't think we had any reason to. But she couldn't have drunk a whole bottleful on the Wednesday, could she?"

"Why are you so interested in this drinking business, Mike? You don't seriously see it as a motive for murder, do you? That Kingman killed her because he'd found out, or been told, that she was a secret drinker?"

"It was a means, not a motive," said Burden. "I know how it was done. I know how Kingman tried to kill her that first time." He grinned. "Makes a change for me to find the answer before you, doesn't it? I'm going to follow in your footsteps and make a mystery of it for the time being, if you don't mind. With your permission we'll go back to the station, pick up those Shaggy Caps, and conduct a little experiment."

MICHAEL BURDEN LIVED IN a neat bungalow in Tabard Road, Kingsmarkham. He had lived there with his wife until her untimely and tragic death and continued to live there still with his sixteen-year-old daughter, his son being away at a university. But that evening Pat Burden was out with her boyfriend, and there was a note left for her father on the refrigerator. "Dad, I ate the cold beef from yesterday. Can you open a tin for yourself? Back by eleven. Love, P."

"I'm glad she hasn't cooked anything," said Burden with what Wexford called his sloppy look, the expression that came over his face whenever he thought his children might be inconvenienced or made to lift a finger on his account. "I shouldn't be able to eat it, and I'd hate her to take it as criticism."

Wexford made the sound that used to be written "Pshaw!" "You've got sensible kids and you treat them like paranoiacs. While you're deciding just how much I'm to be told about this experiment of yours, d'you mind if I phone my wife?"

"Be my guest."

It was nearly six. Wexford came back to find Burden peeling carrots and onions. The four specimens of *Coprinus comatus*, beginning now to look a little wizened, lay on a chopping board. On the stove a saucepanful of bone stock was heating up.

"What the hell are you doing?"

"Making Shaggy Cap stew. My theory is that the stew is harmless when eaten by nondrinkers, and toxic, or toxic to some extent, when taken by those with alcohol in the stomach. How about that? In a minute, when this lot's cooking, I'm going to take a moderate quantity of alcohol, then I'm going to eat the stew. Now say I'm a damned fool if you like."

Wexford shrugged. He grinned. "I'm overcome by so much courage and selfless devotion to the duty you owe the taxpayers. But wait a minute. Are you sure only Hannah had been drinking that night? We know Kingman hadn't. What about those other two?"

"I asked Hood that while you were off in your daydream. He called for Corinne Last at six, at her request. They picked some apples for his mother, then she made him coffee. He did suggest they call in at a pub for a drink on their way to the Kingmans', but apparently she took so long getting ready that they didn't have time."

"Okay. Go ahead then. But wouldn't it be easier to call in an expert? There must be such people. Very likely someone holds a chair of fungology at the University of the South."

"Very likely. We can do that after I've tried it. I want to know for sure *now.* Are you willing, too?"

"Certainly not. I'm not your guest to that extent. Since I've told my wife I won't be home for dinner, I'll take it as a kindness if you'll make me some innocent scrambled eggs."

He followed Burden into the living room, where the inspector opened a door in the sideboard. "What'll you drink?"

"White wine, if you've got any, or vermouth if you haven't. You know how abstemious I have to be."

Burden poured vermouth and soda. "Ice?"

"No, thanks. What are you going to have? Brandy? That was Hannah Kingman's favorite, apparently."

"Haven't got any," said Burden. "It'll have to be whiskey. I think we can reckon she had two double brandies before that meal, don't you? I'm not so brave I want to be as ill as she was." He caught Wexford's eye. "You don't think some people could be more sensitive to it than others, do you?"

"Bound to be," said Wexford breezily. "Cheers!"

Burden sipped his heavily watered whiskey, then tossed it down. "I'll just have a look at my stew. You sit down. Put the television on."

Wexford obeyed him. The big colored picture was of a wood in autumn, pale blue sky, golden beech leaves. Then the camera closed in on a cluster of red-and-white-spotted Fly Agaric. Chuckling, Wexford turned it off as Burden put his head round the door.

"I think it's more or less ready."

"Better have another whiskey."

"I suppose I had." Burden came in and refilled his glass. "That ought to do it."

"Oh, God, I forgot. I'm not much of a cook, you know. Don't know how women manage to get a whole lot of different things brewing and make them synchronize."

"It is a mystery, isn't it? I'll get myself some bread and cheese, if I may."

The brownish mixture was in a soup bowl. In the gravy floated four Shaggy Caps, cut lengthwise. Burden finished his whiskey at a gulp.

"What was it the Christians in the arena used to say to the Roman emperor before they went to the lions?"

"*Morituri te salutamus,*" said Wexford. " 'We who are about to die salute thee.' "

"Well . . ." Burden made an effort with the Latin he had culled from his son's homework. "*Moriturus te saluto.* Would that be right?"

"I daresay. You won't die, though."

Burden made no answer. He picked up his spoon and began to eat. "Can I have some more soda?" said Wexford.

There are perhaps few stabs harder to bear than derision directed at one's heroism. Burden gave him a sour look. "Help yourself. I'm busy."

The chief inspector did so. "What's it like?" he said.

"All right. It's quite nice, like mushrooms."

Doggedly, he ate. He didn't once gag on it. He finished the lot and wiped the bowl round with a piece of bread. Then he sat up, holding himself rather tensely.

"May as well have your telly on now," said Wexford. "Pass the time." He switched it on again. No Fly Agaric this time, but a dog fox moving across a meadow with Vivaldi playing. "How d'you feel?"

"Fine," said Burden gloomily.

"Cheer up. It may not last."

But it did. After fifteen minutes had passed, Burden still felt perfectly well. He looked bewildered. "I was so damned positive. I *knew* I was going to be retching and vomiting by now. I didn't put the car away because I was certain you'd have to run me down to the hospital."

Wexford only raised his eyebrows.

"You were pretty casual about it, I must say. Didn't say a word to stop me, did you? Didn't it occur to you it might have been a bit awkward for you if anything had happened to me?"

"I knew it wouldn't. I said to get a fungologist." And then Wexford, faced by Burden's aggrieved stare, burst out laughing. "Dear old Mike, you'll have to forgive me. But you know me, d'you honestly think I'd have let you risk your life eating that stuff? I knew you were safe."

"May one ask how?"

"One may. And you'd have known, too, if you'd bothered to take a proper look at that book of Corinne Last's. Under the recipe for

Shaggy Cap Stew it said, 'For drinkables, see page 171.' Well, I looked at page 171, and there Miss Last gave a recipe for cowslip wine and another for sloe gin, both highly intoxicating drinks. Would she have recommended a wine and a spirit to drink with those fungi if there'd been the slightest risk? Not if she wanted to sell her book, she wouldn't. Not unless she was risking hundreds of furious letters and expensive lawsuits from her readers."

Burden had flushed a little. Then he too began to roar with laughter.

After a little while Burden made coffee.

"A little logical thinking would be in order, I fancy," said Wexford. "You said this morning that we were not so much seeking to prove murder as attempted murder. Axel Kingman could have pushed her off that balcony, but no one saw her fall and no one heard him or anyone else go up to that flat during the afternoon. If, however, an attempt was made to murder her two weeks before, the presumption that she was eventually murdered is enormously strengthened."

Burden said impatiently, "We've been through all that. We know that."

"Wait a minute. The attempt failed. Now, just how seriously ill was she? According to Kingman and Hood, she had severe stomach pains and she vomited. By midnight she was peacefully sleeping, and by the following day she was all right."

"I don't see where this is getting us."

"To a point which is very important and which may be the crux of the whole case. You say that Axel Kingman attempted to murder her. In order to do so he must have made very elaborate plans— the arranging of the meal, the inviting of two witnesses, the ensuring that his wife tasted the stew earlier in the day, and preparing for some very nifty sleight of hand at the time the meal was served. Isn't it odd that the actual method used should so signally have failed? That Hannah's *life* never seems to have been in danger? And what if the method had succeeded? At postmortem some noxious agent would have been found in her body, or the effects of such. How could he have hoped to get away with that, since, as we know, neither of his witnesses actually watched him serve Hannah and one of them was even out of the room?

"So what I am postulating is that no one *attempted* to murder her, but someone attempted to make her ill so that, taken in conjunction with the sinister reputation of nonmushroom fungi and Hood's admitted suspicion of them, taken in conjunction with the known unhappiness of the marriage, it *would look as if there had been a murder attempt.*"

Burden stared at him. "Kingman would never have done that. He would either have wanted his attempt to succeed or not to have looked like an attempt at all."

"Exactly. And where does that get us?"

Instead of answering him Burden said on a note of triumph, his humiliation still rankling, "You're wrong about one thing. She *was* seriously ill, she didn't just have nausea and vomiting. Kingman and Hood may not have mentioned it, but Corinne Last said she had double vision and black spots before her eyes and . . ." His voice faltered. "My God, you mean—?"

Wexford nodded. "Corinne Last only of the three says she had those symptoms. Only Corinne Last is in a position to say, because she lived with him, if Kingman was in the habit of rinsing plates as soon as he removed them from the table. What does she say? That she doesn't know. Isn't that rather odd? Isn't it rather odd, too, that she chose that precise moment to leave the table and go out into the hall for her handbag?

"She knew that Hannah drank, because Hood had told her so. On the evening that meal was eaten, you say Hood called for her at her own request. Why? She has her own car, and I don't for a moment believe a woman like her would feel anything much but contempt for Hood."

"She told him there was something wrong with her car."

"I see. She asked him to come at six, although they were not due at the Kingmans' till eight. She gave him *coffee.* A funny thing to drink at that hour, wasn't it, and before a meal? So what happens when he suggests calling in at a pub on the way? She doesn't say no or say it isn't a good idea to drink and drive. She takes so long getting ready that they don't have time.

"She didn't want Hood to drink any alcohol, Mike, and she was determined to prevent it. She, of course, would take no alcohol, and she knew Kingman never drank. But she also knew Hannah's habit of having her first drink of the day at about six.

"Now, look at her motive, far stronger than Kingman's. She strikes me as a violent, passionate, and determined woman. Hannah had taken Kingman away from her. Kingman had rejected her. Why not revenge herself on both of them by killing Hannah and seeing to it that Kingman was convicted of the crime? If she simply killed Hannah, she had no way of ensuring that Kingman would come under suspicion. But if she made it look as if he had previously attempted her life, the case against him would become very strong indeed.

"Where was she last Thursday afternoon? She could just as easily have gone up those stairs as Kingman could. Hannah would have admitted her to the flat. If she, known to be interested in gardening, had suggested that Hannah take her onto that balcony and show her the pot herbs, Hannah would willingly have done so. And then we have the mystery of the missing brandy bottle with some of its contents surely remaining. If Kingman had killed her, he would have left that there, as it would greatly have strengthened the case for suicide. Imagine how he might have used it. 'Heavy drinking made my wife ill that night. She knew I had lost respect for her because of her drinking. She killed herself because her mind was unbalanced by drink.'

"Corinne Last took that bottle away because she didn't want it known that Hannah drank, and she was banking on Hood's keeping it dark from us as he had kept it from so many people in the past. And she didn't want it known because the fake murder attempt that *she* staged depended on her victim having alcohol present in her body."

Burden sighed, poured the last dregs of coffee into Wexford's cup. "But we tried that out," he said. "Or I tried it out, and it doesn't work. You knew it wouldn't work from her book. True, she brought the Shaggy Caps from her own garden, but she couldn't have mixed up poisonous fungi with them because Axel Kingman would have realized at once. Or if he hadn't, they'd all have been ill, alcohol or no alcohol. She was never alone with Hannah before the meal, and while the stew was served she was out of the room."

"I know. But we'll see her in the morning and ask her a few sharp questions. I'm going home now, Mike. It's been a long day."

"Shall I run you home?"

"I'll walk," said Wexford. "Don't forget to put your car away, will you? You won't be making any emergency trips to the hospital tonight."

With a shamefaced grin Burden saw him out.

THEY WERE UNABLE TO puncture her self-possession. The languorous Klimt face was carefully painted this morning, and she was dressed as befitted the violinist or the actress or the author. She had been forewarned of their coming, and the gardener image had been laid aside. Her long, smooth hands looked as if they had never touched the earth or pulled up a weed.

Where had she been on the afternoon of Hannah Kingman's death? Her thick, shapely eyebrows went up. At home, indoors, painting. Alone?

"Painters don't work with an audience," she said rather insolently, and she leaned back, dropping her eyelids in that way of hers. She lit a cigarette and flicked her fingers at Burden for an ashtray as if he were a waiter.

Wexford said, "On Saturday, October 29, Miss Last, I believe you had something wrong with your car?"

She nodded lazily.

In asking what was wrong with it, he thought he might catch her. He didn't.

"The glass in the offside front headlight was broken while the car was parked," she said, and although he thought how easily she could have broken that glass herself, he could hardly say so. In the same smooth voice she added, "Would you like to see the bill I had from the garage for repairing it?"

"That won't be necessary." *She wouldn't have offered to show it to him if she hadn't possessed it,* he thought. "You asked Mr. Hood to call for you here at six, I understand."

"Yes. He's not my idea of the best company in the world, but I'd promised him some apples for his mother, and we had to pick them before it got dark."

"You gave him coffee but no alcohol. You had no drinks on the way to Mr. and Mrs. Kingman's flat. Weren't you a little disconcerted at the idea of going out to dinner at a place where there wouldn't even be a glass of wine?"

"I was used to Mr. Kingman's ways." *But not so used,* thought Wexford, *that you can tell me whether it was normal or abnormal for him to have rinsed those plates.* Her mouth curled a little, betraying her a little. "It didn't bother me. I'm not a slave to liquor."

"I should like to return to these—er, Shaggy Caps. You picked them from here on October 28 and took them to Mr. Kingman that evening. I think you said that?"

"I did. I picked them from this garden."

She enunciated the words precisely, her eyes wide open and gazing sincerely at him. The words, or perhaps her unusual straightforwardness, stirred in him a glimmer of an idea. But if she had said nothing more, that idea might have died as quickly as it had been born.

"If you want to have them analyzed or examined or whatever, you're getting a bit late. Their season's practically over." She looked at Burden and gave him a gracious smile. "But you took the last of them yesterday, didn't you? So that's all right."

Wexford, of course, said nothing about Burden's experiment. "We'll have a look in your garden, if you don't mind."

She didn't seem to mind, but she had been wrong. Most of the fungi had grown into black-gilled pagodas in the twenty-four hours that had elapsed. Two new ones, however, had thrust their white oval caps up through the wet grass. Wexford picked them, and still she didn't seem to mind. Why, then, had she seemed to want their season to be over? He thanked her, and she went back into the cottage. The door closed. Wexford and Burden went out into the road.

The fungus season was far from over. From the abundant array on the roadside it looked as if the season would last weeks longer. Shaggy Caps were everywhere, some of them smaller and grayer than the clump that grew out of Corinne Last's well-fed lawn; green and purple Agarics, horn-shaped toadstools, and tiny mushrooms growing in fairy rings.

"She doesn't exactly mind us having them analyzed," Wexford said thoughtfully, "but it seems she'd prefer the analysis to be done on the ones you picked yesterday than on those I picked today. Can that be so or am I just imagining it?"

"If you're imagining it, I'm imagining it too. But it's no good, that line of reasoning. We know they're not potentiated—or whatever the word is—by alcohol."

"I shall pick some more all the same," said Wexford. "Haven't got a paper bag, have you?"

"I've got a clean handkerchief. Will that do?"

"Have to," said Wexford, who never had a clean one. He picked a dozen more young Shaggy Caps, big and small, white and gray, immature and fully grown. They got back into the car, and Wexford told the driver to stop at the public library. He went in and emerged a few minutes later with three books under his arm.

"When we get back," he said to Burden, "I want you to get on to the university and see what they can offer us in the way of an expert in fungology."

He closeted himself in his office with the three books and a pot of coffee. When it was nearly lunchtime, Burden knocked on the door.

"Come in," said Wexford. "How did you get on?"

"They don't have a fungologist. But there's a man on the faculty who's a toxicologist and who's just published one of those popular science books. This one's about poisoning by wild plants and fungi."

Wexford grinned. "What's it called? *Killing for Nothing*? He sounds as if he'd do fine."

"I said we'd see him at six. Let's hope something will come of it."

"No doubt it will." Wexford slammed shut the thickest of his books. "We need confirmation," he said, "but I've found the answer."

"For God's sake! Why didn't you say?"

"You didn't ask. Sit down." Wexford motioned him to the chair on the other side of the desk. "I said you'd done your homework, Mike, and so you had, only your textbook wasn't quite comprehensive enough. It's got a section on edible fungi and a section on poisonous fungi—*but nothing in between*. What I mean by that is, there's nothing in your book about fungi which aren't wholesome yet which don't cause death or intense suffering. There's nothing about the kind which can make a person ill under certain circumstances."

"But we know they ate Shaggy Caps," Burden protested. "And if by 'circumstances' you mean the intake of alcohol, we know Shaggy Caps aren't affected by alcohol."

"Mike," said Wexford quietly, "*do* we know they ate Shaggy Caps?" He spread out on the desk the haul he had made from the roadside and from Corinne Last's garden. "Look closely at these, will you?"

Quite bewildered now, Burden looked at and fingered the dozen or so specimens of fungi. "What am I to look *for*?"

"Differences," said Wexford laconically.

"Some of them are smaller than the others, and the smaller ones are grayish. Is that what you mean? But, look here, think of the differences between mushrooms. You get big flat ones and small button ones and—"

"Nevertheless, in this case it is that small difference that makes all the difference." Wexford sorted the fungi into two groups. "All the small grayer ones," he said, "came from the roadside. Some of the larger white ones came from Corinne Last's garden and some from the roadside."

He picked up between forefinger and thumb a specimen of the former. "This is not a Shaggy Cap, it is an Ink Cap. Now listen." The thick book fell open where he had placed a marker. Slowly and clearly he read: " 'The Ink Cap. *Coprinus atramentarius*, is not to be confused with the Shaggy Cap, *Coprinus comatus*. It is smaller and grayer in color, but otherwise the resemblance between them is strong. While *Coprinus atramentarius* is usually harmless, when cooked, it contains, however, a chemical similar to the active principle in Antabuse, a drug used in the treatment of alcoholics, and if eaten in conjunction with alcohol, would cause nausea and vomiting.' "

"We'll never prove it," Burden gasped.

"I don't know about that," said Wexford. "We can begin by concentrating on the *one lie* we know Corinne Last told, when she said she picked the fungi she gave Axel Kingman from *her own garden*."

Mushroom and Onion Frittata

¼ cup olive oil (divided use)
8 oz. mushrooms, sliced
1 small bunch green onions, roots removed
6 room-temperature eggs, beaten just until the yolks
    and whites are blended
Salt and pepper to taste

TWO 10-INCH SKILLETS are needed for this dish, and the serving plate for the frittata should be warmed and ready.

CAREFULLY WASH THE green onions and remove any bruised or unsavory-looking areas. Slice the green onions into roughly one-inch-long bits.

PUT HALF THE olive oil into each 10-inch skillet. Place both oiled skillets on the stove on low to medium heat. Put the green onion bits into one skillet. Sauté until onion is slightly limp, about one minute, then add the mushrooms. Sauté until the mushrooms are brown and limp, about another two minutes. Pour the onions and mushrooms from the skillet into the beaten eggs. Set greasy skillet aside back on its burner for later. Stir eggs. Pick up the unused heated skillet and roll the olive oil around in the pan until the entire surface has been covered in olive oil. Return skillet to burner. Pour egg mixture into it. Rotate the pan slightly to spread the egg mixture evenly across the skillet surface. If the eggs are not cooking evenly, gently lift the cooked eggs up and move them to the center of the pan, and swirl the pan again until the remaining liquid eggs once again cover the surface. When the bottom of the eggs are set and the top is still glossy and creamy, place the other warm skillet, the greasy one used to cook the mushrooms and onions, upside down over the skillet containing the eggs, and flip the two skillets. The egg mixture should fall out of the pan it is in, its less-cooked side facedown on the onion and mushroom pan. Place the pan back on the stove until the eggs are cooked through, usually one to two minutes.

SERVE IMMEDIATELY ON a warmed platter.

The Cassoulet

Walter Satterthwait

I must speak with you," says Pascal, "regarding a matter of great importance."

"And which matter," I ask him, "might that be?"

Thoughtfully, using forefinger and thumb, he strokes his moustache. "The cassoulet," he says.

"Ah," I say, and within my chest my heart dips a few melancholy millimeters.

We are drinking Pascal's passable filtered coffee in his somewhat too elaborate dining room. The room is situated in a corner of his apartment, and the apartment itself on the top floor of a portly old building along the Quai de Gesvres. A pair of wide windows, running from ceiling to floor, affords us an uninterrupted view of the Île de la Cité and of Notre Dame with its many fine and graceful buttresses. The view no doubt is often charming; but today a gaudy sun is shining, and the river is perfectly reflecting the flawless blue of sky, as though posing for a tourist postcard; and I cannot help but find it all, as I find Pascal's dining room, a trifle overdone.

"You know, of course," says Pascal, "that I have always experienced a certain difficulty with the cassoulet."

"Yes, of course," I say. Pascal's failure with the cassoulet is renowned.

"I have never understood it," he says. As usual, Pascal is wearing black—a silk shirt, a pair of linen slacks—on the mistaken assumption that black makes him appear at once more intellectual and less corpulent.

"I believe," he says, "that I am in all other respects a tolerable cook. The cassoulet, however . . ." he shakes his head ". . . invariably the cassoulet has eluded me. At the market I have purchased the most delectable of beans, the most savory of sausages, the most succulent of pork. When I used fresh duck, I obtained the plumpest of these, and I plucked their feathers myself, with the utmost care. Always, before the final cooking, I rubbed the casserole scrupulously with garlic, like a painter preparing a canvas. Always, as the dish bubbled in the oven, I broke the gratin crust many times—"

"Seven times," I ask him, curious, "as they do in Castelnaudary?"

"On occasion. And on occasion eight times, as they do in Toulouse."

He sits back in his chair and shrugs. "Yet no matter what I assayed, always my cassoulet lacked . . ." Frowning, he holds up his hand and delicately moves his fingers, as though attempting to pluck a thought, like a feather, carefully from the air.

"That certain something?" I offer.

"Exactly, yes," he nods. "That certain something." He smiles sadly. "You recall the party last year, on Bastille Day."

"Only with reluctance," I say. For a moment that evening, after each guest had taken a small tentative taste of the cassoulet, no one could look at anyone else. Silence fell across the table like the blade of a guillotine. Poor Pascal, who had been so embarrassingly hopeful before the presentation, suddenly became quite embarrassingly, quite volubly, apologetic.

"Yes," he nods ruefully. "A disaster."

"I have always," I say, "accounted it rather intrepid of you, this endless combat with the cassoulet."

He wags a finger at me. "Intrepid, yes, perhaps—but confess it, my friend, also rather foolish."

"Ah well," I say, and I shrug. "In this life we are all of us permitted a certain amount of foolishness, no?"

He inclines his head and smiles. "You are, as always, too kind." But then he frowns again. "You know," he says, "it was largely because of this Bastille cassoulet that Sylvie wandered out of my life."

"Come now, Pascal." I smile. "You know very well that Sylvie was wandering long before Bastille Day."

"Certainly. Sylvie was a free spirit and, I agree, a prodigious wanderer. Yet despite our many difficulties, after her wanderings it was to our life here that she invariably returned. Until the day of that fatal cassoulet. The embarrassment was too much for her. The cassoulet was the ultimate of straws."

Pascal's way with a cliché can best be described as unfortunate.

"Nonsense," I tell him. "By her very nature Sylvie was utterly incapable of fidelity."

He smiles sadly. "As you learned yourself, my friend, isn't it so?"

I return his smile, replacing its sadness with curiosity. "Surely, Pascal, you cannot hold that against me, my little incident with Sylvie?"

He lowers his eyebrows and raises his hand, showing me his pale scrubbed palm. "But of course not," he says. "It is inevitable, the attraction between one's friend and one's lover. It is, in a way, a confirmation of one's high regard for both." He shakes his head. "No, my friend, all that is history now. Water far beneath the bridge. But I speak of Sylvie. A few weeks ago, I saw her in the Café de la Paix. She was sitting with her American."

"The American is still in Paris, then?"

"Astounding, is it not? Almost ten months now, and the two of them are as inseparable as ever. You've met the man?"

"I've heard stories only. There are boots, I understand."

"The boots of the cowboy, yes. Constructed from the skin of some unfortunate bird. A turkey, I believe."

"Not a turkey, surely?"

He shrugs. "A bird of some sort. And with them, inevitably, a ridiculous pair of denim trousers. *Gray.* Sitting beside Sylvie, he looked like a circus clown."

"What was Sylvie wearing?" I ask in passing.

"A lovely little sleeveless Versace, red silk, and around her neck a red Hermes scarf."

I smile. "Sylvie and her endless scarves."

"Yes. She saw me, from across the room, and waved to me to join them. I could hardly refuse, not without causing a scene. Not in the Café de la Paix. So I crossed the room, and the American stood to greet me. He's quite excessively tall, you know. He *looms.*"

"It is something they all do, the Americans. Even the women. Even the short ones. They learn it from John Wayne films."

"Doubtless. In any event, we shook hands, the American and I, and naturally he squeezed mine as though it were a grapefruit."

"Naturally."

"His name is Zeke." Frowning, he cocks his head. "That cannot be a common name, can it, even among Americans?"

"I shouldn't think so." I glance at my watch. Eleven thirty now, and I have a one o'clock rendezvous at La Coupole. "So you joined them?" I say. "Sylvie and her Cowboy?"

"What choice had I? The American sat back and crossed his legs, perching his horizontal boot along his knee, so we might all admire the elegant stitchery in the dead turkey."

"I hardly think turkey, Pascal."

"Whatever. The point is the *flamboyance* of the gesture. Why not simply rip the thing from his foot and hurl it, *plonk*, to the center of the table?" Pascal shudders elaborately. "And then he hooked his thumbs over his belt, as they do, these American cowboys, and he said, *'Sylvie tells me you're in chemicals.'*

"I said, 'Not in them, exactly.' "

"*Touché*," I say. "In French, this was, or in English?"

Pascal smiles. "He believed himself to be speaking French. It was execrable, of course. In simple self-defense, I replied in English. 'I have an interest in a small pharmaceutical company,' I told him. 'But naturally I leave the running of it to others.'

"And here Sylvie leaned forward and she said, 'Pascal's primary interest is the kitchen.'

" '*Is that right?*' said the Cowboy. I cannot duplicate the accent. You recall Robert Duvall as Jesse James?"

"Vividly. *The Great Northfield Minnesota Raid*. A Philip Kaufman film."

"Something like Duvall. A combination of Duvall and Marlon Brando in Kazan's *Streetcar*. '*Is that right?*' he said. '*I purely do admire the way you French people cook up your food.*'"

"Pascal," I say. "You exaggerate."

Indignant, he raises his chins. "Indeed I do not."

"And what did you reply?"

"I said, 'We French people are filled with awe at your Big Mac.' "

I smile.

"And then he grinned at me, one of those lunatic American grins that reach around behind the ears, and he said, '*Ain't all that big on burgers myself—*' "

"Pascal!"

"I do not invent this. '*Me,*' he said, '*I like to chow down on a real fine home-cooked meal.*'

"'Perhaps,' I said, 'one day you will permit me to prepare something for you.'

"'*That'd tickle me,*' he said, '*like all get-out.*'"

"Pascal—"

"Wait, wait! Sylvie had been sitting in silence, leaning forward, her elbows on the table, her arms upraised, her fingers locked to form a kind of saddle for her chin. You recall how she nestles her chin against the backs of her fingers? How she watches, with those shrewd blue eyes darting back and forth from beneath that glossy black fringe of hair?"

"I recall, yes," I tell him.

"Suddenly, she spoke. Blinking sweetly, with a perfectly innocent expression, she said, 'Zeke's favorite dish is the cassoulet.'"

"Ah," I say. "I was wondering if we should ever return to the cassoulet."

"I was, of course, stunned," says Pascal. "I had believed us to be friends still, Sylvie and I."

"Possibly your comment about the Big Mac . . . ?"

"Possibly. I was stunned nonetheless. And then the Cowboy, this Zeke creature, said, '*I reckon there ain't no food I like better than a good cassoulet.*'

"And at that point Sylvie, still the picture of innocence, sat up and blinked again and said, 'Why, Pascal would love to prepare a cassoulet, wouldn't you, Pascal?'"

"Clearly," I say, "it was your comment about the Big Mac."

"Very likely. But what could I do?"

"You had no choice, obviously, but to accept."

"None. I invited them to dinner on the following Saturday. As I said goodbye to them both, I could not help but notice in Sylvie's eye that little twinkle she gets when she is anticipating some devilment. You recall that twinkle?"

"I recall it."

"Well. This occurred on a Thursday. That afternoon, and throughout most of Friday, I pored over the literature. Brillat-Savarin. Prosper Montagné. The Larousse. On Friday evening I bought the *lingot* beans, the finest, the most expensive in Paris, and I carried them home—in a taxi, on my lap, so as not to bruise them—and I set

them to soak. Early on Saturday morning I purchased the rest of the
ingredients. Again, all the finest and the most expensive. And then,
when the beans had soaked for exactly twelve hours, I began."

He strokes his mustache, remembering. "First I drained the
beans. Then I cooked them in just enough water for them to swim
comfortably, along with some pork rinds, a carrot, a clove-studded
onion, and a bouquet garni containing three cloves of garlic."

"So far," I say, "the method is unimpeachable."

"Using another pan," he goes on, "in some goose fat I browned
a few pork spareribs and a small boned shoulder of mutton—"

"Mutton? Pascal, this sounds ominously like the cassoulet you
prepared for Jean Claude's birthday."

"The very same recipe." He nods. "I know, I know. A catastrophe."

"You are a brave man, Pascal."

"A desperate man, my friend. But to continue. When the meats
were nicely browned, I transferred them gently to a large skillet,
and I cooked them, covered, with some chopped onion, another
bouquet garni, and two *additional* cloves of garlic—"

"Bravo."

"—as well as three tomatoes, chopped, seeded, and crushed.
Then, when the beans in their separate pan were just approaching tenderness, I removed all the vegetables from them and I
added the pork, mutton, onions, and a fat garlic sausage. And the
preserved goose. It was while I was adding the goose that the accident occurred."

"The accident?"

"Yes." He glances at my empty cup. "Some more coffee, my
friend?"

I look at my watch. Twelve o'clock. "Only a bit," I tell him.

He pours the coffee and sits back, sighing, and then with a
ruminative look he stares out the tall window at the buttresses of
Notre Dame.

"The accident?" I say.

He turns back to me. He smiles. "The accident, yes. It was extraordinary. Really quite extraordinary, in light of what followed. As I
was cutting the leg of preserved goose, my knife slipped, and the
blade went sliding along my left hand. You see?"

He holds out his left hand. Along the base of the thumb is the
clear mark of a recent scar, nearly two inches long, still pink
against Pascal's plump pallor.

"Impressive," I say. "Was it painful?"

"I barely noticed it at the time," he says, "so intent was I upon the cassoulet. And then suddenly I realized that I was bleeding. *Into* the beans."

"Goodness."

"I had bled rather a lot into the beans as it happens. As soon as I understood what had happened, I wrapped my thumb in a dish towel to staunch the flow, and with a spoon I attempted to remove the blood from the beans. This was impossible, of course. Already it had mixed with the liquid in the pot. I had no choice but to mix it in more thoroughly and continue. You understand?"

"Certainly. It was too late in the day for you to begin anew. But still, Pascal . . ."

He raises his brows. "Yes?"

"It is . . . a tad macabre, don't you think?"

"Not at all. Think of blood sausage. Think of civet of hare. Think of sanguette."

"Yes, but human blood. Your own blood."

Dismissively, he shrugs. "I could not afford to be squeamish. As you say, it was late in the day. So, after having mixed everything, I simmered it for another hour, then removed the meat from the beans. I cut the meat, and I arranged all the ingredients in the casserole. A layer of beans, a sprinkling of pepper, a layer of meat, a sprinkling of pepper, a layer of beans—"

"I am familiar with the procedure."

"—and so on. Over the top I sprinkled melted goose fat and bread crumbs—"

"Naturally."

"—and then I placed it in the oven. During the next hour and a half, I broke the gratin crust eight times, at regular intervals. By the time Sylvie and her Cowboy arrived, it was ready."

"And?" I say.

He smiles slyly. "And what?"

"You toy with me, Pascal. The cassoulet. It was a success?"

"Not a success," he says. "A *triumph*. Sylvie took a single bite and closed her eyes—you recall how she closes her eyes when she savors the taste of something, how that little smile spreads across—"

"Yes, yes," I say. "I recall." I had been recalling Sylvie rather more often than I liked. "And the Cowboy?"

"In raptures. He consumed three enormous portions. It was, and I quote, '*the best goldarned cassoulet*' he ever ate."

I sit back and shake my head. "You astound me, Pascal. A remarkable story."

"But no, there is more. Over the weekend, Sylvie and her Cowboy mentioned the cassoulet to everyone they knew. It became a *cause célèbre*. You were gone from Paris at the time."

"In Provence," I say. "I returned, as I told you, only last week."

"I began to receive telephone calls from people—occasionally from people whom I myself had never met—importuning me to prepare for them a cassoulet. You can imagine how gratifying this was to me, after my long and notorious history of failure."

"Certainly. But, Pascal. You could hardly repeat the accident which brought about your one success. The *contretemps* with the knife."

"Ah, but I could, you see."

"Pardon?"

Smiling, he unbuttons the cuff of his left sleeve. With a magician's flourish, he pulls the sleeve up along his thick arm.

Stuck everywhere along the pallid flesh are pink adhesive bandages, eight or nine of them.

For a moment I do not comprehend. And then I do.

"Pascal!" I exclaim. "But this is madness!"

Lowering the arm, he nods sadly. "I agree. I cannot continue. In the morning, I can barely climb from the bed. And yet everyone in Paris, it seems, hungers for my cassoulet."

I pick up my coffee cup, and very much to my surprise I drop it. It falls to my lap, spattering me with warm coffee, then rolls off and tumbles to the floor, shattering against the polished parquet. I look up at Pascal. "How very odd," I say.

He smiles. "The drug begins to take effect." He looks at his watch. "Precisely on time. It requires an hour. It was in your first cup of coffee."

"The drug?" Strangely, this emerges from my throat as a croak.

"A rather interesting variant of curare. A chemist at my pharmaceutical company developed it. Unlike curare, which paralyzes the body's involuntary muscles, this one leaves certain muscles untouched. One can breathe, one can blink one's eyes, one can chew, one can swallow. But one cannot otherwise move."

I open my mouth, attempt to say, "You are joking," but only a shrill sibilant hiss escapes me.

"Nor can one speak," says Pascal, and smiles. Paternally. At me, or at the drug and its effects.

I attempt standing. None of my muscles respond. Suddenly, without my willing it, my body slumps back against the chair. My head topples forward as though it might snap off at the neck, roll down my legs, and go rattling across the floor. I can feel my heart pounding against my ribs like an animal trying, frantically, to escape a trap.

"Relax, my friend," says Pascal. "You will only excite yourself."

With my head lowered, I can see of Pascal only his feet. They move as he stands up. I feel him clap me in a friendly manner upon the shoulder. Then the feet and legs disappear off to my right.

My mind, like my heart, is racing. The rest of me is frozen.

A few moments later I feel myself being lifted into the air. My head flops to the side. Pascal, for all his corpulence, is surprisingly strong. I am placed in what I recognize as a wheelchair. My head lolls back, and I have a view of Pascal's ceiling, and then of Pascal's face as he leans into my line of vision.

"Believe me," he says with an upside-down smile, "this will all go better for you if you simply accept it."

His face vanishes, and the ceiling unscrolls above me as he wheels me from the dining room.

"Perhaps you are asking yourself," I hear him say, "why I should choose you as the source of my—well, let us call it my *special seasoning*.

"First of all," he says, "you commend yourself to this purpose by the sheer emptiness of your life. No one will miss you. No one will ever even suspect that you are gone. Oh, here and there, I imagine, some poor benighted secretary, some simpleminded shopgirl, may wonder why you never telephone. But she will survive this."

We are in another room now. I feel Pascal lift me once again. The ceiling lurches, sways, and then I am lying on a bed. I feel Pascal's hand on my head as he swivels it, gently, to face him.

He stands back, pursing his lips. "And second," he says, "I confess that I have never been terribly fond of you. Your condescension, your arrogance. That metabolism of yours that permits you to eat whatever you like without gaining a gram. Insufferable. And, of course, there is your seduction of Sylvie. Her relationship with me was never the same afterward. You are as much responsible for her leaving me as that cassoulet of Bastille Day."

I want to cry out that it had *not* been a seduction, that Sylvie had been as willing as I, which is very possibly true. But no sound comes.

Smiling again, Pascal leans forward and pats me on the shoulder once more. "Please," he says. "Relax. We shall have a splendid time together, you and I. Like two beans in a pod. We shall have enormous amounts of time to discuss Sylvie. We can analyze her reasons for leaving us both, endlessly. And during the day, before I set off to gather the other ingredients of the cassoulet, I shall prop you up against the pillows, and you can watch the television. Game shows, soap operas. Not your usual fare, I suspect, but it will be great fun, eh?"

He stands upright. "And you need have no fear. I will never take more from you than you can afford to give. A pint here, a pint there. I am not a barbarian. And naturally, to keep up your strength, I shall provide you with the most nutritious and the richest of foods. Tonight you will be enjoying a lovely duckling in orange sauce. With American wild rice and baby peas. A vinaigrette salad of lettuce and arugula. And, I think, a nice Saint Emilion. Until then I bid you adieu."

I watch him walk from the room, pull the door shut behind him.

I stare at the door. I have no choice but to stare at the door. Inside me, horror boils.

Boils and boils and goes screaming through my brain like steam from kettle. And then, finally, like that steam, it exhausts itself. I continue to stare at the door. And all at once it occurs to me that Pascal is, as he says, a tolerable cook. And that his duckling with orange sauce is famous. His wine cellar, of course, is legendary.

Feed the Hungry Hordes Cassoulet

THIS WILL FEED an army, with plenty of leftovers—which is great, because it tastes better the second day. It's also what I call a week-end food. It doesn't take much prep time in the kitchen to fix, but the dish needs to be started the night before you plan to serve it for dinner (put your beans on to soak), and it takes roughly six to seven hours—with excursions into the kitchen on roughly an hourly basis—from the time you start the roast cooking to the earliest possible time you can eat the dish. In other words, you need to be home most of the day to make it. But trust me, the house will smell fabulous.

1 lb. dried white beans, soaked overnight in the refrigerator in 4 quarts water
1 small bunch fresh parsley
1 bay leaf
1 small bunch green onions, washed, cleaned, and with the roots chopped off
2 carrots, scrubbed and with the green tops chopped off
4 large celery stalks, cleaned and rinsed, cut to a length that will fit in your stockpot
Leafy bit from the middle of the celery head
White cotton string—kitchen quality
Optional—unbleached cotton cheesecloth, kitchen quality
3 lbs. pork loin
1 tsp. salt
1 shoulder of lamb
¼ cup butter
1 medium ham shank
1 lb. bacon
Water

½ lb. hard Italian sausage or other heavily flavored
   sausage (I've used browned Jimmy Dean Sage
   Sausage when I can't find authentic Italian hard
   sausage)
Peeled and separated cloves of garlic to taste (I use
   anything from 3 cloves to a whole head, depending
   on who's coming to dinner)
6 white onions, peeled and quartered
1 can tomato sauce
2 cups seasoned bread crumbs

PREHEAT OVEN TO 350 degrees F.

MAKE A BOUQUET garni. First take several sprigs of parsley (reserve
some of the bunch to use as a garnish later) and the bay leaf in
hand. Put them inside the leafy bit from the middle of the celery.
Take the prepared leafy celery bit, the carrots, the green onions,
and set them longwise on two stalks of celery. Top off with two
more celery stalks. Tie the whole thing up with a couple lengths of
string. This will be cooked in your beans to add flavor, then
retrieved and thrown out before the dish is served, so you want to
make the bundle tight and secure enough that you can grab it and
get it out of there. If you want to be absolutely sure it won't fall to
bits and vanish, wrap the whole thing in cheesecloth before tying it
up with string. Set the bouquet garni aside.

RUB THE PORK loin with the salt. Bake in oven for two hours, or until
tender. Meanwhile, put the ham and the bacon in a pan on the
stove. Cover them with cold water. Bring the water to a boil, then
turn it off. This will blanch the ham and bacon. Set the pot aside.

TAKE THE SOAKED beans from the refrigerator. Pour the water the
beans soaked in into a big bowl and reserve for later. Rinse the
soaked beans, drain them, and set the beans aside.

PUT THE WATER the beans soaked in into a stockpot (I soak my
beans in the stockpot—this isn't necessarily the best solution
because it stains the stainless steel. But it does cut down on one
more large dish needed for a dish-intensive meal). Add enough

chicken stock to the pot to make four quarts of liquid. Add the soaked beans. Bring the water to a boil and skim it. Add the blanched ham, the bacon, the bouquet garni, and the garlic, and cover. Simmer for about an hour and a half.

MEANWHILE, BROWN THE lamb shoulder in the butter. Remove the meat from the bone. Place the lamb meat and its bone in the pan with the pork loin. Put the roasts back into the oven and continue cooking them for another hour.

MEANWHILE, ADD THE quartered white onions and the sausage to the beans, simmer for one more hour. Take the roasts from the oven and pour the tomato sauce over them. Return the meat to the oven for about another half an hour. Lower oven temperature to 300 degrees F.

PULL THE MEAT from the oven. Move the roasts from the pan to a platter or cutting board and slice them on the diagonal into individual serving-size slices. Drain the roast pan, reserving the drippings. Pull the ham shank out of the beans and slice the meat, placing it with the sliced pork loin and sliced roast lamb. Pull the sausage out of the beans, and slice it into coin-sized pieces that can be put with the other sliced meats. Discard the lamb bone and ham shank bone. Drain the beans and pull the bouquet garni out of the mixture. Throw the bouquet garni away. Add the roast pan drippings to the drained beans and stir gently. Set aside to let some of the fat pool on the surface. Skim the fat off the bean mixture.

LAYER THE VARIOUS sliced meats into a casserole, alternating layers of meat with the bean mixture. Top the casserole with dried bread crumbs. Place casserole in the oven and cook for about an hour.

REMOVE FROM THE oven when the bread crumbs are a nice golden brown, top with a sprinkling of chopped fresh parsley, and serve.

Tea for Two

M. D. Lake

The door opens and a tall, elegantly clad woman with sleek black hair strides into the restaurant. She glances around, spots Jane already seated at a table against the front window, and marches over to her. Other guests, mostly middle-aged women having late-afternoon tea, glance up at her as she passes and comment in undertones that she looks familiar.

"It's remarkable," she exclaims as she slides into the chair opposite Jane. "I recognized you the moment I came in. You haven't changed at all." She shrugs out of her mink stole, letting it fall over the back of her chair. "You should exercise more, though, Jane—as much for health reasons as for appearance. I exercise an hour every day—even have my own personal masseuse now, an absolutely adorable man!"

She peers into Jane's cup, sniffs. "What're you drinking? Herbal tea!" She shakes her head in mock disbelief. "Same old Jane! You were the first person I ever knew who drank the stuff—you grew the herbs yourself, didn't you? Not for me, thanks. Oh, well, since you've poured it anyway, I suppose I can drink a cup of it for old times' sake. But when the waiter gets here, I want coffee. What are these? Tea cakes? I shouldn't, but I'll take a few. It's my special day, after all."

She puts some on her plate and one in her mouth. "Um, delicious! Did you make them yourself? Of course you did! It's just amazing what a clever cook can do with butter and sugar and—

cardamom? A hint of anise? What else?" She laughs gaily. "You're not going to tell me, are you? Oh, you gourmet cooks and your secret recipes! Well, it would be safe with me, since I don't even know how to turn on the stove in either of my homes."

She eats another cookie, washes it down with a swallow of tea, and then makes a face. "Needs sugar. Oh, look! I haven't seen sugar bowls like this on a restaurant table in years. Nowadays all you see are those hideous little sugar packets that are so wasteful of our natural resources." She spoons sugar into her cup, tastes the result. "That's better," she says.

She looks at her jeweled watch. "Unfortunately, Jane, I don't have a lot of time. I told the escort to be back to pick me up in an hour—one of those damned receptions before the awards banquet tonight, you know. I don't know why I bother going to those things anymore. Vanity, I suppose, but this one is special, after all."

She glances around the room, an amused smile on her lips.

"So this is your little restaurant! Such a cozy place, just like you—and I mean that in the kindest possible way! You started out as a waitress here, didn't you? Then you became the cook, and finally, when you inherited some money and the owner died, you bought the place. See, I didn't cut *all* ties with you when you suddenly dropped out of my life, Jane. I've kept myself informed through our mutual friends."

She smiles. "It's ironic, isn't it? The author of cozy little mysteries featuring the owner of a cozy little restaurant quits writing and becomes the owner of a cozy little restaurant of her own! You've turned fiction into reality, Jane, haven't you? It's usually the other way around."

Becoming more serious, she goes on: "Oh, Jane, I've wanted so much to see you again, to try to clear the air and restore the trust that was lost twenty years ago through misunderstandings—but I wasn't sure you would want to, or that you were ready for it. I was afraid that your wounds, real and imagined, might never heal. But they have, haven't they?

"I can't tell you how happy I was when my secretary told me you'd called and wanted to get together while I'm in New York. 'My cup runneth over,' I thought—isn't that what they say? To get a lifetime achievement award from my peers and, on top of that, to see you again—all on the same day!"

She swallows a cookie, chokes on it, and tries to wash it down with tea.

"It came as such a shock," she continues when she's recovered, "when you threw your writing career away and went to work as a waitress! I mean, over just one little rejection!"

She laughs. "If I'd known it was going to do that to you, I might have accepted the manuscript. I mean, you should have talked to me about it before doing anything so drastic—we could have worked something out. Our relationship, after all, was more than just editor-slash-author. Much more—we were *friends*!

"Your manuscript *was* bad, of course, but your track record was good enough that you could have survived one weak effort like that. Not that I don't think I was right to reject it! As an editor, I had an obligation to my company, and I couldn't let friendship cloud my professional judgment. I did what I thought was right, without considering the consequences. And damn, Jane, there wouldn't have been any consequences if you'd been strong! You could have taken the rejection as a challenge to rise to another plateau. And I thought you were strong—everybody did. 'Strong Jane' we all called you. Quiet, unassuming—maybe even a little dull and drab—but strong. How wrong we were!"

She wags a long, slim finger playfully in Jane's face. "And I don't feel a single twinge of guilt. Don't think for a moment I do, Jane! I'm sure that the rejection couldn't have been the sole reason you gave up writing! Admit it! Doing something that drastic is a lot like suicide. Something had been building up in you for a long time, and my rejection of the manuscript was just the last, but not the only, straw that broke the camel's back. Am I right? Of course I am! You were burned out, or burning out, weren't you? I could sense it in the manuscript. No—no more tea for me or I'll be spending most of the evening in the Ladies, instead of at the head table as guest of honor! Besides, it's a little too bitter, even with the sugar. Well, half a cup, then, since my throat's so dry—probably because I've been doing most of the talking, haven't I? Well, you always were the quiet type, weren't you?"

She spoons sugar into the cup and stirs it, sips tea and scrutinizes Jane across the table, a look of concern on her face. "Are you happy, Jane?"

She rolls her eyes and shakes her head in resignation. "Why do I ask! I don't think you were ever happy, were you? You always went around with a frown on your face, you were always concerned that you weren't writing enough, you were afraid you'd run out of ideas. You once told me you died a little every time you sent in a manuscript, wondering if I'd like it enough to buy it. Well, you look happy now—not happy, exactly, but content—even pleased with yourself, it seems to me. God, I'd give anything to be content! Well, not anything—I don't know any successful author who's content, do you? But you know what I mean. Here I am, about to receive a lifetime achievement award—a *lifetime* achievement award, Jane, after only twenty years, isn't that funny!—and I'm still not content. I don't think I'm writing enough, or good enough, and except for that first book, none of my books have been successfully translated into film. And I'm afraid I'm going to run out of ideas! I've pretty well taken up where you left off in the worry department, haven't I?"

Suddenly, she leans across the table, rests one hand lightly on one of Jane's. "Look, Jane, I accepted your invitation this afternoon because on this, what should be the happiest day of my life, I don't like the thought that you might blame me for your career going into the toilet the way it did. I don't want that shadow over my happiness. I'm here because I want us to be friends again—you do see that, don't you?

"Don't frown at me like that! I know what you're thinking, but you're wrong! When I rejected the manuscript, I didn't have any intention of—of appropriating your plot! I rejected it on its own merits—its own *lack* of merits, I should say."

She lowers her voice. "But then the plot began to haunt me, you see. It was so original, so clever—and you hadn't known what to do with it! You'd played it out with such small people—your heroine, that drab little owner of a cozy little restaurant, for Chrissakes! Her friends, the kitchen help, and her dreary little husband—not to speak of her poodle and her parakeet!"

She laughs harshly. "And all those suspects, the sort of people who patronize restaurants like that—cozy people with cozy middle-class lives and cares and secrets! Who's going to pay good money to read books about characters like that?

"I saw immediately that your plot could be applied to talented and successful characters—characters who were larger than life, the kind that most people want to read about. Characters who own horses and big, expensive cars—not poodles and parakeets! And I took it from there, and it was successful beyond my wildest dreams—and beyond anything you could ever have achieved, Jane!"

She laughs a little wildly. "My God—even I'll admit I've been living off that book ever since. One critic actually went so far as to say that I haven't written seventeen books, I've written the same book seventeen times! That hurt, but there's some truth in it. Even I'll admit it—as I laugh all the way to the bank!

"Oh, I know, I can see that you've caught me in a little contradiction. First I said I didn't have any intention of appropriating your plot and then I said I saw immediately that it could be put to so much better use than you'd put it to. But there's really no contradiction, Jane. Once I'd read your manuscript, I couldn't get the plot out of my head! It haunted me day and night. I couldn't sleep, couldn't think of anything else. I'd been trying to write a mystery for years—God knows, as an editor, I'd read enough of them to know how to do it—but after reading your manuscript my own seemed to turn to ash."

She arranges her mink stole around her shoulders, shivers. "It's cold in here. And where's the damned waiter? I'd like coffee. You'd think he'd be dancing attendance on us, Jane, considering he works for you."

She lowers her voice. "Was what I did so wrong? Your plot was like a succubus, eating away at my creativity. And since your creativity destroyed mine, didn't I have a right to steal from you? But I didn't think it would end your career! I assumed you'd go on writing those miserable little mysteries featuring Maggie O'Hare—or whatever her name was—forever, earning tidy little advances, a steady dribble of royalties, and tepid reviews. Damn it, Jane, I wasn't stealing *everything* from you—just that one brilliant little plot!"

A sheen of perspiration glistens on her forehead and upper lip, and she glances quickly around the room. "Sorry! I didn't mean to raise my voice like that. But you can see how aggravated it still makes me when I think of how you were going to waste it. I thought of you as a bad parent, Jane, and I felt it was my moral obligation to take your child from you to save it. You should have thanked me for that, not quit writing and disappearing without so much as a by-your-leave."

She picks up the teapot and starts to pour tea into Jane's cup, but, when she sees it's full, refills her own instead.

"And when your apartment burned down," she goes on after a moment, "and with it your computer and all the diskettes, it seemed to me that that was a sign from God—or whoever it is who watches over the really creative people in this world—that I should seize the moment! I mean, after the fire your plot was in the air, so to speak, wasn't it—just ashes floating in the air for anybody to grab who had the moral courage to grab it. And I did. I grabbed it, since I was left with the only copy of your manuscript still in existence!"

She dabs at her forehead with the napkin bunched in her hand. "Don't you think it's too hot in here?" she asks, shrugging out of her mink stole again.

"Even then," she continues after a moment, "I'm not sure I would have done it—taken your plot, I mean, changing the names and occupations of the characters—if it hadn't been for your husband. In fact, I'm not sure it wasn't Brad's idea in the first place! You see, he'd grown tired of being the husband of a plump, rather drab, lower midlist mystery author, and one afternoon when we were lying in bed idly chatting about this and that, I happened to mention how possessed I was by the plot of your latest manuscript and how I thought it was bigger, much bigger, than your abilities to do anything with it. It needed larger characters and a larger milieu, I told him—perhaps a strikingly beautiful gourmet cook who has studied with some of the best chefs in France or Italy and is married to a remarkably handsome stockbroker—strong, self-possessed characters who move with casual grace in a world of money, power, and elegance!"

She smiles at a memory. "And you know how it goes when you're lying in bed after sex with your lover. Brad remarked—in all innocence, I'm sure—that unfortunately you weren't equipped to write about such a world. You didn't know it. You only knew the world of the middle class.

"And then I said that, well, *I* knew the world of the beautiful people very well! After all, as an editor I'd had to attend the kind of literary soirees that now, as one of the world's best-selling authors of romantic suspense, I'm forced to attend all the time.

"And that's how it happened, you see, Jane. I rejected your book because it wasn't up to your usual standards. Brad and I discussed what I could do with its marvelous plot—and the next thing I knew, your apartment burned down with all your records! You were lucky to get out with your life, if I remember correctly—

although you did lose the poodle and the parakeet you'd loved so much. I remember that because Brad hated them both and was glad they were gone, although he did feel badly about everything else you lost."

She nibbles a cookie. "And your miscarriage, of course," she adds. "Brad was very, *very* sad about that, as was I. Brad had ceased to love you by that time, of course, but he still *cared* about you. *Deeply.*"

She smiles compassionately across the table at Jane. "If you need money, Jane—for expansion or to get more help—and God knows you could use another waiter!—I'd be glad to give you some. I've got more than I know what to do with now. I'll even give you a little monthly stipend if you want it, even though I don't have to and I certainly don't feel any moral qualms about what I did."

She picks up her cup and brings it to her lips, pauses suddenly, and then puts it down and stares at it thoughtfully for a long moment. Then she laughs uneasily, shrugs, and picks it up again and takes a big swallow.

"Funny," she says, "in your manuscript it's in a pot of tea that Nora Smith puts the poison that kills first her husband and then her husband's lover in Maggie—Margie?—O'Hare's restaurant. Do you remember, or has it been too long ago for you? I'd probably have forgotten about it myself except I had a big quarrel with my editor, who wanted me to make the poison a faster-acting one, cyanide or strychnine. I pointed out that if it acted that fast, the police would have no trouble tracing where the victims ingested it, but by making it take several days, nobody would know—until Maggie or Margie figures it out in the end, that is. Of course, by the time I rewrote it my way, it wasn't Maggie's—Megan's?—drab little restaurant anymore, it was the elegant bistro belonging to my heroine, Titania Oakes, a culinary artist, which attracted only the beautiful people—the trendsetters, the movers and the shakers. And the victims weren't a dowdy schoolteacher and an insurance salesman either—they were famous Broadway stars! That's how I made your wretched little story into a blockbuster, Jane! But I kept the poison the same as yours, except in my book it wasn't in tea, it was in a lovely risotto, for which Titania's restaurant was famous."

She frowns in thought, her eyes moving involuntarily to the teapot. "What was the name of that poison, anyway—do you remember? Something odorless and tasteless that leaves no trace, unless the medical examiner knows what to look for. I remember asking you where you got the idea for it and you said you'd had mushrooms like that growing in your backyard when you were a kid. Your mother had warned you against eating them. Once they got into your system, she said, you were done for—nothing could save you."

She shudders, picks up her teacup, and starts to take another swallow, then changes her mind and puts the cup down with a clatter.

"God, how you must hate me!" she whispers. "First I steal your husband and then your novel. Then you lose your poodle, your parakeet, and your baby—and finally your career. It sounds awful now, in the cold light of a gray autumn day in this cozy Godawful place—but it seemed so right at the time! And I didn't mean to hurt you, Jane! I expected you to bounce back stronger than ever. And probably meaner, too."

She tries to laugh but coughs instead. "I even imagined you'd write a novel in which you murdered me in the most horrible possible way! Isn't that ridiculous? Instead, you just dried up and blew away, didn't you?

"But you did get Brad back! When it didn't work out between us and I was forced to show him the door, right around the time my novel hit the *New York Times* best-seller list, he crawled back to you, didn't he? I seem to recall hearing that somewhere. As I said, I've kept track of you all these years, Jane. I don't know why. I guess I just don't know how to let go of a friend, even one who's turned her back on me the way you did. Call me a fool, but at least I'm a *loyal* fool!"

She frowns at a sudden memory. "But then Brad died, didn't he? I recall hearing that, too. First, you got remarried, and then, a year or so later, he came into some money. And then he died— suddenly, although he wasn't very old."

She's pale and breathing hard now, but she manages a ghastly smile. "Did you have him cremated, Jane?" she asks with forced humor. "So they'd never be able to find out if you'd put something in his food?"

Her voice rising, she asks, "What was it called again—the poison? There's no known antidote for it, is there? And a little goes a long way. Isn't that what your Megan or Maggie or Margie told the homicide inspector? 'No known antidote, Inspector— and a little goes a long way.' " She laughs. "How much better that line sounded in my Titania's mouth than in—in your dreary little protagonist's!

"But once you've got it in your system," she goes on slowly, ominously, "it doesn't do any good to pump your stomach, does it? It doesn't do any good at all! Isn't that right, Jane?"

She jumps up and stares down at Jane in horror. "How long before you begin to feel the effects?" she shouts. "Do you remember? Of course you do—how could you forget? And the symptoms—chills and fever that mimic the flu, aren't they?" She wipes her forehead with her soggy napkin, stares at her shaking hand.

"And then, shortly after Brad died, the owner of this place died too, didn't he, Jane? Suddenly. And you bought the restaurant from his heirs with the money you'd inherited from Brad!"

She looks around the room wildly. "Why hasn't the waiter come over to our table? It's because you told him to leave us alone, didn't you? The tea and cookies were already here, waiting for me. It was in the tea, wasn't it? You never touched a drop of it. Or was it the cookies, or the sugar? Damn you, Jane, tell me!"

Without waiting for an answer, she turns to the others in the room and shouts, "She's killed me! As sure as if she'd pointed a pistol at me and pulled the trigger, she's killed me because I stole her plot, her story, her husband—everything—and she's never forgiven me! And I won't die quickly, either. No—it'll be tomorrow or the next day and I have to live with that knowledge and with the knowledge that it's going to be a slow and painful death. And I'll be conscious every moment of the hideous ordeal!"

She rushes around the table and throws herself on Jane. "Monster!" she screams. "Mass murderer! First your husband, then the owner of the restaurant, now me!"

The waiter runs over and pulls her off Jane. She struggles violently for a moment, then collapses onto the floor.

"Oh, God!" she whispers. "This was supposed to be the happiest day of my life, and now look what you've done! How cleverly you've plotted your revenge, Jane!"

Her face lights up briefly when something occurs to her. "But you won't get away with it this time. They'll do an autopsy! After my long, slow, agonizing death, they'll open me up and find what you murdered me with—and then you'll spend the rest of your life in prison—or worse!"

She chuckles madly and closes her eyes. "Will somebody please cover me with my mink stole?" she says plaintively. "But try not to let it touch the floor. Oh, how like you, Jane, to add insult to injury—poisoning me in such a grubby little place, among such drab people!"

She pulls the stole up over her face, after which her muffled voice can still be heard complaining that the pains have already begun, the poison is acting faster than Ms. Know-It-All thought it would.

As Jane waits for the ambulance and the police to arrive, she stirs sugar into her cold tea (she likes cold tea), helps herself to a couple of the remaining cookies, and begins planning tomorrow's menu. She remembers to turn off the tape recorder in her purse, too. That goes without saying.

Chocolate Surprise Sugar Tea Cakes

---

3 cups flour
1½ tsp. baking powder
1 tsp. salt
1 cup sugar
¾ cup canola oil
2 eggs, beaten
1 tsp. vanilla
½ tsp. almond extract
12-oz. bag of wrapped chocolate miniatures (Hershey's Dark Chocolate Almond are a favorite), unwrapped
½ cup sugar

PREHEAT OVEN TO 375 degrees F.

BLEND FLOUR, BAKING powder, and salt, and set aside. In a large bowl, mix together sugar, oil, eggs, vanilla, and almond extract. Add the flour mixture all at once and stir until blended. Take a miniature chocolate bar and wrap it completely in cookie dough. Roll resulting ball in sugar, set on cookie sheet. Continue until cookie dough and/or candy bars are gone. Bake for 10-15 minutes, until cookie is brown on the bottom and cooked through. Serve warm (the chocolate is nicely melted) or at room temperature.

The Second-Oldest Profession

Linda Grant

*N*o *one in their right mind goes to the market at five o'clock,* Bianca Diamante thought as she surveyed the crowded parking lot. *Unless, of course, they've spent the entire day waiting for the repairman to come fix the dishwasher.*

At four-thirty she had called Angeli's Appliances for the third time to check on Mario's progress toward her home.

"Oh, Mrs. Diamante," an apologetic female voice had said, "he's so sorry. He was really trying to get to you, but this last job has just lasted much longer than he expected. He said to tell you he'd be at your house first thing tomorrow."

I've heard that before, Bianca had thought. Yesterday, in fact. Mario himself had promised to be there "first thing."

She'd felt genuine sympathy for the young woman at the other end of the phone. They both knew that in all likelihood Mario's last job had been performed in the bedroom of some bored housewife. It was too much to wish that the cuckolded husband might arrive home early and armed, but the possibility cheered Bianca.

She knew the repairman well enough to recognize how he prioritized his work orders. Attractive, horny women first, less attractive, horny women second, old ladies last. If she didn't keep after him, it could take weeks to get her dishwasher fixed.

In the parking lot ahead of her a tan station wagon was backing out, but before she could pull forward, a red Miata zipped around her, pulled in front, and took the place.

Bianca honked, then pulled up behind the Miata and got out. "I beg your pardon," she said, "that was my parking place."

A young woman with a shaved skull and a skirt up to her crotch stepped out of the Miata with a snippy smile on her face. "Too bad, Grandma," she said. "Slow folks suck."

The girl turned and headed for the store, and Bianca steamed. She allowed herself a moment to visualize the back of the shaved head in the sights of a rifle, then climbed into her car. The world was producing far too many overindulged, undersocialized young people these days.

It took several turns through the parking lot to find a place and Bianca had thought of at least three nasty ways that the shaved one might meet an early end by the time she pulled her Plymouth into a slot made too narrow by the monstrous sports utility vehicle hulking over the white line. SUV drivers were another category of people the world could do without.

The light on the supermarket's glass door had turned it into a mirror. As she approached it, an old woman walked to meet her. Bianca studied the image with satisfaction. Gray hair framed a wrinkled face, a shapeless dark dress shrouded a short, plump body. Up close she could even see the dark eyebrow pencil that stood in for thinning brows and the lipstick that went slightly outside the line of the lips. The eternal grandma. Harmless and invisible.

Another woman might have regretted the signs of age, maybe considered a visit to the hairdresser or a trip to the mall. Not Bianca. She'd worked hard for that look, plucked her luxurious brows down to next to nothing, and fought off every suggestion of a tint or a more modern hairstyle. No actor had spent more time perfecting the stooped posture and halting movements of old age than Bianca had.

But today she had no need for the stoop or shuffling walk as she pushed the door open and hurried inside. Today, she wasn't working.

The store was as crowded as the parking lot, and half the women had small, whiny children attached to their legs. Bianca was glad she didn't have a lot to buy, just a few things for dinner and apples for the pie.

She headed for the meat counter to get some lamb chops. As she was reaching for the only package that had two chops, a woman in a charcoal power suit stepped forward and grabbed it. She bumped Bianca's arm as she did and gave her a quick look, mumbled "Sorry," and hustled off.

You would be sorry if you knew who you were pushing, Bianca thought. That was the downside of being invisible: You had to put up with people treating you poorly. And you never got the satisfaction of seeing the look on their faces when they realized they'd just insulted someone who killed people for a living.

But it was worth it. Being a harmless old woman was the best possible cover for a hit person. Who else could get close to a powerful Mafia leader without being noticed, or remembered? No man certainly, even an old one. And a young woman would attract notice. But an old woman could go anywhere, and even the most alert bodyguard wouldn't push her out of the way if she passed too close and stumbled.

That's how she'd gotten Johnny the Clam, number three man in the Detroit family. She'd devised a special ring, a gaudy stone on the top, a sharp tack on the back of the band. A tack that she'd dipped in a poison that certain primitive people used on the tips of their arrows. Then it had been a matter of finding the right time and place where she could pass Johnny close enough to grasp his hand when she stumbled. He'd winced when she cut him, but a man like Johnny didn't make a fuss over a cut. In fact, Johnny never made a fuss again.

She'd used a sharp-tipped umbrella with the same poison, and it might have become her favorite weapon if the Bulgarians hadn't used it to assassinate a mark in England and botched the hit. Now everyone knew about umbrellas.

She picked up a quart of milk, a loaf of bread, two tomatoes, and some green beans for dinner, then remembered she'd come for apples.

As she surveyed the neatly stacked pyramids of bright green to deep red apples, a familiar, too-loud voice said, "McIntoshes are the best for pies."

It was Isabel Brasi, she who knew all and couldn't wait to share it. Bianca sighed, then came as close to a smile as she could manage as she turned to greet her neighbor.

Isabel was a constant trial. A bird fanatic, she called at least once a day to complain that Bianca's cats were stalking the birds at her feeders, digging in her garden, or doing something "nasty" in her yard. When she wasn't fussing over the cats, she was gossiping about the other neighbors. Her nosiness knew no bounds, and while Bianca was careful never to have clients come to her house, she didn't like the idea that someone was watching her every move.

Bianca's husband, Tony, had taught her that the first rule of a professional was never to let your personal feelings get involved. "We're probably the world's second-oldest profession," he'd said with a smile. "And we follow the same rules as the oldest profession. Never give it away." No whacking your enemies or those you found intolerably annoying. Isabel was a real test of Bianca's professionalism.

"Of course, the Gravesteins are very nice, too," Isabel said in her annoyingly chirpy voice, "but you can always count on the McIntoshes for flavor. My apple pie has won first place at the church bazaar for the last four years."

Bianca's smile was genuine as she congratulated Isabel; she was thinking of the apple pie she was going to bake. It was a safe bet no one had ever paid $10,000 for one of Isabel's pies.

"The children coming for Mother's Day?" Isabel asked.

Mother's Day! Bianca stared at Isabel in horror. "Mother's Day?" she said. "This Sunday is Mother's Day?"

Sympathy pulled Isabel's face into a somber expression. Poor Bianca. Obviously, her children had forgotten all about Mother's Day.

Jesus, Mary, and Joseph, Bianca thought, *how could I miss that? I must be slipping.* She prided herself on her attention to detail, never leaving any loose ends, and here she was three days from the job and she'd missed completely that Sunday was Mother's Day.

"They get so busy," Isabel was saying. "So many things to remember when you're young. They don't realize how we look forward to their visits."

Speak for yourself, Bianca thought. Cara and Sophia visited quite often enough, thank you. She loved them dearly, but they fussed over her like mother hens. Lately Cara'd started interrogating her about whether she was taking her medicine, how well she was eating, every little thing. You'd think she was an errant teenager the way her daughter fussed. Even her social life was an object of scrutiny. She should get out more, join the bridge club or the garden society, maybe think of moving into one of those nice adult communities.

And Sophia had suggested on two occasions that her friendship with certain members of the Gianni family should be terminated. "You don't know what kind of people they are," she'd said, her lips stretched tight with disapproval.

Bianca knew exactly what kind of people they were. They were the kind of people whose money had bought shoes and put food on the table. Her husband Tony had never been a member of the Gianni family, but favors had been exchanged from time to time, and the Don had been particularly helpful after Tony's cancer had left her a widow with children to support. It was Gianni money that had sent Cara, Sophia, and their brother Robert to college. And her family's connection to the Gianni family had meant that the wild boys stayed away from Cara and Sophia and never challenged Robert.

She and Tony had been careful to shield the children from the realities of Tony's profession. They thought he worked for a company that sold office machines and that his frequent trips were to distant business sites. You couldn't have your kid bringing his father's gun to show-and-tell.

"Maybe Cara's planning to surprise you?" Isabel said, trying to put a good face on things.

Bianca hated surprises, always had. Especially now.

She'd told the client the hit was scheduled for Sunday so that he could arrange an airtight alibi, and she was always careful to deliver exactly what she promised. It hadn't been easy making it as a woman in this field, even with Tony's training and his contacts. Clients were hesitant to trust a woman. For years after Tony's death she'd maintained the fiction that she was just a go-between who set things up with his "brother." At least half her clients still believed that. A hit man could reschedule; a hit woman could not.

She made as quick an escape as possible from Isabel, who was anxious to discuss at length her own children's plans for Mother's Day, and hurried to the checkout counter. There were only four registers open, and long lines of carts were stacked up at each one.

The line at the nine-items-or-less counter was the shortest of the four, an encouraging bit of luck until she realized that the man at the head of it had piled at least twice that many items on the belt. The clerk rolled his eyes at the pile but rang up the goods. It was only as he announced the total that the man pulled out his checkbook.

A ripple of irritation ran up the line. "I could kill him," the woman in front of Bianca muttered.

Bianca nodded agreement. Lucky for him she was a professional.

The checker was pleasant and efficient. The bagger looked to be about fourteen and dropped the tomatoes into the bag first, where they would have been smashed by the milk if Bianca hadn't made him retrieve them.

I'd be doing the world a favor to take that one out of the gene pool, Bianca thought.

"Would you like help to the car with that, ma'am?" the kid asked, indicating the small bag of groceries. She detected a slight smirk on his face.

"I think I can manage, thank you," she said.

Sunday's target was a sleazy lawyer who'd cheated the wrong person once too often. Bianca demanded a fair amount of background on her jobs. She'd developed her own rather quirky code. Abusive husbands were fair game; inconvenient witnesses were not. She needed to know about the marks so she could devise an appropriate exit strategy for them.

You didn't need to know a lot about a guy's habits if you were going to pick him off with a rifle, but Bianca specialized in deaths from natural causes, and for that, you needed background. Sometimes the client supplied it; sometimes she did the research herself. Always, there was a premium for a method that wouldn't attract police attention.

The roads were crammed with cranky drivers working themselves into a frenzy to get home quickly so they could relax. Bianca was deep in thought as she stopped at a traffic light and didn't notice when it changed to green. A loud horn blasted her awake, and a man's angry voice yelled, "Get a move on, Granny. We don't have all day."

At home, she decided the best solution to her problem was to find out what, if anything, her daughters had in mind for Sunday. She called Cara, who was more likely to be home than her sister.

"Mother, I'm so glad you called," Cara said. *She sounded a bit guilty*, Bianca thought. "I've been meaning to call you, but things have been crazy at the office."

"How's your wrist?" Bianca asked. Cara had sprained her wrist when she tripped on the stairs.

"Much better, thanks," Cara said, then launched into a long description of a problem involving a secretary at her office. Bianca made comforting sounds. There was always some problem at the office; she could never keep all the players straight. It was enough to make her glad she worked alone.

"So how are you doing?" Cara asked as she finished her lament.

"The dishwasher's broken," Bianca said. "It stopped midway through the cycle last night. I've been waiting for Mario to come fix it."

"Mario? Is he still fixing appliances? He's such a creep." Cara had gone to school with Mario. They had even dated briefly, until Cara found out he was also dating one of her close friends. No one had ever accused Mario of being long on brains.

"He fixes appliances when he gets around to it," Bianca said. "He's not very reliable."

"Never was," Cara said. "He still have an eye for the ladies?"

"More than an eye," Bianca said. "He's married, but he hasn't let that slow him down."

"He's a creep," Cara repeated. "I don't think he even lives with Sarah—that's his wife. I heard he has a place on Rose Street."

"You mean he's divorced?"

"Oh, no. Mario doesn't believe in divorce; that'd mean child support, and he's not big on sharing his money with his wife and children. Sarah had to take a job, just to get by."

"Why doesn't she file for divorce? She certainly has grounds."

"She won't talk about it," Cara said. "I don't know if she's scared of him or still hopes he'll come back. She just refuses to discuss it. She's one of those women who can't stand up for herself."

Cara told her about another friend who'd filed for divorce only to end up with crushing legal bills and no way to collect child support, then about a colleague who was continuing to date a man who broke her nose. It was all very depressing. Finally, just when Bianca had decided she'd have to bring up the issue of Mother's Day herself, Cara said, "Oh, Sophia and I would like to take you to dinner on Sunday."

"How sweet of you," Bianca said, then added quickly, "How about four o'clock?"

"Uh, fine, four o'clock would be fine."

"Would you like to meet somewhere?"

"No, no. We'll pick you up at the house," Cara said.

As she hung up, Bianca realized they hadn't discussed where they'd go. That meant the girls had already chosen a place, no doubt one that prided itself on combining unlikely ingredients into minuscule servings on gigantic plates. You couldn't even trust the pasta in such places.

But at least she'd gotten the time schedule right. That meant she would be able to use the poisoned pie.

The lawyer was the perfect candidate for a pie. There weren't that many people who were. First off, you couldn't give a poisoned pie to a family man—too much chance of unintended victims. And you couldn't give it to someone who'd take it to a sick friend or ask a buddy over for dinner. Or a gentleman of the old school who'd feel obliged to invite her to have a piece. No, a pie only worked with the selfish loner, the kind of guy who as a kid would have rather eaten lunch by himself than risk having to share his dessert.

The lawyer was just such a guy. Bianca could count on him to keep every bite for himself.

She could drop by with the pie around eleven. She'd already introduced herself as a new neighbor and told him she'd just moved in with her daughter up the block. As she'd expected, he wasn't interested enough to ask the name of her "daughter." He probably didn't know his neighbors' names.

She'd played the lonely widow checking out the prospects. He wasn't bad-looking and had plenty of money, so he'd probably been through that routine before. Sunday, she'd pay a second visit and give him the pie, then scurry off shyly. Just after dark she'd come back to check on him. If the car was there and the lights were out, she'd know she'd succeeded. A call from a phone booth late that night would confirm it.

BIANCA MADE THE APPLE pie Saturday morning so she could bake it before the day heated up. If she'd believed Mario's promise to come by "first thing," she'd have waited, but she knew better than that. In fact, she didn't expect him until Monday. He only worked a half-day on Saturday, and she figured it'd take more than four hours for him to get around to her, so she was surprised when the doorbell rang at eleven o'clock, just as she was taking the pie from the oven.

"Hear the dishwasher's on the fritz," he said. "I got a cancellation so I hurried right over."

"I thought you were coming yesterday," Bianca said sternly.

"I got held up. It's not like a busted dishwasher is an emergency," he said in a tone that suggested *he* was the wronged party.

"No, not like a freezer that's not working," Bianca said, remembering the time she'd had to throw everything out because he'd been "held up."

"Right," he said, no memory of the freezer incident clouding his smile.

Mario spotted the pie as soon as he entered the kitchen. "Boy, that pie sure smells good," he said. "I love apple pie."

"I baked that one for a friend," Bianca said, knowing that Mario was on his way to asking for a piece.

"Aren't I your friend? Come out on a Saturday to fix your dishwasher?"

Bianca smiled thinly and resisted mentioning that he wouldn't have been there at all if he'd come when he was supposed to. Instead, she explained what was wrong with the dishwasher.

Mario dumped his tools on her clean floor and studied the appliance.

"Aw, you got a Kitchen-Aid. I tried to warn you about them. You shoulda bought the GE I tried to sell you. It was a good machine."

Bianca was fairly sure that the "good machine" had fallen off a truck somewhere. Mario had been much too anxious to sell it. "Yes, well, this is the machine I have, so it's the one you'll have to fix."

Mario bent down to pry the front off the dishwasher and continued his complaints about it.

Bianca decided it was time to find something to do in another room before she gave in to the temptation to tap Mario on the head with a cast-iron skillet. "Don't you touch that pie, Mario Angeli," she ordered.

"No need to get overheated," Mario said. He said something else as she was leaving, but he lowered his voice so she couldn't hear it.

When she came back to the kitchen fifteen minutes later, Mario had parts of the motor spread all over the floor and was talking on her phone.

"Tell him you're going to a movie with a girlfriend," he said in a wheedling tone. "Come on, just a couple of hours."

"Mario," Bianca said sternly. "I'm not paying you to arrange your social calendar."

"Gotta go," he said. "Meet me at eight at Phinny's." He gave her his best aw-shucks smile and said, "Sorry, Mrs. D. I won't charge you for the time I was on the phone."

"Very generous of you," Bianca said.

"Speaking of generous, how about a piece of that pie?" Mario moved toward the counter where the pie was cooling.

"No," Bianca said, loudly enough to stop him in his tracks. "Stay away from that pie."

"Just one piece. Your friend wouldn't miss one piece."

Only Mario would imagine it was proper to give a friend a pie with one piece missing. She almost wished she could give it to him, but she was a professional and Tony's second cardinal rule of professionalism was: You never hit someone you know. Tony used to say that anger was one emotion a pro couldn't afford.

"I said no," Bianca said sternly, "and I meant it. You are to stay away from that pie. Do you understand?"

But, of course, he didn't. He only understood what he wanted to understand. Bianca put on the oven mitts, picked up the still-hot pie, and carried it into the study where she could keep an eye on it.

She was going over her plans for Sunday a second time when the phone rang. It was Cara.

"Sophia can't make it at four," she said. "So we had this great idea. She'll take you to brunch at around ten or so, and I'll take you to dinner at four. How's that?"

Dreadful, Bianca thought. *It's just dreadful.* It was hard to imagine a worse schedule.

"Oh, now, you're making much too much of a fuss over me," she said. "Why don't we all just go to brunch?"

"We *want* to make a fuss," Cara said. "We want your Mother's Day to be special."

"Just being with you will be special," Bianca said. "I'd really rather just do the brunch. After all, I get tired easily these days."

"Is something wrong?" Cara asked anxiously. "Aren't you feeling well?"

"I'm fine," Bianca said quickly. "Really. It's just that you don't have as much energy at my age."

"Maybe you should see the doctor."

"Cara, don't be such a worrywart. I'm in excellent health."

"How's your shoulder? Is it still bothering you?"

"It's much better." Bianca had hurt her shoulder six months ago when she'd had to rearrange the body of a minor mob figure who'd lurched the wrong way in his final moments. Cara and Sophia had assumed it was arthritis.

"I really think you should see the doctor. Fatigue can be a symptom of more serious problems."

Bianca sighed. She should have known better than to plead anything remotely connected to poor health. Now she'd have to prove how fit she was or they'd drive her crazy with their fussing. "I'm fine," she said. "And your plans for Mother's Day sound lovely."

"You're sure? We don't want to tire you."

"I'm sure," Bianca said.

As she hung up the phone, she could hear Mario whistling tunelessly in the kitchen. She looked at her watch. He'd been at work for over an hour. At this rate she could have bought a new dishwasher and saved herself a lot of aggravation.

She couldn't use the pie. The timing was too tight. She'd just have to find another way. Aggravating, but not too difficult. Still, it was a shame she'd gone to the work of baking the pie.

For just a moment, she considered offering the pie to Mario.

There was no danger of him sharing it with anyone—he was selfish enough to keep it all for himself. She doubted that the woman he'd been cajoling on the phone would go looking for him when he stood her up, and the poison she'd carefully mixed into the pie filling produced symptoms close enough to food poisoning to confuse all but the most sophisticated autopsy.

She could get away with it, and no one would be the wiser, but it violated the code. No personal hits. It was an indulgence she couldn't afford. Whack Mario and next week it'd be Isabel or the bimbo with the shaved head. One simply had to have standards in this business.

The whole problem with Sunday's job was the deadline. She hated deadlines; they made things so much more difficult. Poisons acted differently on different bodies, even when you tried to adjust the dose to size.

With enough time, she could always come up with a means that would slip by most coroners. The trick was to give them a set of symptoms that looked like a natural cause they recognized. As long as you weren't dealing with a high-profile mark and didn't leave any glaring evidence, you could rely on them to see what they expected.

To ensure that the lawyer was dead by Sunday night, she'd need a fairly fast-acting poison. The ring with the spring-loaded injector was the best bet for a delivery device. She was particularly proud of her latest invention; it was a big step beyond the old ring with the tack on the back. That had been a crude device with no way to measure the dose and too much risk of nicking herself.

She'd found the injector in a medical supply book, another benefit of her volunteer work for the Poison Control Center, and designed the device herself. A hollow glass stone served as the reservoir for the poison; the injector extended down from it, fitting between her fingers. It remained safely sheathed until triggered by the pressure of her hand against a solid surface.

She glanced in the kitchen on her way upstairs to get the ring. Mario seemed to be finishing up—at least there were fewer tools on the floor.

In her bedroom, she carefully removed the ring from its hiding place in the lovely antique bureau with the secret drawer. A note on a yellow Post-it in the box reminded her that it still contained a deadly dose of brown recluse spider venom.

It was a nearly ideal weapon for a local hit. The spider was indigenous to this area, and the venom caused so little pain on injection that by the time the first symptoms appeared a couple of hours later, the victim might not even remember being stuck.

But would it do for this job? She decided it wouldn't. Death usually took more than a day, and the victim could sometimes be saved if he got to a doctor in time.

She slipped the ring on her finger. The safest means to release the venom was to shoot it into an apple or an orange. That wouldn't damage the needle, and the flesh of the fruit would absorb the poison.

As she headed down to the kitchen, the phone summoned her back.

"Mrs. D? This is Jason." Jason, her "social secretary."

"Hello, Jason. How's your daughter?" The question was her signal that it was all right to talk.

"She's fine, thank you. I just learned that my client would like to reschedule the package you were to deliver tomorrow. If you could take care of it today, there'd be a 20-percent bonus."

Bianca considered. She hated changes in plan, but this time it worked to her advantage. She checked her watch. There was still time to deliver the pie.

"I think that would be possible," she said. She didn't ask why the change in plans. She didn't care.

"Excellent. I'll inform my client."

Bianca replaced the receiver and smiled. Everything was working out after all. Now all she had to do was get Mario out of her kitchen, put on her old-lady clothes, and drive the pie across town.

She hurried to the kitchen to tell Mario he had fifteen minutes to finish fixing her dishwasher, but the room was empty. The dishwasher had been reassembled and the tools were back in their box, but the repairman was nowhere to be seen.

Bianca rushed to the study. There, she found Mario by the desk, carefully lifting a fat piece of pie from the pan. She dashed across the room and smacked his hand, knocking the pie from it. The pie landed with a splat on the blotter, spewing crust and filling across the desk. Mario yelped. "Jeeze, Mrs. Diamante," he protested, "don't get so excited. I didn't mean no harm."

He launched into a string of excuses, while Bianca stared at the tiny bright red spot of blood on his hand.

German Apple Cake

Cake:
1 cup sugar
1 cup unsifted, unbleached flour
4 Tbsp. butter, cut into pieces
1 tsp. baking powder
1 tsp. vanilla extract
1 large egg
4 large pippin or Granny Smith apples

Topping:
3 Tbsp. sugar
3 Tbsp. melted butter
1 tsp. cinnamon
1 large egg

IF YOU'RE USING a food processor, put all the cake ingredients, except the apples, into the bowl, and process until the mixture is the consistency of cornmeal. Spread the mixture in the bottom of a well-buttered, 9-inch springform pan. (If you don't have a food processor, mix the dry ingredients together, then cut in the butter, and when the mixture is like cornmeal, add the vanilla and egg.)

PEEL THE APPLES and remove the cores, then slice them.

ARRANGE THE APPLES in layers on top of the crumb mixture. Bake in a pre-heated 350-degree oven for 45 minutes.

MEANWHILE, MIX TOGETHER the topping ingredients. Spoon the mixture over the apples and bake 25 to 30 minutes more or until the top is firm.

Connoisseur

Bill Pronzini

N orman Tolliver was a connoisseur of many things: art, music, literature, gourmet cuisine, sports cars, beautiful women. But above all else, he was a connoisseur of fine wine.

Nothing gave him quite so much pleasure as the bouquet and delicate taste of a claret from the Médoc region of Bordeaux—a 1924 Mouton-Rothschild, perhaps, or a 1929 Haut-Brion; or a brilliant Burgundy such as a Clos de Vougeot 1915. His memory was still vivid of the night in Paris when an acquaintance of his father's had presented him with a glass of the *impériale* claret, the 1878 Latour Pauillac. It was Norman's opinion that a man could experience no greater moment of ecstasy than his first sip of that venerable Latour.

Norman resided in an elegant penthouse in New York that commanded a view of the city best described as lordly. That is, he resided there for six months of the year; the remaining six months were divided among Europe and the pleasure islands of the Caribbean and the Mediterranean. During his travels he expended an appreciable amount of time and money in seeking out new varieties and rare vintages of wine, most of which he arranged to have shipped to New York for placement in his private cellar.

It was his custom every Friday evening, no matter where he might happen to be, to sample an exceptional bottle of claret or Burgundy. (He enjoyed fine whites, of course—the French

Sauterne, the German Moselle—but his palate and his temperament were more suited to the classic reds.) These weekly indulgences were always of a solitary nature; as a connoisseur he found the communion between him and great wine too intimate to share with anyone, too poignant to be blunted by even polite conversation.

On this particular Friday Norman happened to be in New York and the wine he happened to select was a reputedly splendid claret: the Château Margaux 1900. It had been given to him by a man named Roger Hume, whom Norman rather detested. Whereas he himself was the fourth-generation progeny in a family of wealth and breeding, Hume was *nouveau riche*—a large, graceless individual who had compiled an overnight fortune in textiles or some such and who had retired at the age of forty to, as he put it in his vulgar way, "find out how the upper crust lives."

Norman found the man to be boorish, dull-witted, and incredibly ignorant concerning any number of matters, including an understanding and appreciation of wine. Nevertheless, Hume had presented him with the Margaux—on the day after a small social gathering that they had both attended and at which Norman chanced to mention that he had never had the pleasure of tasting that difficult-to-obtain vintage. The man's generosity was crassly motivated, to be sure, designed only to impress; but that could be overlooked and even forgiven. A bottle of Margaux 1900 was too fine a prize to be received with any feeling other than gratitude.

At three o'clock Norman drew his study drapes against the afternoon sun and placed one of Chopin's nocturnes on his quadraphonic record changer. Then, with a keen sense of anticipation, he carefully removed the Margaux's cork and prepared to decant the wine so that it could breathe. It was his considered judgment that an aged claret should be allowed no less than five hours of contact with new air and no more than six. A healthy, living wine must be given time to breathe in order for it to express its character, release its bouquet, become *more* alive; but too much breathing causes a dulling of its subtle edge.

He lighted the candle that he had set on the Duncan Phyfe table, waited until the flame was steady, then began to slowly pour the Margaux, holding the shoulder of the bottle just above the light so that he could observe the flow of the wine as it passed through the neck. There was very little age-crust or sediment. The color, however, did not look quite right; it had a faint cloudiness, a pale brown twinge, as wine does when it has grown old too quickly.

Norman felt a sharp twinge of apprehension. He raised the decanter and sniffed the bouquet. Not good, not good at all. He swirled the wine lightly to let air mix with it and sniffed again. Oh, Lord—a definite taint of sourness.

He poured a small amount into a crystal glass, prepared himself, and took a sip. Let the wine flood over and under his tongue, around his gums.

And then spat the mouthful back into the glass.

The Margaux was dead.

Sour, unpalatable—*dead.*

White-faced, Norman sank onto a chair. His first feelings were of sorrow and despair, but these soon gave way to a sense of outrage focused on Roger Hume. It was Hume who had given him not a living, breathing 1900 Margaux but a desiccated *corpse;* it was Hume who had tantalized him and then left him unfulfilled, Hume who had caused him this pain and anguish, Hume who might even have been responsible for the death of the Margaux through careless mishandling. Damn the man. Damn him!

The more Norman thought about Roger Hume, the more enraged he became. Heat rose in his checks until they flamed scarlet. Minutes passed before he remembered his high blood pressure and his doctor's warning about undue stress; he made a conscious effort to calm himself.

When he had his emotions under control he stood, went to the telephone, found a listing for Hume in the Manhattan directory, and dialed the number. Hume's loud, coarse voice answered on the third ring.

"This is Norman Tolliver, Hume," Norman said.

"Well, Norm, it's been awhile. What's the good word?"

Norm. A muscle fluttered on Norman's cheek. "If you plan to be in this afternoon, I would like a word with you."

"Oh? Something up?"

"I prefer not to discuss it on the telephone."

"Suit yourself," Hume said. "Sure, come on over. Give me a chance to show off my digs to you." He paused. "You shoot pool, by any chance?"

"No, I do not 'shoot pool.' "

"Too bad. Got a new table and I've been practicing. Hell of a good game, Norm, you should try it."

The man was a bloody Philistine. Norman said, "I'll be by directly," and cradled the handset with considerable force.

He recorked the bottle of dead Margaux and wrapped it in a towel. After which he blew out the candle, switched off his quadraphonic unit, and took the penthouse elevator to the street. Fifteen minutes later a taxi delivered him to the East Side block on which Hume's townhouse was situated.

Hume admitted him, allowed as how it was good to see him again, swatted him on the back (Norman shuddered and ground his teeth), and ushered him into a spacious living room. There were shelves filled with rare first editions, walls adorned with originals by Degas and Monet and Sisley, fine Kerman Orientals on the floor. *But all of these works of art,* Norman thought, *could mean nothing to Hume; they would merely be possessions, visible evidence of his wealth.* He had certainly never read any of the books or spent a moment appreciating any of the paintings. And there were cigarette burns (Norman ground his teeth again) in one of the Kerman carpets.

Hume himself was fifty pounds overweight and such a plebeian type that he looked out of place in these genteel surroundings. He wore expensive but ill-fitting clothes, much too heavy for the season because of a professed hypersensitivity to cold; his glasses were rimmed in gold and onyx and quite thick because of a professed astigmatism in one eye; he carried an English walking stick because of a slight limp that was the professed result of a sports car accident. He pretended to be an eccentric, but did not have the breeding, intelligence, or flair to manage even the *pose* of eccentricity. Looking at him now, Norman revised his previous estimate: The man was not a Philistine; he was a Neanderthal.

"How about a drink, Norman?"

"This is not a social call," Norman said.

"No?" Hume peered at him. "So what can I do for you?"

Norman unwrapped the bottle of Margaux and extended it accusingly. "*This* is what you can do for me, as you put it."

"I don't get it," Hume said.

"You gave me this Margaux last month. I trust you remember the occasion."

"Sure, I remember. But I still don't see the point—"

"The point, Hume, is that it's dead."

"Huh?"

"The wine is undrinkable. It's *dead*, Hume."

Hume threw back his head and made a sound like the braying of a jackass. "You hand me a laugh sometimes, Norm," he said, "you really do. The way you talk about wine, like it was alive or human or something."

Norman's hands had begun to tremble. "The Margaux *was* alive. Now it is nothing but seventy-nine-year-old vinegar."

"So what?" Hume said.

"So what?" A reddish haze seemed to be forming behind Norman's eyes. "So what! You insensitive idiot, don't you have any conception of what tragedy this is?"

"Hey," Hume said, "who you calling an idiot?"

"You, you idiot. If you have another Margaux 1900, I demand it in replacement. I demand a *living* wine."

"I don't give a damn what you demand," Hume said. He was miffed too, now. "You got no right to call me an idiot, Norm; I won't stand for it. Suppose you just get on out of my house. And take your lousy bottle of wine with you."

"*My* lousy bottle of wine?" Norman said through the reddish haze. "Oh no, Hume, it's *your* lousy bottle of wine, and I'm going to let *you* have it!"

Then he did exactly that: he let Hume have it. On top of the head with all his strength.

There were several confused moments that Norman could not recall afterward. When the reddish haze dissipated, he discovered that all of his anger had drained away, leaving him flushed and shaken. He also discovered Hume lying quite messily dead on the cigarette-scarred Kerman, the unbroken bottle of Margaux beside him.

It was not in Norman's nature to panic in a crisis. He marshaled his emotions instead and forced himself to approach the problem at hand with cold logic.

Hume was as dead as the Margaux; there was nothing to be done about that. He could, of course, telephone the police and claim self-defense. But there was no guarantee that he would be believed, considering that this was Hume's house, and in any case he had an old-fashioned gentleman's abhorrence of adverse and sensational publicity. No, reporting Hume's demise was out of the question.

Which left the reasonable alternative of removing all traces of his presence and stealing away as if he had never come. It was unlikely that anyone had seen him entering; if he was careful his departure would be unobserved as well. And even if someone *did* happen to notice him in a casual way, he was not known in this neighborhood and there was nothing about his physical appearance that would remain fixed in a person's memory. An added point in his favor was that Hume had few friends and by self-admission preferred his own company. The body, therefore, might well go undiscovered for several days.

Norman used the towel to wipe the unbloodied surfaces of the Margaux bottle—a distasteful but necessary task—and left the bottle where it lay beside the body. Had he touched anything in the house that might also retain a fingerprint? He was certain he had not. He *had* pressed the doorbell button on the porch outside, but it would be simple enough to brush that clean before leaving. Was there anything else, anything he might have overlooked? He concluded that there wasn't.

With the towel folded inside his coat pocket, he went down the hallway to the front door. There was a magnifying-glass peephole in the center of it; he put his eye to the glass and peered out. Damn. Two women were standing on the street in front, conversing in the amiable and animated fashion of neighbors. They might decide to part company in ten seconds, but they might also decide to remain there for ten minutes.

Norman debated the advisability of exiting through the rear. But a man slipping out the back door of someone's house was much more likely to be seen and remembered than a man who departed the front. And there was still the matter of the doorbell button to be dealt with. His only intelligent choice was to wait for the street in front to become clear.

As he stood there he found himself thinking again of the tragedy of the Margaux 1900 (a far greater tragedy to his connoisseur's mind than the unlamented death of Roger Hume). It was considered by many experts to be one of the most superlative vintages in history; and the fact remained that he had yet to taste it. To have come so close and then to be denied as he had was intolerable.

It occurred to him again that perhaps Hume *did* have another bottle on the premises. While presenting the first bottle last month Hume had boasted that he maintained a "pretty well-stocked" wine cellar, though he confided that he had never had "much of a taste for the grape" and seldom availed himself of its contents. Neanderthal, indeed. But a Neanderthal with a good deal of money who had managed, through luck or wise advice, to obtain at least one bottle of an uncommon and classic wine—

Was there another Margaux 1900 in his blasted cellar?

Norman debated a second time. On the one hand it would behoove him to make as rapid an escape as possible from the scene of his impulsive crime; but on the other hand the 1900 Margaux was virtually impossible to find today, and if he passed up this opportunity to secure a bottle for himself he might never taste it. It would be a decision he might well rue for the rest of his days.

He looked once more through the peephole; the two women were still talking together outside. Which only served to cement a decision already made. He was, first and foremost, a connoisseur: he simply *had* to know if Hume had another bottle of the Margaux.

Norman located the wine cellar without difficulty. It was off the kitchen, with access through a door and down a short flight of steps. It was also adequate, he noticed in a distracted way as he descended—a smallish single room, walled and floored in concrete, containing several storage bins filled with at least two hundred bottles of wine.

But no, not just wine; remarkably *fine* wine. Reds from Châteaux Lafite, Haut-Brion, Lascombes, Cos D'Estournel, Mouton-D'Armailhacq, La Tâche, Romanée Saint-Vivant; whites from the Bommes and Barsac communes of France, from the Rhine Hessen of Germany, from Alsace and Italy and the Napa Valley of California. Norman resisted the impulse to stop and more closely examine each of the labels. He had no time to search out anything except the Margaux 1900.

He found two different Château Margaux clarets in the last row of bins, but neither of them was the 1900 vintage. Then, when he was about to abandon hope, he knelt in front of the final section of bins and there they were, a pair of dusty bottles whose labels matched that on the spoiled bottle upstairs.

Norman expelled a breath and removed one of them with care. Should he take the second as well? Yes: if he left it here there was no telling into whose unappreciative hands it might fall. There would doubtless be a paper sack in the kitchen in which to carry both. He withdrew the second bottle, straightened, and started to the stairs.

The door at the top was closed. Blinking, Norman paused. He could not recall having shut the door; in fact he was quite certain he had left it standing wide open. He frowned, went up the steps, set the two living Margaux 1900s down carefully at his feet, and rotated the knob.

It was locked.

It took a moment of futile shaking and rattling before he realized that the top of the door was outfitted with one of those silent pneumatic door closers. He stared at it in disbelief. Only an idiot would put such a device on the door to a wine cellar! But that was, of course, what Hume had been. For whatever incredible reason he had had the thing installed—and it seemed obvious now that he carried on his person the key to the door latch.

There was no other way out of the cellar, no second door and no window; Norman determined that with a single sweep of his gaze. And the door looked to be fashioned of heavy solid wood, which made the task of forcing it or battering it down an insurmountable one.

He was trapped.

The irony was as bitter as the taste of the dead Margaux: trapped in Roger Hume's wine cellar with the man's murdered corpse in the living room upstairs. He had been a fool to come down here, a fool to have listened to the connoisseur in him. He could have been on his way home to his penthouse by now. Instead, here he was, locked away awaiting the eventual arrival of the police . . .

As he had done earlier, Norman made an effort to gather his wits. Perhaps all was *not* lost, despite the circumstances. He could claim to have been visiting Hume when two burly masked men entered the house; and he could claim that these men had locked him in the cellar and taken Hume away to an unknown fate. Yes, that was plausible. After all, he was a respected and influential man. Why shouldn't he be believed?

Norman began to feel a bit better. There remained the problem of survival until Hume's body was found; but as long as that did not take more than a week—an unlikely prospect—the problem was not really a serious one. He was surrounded by scores of bottles of vintage wine, and there *was* a certain amount of nourishment to be had from the product of the vintner's art. At least enough to keep him alive and in passable health.

Meanwhile, he would have to find ways to keep himself and his mind occupied. He could begin, he thought, by examining and making a mental catalogue of Hume's collection of vintages and varieties.

He turned from the door and surveyed the cellar again. And for the first time, something struck him as vaguely odd about it. He had not noticed it before in his haste and purpose, but now that he was locked in here with nothing to distract him—

A faint sound reached his ears and made him scowl. He could not quite identify it or its source at first; he descended the stairs again and stood at the bottom, listening. It seemed to be coming from both sides of the cellar. Norman moved to his left—and when the sound became clear the hackles rose on the back of his neck.

What it was, was a soft hissing.

ROGER HUME'S BODY WAS discovered three days later by his twice-weekly cleaning lady. But when the police arrived at her summons, it was not Hume's death which interested them quite so much as that of the second man, whose corpse was found during a routine search of the premises.

This second "victim" lay on the floor of the wine cellar, amid a rather astonishing carnage of broken wine bottles and spilled wine. His wallet identified him as Norman Tolliver, whose name and standing were recognized by the cleaning lady, if not by the homicide detectives. The assistant medical examiner determined probable cause of death to be an apoplectic seizure, a fact which only added to the consternation of the police. Why was Tolliver locked inside Roger Hume's wine cellar? Why had he evidently smashed dozens of bottles of expensive wine? Why was he dead of natural causes and Hume dead of foul play?

They were, in a word, baffled.

One other puzzling aspect came to their attention. A plain-clothes officer noticed the faint hissing sound and verified it as forced air coming through a pair of wall ducts; he mentioned this to his lieutenant, saying that it seemed odd for a wine cellar to have heater vents like the rest of the rooms in the house. Neither detective bothered to pursue the matter, however. It struck them as unrelated to the deaths of the two men.

But it was, of course, the exact opposite: it was the key to everything. Along with several facts of which they were not yet aware: Norman's passion for wine and his high blood pressure, Roger Hume's ignorance in the finer arts and *his* hypersensitivity to cold—and the tragic effect on certain wines caused by exposure to temperatures above 60 degrees Fahrenheit.

No wonder Norman, poor fellow, suffered an apoplectic seizure. Can there be any greater horror for the true connoisseur than to find himself trapped in a cellar full of rare, aged, and irreplaceable wines that have been stupidly turned to vinegar?

Mulled Wine

⅔ cup sugar
⅓ cup water
1 dozen whole cloves
2 cinnamon sticks
1 crushed nutmeg
1 orange
1 lemon
1 cup lime or lemon juice, heated
1 bottle red wine, heated

CUT THE ORANGE and lemon in half. Juice one half of the orange and one half of the lemon. Add juice to the lime or lemon juice.

SLICE THE REMAINING half of the lemon and orange, and set aside. The citrus slices will be used to garnish the final product.

PUT THE SUGAR, water, cloves, cinnamon sticks, nutmeg, and the peels of the juiced halves of the lemon and orange in a saucepan. Bring to a boil over low to medium heat and boil for about five minutes, until the sugar melts and forms a syrup. Let cool slightly and strain. Return the strained syrup to the pan. Add the hot lemon or lime juice slowly to the syrup while stirring. Add the heated wine and stir. Serve hot, garnished with citrus slices.

Gored

Bill Crider

N o one ever invited Sheriff Dan Rhodes to the annual Blacklin County Stag BBQ. It wasn't that no one liked him. The truth was that the Stag BBQ was something of a scandal, and everyone wanted to be sure that the sheriff ignored it.

And he did. He would never have been there if it hadn't been for the dead man.

THE STAG BBQ WAS held at a different location every year. This year's site was the camphouse on George Newberry's ranch, about ten miles out of Clearview and just off a paved two-lane highway that ran practically straight as an arrow thanks to the fact that it was built on an old narrow-gauge railroad bed.

Rhodes pulled the county car up to a lightweight metal gate. There was a blue-and-white metal sign on the gate to let the world know that George Newberry was a member of the ABBA, the American Brahman Breeders Association.

Newberry himself got out of a red-and-cream-colored Ford pickup and opened the gate. Rhodes drove through. Newberry closed the gate and got in the car beside Rhodes.

"I'll just ride down with you," he said. "I'll come back for the truck later."

Newberry was a big man, over two hundred pounds, very little of which appeared to be muscle. The car sagged slightly to the side when he sat down.

"I'll show you where to go," he said. He pointed to the barn. "It's around that way."

He sounded nervous, and Rhodes didn't blame him. It wasn't every day that someone found a dead man on your property.

The road they were following wasn't much of a road after it passed by the dilapidated sheet-metal barn. It was really just a pair of ruts through a pasture blooming with yellow bitterweed and goldenrod.

Every now and then the county car hit a bump, and Newberry had to take off his Western-style straw hat to keep it from being crushed against the roof. He wiped the sweat off his forehead with his blue bandanna and stuck the bandanna in his pocket.

"It's Gabe Tolliver," he said.

So it wasn't just any dead man, not some homeless drifter that just happened to turn up on Newberry's property looking for a place to rest for a day or so and praising his luck at finding the empty camphouse. No, it was a Somebody. It was Gabe Tolliver, who had been a loan officer at the larger of Clearview's two banks.

"What happened?" Rhodes asked.

"I'll let you be the judge of that," Newberry said. Though the car's air conditioner was running full blast, Newberry was still sweating. His western shirt had dark circles under the armpits. "All I know for sure's that Ben Locklin found him lyin' by a brush pile, and Bo Peevehouse called you on that cellular phone of his that he's so proud of."

Ben Locklin was a vice president of the bank where Tolliver worked. Or *had* worked. He wouldn't be reporting in on Monday. Peevehouse sold life and accident insurance. Newberry was also a big man in Clearview. He owned three of the most prosperous businesses in town: two convenience stores and a video store.

In fact, that was what the Stag BBQ was all about. It was a chance for the movers and shakers to get together and drink a lot of beer, eat some BBQ and homemade ice cream, tell a few dirty jokes, and do a little gambling.

It was the gambling that no one wanted the sheriff to know about, though it was an open secret. If the men wanted to lose a few dollars to one another shooting craps or playing jacks-or-better-to-open, Rhodes didn't really see the harm in it.

But it seemed that this year there had been some harm after all, at least for Gabe Tolliver.

The BBQ was the social event of the year for the men in Blacklin County, and everyone who was anyone got invited. Everyone who was anyone and male, that is. Women weren't allowed. Blacklin County was becoming more conscious of women's rights every day, but Blacklin County was, after all, in Texas, where a great many men still believed that some activities just weren't appropriate for women. Maybe they were okay in Las Vegas, but that was different.

Rhodes looked over at Newberry, who was holding his hat in his lap. The businessman was wearing jeans and a pair of expensive-looking boots that were covered with dust. It hadn't rained in Blacklin County for nearly a month.

"Don't worry," Newberry said, noticing Rhodes's glance. "I haven't stepped in anything."

"I didn't think you had," Rhodes told him.

Rhodes figured he'd be the only man at the ranch without a pair of boots. He was pretty certain that he was the only sheriff in Texas who didn't wear them. But they hurt his toes and he couldn't walk in them very well, so he was wearing an old pair of scuffed Rockports.

The car went up over a low rise, and Rhodes could see Newberry's camphouse, painted dark green and sitting on top of a hill not far from a big stock tank and in front of a thickly wooded area that began about thirty yards away and ran down the hill. There was a four-strand barbed-wire fence around the camphouse.

"Any fish in the tank?" Rhodes asked.

"Bass," Newberry said. "A couple of the guys have tried it today, but nobody's caught anything. I caught a five-pounder last spring, though."

Rhodes wished that he'd brought his rod and reel along, but it wouldn't have been very professional to go fishing while he was supposed to be conducting a murder investigation.

There were white Brahman cattle scattered out over the pasture, crunching the grass with their heads down or looking at whatever it was that cows looked at. Rhodes couldn't tell whether they were purebred or not. They paid no attention to his car.

"Nice-looking herd," he said.

"Yeah," Newberry said, sounding a little distracted. "Kind of wild, though."

"Wild?"

"You'll see," Newberry said.

RHODES SAW WHEN THEY got to the body, which was located just inside the woods. Gabe Tolliver was lying on his back, and there was a terrible wound in his stomach, as if a horn had twisted his insides. Black flies buzzed around the wound, and a couple of them were crawling on it, near a curling brown leaf that stuck to the torn skin. Rhodes hadn't known Tolliver well, and what he'd heard about, he didn't much like. Tolliver was said to be a womanizer and a bully, and that might have been true. But even if it was, Tolliver hadn't deserved to die like this.

"Did you call a doctor?" Rhodes asked Newberry.

They were standing over the body. Everyone else was in the fenced yard of the house, and Rhodes could almost feel their eyes boring into his back.

"Didn't see any need of a doctor," Newberry said. His face was white. "Not much doubt that Gabe's dead. But listen, Sheriff, as wild as those braymahs are, I don't think any of them did this. What about you?"

Rhodes didn't think so either. He knelt down by the body and shooed the flies away with his hand. There were wood splinters in the twisted flesh, and there was a sliver of bark on Tolliver's blue western shirt.

There was a dark stain by the back of Tolliver's head, and his hair was wet with blood. He'd been hit, probably before the goring.

Rhodes stood up. The trees were native hardwoods, oak and elm mostly, with a few pecan trees thrown in. There were several dead tree limbs lying near where Rhodes was standing and more in the brush pile near the body, but nothing that looked as if it had been used to kill Tolliver.

"Cows didn't do this," Rhodes said.

He looked around the area carefully. There was a place nearby where the ground was gouged up as if an armadillo had been rooting around, though Rhodes suspected that no animal was responsible. He'd have to get soil samples to be sure.

He turned to Newberry. "Let's get back to your camphouse."

Newberry looked glad of the chance to leave the body. They walked up a little cattle trail, and Newberry sidestepped a cow pie, the same one he had avoided on their way down to see the body. Someone had stepped in the manure earlier, but not Rhodes, which was surprising to the sheriff. Whenever he visited a pasture, he generally stepped in something within ten seconds of getting out of his car.

He stopped and looked down at the cow pie. There was another one just to the side of it, and that one had been kicked to pieces. Both were fairly fresh, and the one that had been shattered wasn't yet entirely dry.

"What was Tolliver doing in the woods, anyway?" Rhodes asked Newberry.

Newberry turned around. "I don't know. There's not any bathroom up there at the camphouse, so nearly ever'body's goin' to come to the woods once or twice."

Rhodes hadn't seen any signs of that kind of activity, and said so.

"Well, mostly people just go behind the tank dam. But I know some of 'em have come down here to get wood for the fire. Maybe that's what Gabe was after."

"Who's the cook?"

"Jerry Foster."

Foster ran a discount auto parts store. He was the one Rhodes wanted to talk to.

Just before they got back to the house, an armadillo shot out of the weeds beside the trail and charged through the goldenrods and bitterweeds. Little puffs of dust flew from its feet. Rhodes had never understood how something with such short legs could go so fast. He wondered if he could have been wrong about the gouges in the earth near Tolliver's body, but he didn't think so. No armadillo had done that.

I⹁ WAS NEARLY FIVE o'clock, but because it was the first week in October it wouldn't be dark for more than two hours. The shadows in the woods were beginning to deepen, but there was a pleasant glow to the light that belied the circumstances. Newberry's cattle grazed peacefully in the pasture, unable to get near the house thanks to the barbed-wire fence.

Rhodes didn't have time to enjoy the deceptive peacefulness of the scene. He went to the county car, which was parked outside the fence. He opened the car door, got in, and called the jail on the radio. Then he told Hack Jensen, the dispatcher, to send the justice of the peace to Newberry's ranch. And an ambulance.

"You think an ambulance can make it up to that camphouse?" Hack asked.

Rhodes said that he hoped so. He didn't want to have to haul Tolliver's body out in the back of someone's pickup.

"I'll tell 'em then," Hack said. "You gonna solve this and be home in time for supper, or do you want me to call Ivy for you?"

Rhodes thought about the barbecue that Jerry Foster was cooking. He thought about bread soaked in barbecue sauce and about potato salad and pinto beans and cool, thick slices of white onion. He thought about homemade ice cream. And he thought about the low-fat diet he was on at home.

"You better call her," he said. "This might take a while."

THE GIANT BARBECUE GRILL was made from three fifty-five-gallon drums split in half and welded together end to end. There was a stovepipe on one end. Rhodes could smell the mesquite smoke as he walked over to talk to Jerry Foster, who stood by the grill.

Foster was taller than Rhodes's six feet, and he was wearing a chef's hat that had once been white but which was now mostly gray and stained with smoke and grease. He was also wearing an equally stained apron that had "Kiss the Cook" printed on it in red. Someone had used a black marking pen to add the word "Don't" to the front of the sentence and an exclamation mark at the end.

Foster opened the grill as Rhodes walked up. Smoke billowed out, enveloping them and stinging the sheriff's eyes. Rhodes waved a hand in front of his face to push the smoke away.

Coals glowed under the slow-cooked meat. Rhodes looked hungrily at the juicy pork ribs while Foster poked a brisket with a long fork. Satisfied that everything was all right, Foster lowered the lid.

"Still planning to eat?" Rhodes asked.

"I expect we will, but Gabe's dyin' has pretty much put a damper on the festivities." Foster had a raspy smoker's voice. "There's no need to let the meat burn up even if we don't eat it today, though."

Foster was right about the festivities. There weren't any that Rhodes could see. He looked over at a big oak tree by the camphouse. The ground beneath it was worn smooth and packed hard, but there were no crapshooters gathered there. Everyone was standing around in small groups, whispering and looking over at Rhodes and Foster.

The shaded tables under the other trees were clear of cards and poker chips, but Rhodes wasn't entirely sure whether the gambling had come to a stop because he was there or because of Tolliver's murder.

Also in the shade of the oak were three washtubs covered with thick quilts. Rhodes knew that the tubs would be full of ice and that under the quilts were hand-cranked wooden ice cream freezers. Rhodes hadn't had any homemade ice cream in years. The thought of its cold smoothness made his mouth water.

"What kind of ice cream in the freezers?" he asked.

"Peach," Foster said. "Last of the Elbertas came in back in August, and my wife put some up in the freezer for us to use for the barbecue."

Peach was Rhodes's favorite.

"Did Ben Locklin bring you any firewood?" Rhodes asked.

"Nope." Foster pushed up his chef's hat and wiped his forehead. "Who did?"

"I brought the mesquite myself, in my truck. Got it from my place. Newberry doesn't have any mesquite trees, or if he does you can't see 'em from here. You need some mesquite for the flavor."

"I wasn't talking about the mesquite," Rhodes said, thinking how the smoked ribs would taste. "I was talking about wood from the trees down the hill."

Foster gave it some thought. "Bo Peevehouse. Brian Colby. Hal Janes. Ben Locklin was goin' to, but he got a little sidetracked, what with findin' Gabe dead like that. There might've been a few more. I didn't try to keep up. They just dumped it on the pile and left it. I didn't look to see who brought it."

There was a little stack of twigs at one end of the grill.

"Looks like you're about out of wood," Rhodes said.

"Yeah. I've used most of it. But the brisket's about done. We won't need any more."

Rhodes supposed that was good, but it was too bad that all the wood had been burned, not that he'd expected to find anything.

"Any idea who'd want to kill Gabe?" he asked.

Foster readjusted his chef's hat. "Sheriff, you know as well as I do that half the people here've known each other since they were kids. They've got reasons to kill each other that go all the way back to high school, if not before. And the other half didn't like Gabe all that much. He wasn't bein' any too lenient with his loans these days."

Rhodes had heard the same thing. He left Foster and went looking for Newberry, whom he found talking to Bo Peevehouse.

"I need to talk to a few people," Rhodes told Newberry. "I'll do it inside if that's all right."

"Don't see any reason why not," Newberry said. "Who did you want to see?"

"I'll start with Bo," Rhodes said.

BO PEEVEHOUSE, WHO HAD the cellular phone, also had the biggest TV set in Blacklin County, or so Rhodes had heard. He'd never seen it, himself. Bo had done very well in insurance, which Rhodes knew about in the same way he knew about the TV set: through Ivy, Rhodes's wife, who worked at a rival insurance agency.

Peevehouse had red hair that he wore in a spiky crew cut that Rhodes thought looked pretty strange with his western garb. Bo's boots were dusty but otherwise clean. His hands were smooth and white. Not the hands of a cowboy.

"Did you see the body?" Rhodes asked him.

They were sitting at a small wooden table in the camphouse, which had only one big room with a concrete floor. The rafters were covered with antlers, some of them small, some of them having five or six points, and the walls held pictures of wolves, deer, mountain lions, and Rocky Mountain sheep. There was a cot in one corner, a fireplace with more antlers nailed to the rough wooden mantel, and some metal folding chairs.

"Nope," Peevehouse said. "I didn't see it, and I sure didn't want to. Ben Locklin threw up, they told me, and I would've done the same thing. I don't need to see any bodies. All I did was call your office on my phone."

He patted his shirt pocket, where Rhodes could see the slim outline of the telephone.

"Flip model," Peevehouse said. "You wanta have a look?"

Rhodes didn't. "You brought some wood for the fire?"

"Sure did. Somebody gotta do it, and I figured it might as well be me. I don't mind working for my dinner."

"Who else brought wood up?"

Peevehouse didn't know. "I was busy shootin' di—I mean, I was doin' somethin' else."

"Who do you know that might want to kill Gabe Tolliver?"

Peevehouse didn't want to talk about it. He looked at the antlers, at the pictures, and at the concrete floor. Finally, he said, "Sheriff, you know what it's been like in this county for the last ten years? People haven't had much money, and when the bank was sold to that holdin' company, a lot of the old guys who'd been there for years lost their jobs. Gabe held onto his, but he had to be tough to do it. He couldn't do business the way he had before. You might say he was foreclosin' on the widows and orphans, and the only people who could get a loan were the folks who didn't need one. There were plenty of people who didn't like Gabe."

Rhodes knew Tolliver's reputation. But the word was that Gabe *liked* being tough. Foster had already hinted at it, and Rhodes had been hearing it for a long time before that. That wasn't really what he was interested in.

"Anybody here today get turned down for money he needed to keep his doors open?" he asked. "Anybody here today lose a house or a car because of Gabe?"

Peevehouse shook his head. "Not that I know of."

"I didn't think so. Now, what about other things? The kind of things that people get really upset about."

"I don't like to gossip, Sheriff," Peevehouse said. "When you sell insurance, you meet a lot of people and you hear a lot of stories. I don't pay 'em much attention."

He was looking at the fireplace while he talked. Rhodes figured he was lying.

"I think you should tell me if you've heard anything," Rhodes said. "I'll just find out from someone else."

"I guess you're right," Peevehouse said. He looked away from the fireplace and sighed. And then he told Rhodes what he'd heard.

BEN LOCKLIN WAS FIVE inches over six feet, but his hands were as small and soft as those of a teenage girl.

"It was a hell of a shock," he said. "Seeing Gabe lying there, like that, his stomach ripped open. I don't mind telling you I lost my lunch. It was a hell of a mess. Looked like he got gored by a bull to me, but I hadn't seen any bull down there in the woods, or any cows either. That's why I told Bo he'd better call you."

"You thought somebody had a reason to kill him?" Rhodes asked.

"Gabe was a good man," Locklin said, folding his arms across his wide chest. "I know what people think about him, but they think worse of me. I'm his boss, after all. I could tell him to do different if I wanted to."

Rhodes didn't really believe that. Locklin had been with the bank for twenty years, but everyone knew that didn't make a bit of difference to the new owners, who were probably planning to get rid of him as soon as they got more of their own men in place.

"I wasn't wondering about his business practices," Rhodes said. "I wanted to hear about his troubles with women."

Locklin looked at him.

"You know what I mean," Rhodes said. "He had a wandering eye, from what I hear."

"I don't know about that," Locklin said. "What my employees do on their own time is their own business."

"In a town the size of Clearview it isn't. I've already heard about it from Bo."

Ben waved a dismissive hand. "Gutter talk."

"Maybe. You've heard about it too, though, haven't you?"

"I've heard. That doesn't mean I believe it."

"That kind of talk gets under people's skin," Rhodes said. "Whether it's true or not." He told Locklin what he'd heard.

Locklin thought for a second or two and then admitted that he'd heard more or less the same things. Rhodes asked if he'd mentioned the talk to Gabe.

"Yeah, I said something. He told me to mind my own damn business, not that I blame him. Whatever he was doing, it didn't affect his work at the bank."

"And those men I mentioned, they had loans they'd missed a payment or two on?"

Locklin shrugged. "Yeah, I guess that's right."

That was all Rhodes wanted to know.

GEORGE NEWBERRY WAS JUST as reluctant to talk as Peevehouse and Locklin had been, but when Rhodes told him that he'd already heard the gossip, Newberry gave in. He confirmed everything that Peevehouse and Locklin had said.

"But it's just gossip," he said. "Stuff you hear if you hang around a convenience store all day like I do. I don't know that a word of it's true. You know what it is like when stories get started."

Rhodes knew. But there was generally a factual basis for things, even if the facts weren't as juicy as the story that finally made the rounds of the entire community.

"Both those men went down for firewood, according to Foster," Rhodes said.

"Maybe so," Newberry agreed, "but that doesn't make them killers."

That was true enough, but it put them in the vicinity of the murder. Right now that was about all Rhodes had to go on, that and the gossip.

"Send them in," he told Newberry. "I'll talk to them together."

"You think that's a good idea?"

"Maybe not," Rhodes said. "But it's the only one I have."

N<small>EITHER</small> H<small>AL</small> J<small>ANES</small> <small>NOR</small> Brian Colby looked like a killer. They were young and skinny, and in their tight jeans and western hats, they looked as if they were just about to go to a rodeo and ride a bronc or maybe enter the calf-roping event. Colby had a red-and-white bandanna tied around his neck.

They came into the camphouse and stood awkwardly until Rhodes told them to sit at the table. He stood by the fireplace and watched them.

Janes was a little taller than Colby, but Colby was a lot wider through the shoulders. Either one of them looked big enough to have killed Gabe without too much trouble. Colby's boots were dirty, but Janes's were spotless.

Both men were nervous. Colby fidgeted in the folding chair, and Janes rubbed his hands together as if he were washing them.

Rhodes gave them a few seconds to wonder about what he was going to ask them. Then he said, "I know that you both went down to bring in some wood for the fire, and I know that one of you killed Gabe Tolliver. What I don't know is which one of you did it."

"Jesus Christ," Colby said, standin, up and knocking over his chair. It clanged on the hard floor. "You must be crazy, Sheriff."

"Lots of people think so," Rhodes said. "What about you, Hal?"

Janes was still sitting at the table, still dry-washing his hands.

"I wouldn't know about that," he said. "I think you're makin' a big mistake, though, accusin' two innocent men without any evidence."

"How would you know I don't have any evidence?" Rhodes asked.

Colby picked up his chair and sat back down. He looked at Janes and seemed as interested in his answer to the question as Rhodes did.

Janes gripped the edge of the table with his fingers, looking down at his nails. "The way I heard it, Gabe's just lyin' down there dead. Nobody saw him get killed, so there's no witnesses." He looked up at Rhodes. "Ben Locklin found the body, and he said it looked like a cow did it, or a bull. Said Gabe looked like he'd been gored."

"So there must not be any evidence of any murder," Colby said, more relaxed now and tipping back his chair. "Ben would've seen it if there was."

"Ben's not a trained lawman," Rhodes said. "He works in a bank."

"So did Gabe," Janes pointed out. "The same bank. Maybe they had a fight and Ben killed Gabe."

"Ben found the body, all right," Rhodes said. "He didn't kill anybody, though."

"Did you ask him?"

"I didn't have to," Rhodes said. "Now, let me tell you what I think happened."

"It won't do you any good," Colby told him. "I didn't kill anybody, and I don't have to listen to you."

"Me neither," Janes said. "I don't see why you're pickin' on us."

"Because of your wives," Rhodes said.

"You son of a bitch," Janes said.

Colby didn't say anything. He just sat there and looked as if he'd like to be somewhere else.

"Tolliver was after both of them," Rhodes went on, ignoring Janes. He'd been called worse. "You were both behind on loans, and he was using that to get at your wives. That's the way he was. He'd promise a little leeway if the woman would meet him somewhere for a drink."

"I think you'd better shut up, Sheriff," Colby said.

Rhodes ignored him the way he'd ignored Janes and leaned an elbow on the mantel in a space that was free of antlers.

"I think it happened this way," he said. "One of you saw Tolliver going for wood and followed him down there. Maybe you already had in mind what you were going to do, but I don't know about that. Maybe you just wanted to talk to him, tell him to stay away from your wife."

"So what?" Colby said. "What'd be wrong with that? If he was messin' where he shouldn't have been, he needed tellin'."

Rhodes agreed. "There's nothing wrong with telling. But that's not what happened. Whoever followed Gabe got so mad that he killed him. Maybe there was an argument first, and maybe Gabe said a few things he shouldn't have said. I don't know about that, either. I do know that somebody took a tree limb and clubbed Gabe in the back of the head."

"That wouldn't look like a bull gored him," Colby pointed out.

"No, so someone tried to cover up. Not that it did any good. That mark on the back of the head couldn't be hidden."

"Maybe he hit his head when he fell," Janes said. "After he got gored."

"That's a good argument, but it's not what happened. If he hadn't been hit first, he would have screamed. Somebody hit

Tolliver and then gored him with a tree limb. Maybe with the same one he hit him with."

"Where's the limb, then?" Colby asked.

"Burned up," Rhodes said. "The killer broke it up and took it to Jerry for firewood."

Colby didn't believe it. "Wouldn't Jerry have noticed the blood on the pieces of the limb when he put it in the fire?"

"Whoever killed Gabe jammed the limb in the dirt to clean the blood off," Rhodes said. "If there was any blood still on it, the dirt covered it up. Foster wouldn't have been looking for it."

"Sounds like you don't have any evidence, then, Sheriff," Janes said.

"Maybe not. But I know who killed Gabe Tolliver."

"Who?" Janes asked.

"You did," Rhodes said, stepping toward the table.

Janes shoved back his chair, kicked over the table, and threw Brian Colby at Rhodes.

Colby and Rhodes went down in a heap on the floor. Rhodes banged his elbow, and Janes ran out the door.

NO ONE IN THE yard tried to stop Janes. They didn't even know for sure what was going on until Rhodes came running out after him.

By that time Janes had vaulted the fence and headed across the pasture. Rhodes knew that if Janes made it to the river bottoms, about a mile away, they might never catch him. The bottom land was thick with trees and if a man was careful and knew the woods, he could stay hidden in the trees most of the way across the state.

Rhodes knew better than to try vaulting the fence. He valued the more delicate parts of his anatomy too much for that. He went through the gate, but that put him even farther behind Janes.

He probably wouldn't have caught him if it hadn't been for the armadillo. The armored mammal, frightened by Janes's approach, sprang up out of nowhere and shot across Janes's path.

It was too late for Janes to try to avoid the armadillo. He kicked it, tripped, and went sprawling in the bitterweed. The armadillo rolled a few feet and then it was on its way again.

Janes got to his knees, but Rhodes reached him before he could get up, put an armlock on him, and then slapped on the cuffs. After that it was easy to march him back to the camphouse.

They got there at the same time that the ambulance arrived, followed closely by the J. P., another county car carrying Deputy Ruth Grady, and Red Rogers, a reporter for the local radio station who was looking for a good story. Rhodes figured he would get one.

IT WAS NEARLY DARK before things were straightened out, but no one left. They were all too curious to know the story, and besides, there was all that barbecue to eat, not to mention peach ice cream.

They were so eager to hear the story that they even invited Rhodes to stay.

Red Rogers tried to get Rhodes on tape, but Rhodes didn't want to talk for the radio. He wanted to eat ribs and ice cream.

"You owe it to the community," Rogers said. "You have to tell us how you knew that Hal Janes was the killer."

Rhodes could smell the barbecue and he looked longingly at the ice cream freezers under their quilt covers.

"We'll save you some cream," Newberry assured him. "You go on and talk."

"Great," Rogers said. "So how did you know it was Janes?"

"His boots were too clean," Rhodes said. "He was the only one here with clean boots. Which meant that he'd cleaned them off. I think he stepped in a cow patty on the trail and left a boot print in it. But he noticed the print and kicked the patty to pieces, so naturally he had to clean his boots. Deputy Grady is looking around for his bandanna right now. I think she'll find it."

Rogers was incredulous. "And that's it? You know he did it because his boots were clean?"

"That and his hands," Rhodes said. "You look at all these men here, they're dressed up in cowboy clothes, but they're not cowboys. They're bankers and salesmen and store owners. There's not a callused hand in the bunch. Janes didn't want me to see his hands because he'd scratched them up on the limb he used to kill Tolliver with. You can't fool with that rough bark like that, not without marking your hands."

"But what about hard evidence?" Rogers asked.

"We'll find that bandanna," Rhodes said. "And we'll find traces of bark in the scratches on Janes's hands. We'll find cow manure on his boots, too, in the cracks and crevices. He couldn't get it all off."

"But will that prove he killed Gabe Tolliver?"

"He had a motive, the means, and the opportunity," Rhodes said. "We'll see what a jury thinks."

There was more that Rogers wanted to say, but Rhodes didn't listen. Everyone was eating from paper plates heaped with ribs and brisket, beans and potato salad, and the covers were off the ice cream freezers. Rhodes wanted to get his share.

It turned out to be even better than he'd thought. The ribs were smoky and spicy, and the ice cream was so smooth and sweet and cold that he could have eaten a whole gallon.

It was too bad, he thought, that Hal Janes and Gabe Tolliver weren't there to enjoy it.

Peach Ice Cream

Makes one gallon

5 eggs
2 cups sugar
Pinch of salt
3 tsp. vanilla
1 can sweetened condensed milk
1 large can evaporated milk (13 ounces)
1 quart mashed peaches
Enough whole milk to fill freezer can within 2 inches
   of top (about 3 cups)

BEAT EGGS UNTIL thick, adding sugar gradually. Add remaining ingredients and pour into freezer can. Put dasher in freezer can. Put freezer can in bucket and fill bucket with ice (add salt to ice about every six inches). Attach freezer crank, and turn until mixture is hard. Remove dasher and keep the freezer can iced down until serving.

USE A WOODEN freezer with a hand crank. Whoever turns the crank gets to lick the dasher.

Day for a Picnic

Edward D. Hoch

I suppose I remember it better than the other, countless other, picnics of my childhood, and I suppose the reason for that is the murder. But perhaps this day in mid-July would have stood out in my mind without the violence of sudden death. Perhaps it would have stood out simply because it was the first time I'd ever been out alone without the ever-watching eyes of my mother and father to protect me. True, my grandfather was watching over me that month while my parents vacationed in Europe, but he was more a friend than a parent—a great old man with white hair and tobacco-stained teeth who never ceased the relating of fascinating tales of his own youth out West. There were stories of Indians and warfare, tales of violence in the youthful days of our nation, and at that youthful age I was fully content in believing that my grandfather was easily old enough to have fought in all those wars as he so claimed.

It was not the custom in the thirties, as it is today, for parents to take their children along when making their first tour of Europe, and so as I've said I was left behind in Grandfather's care. It was really a month of fun for me, because the life of the rural New York town is far different from the hustle of the city, even for a boy of nine or ten, and I was to spend endless days running barefoot along dusty roads in the company of boys who never—hardly ever—viewed me strangely because of my city background. The days were sunny with warmth, because it had been a warm summer

even here on the shores of a cooling lake. Almost from the beginning of the month my grandfather had spoken with obvious relish
of the approach of the annual picnic, and by mid-month I was
looking forward to it also, thinking that here would be a new
opportunity of exploring the byways of the town and meeting
other boys as wild and free as I myself felt. Then too, I never
seemed to mind at that time the company of adults. They were
good people for the most part, and I viewed them with a proper
amount of childish wonder.

There were no sidewalks in the town then, and nothing that
you'd really call a street. The big touring cars and occasional late-
model roadsters raised endless clouds of dust as they roared
(seemingly to a boy of ten) through the town at fantastic speeds
unheard of in the city. This day especially, I remember the cars
churning up the dust. I remember Grandfather getting ready for
the picnic, preparing himself with great care because this was to be
a political picnic, and Grandfather was a very important political
figure in the little town.

I remember standing in the doorway of his bedroom (leaning,
really, because boys of ten never stood when they could lean),
watching him knot the black string tie that made him look so
much like that man in the funny movies. For a long time I watched
in silence, seeing him scoop up coins for his pockets and the solid
gold watch I never tired of seeing, and the little bottle he said was
cough medicine even in the summer, and, of course, his important
speech.

"You're goin' to speak, Gramps?"

"Sure am, boy. Every year I speak. Give the town's humanitarian
award. It's voted on by secret ballot of all the townspeople."

"Who won it?"

"That's something no one knows but me, boy. And I don't tell
till this afternoon."

"Are you like the mayor here, Gramps?"

"Sort of, boy," he said with a chuckle. "I'm what you call a select-
man, and since I'm the oldest of them here I guess I have quite a
lot to say about the town."

"Are you in charge of the picnic?"

"I'm in charge of the awards."

"Can we get free Coke and hot dogs?"

He chuckled at that. "We'll see, boy. We'll see."

Grandfather didn't drive, and as a result we were picked up for the picnic by Miss Pinkney and Miss Hazel, two old schoolteachers who drove a white Ford with a certain misplaced pride. Since they were already in front, the two of us piled in back, a bit crowded but happy. On the way to the picnic grounds we passed others going on foot, and Grandfather waved like a prince might wave.

"What a day for a picnic!" Miss Hazel exclaimed. "Remember how it rained last year?"

The sun was indeed bright and the weather warm, but with the contrariness of the very young I remember wishing that I'd been at the rainy picnic instead. I'd never been at a rainy picnic for the very simple reason that my parents always called them off if it rained.

"It's a good day," my grandfather said. "It'll bring out the voters. They should hold elections in the summertime, and we'd win by a landslide every time."

The Fourth of July was not yet two weeks past, and as we neared the old picnic grounds we could hear the belated occasional crackling of leftover fireworks being set off by the other kids. I was more than ever anxious to join them, though I did wonder vaguely what kind of kids would ever have firecrackers unexploded and left over after the big day.

We traveled down a long and dusty road to the picnic property, running winding down a hillside to a sort of cove by the water where brown sandy bluffs rose on three sides. There was room here for some five hundred people, which is the number that might be attracted by the perfect weather, and already a few cars were parked in the makeshift parking area, disgorging there the loads of children and adults. Miss Pinkney and Miss Hazel parked next to the big touring car that belonged to Dr. Stout, and my grandfather immediately cornered the doctor on some political subject. They stood talking for some minutes about—as I remember—the forthcoming primary election, and all the while I shifted from one foot to the other, watching the other kids at play down by the water, watching the waves of the lake whitened by a brisk warming breeze that fanned through the trees and tall uncut grass of the bluffs.

Finally, with a nod of permission from my grandfather, I took off on the run, searching out a few of the boys I'd come to know best in these weeks of my visit. I found them finally, playing in a

sort of cave on the hillside. Looking back now I realize it was probably no more than a lovers' trysting place, but at the time it held
for us all the excitement and mystery of a smuggler's den. I played
there with the others for nearly an hour, until I heard my grandfather calling me from down near the speakers' platform.

Already as I ran back down the hill I saw that the campaign
posters and patriotic bunting were in place. The picnic crowd was
gradually drifting down to the platform, clutching hot dogs and
bottles of soda pop and foaming mugs of beer. Over near the cars I
could see the men tapping another keg of beer, and I watched as a
sudden miscalculation on the part of the men sent the liquid
shooting up into a fizzing fountain. "It's raining beer," shouted
one of the men, standing beneath the descending stream with his
mouth open. "This must be heaven!"

Frank Coons, the town's handyman and occasional black sheep,
had cornered my grandfather and was asking him something.
"Come on, how about some of your gin cough medicine? I been
waitin' all afternoon for it!"

But my grandfather was having none of it. "None today, Frank."

"Why not? Just a drop."

"Have some beer instead. It's just as good." He moved off, away
from Frank, and I followed him. There were hands to be shaken,
words to be spoken, and in all of it Grandfather was a past master.

"When's your speech, Gramps?" I asked him.

"Soon now, boy. Want a soda pop?"

"Sure!"

He picked a bottle of cherry-colored liquid from the red and
white cooler and opened it for me. It tasted good after my running
and playing in the hot dirt of the hillside. Now Grandfather saw
someone else he knew, a tall handsome man named Jim Tweller,
whom I'd seen at the house on occasion. He had business dealings
with my grandfather, and I understood that he owned much of the
property in the town.

"Stay close to the platform, Jim," Grandfather was saying.

"Don't tell me I won that foolish award!"

"Can't say yet, Jim. Just stay close."

I saw Miss Pinkney and Miss Hazel pass by, casting admiring
glances at Jim Tweller. "Doesn't he have such a *mannish* smell about
him!" Miss Pinkney whispered loudly. Tweller, I gathered even at
that tender age, was much admired by the women of the town.

"Come, boy," Grandfather was saying. "Bring your soda and I'll find you a seat right up in front. You can listen to my speech."

I saw that the mayor, a Mr. Myerton, was already on the platform, flanked by two men and a woman I didn't know. In the very center was a big microphone hooked up to an overhead loudspeaker system borrowed from the sole local radio station. Empty beer mugs stood in front of each place. My grandfather's chair was over on the end, but right now he strode to the speaker's position, between Mayor Myerton and the woman.

"Ladies and gentlemen," he began, speaking in his best political voice. "And children, too, of course. I see a lot of you little ones here today, and that always makes me happy. It makes me aware of the fact that another generation is on the rise, a generation that will carry on the fine principles of our party in the decades to come. As many of you know, I have devoted the years since the death of my wife almost exclusively to party activities. The party has been my lifeblood, as I hope it will be the lifeblood of other, future generations. But enough of that for the moment. Mayor Myerton and Mrs. Finch of the school board will speak to you in due time about the battle that lies ahead of us this November. Right now, it's my always pleasant duty to announce the annual winner of the party's great humanitarian award, given to the man who has done the most for this community and its people. I should say the man or woman, because we've had a number of charming lady winners in past years. But this year it's a man, a man who has perhaps done more than any other to develop the real estate of our town to its full potential, a man who during this past year donated—yes, I said donated—the land for our new hospital building. You all know who I mean, the winner by popular vote of this year's humanitarian award—Mr. Jim Tweller!"

Tweller had stayed near the speakers' stand and now he hopped up, waving to a crowd that was cheering him with some visible restraint. Young as I was, I wondered about this, wondered even as I watched Grandfather yield the honored speaker's position to Tweller and take his chair at the end of the platform. Tweller waited until the scattered cheers had played themselves out in the afternoon breeze and then cheerfully cleared his throat. I noticed Frank Coons standing near the platform and saw Grandfather call him over. "Get a pitcher of beer for us, Frank," he asked. "Speeches make us thirsty."

While Frank went off on his mission, Jim Tweller adjusted the wobbly microphone and began his speech of thanks and acceptance. I was just then more interested in two boys wrestling along the water's edge, tussling, kicking sand at each other. But Tweller's speech was not altogether lost on me. I remember scattered words and phrases, and even then to me they seemed the words and phrases of a political candidate rather than simply an award winner. ". . . Thank you from the bottom of my heart for this great honor . . . I realize, I think, more than anyone else the fact that our party needs a rebirth with new blood if it is to win again in November . . . loyal old horses turned out to pasture while the political colts run the race . . ." I saw Mayor Myerton, a man in his sixties, flinch at these words, and I realized that the simple acceptance speech was taking a most unexpected turn.

But now my attention was caught by the sight of Frank Coons returning with the foaming pitcher of beer. He'd been gone some minutes and I figured he'd stopped long enough to have one himself, or perhaps he'd found someone else who carried gin in a cough medicine bottle. Anyway, he passed the pitcher up to the man at the end of the platform, the opposite end from my grandfather. I wondered if this was his revenge for being refused that drink earlier. The man on the end filled his glass with beer and then passed it on to the mayor who did likewise. Jim Tweller interrupted his speech a moment to accept the pitcher and fill his glass, then pass it to Mrs. Finch of the school board who was on his right. She shook her head with a temperant vigor and let it go on to the man I didn't know, sitting next to Grandfather at the end of the platform.

Tweller had taken a drink of his beer and shook his head violently as if it were castor oil. "Got a bad barrel here," he told the people with a laugh. "I'm going to stick to the hard stuff after this. Or else drink milk. Anyway, before I finish I want to tell you about my plans for our community. I want to tell you a little about how . . ." He paused for another drink of the beer ". . . about how we can push back the final remains of the depression and surge ahead into the forties with a new prosperity, a new ve . . . agh . . ."

Something was wrong. Tweller had suddenly stopped speaking and was gripping the microphone before him. Mayor Myerton put down his own beer and started to get up. "What's wrong, man?" he whispered too near the microphone. "Are you sick?"

"I . . . gnugh . . . can't breathe . . . help me . . ." Then he toppled backward, dragging the microphone with him, upsetting his
glass of beer as he fell screaming and gasping to the ground.

Somewhere behind me a woman's voice took up the scream, and
I thought it might have been Miss Hazel. Already Dr. Stout had
appeared at the platform and was hurrying around to comfort the
stricken man. As I ran forward myself I caught a funny odor in the air
near the platform, near where the beer had spilled from Tweller's
overturned glass. It was a new smell to me, one I couldn't identify.

Behind the platform, Dr. Stout was loosening the collar of the
convulsed man as Grandfather and the mayor tried to assist him.
But after a moment the thrashing of arms and legs ceased, and the
doctor straightened up. The bright overhead sun caught his
glasses as he did so, reflecting for an instant a glare of brilliance.
"There's nothing I can do," he said quietly, almost sadly. "The man
is dead."

SUDDENLY, I WAS BUNDLED off with the other children to play where
we would, while the adults moved in to form a solid ring of curiosity about the platform. The children were curious too, of course,
but after a few minutes of playing many of the younger ones had
forgotten the events with wonder at their newly found freedom.
They ran and romped along the water's edge, setting off what few
firecrackers still remained, wrestling and chasing each other up
the brilliant brown dunes to some imagined summit. But all at
once I was too old for their games of childhood and longed to be
back with the adults, back around the body of this man whom I
hadn't even known a few weeks earlier.

Finally, I did break away, and hurried back to the edges thinning now as women pulled their husbands away. I crept under the
wooden crossbeams of the platform, became momentarily entan-
gled in the wiles of the loudspeaker system, and finally freed
myself to creep even closer to the center of the excitement. A big
man wearing a pistol on his belt like a cowboy had joined them
now, and he appeared to be the sheriff.

"Just tell me what happened," he was saying. "One at a time, not
all it once."

Mayor Myerton grunted. "If you'd been at the picnic, Gene, instead of chasing around town, you'd know what happened."

"Do you pay me to be the sheriff or to drink beer and listen to speeches?" He turned to one of the other men. "What happened, Sam?"

Sam was the man who'd been on the end of the platform, the opposite end from Grandfather. "Hell, Gene, you know as much about it as I do. He was talkin' and all of a sudden he just toppled over and died."

At this point Dr. Stout interrupted. "There's no doubt in my mind that the man was poisoned. The odor of bitter almonds was very strong by the body."

"Bitter almonds?" This from Mayor Myerton. He was wiping the sweat from his forehead, though it didn't seem that hot to me.

Dr. Stout nodded. "I think someone put prussic acid in Tweller's beer. Prussic acid solution or maybe bitter almond water."

"That's impossible," the mayor insisted. "I was sitting right next to him."

Grandfather joined in the discussion now, and I ducked low to the ground so he wouldn't see me. "Maybe the whole pitcher was poisoned. I didn't get around to drinking mine."

But the mayor had drunk some of his without ill effects, as had the man on the end named Sam. Someone went for the pitcher of beer, now almost empty, and Dr. Stout sniffed it suspiciously. "Nothing here. But the odor was on the body, and up there where his glass spilled."

"Maybe he killed himself," Frank Coons suggested, and they seemed to notice him for the first time. Frank seemed to be a sort of town character, lacking the stature of the others, an outsider within the party. And—I knew they were thinking it—after all, he was the one who went for the pitcher of beer in the first place.

"Frank," the sheriff said a little too kindly, "did you have any reason to dislike Jim Tweller?"

"Who, me?"

"Don't I remember hearing something a few years back about a house he sold you? A bum deal on a house he sold you?"

Frank Coons waved his hands airily. "That was nothing, a misunderstanding. I've always liked Jim. You don't think I could have killed him, do you?"

The sheriff named Gene said, "I think we'd all better go down to my office. Maybe I can get to the bottom of things there."

Some of them moved off then, and I saw that the undertaker's ambulance had come for Jim Tweller's body. The undertaker discussed the details of the autopsy with the sheriff, and the two of them proceeded to lift the body onto a stretcher. At that time and that place, no one worried about taking pictures of the death scene or measuring critical distances.

But I noticed that the woman from the school board, Mrs. Finch, pulled Grandfather back from the rest of the group. They paused just above me, and she said, "You know what he was trying to do as well as I do. He was using the acceptance of the award to launch a political campaign of his own. All this talk about rebirth and new blood meant just one thing—he was getting to the point where he was going to run against Mayor Myerton."

"Perhaps," my grandfather said.

"Do you think it's possible that the mayor slipped the poison into his beer?"

"Let me answer that with another question, Mrs. Finch. Do you think the mayor would be carrying a fatal dose of prussic acid in his pocket for such an occasion?"

"I don't know. He was sitting next to Tweller, that's all I know."

"So were you, though, Mrs. Finch," my grandfather reminded her.

They moved off with that, and separated, and I crawled back out to mingle with the children once more. Over by the beer barrel, the man named Sam was helping himself to a drink, and I saw a couple of others still eating their lunch. But for the most part the picnic had ended with Tweller's death. Even the weather seemed suddenly to have turned coolish, and the breeze blowing off the water had an uncomfortable chill to it. Families were folding up their chairs and loading picnic baskets into the cars, and one group of boys was helpfully ripping down the big colored banners and campaign posters. Nobody stopped them, because it was no longer a very good day for a picnic.

THE TWO REMAINING WEEKS of my visit were a blur of comings and goings and frequent phone calls at my grandfather's house. I remember the first few days after the killing, when the excitement of the thing was still on everybody's lips, when one hardly noticed the children of the town and we ran free as birds for hours on end. Frank Coons was jailed by the sheriff when they learned for certain that the beer had been poisoned, but after a few days of questioning they were forced to release him. No one could demonstrate just how he would have been able to poison only the beer poured into Jim Tweller's glass while leaving the mayor and the others unharmed.

I knew that Mrs. Finch still harbored her suspicion of the mayor, and it was very possible that he suspected her as well. All of them came to Grandfather's house, and the conversations went on by the hour. The fact that no one much regretted the death of Tweller did little to pacify things in those first two weeks. The man still had his supporters outside of the political high command, all the little people of the town who'd known him not as a rising politician but only as the donor of land for a hospital. These were the people who'd voted him his humanitarian award, and these were the people who publicly mourned him now, while the top-level conferences at Grandfather's house continued long into the night.

At the end of two weeks I departed, and Grandfather took me down to the railroad station with what seemed a genuine sadness at my going. I stood in the back of the train waving at him as we pulled out of the station, and he seemed at that moment as always to be a man of untried greatness. His white hair caught the afternoon sunlight as he waved, and I felt a tear of genuine feeling trickle down my cheek.

If this had been a detective novel instead of a simple memoir of youth, I would have provided a neat and simple solution to the poisoning of Jim Tweller. But no such solution was ever forthcoming. I heard from my mother and father that the excitement died down within a few weeks, and the life of the town went on as it had before. That November, the mayor and my grandfather and the other town officials were reelected.

I saw my grandfather only briefly after that, at annual family reunions and his occasional visits to our home. When I was sixteen he died quietly in his sleep, and we went up to the town once more. It hadn't changed much, really, and the people seemed much the same as I remembered them. In the cemetery, I stood between Father and Mrs. Finch, who commented on how much I'd grown. The mayor was there, of course, and Dr. Stout, and even

Miss Pinkney and Miss Hazel. I understood from the talk that Frank Coons no longer lived in town. He'd moved south shortly after the murder investigation.

So I said good-bye to my grandfather and his town forever, and went back to the city to grow into manhood.

I SAID A MOMENT ago that this was a memoir and not a mystery and as such would offer no solution to the death of Jim Tweller. And yet—I would not be honest either as a writer or a man if I failed to set down here some thoughts that came to me one evening not long ago, as I sat sipping a cocktail in the company of a particularly boring group of friends.

I suppose it was the sight of cocktails being poured from an icy pitcher that made me remember that other occasion, when the beer had passed down the line of speakers. And remembering it, as the conversation about me droned on, I went over the details of that day once more. I remembered especially that pitcher of beer, and the pouring of Tweller's drink from it. I remembered how he drank from the glass almost immediately, and commented on the bad taste. Certainly, no poison was dropped into the glass *after* the beer had been poured. And yet it was just as impossible to believe that the poison had gone into the glass *with* the beer, when others had drunk unharmed from the same pitcher. No, there was only one possibility—the poison had been in the glass before the beer was poured in.

I imagined a liquid, colorless as water, lying in the bottom of the glass. Just a few drops perhaps, or half an ounce at most. The chances were that Jim Tweller never noticed it, or if he did he imagined it to be only water left from washing out the glass. He would pour the beer in over the waiting poison, in all likelihood, or at worst empty the glass onto the grass first. In any event, there was no danger for the poisoner, and the odds for success were in his favor.

And I remembered then who had occupied the speaker's position immediately before Tweller. I remembered Grandfather with the empty glass before him, the empty beer mug with its thickness of glass to hide the few drops of liquid. I remembered Grandfather with his little bottle of cough medicine, clear cough medicine that usually was gin. Remembered his reluctance that day to give Frank Coons a drink from it. Remembered that I hadn't seen the bottle again later. Remembered most of all Grandfather's devotion to the party, his friendship with Tweller that must have warned him earlier than most of the man's political ambitions. Remembered, finally, that of all the people at the picnic, only Grandfather had known that Tweller was the winner of the award, that Tweller would be on the speaker's platform that day. Grandfather, who called out to Coons for the pitcher of beer. Grandfather, the only person with the motive and the knowledge and the opportunity. And the weapon, in a bottle that might have been cough medicine or gin—or prussic acid.

But that was a long time ago, a generation ago. And I remember him best standing at the station, waving good-bye. . . .

Home-Brewed Beer

THIS IS NOT a recipe. Given that those of you who wish to brew your own beer are going to need specialized ingredients (just try buying malted hops at your grocery store!), as well as equipment, it's best to get both from a reputable home-brewing shop, which will happily bury you in recipes for home-brewed beer and ales. After all, the better the recipes, the more supplies you'll buy. You can check the Yellow Pages for a nearby supplier, but many towns don't have access to a local shop. But, thanks to the magic of the Internet and decent mail service, everybody with access to a computer also has access to all the resources they could possibly want to brew their own beer. Just type home-brew beer into your search engine and have fun!

Guardian Angel

Caroline Benton

People react to death in various ways. Me, I stare through a window. I've always done it, even when I was a small girl. I stare out at the view, sometimes for hours at a time, thinking, adapting, willing myself to cope. Like when I was eight and my father died. I spent whole days in my bedroom then, staring out across cold, January fields. Shortly after his death we moved.

The view from my next bedroom was less exciting—vegetable gardens, allotments, the back of the row of houses in the next street. I felt squeezed and hemmed in. So I cast my eyes upward and watched the sky. It was constantly changing. From my encyclopedia I learned the names of clouds—cirrus, nimbostratus, cumulonimbus. Such wonderful names. They were cumulonimbus some nine years later on the day of my mother's funeral.

The clouds that afternoon were spectacular, rising in vast towering peaks like snowcapped mountains. I pretended they were mountains. I stared out through my window, imagining myself in Switzerland, Austria, the Himalayas—anywhere rather than that gloomy house which overnight had become so empty.

Shortly after her death I moved.

For the next few years the sky was my salvation, drawing my eyes from dismal streets beneath countless bed-sitting rooms. Then I married and once again had a view. It was my husband who found the small house overlooking the town.

As soon as I walked in I made a beeline for the window. You could see the cathedral, Saint Mary's, the bend in the river where the boats are moored. I turned to him and grinned.

"I think she likes it," he told the agent before coming over and putting his arm around my shoulder, giving me a hug.

Like it? I loved it. From the day we moved in, the view was a constant source of delight. In the evenings we would sit side by side watching the darkness gather, the lights come on in the city spread out below. Holding hands, touching. We became so close. It was *our* view, a symbol of our togetherness. We even had our special view-watching music—Pink Floyd, "Dark Side of the Moon."

WHEN I HEARD HE'D been killed in a road accident I was numbed. It couldn't be happening, not to me. Hadn't I already suffered enough?

Instinctively, I turned to the window. But the view just mocked me, reminding me of what had been and would never be again, and I knew I couldn't stay in the house. It seemed that every time someone died, I had to move.

IT WAS AFTER HIS death that I bought this cottage. It's not much to look at, but its setting is superb, tucked into a hillside overlooking pasture fields and beyond that the moor. When I moved in—emotionally drained, desperately trying to adjust—it never occurred to me that I would ever share it with anyone, let alone another man. Three years later I met Marcus.

I was out walking in nearby woods and had stopped to look at a strange fungus growth on a fallen tree, when a dog came rushing up.

"It's okay, she's friendly," called a voice from farther up the track. "But don't let her jump up, she's been in the water."

The bedraggled mass of hair at my feet belonged to a springer spaniel, the voice to a man dressed in jeans and a Barbour. He came striding up, six-foot-one in his Wellingtons, smiling broadly.

"She hasn't made you muddy? Good. She loves the water. Can't keep her out, can I, Tess?"

He looked from me to the fungus. "Know what it is?"

I shook my head. "The only mushrooms I know are the ones I buy in the supermarket."

"Me, too. I keep meaning to buy a book, but . . ." He broke off, squinted. "I've seen you before. That cottage on the hill. You were outside trimming the hedge."

It turned out he lived in the next village and regularly drove past the gate. Not that I discovered that then. I had to wait till the next evening when I answered my doorbell and found him standing on the step.

"*Clitocybe flaccida,*" he said, holding out a book.

"I'm sorry?"

"*Clitocybe flaccida*—that fungus you were looking at. At least I think it is. A lot of them look the same."

I took the book, flipped absently through the pages.

"It's for you," he added. "I thought you might like it."

It seemed rude not to invite him in.

HE STAYED ABOUT TWO hours. I found him easy to talk to, relaxed, perhaps because of what we had in common. He was thirty-six, a lecturer, a divorcé; I was twenty-seven and a widow. We both preferred the country. We both loved a house with a view. When he left he suggested we return to the woods with the newly acquired book to make an accurate identification, and before I knew it I'd agreed. We went on the Saturday.

The weather was perfect for fungi (though we didn't know that at the time), a warm autumnal day following rain, and once we started looking we found a whole host of them. Many were beautiful, others grotesque, one or two smelled disgusting. Some, like the Fly Agaric with its white-spotted scarlet cap, we could identify immediately, but most were less distinctive. We were amazed at how many were edible.

"Perhaps we should buy a recipe book," he said jokingly, and a few days later he did.

And that's how it started. On a fungus foray. God knows I didn't intend to get involved, but these things happen, creeping up on us unawares until it's too late. Even so, it was more than a year before I allowed him to move in.

Marcus loved the cottage as much as I did, especially the view, the way it constantly changes. On rainy days the moor is obscured by mist, but on clear days you can make out sheep grazing the lower slopes. And the skies! Have you ever noticed the proportion of sky to land? About eighty-twenty if you get really close to the window. And we did get close—to the window and to each other. Often we would pick out patterns in the clouds, the way some people find faces in a fire. "That looks like my aunt," he once said, and I laughed. "It does," he insisted, tracing the outline on the glass with his finger. "See the nose and the hair?"

One day I came in from shopping and found him playing Pink Floyd. I stopped dead in my tracks. I'd no idea he had it in his collection. I'd thrown my own copy away. "What's wrong?" he asked when he saw my face. "Nothing," I assured him. And there wasn't; truly, there wasn't. As time went on I even began to play it myself.

I could hardly believe it when Marcus said he thought we should move, though his reason was perfectly valid. This was *my* cottage, and he wanted a home we could share, one he could feel a part of. He had my sympathy. Yet it seemed silly to move when we were both so happy here. Adding his name to the deeds seemed like the obvious solution.

We never lost our interest in fungi. Every year, spring and autumn, we tramped the fields and woods, searching them out. Last year we found morels for the first time, but we've yet to find an Earth Star. I know they're around somewhere.

It was with extreme caution that we first began to cook and eat our finds. Some proved edible but disappointing; others were delicious. Parasols *à la Jane Grigson* are a culinary delight. Our friends regard our eating habits mistrustfully and I suspect are wary of accepting invitations to dinner. The timid amongst them still refuse to taste my exciting side dishes, and even the more adventurous usually wait for us to eat the first mouthful. "It's perfectly safe," I assure them. "The most important thing is knowing which ones to avoid."

And it's true. Most so-called poisonous mushrooms are merely indigestible and will cause, at worst, a bad attack of stomachache. Only a few are deadly, like the Death Cap and the aptly named Destroying Angel, where one mouthful can be fatal. Both are *amanitas; amanita phalloides* and *amanita virosa.* The Destroying Angel is pure white. It's quite rare in this part of the country, but I know where it can be found. I discovered it on one of my forays.

It was his attitude to the forays that first made me realize something was wrong. Normally, we look forward to autumn, to the new season's crop, but this year he seemed indifferent.

"You go," he said, when I suggested an expedition.

"But we might find an Earth Star."

"I've work to do. Can't you go alone?"

So I did—me and Tess together. How convenient!

LAST WEEK HE TOLD me the reason for his indifference. Her name's Laura. She's one of his students, just twenty-one years old. He'll need money, he told me, to start a new life, so regretfully—he knows how much it means to me—the cottage will have to be sold. I went to the window.

The clouds were extraordinary, cirrocumulus, lit from behind by the setting sun. Above the horizon their formation resembled an angel with outspread wings. True, the wings were different sizes, the halo tilted to one side, but it was undoubtedly an angel, of the purest white. The edges of the wings were silver.

I'M AT THE WINDOW now, listening to Pink Floyd, waiting for Marcus to arrive. He's not moving out until the end of the week. He's so relieved at the way I've taken the news, he'd been afraid I wouldn't understand.

Me? Not understand?

I'm cooking us a risotto of wild mushrooms for supper, with lots of garlic and herbs. It smells delicious. The Destroying Angel is already sautéed and waiting in the microwave. I couldn't cook it with the others; there would be no way of separating it out.

Today's clouds are truly remarkable. They're stratified, in three distinct layers, all traveling at different speeds. The uppermost layer is white but slow, the middle one grayer and faster. But it's

the bottom layer that is most beautiful, sheer and ethereal, forming and re-forming into delicate wispy patterns as it races across
the sky. Like dark gray widow's lace.

It's all about patterns, you see . . . I really must break the pattern. I'm damned if I'll let it happen again. This time death will
mean I *don't* have to move.

Mushroom Risotto

---

2 14.5-oz. cans chicken stock, or 5 cups homemade
    stock
½ tsp. saffron threads
1 clove garlic, peeled and smashed
¼ cup olive oil
1 small white onion, finely chopped
1 bunch olives, diced (about ½ cup, divided use)
8 oz. mushrooms, sliced
1½ cups Aborio rice
2 cups dry white wine (divided use)
Water as needed
¼ cup Parmesan cheese, grated
Salt and pepper to taste

HEAT THE CHICKEN stock, and add the saffron. Steep the saffron
until the stock is a deep golden color. Strain and reserve the
stock. In a large skillet, heat the olive oil, add the garlic and
onions, and sauté until the onions are clear and soft, about two
minutes. Add the mushrooms and the chives, reserving two tablespoons of the chives to be used as a garnish on the finished dish.
Sauté the vegetables until the mushrooms are limp and brown,
about a minute. Add the rice to the pan, and sauté until the rice is
coated evenly with oil. Add two cups chicken stock and one cup of
the wine. Reserve the remaining liquids for now. Stirring constantly, simmer until almost all of the liquid has been absorbed.
Taste the rice. Continue stirring. Add chicken stock as needed
until the rice grains are softened and chewy and yet distinct and

firm. Don't let the rice dry out. Because the moisture content of rice differs dramatically from bag to bag, it is impossible to give exact quantities of liquid needed to make a good risotto. Simply keep adding chicken stock until it runs out, then water, stirring all the while, until the rice feels and tastes the way you like it. Typically, you should add about two-thirds of the liquid in about 10 minutes, and the remainder over about eight more minutes, at which point the rice should be done. Once the rice is cooked to your liking, add the reserved cup of white wine. Bring the dish to a simmer, stirring constantly, until the rice has absorbed most of the liquid. Add cheese, stirring, until the risotto has a creamy texture. Adjust seasoning with salt and pepper. Serve immediately.

The Main Event

Peter Crowther

W e gonna go bed now, baby?" Dolores trilled sleepily as she slouched around the table and lifted the Calvados from the after-dinner wreckage. "Dosie tired."

Vince watched her pour two fingers into a goblet that still held traces of claret, then he turned around to the window. Listening to his wife slurp and hiccup, Vince pulled the corner of the curtain aside and watched the Cadillac's taillights move off down the drive. The tension in his stomach subsided only when he saw the car pull out into the street and disappear. The sharp sound of breaking glass made him spin around in time to see Dolores, having staggered against the table, picking pieces of cut glass out of the Roquefort cheese. "Jesus, Dolores!" he snapped.

Dolores straightened up and pouted. "Hey, no need to get spikey, honey," she said, slurring the words. "Just a little accident." She dropped the shards of glass onto a side plate and giggled, lifting a hand to cover her mouth. Vince saw that she had smudged her lipstick, and he was annoyed to find that it aroused him. Despite the effects of the alcohol, Dolores noticed it, saw it in his eyes. She leaned against the table and ran her hand through her hair. "We gonna go up and make Buster warm, huh? We gonna have, you know, the main event now? Are we, honey?"

Buster was Vince's penis. Making Buster warm entailed jamming it inside Dolores as far as it would go. And then some. That was Dolores's main event. Vince sometimes thought that she had some kind of dimensional warp up there, the same way that the inside of Doctor Who's phonebox looked like the Cape Canaveral operations room. Maybe you could ram a broom handle up inside her, right to the bristles, and still not encounter any obstacles, and even if he stared down her throat there would be no trace of the end.

Dolores ran a hand down her camel-colored cashmere rib-knit dress until she reached the outside of her thigh, then she moved it over to her crotch and started to rub between her legs, pushing the material in and out, in and out. Vince moved away from the window and brushed past her. "You're sick, you know that?" he said. "And you said you needed oysters."

"Hey, I di'n't say I *needed* the oysters, honey, I said I *wanted* them. I still can't understand why you wouldn't let me have none." She took another drink of brandy, swallowed hard, and asked, "Why was that, honey? Why di'n't you let me have no oysters? Why'd we haveta have chowder insteada oysters, like Jerry an' Estelle did, huh?"

"There weren't enough." Vince shook a Marlboro out of the packet and tossed it back onto the table, leaned over, and lit the cigarette from the burning candle. "I told you that."

"Yeah, I heard you say there wasn't enough, and that you knew how much they liked oysters so they should just eat and enjoy. 'Eat and enjoy, Jer,' you said." Dolores swept her arm expansively as she mimicked Vince. " 'Cept I know there was enough. I saw them when you were preparing them. You threw a whole bunch out with the trash."

Blowing a thick column of smoke across the table, Vince looked at his watch and said, "They were bad. I threw them out because they were bad."

Dolores thought about that for a moment. "How'd you know they was bad?"

Vince looked at her and narrowed his eyes. "I just knew, okay? I know these things. It's what I used to do for a living, remember?"

The truth of the matter was there was nothing wrong with the oysters. None of them. At least, not the ones that Vince had thrown out. He'd just wanted only Jerry and Estelle to eat those he'd saved. Those were the ones with the small capsules inside. Vince couldn't take the chance of his guests getting the wrong ones—the safe ones—if Dolores screwed up the portions. Worse than that, he couldn't take the chance of getting one of the capsules himself. Taken alone, they probably wouldn't do much harm, just an upset stomach or maybe a bad dose of the runs. But if he and Dolores had eaten them then Jerry and Estelle wouldn't have. And it was important—crucial—that the guests ate all the ingredients.

"Mmm." Dolores plopped onto a chair and hoisted her dress up above the tops of her hose, wafting the pale flesh at the tops of her legs with her free hand. "It was a nice meal though, honey. I meant to tell you that."

Vince nodded.

"Real nice meal."

"So you said," he snapped, glancing at the clock on the wall. "Thanks for the compliment, okay? I appreciate it."

Dolores shook her head and pulled down her dress. "That salad—what was the name of that salad again? Nishsomethin' or other?"

"Niçoise. Salad Niçoise."

"I liked that," Dolores slurred.

"Good," Vince said. He stubbed out his cigarette and adjusted his tie.

"Maybe it was just a little salty, though."

"You just said you liked it."

"I did too like it. All I said was that maybe it was just a little bit salty. That's all." She stood up from the table and walked to the bar and the bourbon.

Vince shook his head as he watched her stagger across the room. "You're drunk."

"I'm getting there," she said, unscrewing the cap. "If we ain't gonna have no main event, then I just might as well have a few drinks." Pouring whiskey into a shot glass, Dolores said, "The cheese tasted the same way."

"Like salad?"

Dolores glared at him. "Like salty," she said. "Salty like the fucking nishwahrs salad."

"Go to bed, will you?"

Dolores shook the liquid in her glass from side to side, watching it climb and fall, climb and fall. "The curry was good."

"You liked the curry. I'm glad. I feel whole again."

She pulled a face. "Smelly, though."

"It was a Korma."

"Not a curry?"

Vince sighed and reached for the Marlboros. "A Korma is a kind of curry, okay? Cream, coconut, lampasander, buttered chicken. Curry. Korma. All the same." He lit a cigarette with a match and shook out the flame.

Dolores looked into her drink some more.

Vince said, "Smelled how?"

"Huh?"

"You said it smelled. You said it was smelly, the Korma. How was it smelly?"

For a moment Dolores looked blank, like someone had reached into her head and turned off the generator. Then she started to laugh.

"What?"

She kept on laughing.

Vince ruffled his hair in frustration and marched across to the window. "Suddenly I'm—what am I? Woody Allen? I ask you—"

"Like a fart," Dolores said amidst chuckles. "It smelled a little like a fart."

Vince turned around and looked at her.

"I'm sorry, hon—"

"Did anybody else think it smelled?"

"Oh, hey, I—"

"Look! I'm fucking asking you if anybody else thought the Korma smelled funny, okay?"

Her smile faded. "Okay," she said. "There's no need—"

"And the answer is? I'm waiting for the answer, Dolores."

She shrugged. "Nobody said nothin'."

He nodded and took a pull on the Marlboro. "Good," he said, around a mouthful of smoke. "That's good."

Silence again.

"He's funny isn't he, you know . . . Jerry."

"How is Jerry funny?"

Dolores drained her glass and reached for the bottle. "His ways, you know."

"He's a very busy, very important man, Dolores."

Dolores laughed as she swallowed, spraying liquor in a fine mist. "He's a crook."

"Look, we've been through all this a dozen times. Maybe a hundred times. Jerry is a businessman."

"In a pig's eye." She hiccuped, and then added, disdainfully, "Businessman! Hmph!"

"I'm not going to argue, Dolores, I'm—"

"Why d'you keep looking at your watch?"

Vince lowered his arm and shook it until his shirtsleeve slid down over his wrist. "I'm not looking at my watch."

"You were too. I saw—"

"Okay, I was looking at my watch. I wanted to know what time it was, for crissakes."

Dolores took a slug of bourbon and swallowed hard. "It's about thirty seconds later than it was when you last looked at it," she said.

"What are you? My—" He was going to say "timekeeper" but realized immediately that it sounded stupid. The same with "watchman." Instead, he pulled on his cigarette and shook his head some more. Then he looked out of the window.

"He's a crook, Vinny. You know it and I know it." She swirled the liquor around the glass and then threw it into her mouth. "And you're a crook, too."

Vince looked around at her and smiled. "Hey, we both enjoy the fruits of my labor. I don't see you complaining any about where the money comes from."

She poured some more bourbon into her glass silently.

"He's a businessman. Got a lot of contacts, sees a lot of people, makes a lot of deals. That's how he makes his money. That's how I make my money. I'm not ashamed of it."

"He know a lot of people?"

"A *lot* of people. He knows everybody. And I mean *every*body."

"They all crooks, too?"

"Dolores, not everybody is a crook." Vince pulled one of the chairs away from the table and sat down, loosening his tie. He was starting to feel a little easier. This one was the one. He'd thought about every way he could do it—shooting, knifing, even poison— but each of those methods could have led back to him. But not this way. This way there would be nothing left to lead anyone anywhere. He smiled across the table at his wife, watched her backside stretch the clinging material of her dress, saw the small metal clips of her garters outlined against her thighs.

"He keep all their names in his goddamned book?"

Vince shrugged. "It's his way, okay? He calls it his memory bank." He blew smoke out in small rings and watched them swirl up to the ceiling. "Takes it everywhere he goes. I never seen him without that book. It's like it's attached to him surgically, you know what I'm saying?"

"Yeah, I hear you."

Vince softened his voice. "Hey."

"What?"

"C'm'ere. "

"What?"

"I said, c'm'ere." A little harder now.

Dolores stood up and walked across to him. She was trying to look disinterested but the first faint signs of a smile were pulling at her mouth. When Dolores had reached him, Vince patted his knees and shuffled the chair farther from the table. "Siddown."

"I'm fine standing right here," she said petulantly, swaying her body from side to side, legs stretched wide. Vince looked at her, allowing his eyes to travel up and down the curves and bulges. He liked what he saw. Buster liked it, too, uncoiling himself from Vince's Calvin Klein briefs and fighting off the effects of the booze.

He felt good, suddenly. A good evening. He remembered the dessert, remembered thinking it tasted fine and wondering—as he watched Jerry and Estelle gorge themselves on two pieces—if they noticed anything unusually gritty about it. He reached out to trace a finger across Dolores's lower stomach, and said, "My, how'd you like the chocolate gateau?"

She stopped swaying and said, "You still wanna talk about the food? I thought we was getting ready for the main event . . . getting ready to warm up li'l Buster, honey."

"We are, we are. I just wondered how you liked the dessert is all."

"I liked it, okay?"

She started swaying again, moving her body closer to him with each pass.

"You didn't think . . . you didn't think that maybe it tasted a little gritty?"

Dolores placed her glass on the table and pulled up her dress, slowly, inch by loving inch, until she exposed the tops of her hose, then the pale flesh of her upper thighs, and then, last but by no means least, the soft blue of her panties. Vince could see thin, spindly hairs curling their way out of the crotch, could see the first faint traces of wet on it, could smell the deodorant she used down there, could smell it wafting across at him. Buster could smell it too, apparently, and he stretched against Vince's trousers wanting to be out. Out and in. "Gritty?" she said. The word came out as a whisper.

Without watching what he was doing, but rather keeping his eyes focused on the endless sky of those briefest of bikini panties, Vince reached out his right hand to lower his glass to the floor beside the large wing chair. As he removed his hand from the glass, he heard it topple over with a dull thud. He turned around to see if there was much of a mess on the carpet, and saw the polished black of Jerry's memory bank half-covered by the chair.

At first
takes it everywhere he goes
it didn't register
never seen him without that book
and then
it's like it's attached to him surgically
he looked up at Dolores. She was turning around to look at the window, shuffling her dress back down her legs. "A car, Vinny," she said, simply. "Now who the hell—"

Vince grabbed the book and jumped off his chair. "It's Jerry," he said, "come for his damned book."

"Jesus H. Christ on a fucking bicycle," Dolores snarled, spitting out the words like bad food.

Vince ran into the hall, heading for the door, trying to beat Jerry's having to get out of the car, having to walk up to the house, having to ring the bell, having to waste all that time . . . precious time. As he ran, seeming to take forever, every step like running in slow motion or through water, his life flashed before him. Not his whole life, just the afternoon. One afternoon.

He saw himself working tiny lumps of elemental sodium into small gelatin capsules of oil and then inserting them almost lovingly into the oysters.

He saw himself sprinkling potassium and more sodium onto the anchovies, eggs, and olives. And then more—just to be safe—smeared inside the Roquefort cheese.

He saw himself mixing liberal quantities of sulphur into the buttered chicken.

He saw himself grinding up lumps of charcoal for the chocolate gateau.

Reaching for the key to the front door, he shook his head, trying to convince himself it had all been a stupid idea. It wouldn't work. Why the hell was he panicking?

He saw his arm reach out in front of him, reach out toward the door, the key held in his hand, reaching to the small lock.

He heard the footsteps on the steps, someone coming to the front door. "With you in a second, Jer," he shouted. "Forgot your fucking book, didn't you?"

He heard Jerry laugh. And then the laugh stopped. Abruptly. Jerry gasped. The sound was a mixture of pain and surprise.

Vince's hand had reached the door, inserted the key. He began to turn his hand and reach for the handle. Then the world turned bright white . . .

The

and somewhere, far off in the distance but getting closer with every millionth of a second . . .

Main

a shuddering growl of thunder sounded, traveling toward him at ten times the speed of light . . .

Event!

traveling with the shards of door and lumps of masonry and a billion tiny spears of glass.

Vince didn't hear the second explosion. Nor did he notice the small pieces of perfumed meat, leather upholstery, and blackened metal that rained on the burning ruins of his house.

The Menu

PRE-DINNER: CHAMPAGNE
Dom Perignon, 1970

Appetizer: Oysters Rockefeller

2 dozen fresh oysters in shells
½ small onion, minced
3 Tbsp. parsley, finely chopped
½ stick celery
¼ cup butter
2 oz. fresh raw spinach, finely chopped
2 oz. fine dry bread crumbs
¼ tsp. salt
4 Tbsp. butter
Paprika
Olive oil
8 oz. gelatin, heated

PRY OPEN THE oyster shells with a sharp knife, remove oysters, and drain them. Wash the deep halves of the shells and place an oyster on each.

Fry onion, parsley, and celery in ¼ cup butter until tender. Add spinach, bread crumbs, and salt, and cook, stirring constantly for one minute. Place a spoonful of spinach mixture on each oyster, top with ½ teaspoon of butter, and sprinkle lightly with paprika. Bake in a hot oven (450 degrees F.) for 10 minutes or until browned.

Serve in shells.

Wine: A chablis
(Vince provided two bottles of Le Montrachet, 1971.)

Main Course: Chicken Korma (Moorgee Korma)

CUT UP A fair-sized chicken and marinade it for one hour in a mixture of two or three tablespoons of Dhye (sour curds), one heaped teaspoon of ground turmeric, and one clove of garlic (either ground into a paste or finely mixed).

USING A STEW pan, combine:

> 2 oz. ghee or other fat
> 1 large onion, halved and finely sliced
> 1 clove garlic, finely sliced lengthwise
> Several 1-inch pieces of fresh or pickled ginger, finely sliced
> 6 whole cloves
> 6 whole cardamom pods
> One 2-inch stick of cinnamon

COOK UNTIL THE onions are half-done, then add one heaped tablespoon of Korma mixture. Stir well and cook on a low flame for three or four minutes longer.

Now add the chicken and marinade. Mix lightly but thoroughly. Cover the pan tightly and simmer until the chicken is done. Add salt and lemon juice to taste . . . and to try to minimize the smell of the sulphur.

Serve with a Salad Niçoise:
Rub your salad bowl with garlic and then place in it:

> 2 tomatoes, peeled and quartered
> 1 cucumber, peeled and finely cut
> 6 fillets of anchovy, coarsely chopped
> 12 pitted black olives, coarsely chopped
> 1 cup bibb lettuce
> 1 cup romaine

Now toss in a store-bought French dressing.

Wine: A fine claret
(Vince served Chateau Lafite-Rothschild, 1962.)

Dessert: Chocolate Gateau

3 large eggs
3 oz. caster sugar
3 oz. all-purpose flour
1 Tbsp. cocoa
3 oz. flaked almonds
3 oz. butter cream or ½ pint fresh cream, whipped
Chocolate icing
8-oz. can finely chopped fruit in syrup

WHISK THE EGGS and sugar until thick and creamy. Fold in the sieved flour and cocoa. Divide the mixture into three greased six-inch cake tins. Bake in a hot oven (400 degrees) for about 10 minutes and then turn out onto a cooling tray.

When cold, sandwich two cakes together with cream. Cut a circle one-inch wide around the edge of the third cake and sandwich the "circle" to the other two cakes. Spread cream around the outside edge of the cake and roll in flaked almonds. Pipe whirls of cream around the edge, strain the canned fruit, and pile in the center. Cover the remaining sponge with chocolate icing, pipe whirls of cream around the edge, and place on top of the fruit.

Wine: A good sauterne
(Vince served Chateau Yquem [pronounced *Dick-emm*] 1955.)

Cheese: Roquefort

Wine: A vintage red sherry
(Vince's choice was Manzanilla from San Lucar de Barrameda.)

The Deadly Egg

Janwillem van de Wetering

T he siren of the tiny dented Volkswagen shrieked forlornly
between the naked trees of the Amsterdam Forest, the
city's largest park, set on its southern edge: several square
miles of willows, poplars, and wild-growing alders, surrounding
ponds and lining paths. The paths were restricted to pedestrians
and cyclists, but the Volkswagen had ignored the many No Entry
signs, quite legally, for the vehicle belonged to the Municipal
Police and more especially to its Criminal Investigation Department, or the Murder Brigade. Even so, it looked lost, and its howl
seemed defensive.

It was Easter Sunday and it rained, and the car's two occupants,
Detective Adjutant Grijpstra and Detective Sergeant de Gier, sat
hunched in their overcoats, watching the squeaky, rusted wipers
trying to deal with the steady drizzle. The car should have been
junked some years before, but the adjutant had lost the form that
would have done away with his aging transport, lost it on purpose
and with the sergeant's consent. They had grown fond of the Volkswagen, of its shabbiness and its ability to melt away in traffic.

But they weren't fond of the car now. The heater didn't work, it
was cold, and it was early. Not yet nine o'clock on a Sunday is early,
especially when the Sunday is Easter. Technically they were both
off duty, but they had been telephoned out of warm beds by headquarters' radio room. A dead man dangling from a branch in the
forest; please, would they care to have a look at the dead man?

163

Grijpstra's stubby index finger silenced the siren. They had followed several miles of winding paths so far and hadn't come across anything alive except tall blue herons, fishing in the ponds and moats and flapping away slowly when the car came too close for their comfort.

"You know who reported the corpse? I wasn't awake when the radio room talked to me."

De Gier had been smoking silently. His handsome head with the perfect curls turned obediently to face his superior. "Yes, a gentleman jogger. He said he jogged right into the body's feet. Gave him a start. He ran all the way to the nearest telephone booth, phoned headquarters, then headquarters phoned us, and that's why we are here, I suppose. I am a little asleep myself—we are here, aren't we?"

They could hear another siren, and another. Two limousines came roaring toward the Volkswagen, and Grijpstra cursed and made the little car turn off the path and slide into a soggy lawn; they could feel its wheel sink into the mud.

The limousines stopped and men poured out of them; the men pushed the Volkswagen back on the path.

"Morning, Adjutant, morning, Sergeant. Where is the corpse?"

"Shouldn't you know, too?"

"No, Adjutant," several men said simultaneously, "but we thought maybe you know. All we know is that the corpse is in the Amsterdam Forest and that this is the Amsterdam Forest."

Grijpstra addressed the sergeant. "You know?"

De Gier's well-modulated baritone chanted the instructions. "Turn right after the big pond, right again, then left. Or the other way round. I think I have it right, we should be close."

The three cars drove about for a few minutes more until they were waved down by a man dressed in what seemed to be long blue underwear. The jogger ran ahead, bouncing energetically, and led them to their destination. The men from the limousines brought out their boxes and suitcases, then cameras clicked and a video recorder hummed. The corpse hung on and the two detectives watched it hang.

"Neat," Grijpstra said, "very neat. Don't you think it is neat?"

The sergeant grunted.

"Here. Brought a folding campstool and some nice new rope, made a perfect noose, slipped it around his neck, kicked the stool. Anything suspicious, gentlemen?"

The men from the limousines said there was not. They had found footprints—the prints of the corpse's boots. There were no other prints, except the jogger's. The jogger's statement was taken, he was thanked and sent on his sporting way. A police ambulance arrived and the corpse was cut loose, examined by doctor and detectives, and carried off. The detectives saluted the corpse quietly by inclining their heads.

"In his sixties," the sergeant said, "well dressed in old but expensive clothes. Clean shirt. Tie. Short gray beard, clipped. Man who took care of himself. A faint smell of liquor—he must have had a few to give him courage. Absolutely nothing in his pockets. I looked in the collar of his shirt—no laundry mark. He went to some trouble to be nameless. Maybe something will turn up when they strip him at the mortuary; we should phone in an hour's time."

Grijpstra looked hopeful. "Suicide?"

"I would think so. Came here by himself, no traces of anybody else. No signs of a struggle. The man knew what he wanted to do, and did it, all by himself. But he didn't leave a note; that wasn't very thoughtful."

"Right," Grijpstra said. "Time for breakfast, Sergeant! We'll have it at the airport—that's close and convenient. We can show our police cards and get through the customs barrier; the restaurant on the far side is better than the coffee shop on the near side."

De Gier activated the radio when they got back to the car.

"Male corpse, balding but with short gray beard. Dentures. Blue eyes. Sixty-odd years old. Three-piece blue suit, elegant dark gray overcoat, no hat. No identification."

"Thank you," the radio said.

"Looks very much like suicide. Do you have any missing persons of that description in your files?"

"No, not so far."

"We'll be off for breakfast and will call in again on our way back."

"Echrem," the radio said sadly, "there's something else. Sorry."

De Gier stared at a duck waddling across the path and trailing seven furry ducklings. He began to mumble. Adjutant Grijpstra mumbled with him. The mumbled four-letter words interspersed with mild curses formed a background for the radio's well-articulated message. They were given an address on the other side of the city. "The lady was poisoned, presumably by a chocolate Easter egg. The ambulance that answered the distress call just radioed in. They are taking her to hospital. The ambulance driver thought the poison was either parathion, something used in agriculture, or arsenic. His assistant is pumping out the patient's stomach. She is in a bad way but not dead yet."

Grijpstra grabbed the microphone from de Gier's limp hand. "So if the lady is on her way to hospital, who is left in the house you want us to go to?"

"Her husband, man by the name of Moozen, a lawyer, I believe."

"What hospital is Mrs. Moozen being taken to?"

"The Wilhelmina."

"And you have no one else on call? Sergeant de Gier and I are supposed to be off duty for Easter, you know!"

"No," the radio's female voice said, "no, Adjutant. We never have much crime on Easter day, especially not in the morning. There are only two detectives on duty, and they are out on a case too—some boys have derailed a streetcar with matches."

"Right," Grijpstra said coldly, "we are on our way."

The old Volkswagen made an effort to jump away, protesting feebly. De Gier was still muttering but had stopped cursing. "Streetcar? Matches?"

"Yes. They take an empty cartridge, fill it with matchheads, then close the open end with a hammer. Very simple. All you have to do is insert the cartridge into the streetcar's rail and when the old tram comes clanging along, the sudden impact makes the cartridge explode. If you use two or three cartridges the explosion may be strong enough to lift the wheel out of the rail. Didn't you ever try that? I used to do it as a boy. The only problem was to get the cartridges. We had to sneak around on the rifle range with the chance of getting shot at."

"No," de Gier said. "Pity. Never thought of it, and it sounds like a good game."

He looked out of the window. The car had left the park and was racing toward the city's center through long empty avenues. There

was no life in the huge apartment buildings lining the old city—
nobody had bothered to get up yet. Ten o'clock and the citizenry
wasn't even considering the possibility of slouching into the
kitchen for a first cup of coffee.

But one man had bothered to get up early and had strolled into
the park, carrying his folding chair and a piece of rope to break
off the painful course of his life, once and for all. An elderly man
in good but old clothes. De Gier saw the man's beard again, a
nicely cared-for growth. The police doctor had said that he hadn't
been dead long. A man alone in the night that would have led him
to Easter, a man by himself in a deserted park, testing the strength
of his rope, fitting his head into the noose, kicking the campstool.

"Bah!" he said aloud.

Grijpstra had steered the car through a red light and was turning the wheel.

"What's that?"

"Nothing. Just bah."

"Bah is right," Grijpstra said.

They found the house, a bungalow, on the luxurious extreme
north side of the city. Spring was trying to revive the small lawn
and a magnolia tree was in hesitant bloom. Bright yellow crocuses
off the path. Grijpstra looked at the crocuses. He didn't seem
pleased.

"Crocuses," de Gier said, "very nice. Jolly little flowers."

"No. Unimaginative plants, manufactured, not grown. Computer plants. They make the bulbs in a machine and program
them to took stupid. Go ahead; Sergeant, press the bell."

"Really?" the sergeant asked.

Grijpstra's jowls sagged. "Yes. They are like mass-manufactured
cheese, tasteless; cheese is probably made with the same
machines."

"Cheese," de Gier said moistly, "there's nothing wrong with
cheese either, apart from not having any right now. Breakfast has
slipped by, you know." He glanced at his watch.

They read the nameplate while the bell rang. *H. F. Moozen, Attorney at Law.* The door opened. A man in a housecoat made out of
brightly striped towel material said good morning. The detectives
showed their identifications. The man nodded and stepped back.
A pleasant man, still young, thirty years or a bit more. The ideal
model for an ad in a ladies' magazine. A background man, show-

ing off a modern house, or a minicar, or expensive furniture. The sort of man ladies would like to have around. Quiet, secure, mildly good-looking. Not a passionate man, but lawyers seldom are. Lawyers practice detachment; they identify with their clients, but only up to a point.

"You won't take long, I hope," Mr. Moozen said. "I wanted to go with the ambulance, but the driver said you were on the way, and that I wouldn't be of any help if I stayed with my wife."

"Was your wife conscious when she left here, sir?"

"Barely. She couldn't speak."

"She ate an egg, a chocolate egg?"

"Yes. I don't care for chocolate myself. It was a gift, we thought, from friends. I had to let the dog out early this morning, an hour ago, and there was an Easter bunny sitting on the path. He held an egg wrapped up in silver paper. I took him in, woke up my wife, and showed the bunny to her, and she took the egg and ate it, then became ill. I telephoned for the ambulance and they came almost immediately. I would like to go to hospital now."

"Come in our car, sir. Can I see the bunny?"

Mr. Moozen took off the housecoat and put on a jacket. He opened the door leading to the kitchen and a small dog jumped around the detectives, yapping greetings. The bunny stood on the kitchen counter; it was almost a foot high. Grijpstra tapped its back with his knuckles; it sounded solid.

"Hey," de Gier said. He turned the bunny around and showed it to Grijpstra.

"Brwah!" Grijpstra said.

The rabbit's toothless mouth gaped. The beast's eyes were close together and deeply sunk into the skull. Its ears stood up aggressively. The bunny leered at them, its torso crouched; the paws that had held the deadly egg seemed ready to punch.

"It's roaring," de Gier said. "See? A roaring rabbit. Easter bunnies are supposed to smile."

"Shall we go?" Mr. Moozen asked.

They used the siren, and the trip to hospital didn't take ten minutes. The city was still quiet. But there proved to be no hurry. An energetic, bright young nurse led them to a waiting room. Mrs. Moozen was being worked on; her condition was still critical. The nurse would let them know if there was any change.

"Can we smoke?" Grijpstra asked.

"If you must." The nurse smiled coldly, appraised de Gier's tall, wide-shouldered body with a possessive feminist glance, swung her hips, and turned to the door.

"Any coffee?"

"There's a machine in the hall. Don't smoke in the hall, please."

There were several posters in the waiting room. A picture of a cigarette pointing to a skull with crossed bones. A picture of a happy child biting into an apple. A picture of a drunken driver (bubbles surrounding his head proved he was drunk) followed by an ambulance. The caption read: "Not *if* you have an accident, but *when* you have an accident."

De Gier fetched coffee and Grijpstra offered cigars. Mr. Moozen said he didn't smoke.

"Well," Grijpstra said patiently and puffed out a ragged dark cloud, "now who would want to poison your wife, sir? Has there been any recent trouble in her life?"

The question hung in the small white room while Moozen thought. The detectives waited. De Gier stared at the floor, Grijpstra observed the ceiling. A full minute passed.

"Yes," Mr. Moozen said, "some trouble. With me. We contemplated a divorce."

"I see."

"But then we decided to stay together. The trouble passed."

"Any particular reason why you considered a divorce, sir?"

"My wife had a lover." Mr. Moozen's words were clipped and precise.

"*Had*," de Gier said. "The affair came to an end?"

"Yes. We had some problems with our central heating, something the mechanics couldn't fix. An engineer came out, and my wife fell in love with him. She told me—she doesn't like to be secretive. They met each other in motels for a while."

"You were upset?"

"Yes. It was a serious affair. The engineer's wife is a mental patient; he divorced her and was awarded custody of his two children. I thought he was looking for a new wife. My wife has no children of her own—we have been married some six years and would like to have children. My wife and the engineer seemed well matched. I waited a month and then told her to make up her mind—either him or me, not both, I couldn't stand it."

"And she chose you?"

"Yes."

"Do you know the engineer?"

A vague pained smile floated briefly on Moozen's face. "Not personally. We did meet once and discussed central heating systems. Any further contact with him was through my wife."

"And when did all this happen, sir?"

"Recently. She only made her decision a week ago. I don't think she has met him since. She told me it was all over."

"His name and address, please, sir."

De Gier closed his notebook and got up. "Shall we go, Adjutant?"

Grijpstra sighed and got up, too. They shook hands with Moozen and wished him luck. Grijpstra stopped at the desk. The nurse wasn't helpful, but Grijpstra insisted and de Gier smiled, and eventually they were taken to a doctor who accompanied them to the next floor. Mrs. Moozen seemed comfortable. Her arms were stretched out on the blanket. The face was calm. The detectives were led out of the room again.

"Bad," the doctor said. "Parathion is a strong poison. Her stomach is ripped to shreds. We'll have to operate and remove part of it, but I think she will live. The silly woman ate the whole egg, a normal-size egg. Perhaps she was still too sleepy to notice the taste."

"Her husband is downstairs. Perhaps you should call him up, especially if you think she will live." Grijpstra sounded concerned. *He probably was*, de Gier thought. He felt concerned himself. The woman was beautiful, with a finely curved nose, very thin in the bridge, and large eyes and a soft and sensitive mouth. He looked at her long delicate hands.

"Husbands," the doctor said. "Prime suspects in my experience. Husbands are supposed to love their wives, but usually they don't. It's the same the other way around. Marriage seems to breed violence—it's one of the impossible situations we humans have to put up with."

Grijpstra's pale blue eyes twinkled. "Are you married, Doctor?"

The doctor grinned back. "Very. Oh, yes."

"A long time?"

"Long enough."

Grijpstra's grin faded. "So am I. Too long. But poison is nasty. Thank you, Doctor."

There wasn't much conversation in the car when they drove to the engineer's address. The city's streets had filled up. People were stirring about on the sidewalks and cars crowded each other, honking occasionally. The engineer lived in a block of apartments, and Grijpstra switched off the engine and lit another small black cigar.

"A family drama. What do you think, Sergeant?"

"I don't think. But that rabbit was most extraordinary. Not bought in a shop. A specially made rabbit, and well made, not by an amateur."

"Are we looking for a sculptor? Some arty person? Would Mr. Moozen or the engineer be an artist in his spare time? How does one make a chocolate rabbit, anyway?"

De Gier tried to stretch, but didn't succeed in his cramped quarters. He yawned instead. "You make a mold, I suppose, out of plaster of Paris or something, and then you pour hot chocolate into the mold and wait for it to harden. That rabbit was solid chocolate, several kilos of it. Our artistic friend went to a lot of trouble."

"A baker? A pastry man?"

"Or an engineer—engineers design forms sometimes, I believe. Let's meet this lover man."

The engineer was a small nimble man with a shock of black hair and dark lively eyes, a nervous man, nervous in a pleasant childlike manner. De Gier remembered that Mrs. Moozen was a small woman, too. They were ushered into a four-room apartment, They had to be careful not to step on a large number of toys, spread about evenly. Two little boys played on the floor; the eldest ran out of the room to fetch his Easter present to show it to the uncles. It was a basketful of eggs, homemade, out of chocolate. The other boy came to show his basket, identical but a size smaller.

"My sister and I made them last night," the engineer said. "She came to live here after my wife left and she looks after the kids, but she is spending the Easter weekend with my parents in the country. We couldn't go because Tom here had measles, hadn't you, Tom?"

"Yes," Tom said. "Big measles. Little Klaas here hasn't had them yet."

Klaas looked sorry. Grijpstra took a plastic truck off a chair and sat down heavily after having looked at the engineer, who waved him on. "Please, make yourself at home." De Gier had found himself a chair, too, and was rolling a cigarette. The engineer provided coffee and shooed the children into another room.

"Any trouble?"

"Yes," Grijpstra said. "I am afraid we usually bring trouble. A Mrs. Moozen has been taken to hospital. An attempt was made on her life. I believe you are acquainted with Mrs. Moozen?"

"Ann," the engineer said. "My God! Is she all right?"

De Gier had stopped rolling his cigarette. He was watching the man carefully; his large brown eyes gleamed, but not with pleasure or anticipation. The sergeant felt sorrow, a feeling that often accompanied his intrusions into the private lives of his fellow citizens. He shifted, and the automatic pistol in his shoulder holster nuzzled into his armpit. He impatiently pushed the weapon back. This was no time to be reminded that he carried death with him, legal death.

"What happened?" the engineer was asking. "Did anybody hurt her?"

"A question," Grijpstra said gently. "A question first, sir. You said your sister and you were making chocolate Easter eggs last night. Did you happen to make any bunnies, too?"

The engineer sucked noisily on his cigarette. Grijpstra repeated his question.

"Bunnies? Yes, or no. We tried, but it was too much for us. The eggs were easy—my sister is good at that. We have a pudding form for a bunny, but all we could manage was a pudding. It is still in the kitchen, a surprise for the kids later on today. Chocolate pudding—they like it."

"Can we see the kitchen, please?"

The engineer didn't get up. "My God," he said again, "so she was poisoned, was she? How horrible! Where is she now?"

"In the hospital, sir."

"Bad?"

Grijpstra nodded. "The doctor said she will live. Some sort of pesticide was mixed into chocolate, which she ate."

The engineer got up; he seemed dazed. They found the kitchen. Leftover chocolate mix was still on the counter. Grijpstra brought out an envelope and scooped some of the hardened chips into it.

"Do you know that Ann and I had an affair?"

"Yes, sir."

"Were you told that she finished the affair, that she decided to stay with her husband?"

"Yes, sir."

The engineer was tidying up the counter mechanically. "I see. So I could be a suspect. Tried to get at her out of spite or something. But I am not a spiteful man. You wouldn't know that. I don't mind being a suspect, but I would like to see Ann. She is in the hospital, you said. What hospital?"

"The Wilhelmina, sir."

"Can't leave the kids here, can I? Maybe the neighbors will take them for an hour or so. Ann. This is terrible."

Grijpstra marched to the front door with de Gier trailing behind him. "Don't move from the house today if you please, sir, not until we telephone or come again. We'll try and be as quick as we can."

"Nice chap," de Gier said when the car found its parking place in the vast courtyard of headquarters. "That engineer, I mean. I rather liked Mr. Moozen, too, and Mrs. Moozen is a lovely lady. Now what?"

"Go back to the Moozen house, Sergeant, and get a sample of the roaring bunny. Bring it to the laboratory together with this envelope. If they check we have a heavy point against the engineer."

De Gier restarted the engine. "Maybe he is not so nice, eh? He could have driven his wife crazy and now he tries to murder his girlfriend, his ex-girlfriend. Lovely Ann Moozen, who dared to stand him up. Could be, do you think so?"

Grijpstra leaned his bulk against the car and addressed his words to the emptiness of the yard. "No. But that could be the obvious solution. He was distressed, genuinely distressed, I would say. If he hadn't been and if he hadn't had those kids in the house, I might have brought him in for further questioning."

"And Mr. Moozen?"

"Could be. Maybe he didn't find the bunny on the garden path; maybe he put it there, or maybe he had it ready in the cupboard and brought it to his wandering wife. He is a lawyer—lawyers can be devious at times. True?"

De Gier said, "Yes, yes, yes . . ." and kept on saying so until Grijpstra squeezed the elbow sticking out of the car's window. "You are saying *yes*, but you don't sound convinced."

"I thought Moozen was suffering, too."

"Murderers usually suffer, don't they?"

De Gier started his "Yes, yes," and Grijpstra marched off.

They met an hour later, in the canteen in headquarters. They munched rolls stuffed with sliced liver and roast beef and muttered diligently at each other.

"So it is the same chocolate?"

"Yes, but that doesn't mean much. One of the lab's assistants has a father who owns a pastry shop. He said that there are only three mixes on the market and our stuff is the most popular make. No, not much of a clue there."

"So?"

"We may have a full case on our hands. We should go back to Mr. Moozen, I think, and find out about friends and relatives. Perhaps his wife had other lovers, or jealous lady friends."

"Why her?"

Grijpstra munched on. "Hmm?"

"Why *her*?" de Gier repeated. "Why not him?"

Grijpstra swallowed. "Him? What about him?"

De Gier reached for the plate, but Grijpstra restrained the sergeant's hand. "Wait, you are hard to understand when you have your mouth full. What about him?"

De Gier looked at the roll. Grijpstra picked it up and ate it.

"Him," de Gier said unhappily. "He found the bunny on the garden path, the ferocious bunny holding the pernicious egg. A gift, how nice. But he doesn't eat chocolate, so he runs inside and shows the gift to his wife and his wife grabs the egg and eats it. She may have thought *he* was giving it to her, she was still half asleep. Maybe she noticed the taste, but she ate on to please her husband. She became ill at once and he telephoned for an ambulance. Now, if he had wanted to kill her he might have waited an hour or so, to give the poison a chance to do its job. But he grabbed his phone, fortunately. What I am trying to say is, the egg may have been intended for him, from an enemy who didn't even know Moozen had a wife, who didn't care about killing the wife."

"Ah," Grijpstra said, and swallowed the last of the roll. "Could be. We'll ask Mr. Moozen about the enemies. But not just now. There is the dead man we found in the park—a message came in while you were away. A missing person has been reported and the description fits our corpse. According to the radio room a woman phoned to say that a man who is renting a room in her house has been behaving strangely lately and has now disappeared. She traced him to the corner bar, where he spent last evening until 2:00 A.M., when they closed.

"He was a little drunk, according to the barkeeper, but not blind drunk. She always takes him tea in the morning, but this morning he wasn't there and the bed was still made. But she does think he's been home, for she heard the front door at a little after 2:00 A.M., opening and closing twice. He probably fetched the rope and his campstool then."

"And the man was fairly old and has a short gray beard?"

"Right."

"So we go and see the landlady. I'll get a photograph—they took dozens this morning and they should be developed by now. Was anything found in his clothes?"

"Nothing." Grijpstra looked guiltily at the empty plate. "Want another roll?"

"You ate it."

"That's true, and the canteen is out of rolls; we got the last batch. Never mind, Sergeant. Let's go out and do some work. Work will take your mind off food."

"That's him," the landlady with the plastic curlers said. Her glasses had slipped to the tip of her blunt nose while she studied the photograph. "Oh, how horrible! His tongue is sticking out. Poor Mr. Marchant, is he dead?"

"Yes, ma'am."

"For shame, and such a nice gentleman. He has been staying here for nearly five years now, and he was always so polite."

Grijpstra tried to look away from the glaring pink curlers pointing at his forehead from the woman's thinning hair.

"Did he have any troubles, ma'am? Anything that may have led him to take his own life?"

The curlers bobbed frantically. "Yes. Money troubles. Nothing to pay the tax man with. He always paid the rent, but he hadn't been paying his taxes. And his business wasn't doing well. He has a shop in the next street; he makes things—ornaments, he calls them, out of brass. But there was some trouble with the neighbors. Too much noise, and something about the zoning, too; this is a residential area now, they say. The neighbors wanted him to move, but he had nowhere to move to, and he was getting nasty letters, lawyers' letters. He would have had to close down, and he had to make money to pay the tax man. It was driving him crazy. I could hear him walk around in his room at night, round and round, until I had to switch off my hearing aid."

"Thank you, ma'am."

"He was alone," the woman said and shuffled with them to the door. "All alone, like me. And he was always so nice." She was crying.

"Happy Easter," de Gier said, and opened the Volkswagen's door for the adjutant.

"The same to you. Back to Mr. Moozen again—we are driving about this morning. I could use some coffee again. Maybe Mr. Moozen will oblige."

"He won't be so happy either. We aren't making anybody happy today," the sergeant said, and tried to put the Volkswagen into first gear. The gear slipped and the car took off in second.

They found Mr. Moozen in his garden. It had begun to rain again, but the lawyer didn't seem to notice that he was getting wet. He was staring at the bright yellow crocuses, touching them with his foot. He had trampled a few of them into the grass.

"How is your wife, sir?"

"Conscious and in pain. The doctors think they can save her, but she will have to be on a stringent diet for years and she'll be very weak for months. I won't have her back for a while."

Grijpstra coughed. "We visited your wife's, ah, previous lover, sir." The word *previous* came out awkwardly, and he coughed again to take away the bad taste.

"Did you arrest him?"

"No, sir."

"Any strong reasons to suspect the man?"

"Are you a criminal lawyer, sir?"

Moozen kicked the last surviving crocus, turned on his heels, and led his visitors into the house. "No, I specialize in civil cases. Sometimes I do divorces, but I don't have enough experience to point a finger in this personal case. Divorce is a messy business, but with a little tact and patience reason usually prevails. To try and poison somebody is unreasonable behavior. I can't visualize Ann provoking that type of action—she is a gentle woman, sensuous but gentle. If she did break her relationship with the engineer she would have done it diplomatically."

"He seemed upset, sir, genuinely upset."

"Quite. I had hoped as much. So where are we now?"

"With you, sir. Do you have any enemies? Anybody who hated you so badly that he wanted you to die a grotesque death, handed to you by a roaring rabbit? You did find the rabbit on the garden path this morning, didn't you, sir?"

Moozen pointed. "Yes, out there, sitting in between the crocuses, leering and, as you say, roaring. Giving me the egg."

"Now, which demented mind might have thought of shaping that apparition, sir? Are you dealing with any particularly unpleasant cases at this moment? Any cases that have a badly twisted undercurrent? Is anyone blaming you for something bad that is happening to them?"

Moozen brushed his hair with both hands. "No. I am working on a bad case having to do with a truckdriver who got involved in a complicated accident; his truck caught fire and it was loaded with expensive cargo. Both his legs were crushed. His firm is suing the firm that owned the other truck. A lot of money in claims is involved and the parties are becoming impatient, with me mostly. The case is dragging on and on. But if they kill me the case will become even more complicated, with no hope of settlement in sight."

"Anything else, sir?"

"The usual. I collect bad debts, so sometimes I have to get nasty. I write threatening letters, sometimes I telephone people or even visit them. I act tough—it's got to be done in my profession. Usually they pay, but they don't like me for bothering them."

"Any pastry shops?"

"I beg your pardon?"

"Pastry shops," Grijpstra said, "people who make and sell confectionery. That rabbit was a work of art in a way, made by a professional. Are you suing anybody who would have the ability to create the roaring rabbit?"

"*Ornaments!*" de Gier shouted. His shout tore at the quiet room. Moozen and Grijpstra looked up, startled.

"Ornaments! Brass ornaments. Ornaments are made from molds. We've got to check his shop."

"Whose shop?" Grijpstra frowned irritably. "Keep your voice down, Sergeant. What shop? What ornaments?"

"Marchant!" de Gier shouted. "Marchant's shop."

"Marchant?" Moozen was shouting too. "Where did you get that name? *Emil* Marchant."

Grijpstra's cigar fell on the carpet. He tried to pick it up and it burned his hand, sparks finding their way into the carpet's strands. He stamped them out roughly.

"You know a Mr. Marchant, sir?" de Gier asked quietly.

"No, I haven't met him. But I have written several letters to a man named Emil Marchant. On behalf of clients who are hindered by the noise he makes in his shop. He works with brass, and it isn't only the noise, but there seems to be a stink as well. My clients want him to move out and are prepared to take him to court if necessary. Mr. Marchant telephoned me a few times, pleading for mercy. He said he owed money to the tax department and wanted time to make the money, that he would move out later; but my clients have lost patience. I didn't give in to him—in fact, I just pushed harder. He will have to go to court next week, and he is sure to lose out."

"Do you know what line of business he is in, sir?"

"Doorknobs, I believe, and knockers for doors, in the shape of lions' heads—that sort of thing. And weather vanes. He told me on the phone. All handmade. He is a craftsman."

Grijpstra got up. "We'll be on our way, sir. We found Mr. Marchant this morning, dead, hanging from a tree in the Amsterdam Forest. He probably hanged himself around 7:00 A.M., and at some time before he must have delivered the rabbit and its egg. According to his landlady he has been behaving strangely lately. He must have blamed you for his troubles and tried to take his revenge. He didn't mean to kill your wife, he meant to kill you. He didn't know that you don't eat chocolate, and he probably didn't even know you were married. We'll check further and make a report. The rabbit's mold is probably still in his shop, and if not we'll find traces of the chocolate. We'll have the rabbit checked for fingerprints. It won't be difficult to come up with irrefutable proof. If we do, we'll let you know, sir, a little later today. I am very sorry all this has happened."

"Nothing ever happens in Amsterdam," de Gier said as he yanked the door of the Volkswagen open, "and when it does it all fits in immediately."

But Grijpstra didn't agree.

"We would never have solved the case, or rather *I* wouldn't have, if you hadn't thought of the rabbit as an ornament."

"No, Grijpstra, we would have found Marchant's name in Moozen's files."

The adjutant shook his heavy grizzled head. "No, we wouldn't have checked the files. If he had kept on saying that he wasn't working on any bad cases I wouldn't have pursued that line of thought. I'd have reverted to trying to find an enemy of his wife. We might have worked for weeks and called in all sorts of help and wasted everybody's time. You are clever, Sergeant."

De Gier was studying a redheaded girl waiting for a streetcar.

"Am I?"

"Yes. But not as clever as I am," Grijpstra said and grinned. "You work for me. I personally selected you as my assistant. You are a tool in my expert hands."

De Gier winked at the redheaded girl and the girl smiled back. The traffic had jammed up ahead and the car was blocked. De Gier opened his door.

"Hey! Where are you going?"

"It's a holiday, Adjutant, and you can drive this wreck for a change. I am going home. That girl is waiting for a streetcar that goes to my side of the city. Maybe she hasn't had lunch yet. I am going to invite her to go to a Chinese restaurant."

"But we have reports to make, and we've got to check out Marchant's shop; it'll be locked, we have to find the key in his room, and we have to telephone the engineer to let him off the hook."

"I am taking the streetcar," de Gier said. "You do all that. You ate my roll."

Chocolate Cherry Truffles

⅓ cup whipping cream

12 oz. good milk chocolate, broken or chopped into small pieces (Milk chocolate chips will work, but get the best available. The better the chocolate, the better the truffle!)

3 Tbsp. kirsch

½ cup maraschino cherries, drained and finely chopped

Large cookie sheet lined with waxed paper

½ cup of something—cocoa, or confectioner's sugar, or shredded coconut, or finely chopped nuts, or chocolate sprinkles—as desired, to coat completed truffles

Paper candy cups—paper mini-muffin cups work well if you can't find candy cups

PLACE CREAM IN small saucepan over low to medium heat. Bring just to boiling, stirring constantly. Turn off burner and remove pan from heat. Mix chopped chocolate in the hot cream. Cover and set aside for three to four minutes, just until chocolate is melted. Stir the mixture until smooth. Stir in kirsch and chopped cherries. Refrigerate for an hour. Remove mixture from refrigerator and beat until fluffy. (Using a hand mixer on high speed for about three minutes will do the job, as will beating for four to five minutes by hand.) Refrigerate until firm. Using a melon baller or a rounded measuring spoon or a teaspoon, scoop tablespoon-sized rounded balls of the chocolate mixture onto the waxed paper. Roll the chocolate balls in the chosen coating material and place completed truffles in the paper candy cups.

TRUFFLES WILL KEEP for up to three weeks in the refrigerator if placed in a tightly sealed container. But the container must be absolutely sealed, otherwise the truffles will absorb any stray odors floating around your fridge (I discovered this when I accidentally served garlic and onion-flavored truffles to guests right after the nice lasagna that tainted the chocolate.)

Dead and Breakfast

Barbara Collins

L aura sat in the front on the passenger's side of the white Transport minivan in the Holiday Inn parking lot, waiting for her husband to come out of the lobby.

In the back seat, their son, Andy, a dark-haired, round-faced, eleven-year-old boy with glasses, was hunched over, peering into the small screen of his Turbo Express, moving the expensive video game back and forth in his hands to catch the last fading rays of the sun.

Even with the volume turned down, Laura could hear the frantic tune of the game he was playing, "Splatterhouse": a particularly violent one she didn't approve of (and wouldn't have allowed her husband to buy for the boy, if *she'd* been along on that shopping trip). She mentally blocked the sound out, gazing toward the horizon at the picture-postcard sunset descending on lush green trees.

Wisconsin was a beautiful state, and the weather had been perfect; but now, dark, threatening clouds were moving quickly in, bringing to an end a memorable summer-vacation day.

She spotted her husband, Pete, coming out of the lobby. He'd only been in there a minute or so . . . not very long.

It wasn't a good sign.

"We're in trouble," he said, after opening the van's door and sliding in behind the wheel. The brow of his ruggedly handsome face was furrowed.

"No room?" she asked.

"No room."

"Let's try another."

Pete turned toward her. "Honey," he said, his expression grave, "according to the desk clerk, there's not a vacancy between Milwaukee and Minneapolis."

"But that's impossible!" Laura said, astounded. "What's going on?"

Pete started the van. "A country festival, for one thing," he replied. "And this *is* the tourist season . . ."

"Aren't we staying here?" Andy asked from the back seat.

"No, son," his dad answered, as he wheeled the van out of the packed hotel parking lot and toward the Interstate ramp. "We have to go on."

"But I'm tired," the boy whined, "and there's not enough light anymore to play my game!"

Annoyed—more with their current predicament than with her son—Laura picked up a small white sack on the seat next to her and threw it to Andy, hitting him on the arm. "Here . . . have some fudge," she said flatly.

"I don't *like* fudge!" the boy retorted, and threw the sack back at his mom, smacking her on the head.

"Andy!" Pete said sharply, looking at his son in the rearview mirror. "That's five points! When you get to ten, you lose your Turbo Express for a week, remember?"

"Well, *she* started it!" he protested.

"Six," his father said.

The van fell silent, the air tense and heavy with more than the humidity of the oncoming storm. Big drops of rain splattered on the windshield. The sky was crying, and suddenly Laura felt like crying, too. She stared at the dark highway before her, upset that their wonderful day had turned sour.

"We shouldn't have stopped at the Dells," she sighed.

It had to be said, and it might as well be said by her, because she was the one who first suggested the detour to the expensive touristy playground . . .

A sign on the road advertising the Oak Street Antiques Mall had caught her attention, but Pete and Andy had just groaned.

Then Andy saw the gigantic 3-D billboard for Pirate's Cove—a seventy-two-hole miniature golf course set in tiers of sandstone and waterfalls that overlooked the Wisconsin River. Quickly, he defected to his mother's side.

Pete, reminding them both of their agreement to make it from Illinois to Minnesota by nightfall, where a coveted condominium at Kavanaugh's Resort in Brainerd awaited them, held firm . . . until he drove over the next hill on the highway.

There, among the trees, was a pretty blonde, braided billboard *Fräulein* wearing an alluring peasant dress; she beckoned to him with her wooden finger, teasingly, tempting him to taste the homemade fudge (sixteen flavors) at the German Candy Shoppe.

"Well," Pete had said, slowly, "maybe we can stop for just a little while."

But "just a little while" had turned into all afternoon, because there was much more to the Wisconsin Dells than antiquing and golfing and rich gooey fudge, like river rides and go-carts, wax museums and haunted houses . . .

"Let's try that one," Laura suggested, as a roadside motel materialized in the mist. Three hours earlier, she wouldn't have dreamed of ever stopping at such a scuzzy place; but now they were desperate, and *any* bed looked good, even this biker's haven.

Pete pulled off the highway and into the motel—a long, single-story, rundown succession of tiny rooms. The lot was full of pickup trucks and motorcycles, so he parked in front of the entrance and got out of the van, leaving the engine running.

Laura locked the doors behind him and waited. Rain pelted the windshield. The van's huge wipers moved back and forth spastically, like gigantic grasshopper legs, grating on her nerves. She leaned over and shut the engine off.

Behind her, Andy sighed wearily.

Please, dear God, she thought, *let there be a room so we don't have to sleep in the car.*

She strained to see through the rain-streaked window, trying to spot Pete. He'd been gone a long time this time . . . too long.

That wasn't a good sign, either.

Suddenly, Laura saw him dart in front of the van, and quickly she unlocked the doors. He jumped inside. His clothes were soaked, hair matted, but he wore a grin.

"You got us a room!" Laura cried, elated.

Pete nodded, wiping wetness from his face with the back of one hand. "But not here."

"Then where?"

He looked at her. "When I went in," he explained, "the desk clerk was telling another family they had no rooms. So naturally, I turned around to leave. Then a maintenance man gave me a tip on a place . . . a *bed and breakfast.*"

"Oh, really?" They'd never stayed at one.

"I used the pay phone and called," Pete continued. "The woman sounded very nice. They had one room left and promised to save it for us. I got the directions right here."

He fished around in his pocket and drew out a piece of paper.

"We gotta go back about forty miles, and it's a little out of our way, but—"

"But it's a *bed.*" She smiled, relieved, throwing her arms around Pete, hugging him.

"And *breakfast.*" He smiled back, and kissed her.

"What's a bed and breakfast?" Andy asked.

Laura looked at her son. "A bed and breakfast is not really a hotel," she answered. "It's somebody's home." She paused. "It'll be like staying at your Aunt Millie's house."

"Oh," the boy said sullenly, "then I gotta be good."

"You've got to be *especially* good," Pete said, "because these people don't usually take children, but they're going to make an exception for us. Okay, son?"

"I'll try," he said, but not very convincingly.

An hour later, as the storm began to die down, the little family drove into the small quaint town of Tranquillity, its old cobblestone streets shiny from the rain.

At a big County Market grocery store, Pete turned left, down an avenue lined with sprawling oak trees and old homes set back from the street.

They pulled up in front of a many-gabled house. An outside light was on, illuminating the large porch, which wrapped around the front of the home. On either side of the steps sat twin lions, their mouths open in a fierce frozen roar as they guarded the front door.

Laura clasped her hands together, gazing at the house. "Oh, isn't it *charming*? This will be such fun!"

Pete nodded, then read the wooden sign attached to the sharp spears at the wrought-iron gate. "*Die Gasthaus*?"

"That's German for 'the inn,' " Laura said, utilizing her high school foreign language class for the very first time.

"So let's go in," smiled Pete.

"What's German for 'Splatterhouse'?" said a small sarcastic voice from the back seat.

Anger ignited in Laura—why did the boy have to ruin things? And after all they had done for him today! She turned to reprimand Andy, but her husband beat her to it.

"*Shape up*," Pete shouted at the boy. "You already have six points—wanna try for seven?"

"No."

"It's going to be a mighty long trip without your Turbo Express," his father threatened.

"I'm sorry," Andy said. "It's not *my* fault this place looks like a spook house."

Pete wagged a finger at his son. "Now we're going to go in, and you're going to behave, and, goddamnit, we're all going to have a *good time!*"

There was a long silence.

Laura couldn't stand it, so she reached back and patted Andy on the knee. "Now gather up your things, honey," she said cheerfully. "Don't you know how lucky we are to be here?"

IN THE PARLOR OF Die Gasthaus Bed and Breakfast, Marvin Butz sipped his tea from a china cup as he sat in a Queen Anne needlepoint chair in front of a crackling fireplace.

A bachelor, pushing fifty, slightly overweight, with thinning gray hair and a goatee, the regional sales manager of Midwest Wholesale Grocery Distributors was enjoying the solitude of the rainy evening.

Whenever he went on the road, Marvin always stayed at bed and breakfasts, avoiding the noisy, crowded, kid-infested chain hotels. The last thing he needed in his high-pressure job was being kept awake all night by a drunken wedding reception, or rowdy class reunion, or loud bar band.

Besides, he delighted in being surrounded by the finer things in life—rare antiques, crisply starched linens, delicate bone china—which reminded him of his mother's home, before the family went bankrupt and had to sell everything.

He couldn't find these "finer things in life" in a regular hotel, where lamps and pictures and clock radios were bolted down, like he might be some common thief. (Besides which, who would want such *bourgeois* kitch, anyway?) And he could *never* get any satisfaction—or compensation—for the many inconveniences that always happened to him in the usual hotels. Whenever he complained, all he ever got was rude behavior from arrogant desk clerks.

But at most bed and breakfasts, even the smallest complaint, Marvin found, almost guaranteed a reduction in his bill. Why, half the time, he stayed for free! (Charging his expense account the full amount, of course.)

"More tea, Mr. Butz?"

Mrs. Hilger, who owned and ran the establishment with her husband, stood next to Marvin, a Royal Hanover green teapot in her hand, a white linen napkin held under its spout to catch any drip. She was a large women, not fat, just big. Marvin guessed her age to be about sixty, and at one time she must have been a looker, but now her skin was wrinkled and spotted with old-age marks, her hair coarse and gray and pulled back in a bun.

He nodded and held out his cup. "With sugar."

"I'll bring you some."

He watched her walk away. She was nice enough, he thought, but the woman would talk his ear off if he let her. When he first arrived around 6:00 P.M., she started in lecturing him about how everybody should be nice to one another and do what they could to make the world a better place to live. If he had known he was going to be staying with a religious fanatic, he never would have come here!

He frankly told her *his* world would be a better place to live if she would leave him alone while he unpacked.

She had acted hurt and scurried off, and he hadn't seen her until about eight o'clock, when she had offered him tea.

Mrs. Hilger came back into the parlor, carrying a silver sugar bowl. She handed Marvin an unusual sterling sugar spoon with what appeared to be real rubies set into the handle.

He took the spoon and looked at it closely. "I've never seen anything like this before," he mused.

"That's because it's one of a kind," she replied.

He used the spoon to sugar his tea, then set it on the side of his saucer.

"There'll be another party coming in this evening," the woman informed him. "A couple with their young son."

About to take a sip of tea, Marvin looked at her sharply. "But you advertised 'no children,' " he complained.

"Yes, I know," the woman said, "but this poor family is caught out in the storm without hotel accommodations."

"So *I'm* to be inconvenienced because some dumb hicks didn't have the common sense to make reservations?"

There was a brief silence. Then Mrs. Hilger said, "If that's how you feel, Mr. Butz, your stay with us will be complimentary."

Marvin smiled.

And Mrs. Hilger smiled back, but he wasn't at all sure that the smile was friendly.

Mr. Hilger's large form filled the doorway to the parlor. He looked more like a handyman than the proprietor of a bed and breakfast, in his plaid shirt and overalls.

Marvin had had a brief conversation with the bald, bespectacled man earlier, when Marvin had gone into the kitchen to admire an old butcher's block. Mr. Hilger had come up from the basement.

"It's from our store," Mr. Hilger had said. "We had a little corner grocery before County Market came in and put us out of business."

"What a pity," Marvin had said, shrugging. "But personally, I don't believe anybody gets 'put out of business' by anybody else."

"Oh?"

"Yes. You do it yourself, by not keeping up. Survival of the fittest."

"You're probably right," Mr. Hilger had said, getting a butcher's apron out of a narrow closet by the pantry. The big man slipped it on and went back down into the basement.

Marvin had frowned—was food preparation going on down there? If so, he hoped conditions were sanitary.

"Those folks with the child are here," Mr. Hilger was saying to his wife. The apron was gone now. "I'm going to help them with their luggage."

"Thank you, dear," Mrs. Hilger replied.

Marvin quickly finished the last of his tea and stood up. "I'll be retiring now," he informed her. He'd rather die than spend one minute in boring, pointless small talk with these new people. "Please inform that family I will be using the bathroom at six in the morning. And I'd like my breakfast served promptly at seven, out in the garden."

"Yes, Mr. Butz." Mrs. Hilger nodded. "Good night."

Marvin left the parlor, through the main foyer and past a large, hand-carved grandfather clock. He climbed the grand oak staircase to the second floor.

To the left was the Gold Room, where an elderly couple from Iowa was staying. They had gone to bed already, the little woman not feeling well, and so their door was shut. But behind the door was a grandiose three-piece Victorian bedroom set of butternut and walnut, with a carved fruit cluster at the top of the headboard and dresser. (He had peeked in, earlier, when they were momentarily out.) He wished he had that room, because it had its own bath . . . but the old farts had gotten there first.

At the end of the hall on the left was the White Room. The bridal suite. Everything in it was white—from the painted four-poster bed with lace canopy to the white marble-topped dresser. It also had its own bathroom. He'd gotten to see the exquisite room when he first arrived and wouldn't have minded his company paying a little extra for such fine accommodations. But some new-lyweds on a cross-country honeymoon were in there right now—doing God only knows what behind their closed door.

Across the hall from the White Room was the Blue Room, the least impressive (or so he thought). It was decorated in wicker, with a Battenburg lace comforter, and a collection of old cast-iron toys showcased on the ledges of the beveled glass windows. Mrs. Hilger had tried to put him in there, but he protested. (The furnishings were so informal, it would have been like sleeping on a porch!) He demanded a different room.

The door to the Blue Room stood open, awaiting the inconsiderate family that would soon be clomping nosily up the steps.

To the immediate right was the Red Room, his room, which had a massive oak bedroom set with eight-inch columns and carved capitals, and a beautiful red oriental rug on the floor. It was satisfactory.

Marvin used an old skeleton key to open his door: he had locked it to protect his belongings, even though the other skeleton room keys could also open his door. He would have to speak to Mrs. Hilger, later, about this little breach in security.

He entered the room, leaving the door open. He was planning on getting his shaving kit and using the bathroom, which he shared with the Blue Room, before turning in for the night, but he stopped at a small mahogany table next to the door. On the table was a lovely cranberry lamp with thumbprint shade and dropped crystals.

Marvin dug into his jacket pocket and pulled out the sweet little sugar spoon, leaned over, and turned on the lamp to examine the spoon better. Its red ruby handle sparkled in the light.

A nice addition to his spoon collection.

Suddenly, something caught his attention in the hallway. Flustered, caught off guard, Marvin shoved the spoon back into his pocket and looked up from the light.

A young boy stood in the hall, not six feet away. How long the kid had been there, watching, Marvin didn't know.

Marvin reached out with one hand and slammed his door in the boy's face.

How he hated children! They were a bunch of sneaky, snooping, immature brats.

Marvin yawned, aware for the first time of how tired he was. He got his toiletries and went off to the bathroom, then came back and got into a pair of burgundy silk pajamas.

He crawled under the beige crocheted bedspread and lace-trimmed sheets. He wanted to read awhile, but his eyes were too heavy. He got out of bed and turned off the push-button light switch on the wall by the door.

Then he went back to bed.

Soon, Marvin was fast asleep.

It was a deep sleep. So deep he didn't hear the skeleton key working in the keyhole of his door. Or see the dark form of Mr. Hilger poised over him, large hands outstretched.

But not so deep that he didn't feel those hands tighten around his neck like a vise, slowly squeezing him into the deepest of all deep sleeps.

A NOISE WOKE ANDY. It was a bump, or a thump, or *something*. He lay quietly in the dark on the cot Mrs. Hilger fixed up for him, and listened.

All was silent now, except for the soft breathing of his parents across the room in that great big bed. Whatever the noise had been, Andy was glad it woke him. He'd been having a nightmare. A bad dream where he'd been sucked into the video game, "Splatterhouse," he'd been playing. And ghouls and monsters were chasing him with butcher knives and stuff.

Andy reached under the cot, got his glasses, and put them on. A fancy clock on a table read a quarter to three in the morning. He sat up farther and looked at the window next to him. On the ledge was a row of small toys—little cars, and airplanes and trains. His mother had told him they were antiques and not to touch them.

Andy's favorite was the train. You could actually see the conductor standing inside! He picked the heavy toy up and held it in his hand. It was so much cooler than anything you ever saw in a toy store today! He reached under the cot again, opened his suitcase, and tucked the train inside. Then he lay back down.

There were so many of the toys—thirty-two, he'd counted—that he was sure the Hilgers wouldn't miss it. Besides, the boy thought, wasn't his mom always saying to his dad when they stayed in hotels, "Honey, take the soap, take the shampoo, get the Kleenex . . ."? This wasn't exactly soap, or shampoo, or Kleenex, but then this wasn't exactly a hotel. So it had to be kind of the same.

And if that nasty, mean man in the room next to them could cop a spoon, why couldn't he have the train? Andy *knew* the man had stolen it, because of the look on his face—there was guilt written all over it!

Andy had to pee. He remembered his mother telling him that if he woke up in the night to be sure and go, because someone else might be in the bathroom in the morning.

The boy got up from the cot and quietly slipped out of the room. He tiptoed down the dark hallway to the bathroom.

Inside, he used the toilet, which had a funny chain he had to pull to flush it. Then he washed his hands at a neat faucet where the water came out of a fish's head. He turned out the bathroom light, opened the door, and stepped into the hallway.

That's when he saw Mrs. Hilger coming out of the crabby man's room. She had some wadded-up sheets in her arms.

The woman didn't see him, because she had her back to the boy, heading toward the stairs with her bundle.

Andy stood frozen for a moment, and when the woman was gone, he walked down to that mean man's room.

The door was wide open. And even though the only light came from the moon that shone in through the windows, he could see that the bed had been made. There was no sign of that man *or* his things.

Andy tiptoed to the top of the stairs which yawned down into the blackness. Below, somewhere, he could hear noises—faint pounding and the sound of something electrical, something sawing, maybe, like his father sometimes used in the garage.

Quietly, he crept down the stairs, staying close to the railing, until he reached the bottom.

Suddenly, the big clock by the stairs bonged three times, scaring Andy nearly out of his skin. He waited until he'd calmed down, then moved silently along, toward the back of the dark house, through the dining room with its big, long table. He bumped into a chair, and its legs went *screech* on the wooden floor.

Andy froze. The faint noises below him stopped. He held his breath. Seconds felt like minutes. Then the sounds started up again.

He went into the kitchen.

There was a light coming from under the door that led to the basement. That's where the noises were coming from.

Andy thought about a movie he had seen last year with his father. At one point a kid—a boy a lot like himself—was going to go down in a basement where bad, evil people lived. Andy had turned to his dad and said, "Why's he going down there?" And Andy's father had said, "Because it's a story, and he just has to *know.*"

And now, just like the boy in that scary movie, Andy reached his hand out for the doorknob. He didn't know why—he was certainly frightened—but he couldn't seem to stop himself.

Slowly, he opened the door to the basement, and the sound of sawing increased as the crack of bright light widened until Andy was washed in illumination. *What am I doing?* he thought, *I don't have to know!* And as he was starting to ease the door shut again, a hand settled on his shoulder.

He jumped. Someone was beside him! Shaking, he looked back at the shape of a figure with a knife in its hand, and gasped.

"What are you doing, young man?" the figure demanded.

The voice was low and cold—but a lady's voice.

Then there was a click and he saw her, one hand on the light switch, the other holding the butcher knife: Mrs. Hilger. The face that had been so friendly before was now very cross.

Even though Andy was trembling badly, he managed to say, "Wh-where am I? I . . . I must be sleepwalking again."

There was a long, horrible moment.

Then the knife disappeared behind Mrs. Hilger's back and she said sweetly, "You're in the kitchen, my boy. I'll see that you get back to your room."

"Th-that's all right, now I know where I am."

He backed away from her, and turned, and hurried through the dining room, and when he got to the stairs, he bolted up them, and dashed down the hallway, past the man's room who had stolen the spoon, to his parents' room, where he opened the door, then slammed it shut, ran to their bed, and jumped in between them.

"Andy!" his mother moaned. "What in the world . . . ?"

"Can I please sleep here, Mom?" he pleaded. "I had a terrible nightmare."

She sighed. "Well, all right, get under the covers."

Andy started to crawl beneath the sheets, but stopped.

"Wait," he said. "There's something I gotta do first."

He climbed out of the bed and went over to the cot, dug beneath it, and got into his suitcase.

He put the toy train back on the ledge of the window.

PETE WOKE TO A sunny morning, the smell of freshly brewed coffee, and the unmistakable aroma of breakfast. He breathed deeply, taking in the wonderful smells.

He looked over at Laura, still sleeping soundly in the big bed next to him, her hair spread out on the lace pillowcase like a fan. She was so beautiful—even snoring, with her mouth open.

He propped himself up with both elbows and noticed his son sitting on the cot across the room, fully dressed, his little suitcase, packed, by his feet. The boy was staring at him.

"Hey, partner," Pete said, still a little groggy, "what's the hurry?"

Andy didn't respond.

Now Pete realized something was wrong with the boy, and vaguely remembered his son sleeping with them in the night.

Pete sat up farther in the bed, letting the bedspread fall down around his waist. "Did you have a bad dream?" he asked.

The boy nodded. "Sort of."

"Well, why don't you come over here and tell me about it?" Pete patted a place on the bed next to himself. "Most bad dreams sound pretty silly in the light of day."

Andy stood up slowly, went to the bed, and sat on it. The springs made a little squeak.

Pete gazed at his son's face—his large brown eyes, made larger by the glasses, his little pug nose, the tiny black mole on the side of his cheek—the depth of Pete's love for the child was sometimes frightening.

"You know that man in the room next to us?" Andy said almost in a whisper, looking at his hands in his lap.

"The one who had dibs on the bathroom from six to seven this morning?"

Andy nodded.

Pete waited.

"When I went to the bathroom in the middle of the night," Andy said, "he was *gone.*"

"Gone?"

Now the boy looked at his father. "His room was all made up, Dad . . . like he'd never been there!"

"Soooo," Pete said slowly, "what do you think happened?"

"I don't know," Andy said softly.

Pete looked toward the door of their room, and then back at his son. "Do you think somebody chopped him up with a meat cleaver," Pete said with a tiny smile, "and buried him in the garden, like in that movie we saw?"

Andy's eyes went wide, but then he smiled. "No," he said. "I guess not." He paused. "But where *did* he go?"

Pete put an arm around the boy. "Son, Mrs. Hilger told me about that man. He was very unhappy. And unhappy adults sometimes do unpredictable things. He just packed up and left."

"Really?"

"Sure." Pete hugged his son. "Now do you feel better?"

"Uh-huh."

"Okay." Pete slapped Andy's knee with one hand. "Let's wake up your mom and get down to breakfast, so we can get on the road!"

Breakfast at Die Gasthaus was offered in either the formal dining room, outside on the patio, or in the privacy of the rooms.

The elderly couple staying in the Gold Room had decided to eat in the dining room; the wife was feeling much better this morning after a good night's sleep.

The newlyweds, not surprisingly, were being served in their room.

Pete let Laura decide where they would eat—that was the kind of decision she always made, anyway—and she wanted to go out on the patio.

The three sat at a white wrought-iron table, with comfortable floral cushions on their chairs, surrounded by a variety of flowers.

Pete leaned toward Andy, and whispered that there didn't appear to be any new additions in the garden today.

Andy smiled. Laura asked what the two of them were talking about, and they both said, "Nothing."

Then Mrs. Hilger appeared in a starched white apron, carrying a casserole dish which she placed in the center of the table. Pete leaned forward.

It was an egg dish, a soufflé or something, and looked delicious—white and yellow cheeses baked over golden eggs with crispy bits of meat. Pete's mouth began to water.

"Oh, Mrs. Hilger," Laura said, "our stay here has been so wonderful!"

"I'm glad, dear," Mrs. Hilger replied, as she gave each of them a serving on a china plate. "My husband and I enjoy making other people happy . . . people who are appreciative, that is. And we try, in our small way, to do what we can to make this world a better place to live."

Pete, wolfing down the eggs, said, in between bites, "What's in this, Mrs. Hilger? Is it ham?"

"No," Mrs. Hilger said.

"Well, it's not sausage," Pete insisted.

Mrs. Hilger shook her head.

"Then, what is it?"

Mrs. Hilger smiled. "I'm sorry, but we never give out our recipes," she said. "Our unique dishes are one of the reasons people come back. Most of them, that is."

Mrs. Hilger reached for the silver coffee pot on the table. "More coffee?" she asked Laura.

"Please," Laura said. "With sugar."

The woman reached into the pocket of her apron and pulled out a spoon—a silver one with red stones on the handle. She handed the spoon to Laura.

"Oh, how beautiful," Laura said, looking at the spoon.

"There's not another like it," Mrs. Hilger said.

Suddenly, Andy began to gag and cough, and the boy leaned over his plate and spit out a mouthful of food.

"Andrew!" Laura cried, shocked.

"Son, what's the matter?" Pete asked, alarmed. The boy must have choked on his breakfast.

"I . . . I'm not hungry," Andy said, his face ashen as he pushed his plate away from himself.

"Andy!" Laura said, sternly. "You're being rude!"

But Pete stepped in to defend the boy. "He had kind of a rough night, Laura. That's probably why he doesn't have an appetite. Let's just forget it."

Laura smiled. "Well, *I* certainly have an appetite! Mrs. Hilger, I'd love some more of your delicious eggs, but I don't want to trouble you, I can get it myself." Laura started to reach for the dish, but Mrs. Hilger picked it up.

"Nonsense, my dear," the woman said with a tiny smile, and she put another huge spoonful of eggs with cheeses and succulent meat on Laura's plate. "It's no trouble. We at Die Gasthaus just love to serve our guests!"

Die Gasthaus Breakfast Eggs

8 to 10 slices white bread
1 lb. meat (optional)
6 to 8 eggs, slightly beaten
½ cup sharp cheddar cheese
½ cup Swiss cheese
½ cup mushrooms, drained
¾ cup Half & Half
1¼ cup milk
1 tsp. Worcestershire sauce
1 tsp. prepared mustard
Salt & pepper to taste

BUTTER A 9" X 13" PAN. Cube bread, removing crusts, and line the bottom of the pan. Cook meat until done; crumble over bread. Add the remaining ingredients to the slightly beaten eggs. Pour into pan. Bake at 350 degrees F. for 35 to 40 minutes.

Recipe for a
Happy Marriage

Nedra Tyre

Today is just not my day.

And it's not even noon.

Maybe it will take a turn for the better.

Anyway, it's foolish to be upset.

That girl from the *Bulletin* who came to interview me a little while ago was nice enough. I just wasn't expecting her. And I surely wasn't expecting Eliza McIntyre to trip into my bedroom early this morning and set her roses down on my bedside table with such an air about her as if I'd broken my foot for the one and only purpose of having her arrive at 7:30 to bring me a bouquet. She's been coming often enough since I broke my foot, but never before eleven or twelve in the morning.

That young woman from the *Bulletin* sat right down, and before she even smoothed her skirt or crossed her legs she looked straight at me and asked if I had a recipe for a happy marriage. I think she should at least have started off by saying it was a nice day or asking how I felt, especially as it was perfectly obvious that I had a broken foot.

I told her that I certainly didn't have any recipe for a happy marriage, but I'd like to know why I was being asked, and she said it was almost Saint Valentine's Day and she had been assigned to

197

write a feature article on love, and since I must know more about love than anybody else in town she and her editor thought that my opinions should have a prominent place in the article.

Her explanation put me more out of sorts than her question. But whatever else I may or may not be, I'm a good-natured woman. I suppose it was my broken foot that made me feel irritable.

At that very moment Eliza's giggle came way up the back stairwell from the kitchen, and it was followed by my husband's laughter, and I heard dishes rattle and pans clank, and all that added fire to my irritability.

The one thing I can't abide, never have been able to stand, is to have somebody in my kitchen. Stay out of my kitchen and my pantry, that's my motto. People always seem to think they're putting things back in the right place, but they never do. How well I remember Aunt Mary Ellen saying she just wanted to make us a cup of tea and to cut some slices of lemon to go with it. I could have made that tea as well as she did, but she wouldn't let me. I couldn't tell a bit of difference between her tea and mine, yet she put my favorite paring knife some place or other and it didn't turn up until eight months later, underneath a stack of cheese graters. That was a good twenty years ago and poor Aunt Mary Ellen has been in her grave for ten, and yet I still think about that paring knife and get uneasy when someone is in my kitchen.

Well, that young woman leaned forward and had an equally dumbfounding question. She asked me just which husband I had now.

I don't look at things—at husbands—like that. So I didn't answer her. I was too aghast. And then again from the kitchen came the sound of Eliza's giggle and Lewis's whoop.

I've known Eliza Moore, now Eliza McIntyre, all my life. In school she was two grades ahead of me from the very beginning, but the way she tells it now she was three grades behind me; but those school records are somewhere, however yellowed and crumbled they may be, and there's no need for Eliza to try to pretend she's younger than I am when she's two years older. Not that it matters. I just don't want her in my kitchen.

That young woman was mistaking my silence. She leaned close as if I were either deaf or a very young child who hadn't paid attention. How many times have you been married? she asked in a very loud voice.

When she put it like that, how could I answer her? Husbands aren't like teacups. I can't count them off and gloat over them the way Cousin Lutie used to stand in front of her china cabinets, saying she had so many of this pattern and so many of that.

For goodness sake, I had them one at a time, a husband at a time, and perfectly legally. They all just died on me. I couldn't stay the hand of fate. I was always a sod widow—there weren't any grass widows in our family. As Mama said, it runs in our family to be with our husbands till death us do part. The way that girl put her question, it sounded as if I had a whole bunch of husbands at one time like a line of chorus men in a musical show.

I didn't know how to answer her. I lay back on my pillows with not a word to say, as if the cat had run off with my tongue.

It's sheer accident that I ever married to begin with. I didn't want to. Not that I had anything against marriage or had anything else special to do. But Mama talked me into it. Baby, she said, other women look down on women who don't marry. Besides, you don't have any particular talent and Aunt Sallie Mae, for all her talk, may not leave you a penny. I don't think she ever forgave me for not naming you after her, and all her hinting about leaving you her money may just be her spiteful way of getting back at me.

Besides, Mama said, the way she's held on to her money, even if she did leave it to you, there would be so many strings attached you'd have to have a corps of Philadelphia lawyers to read the fine print before you could withdraw as much as a twenty-five-cent piece. If I were you, Baby, Mama said, I'd go and get married. If you don't marry you won't get invited any place except as a last resort, when they need somebody at the last minute to keep from having thirteen at table. And it's nice to have somebody to open the door for you and carry your packages. A husband can be handy.

So I married Ray.

Well, Ray and I hadn't been married six months when along came Mama with a handkerchief in her hand and dabbing at her eyes. Baby, she said, the wife is always the last one to know. I've just got to tell you what everyone is talking about. I know how good you are and how lacking in suspicion, but the whole town is buzzing. It's Ray and Marjorie Brown.

Ray was nice and I was fond of him. He called me Lucyhoney, exactly as if it were one word. Sometimes for short he called me

Lucyhon. He didn't have much stamina or backbone—how could he when he was the only child and spoiled rotten by his mother and grandma and three maiden aunts?

Baby, Mama said, and her tears had dried and she was now using her handkerchief to fan herself with, don't you be gullible. I can't stand for you to be mistreated or betrayed. Should I go to the rector and tell him to talk to Ray and point out where his duty lies? Or should I ask your uncle Jonathan to talk to Ray man-to-man?

I said, Mama, it's nobody's fault but my own. For heaven's sake let Ray do what he wants to do. He doesn't need anyone to tell him when he can come and go and what persons he can see. It's his house and he's paying the bills. Besides, his taking up with Marjorie Brown is no discredit to me—she's a lot prettier than I am. I think it's romantic and spunky of Ray. Why, Marjorie Brown is a married woman. Her husband might shoot Ray.

I don't know exactly what it was that cooled Ray down. He was back penitent and sheep-eyed, begging forgiveness. I'm proud of you, Ray, I said. Why, until you married me you were so timid you wouldn't have said boo to a goose, and here you've been having an illicit affair. I think it's grand. Marjorie Brown's husband might have horsewhipped you.

Ray grinned and said, I really have picked me a wife.

And he never looked at another woman again as long as he lived. Which, unfortunately, wasn't very long.

I got to thinking about him feeling guilty and apologizing to me, when I was the one to blame—I hadn't done enough for him, and I wanted to do something real nice for him, so I thought of that cake recipe. Except we called it a receipt. It had been in the family for years—centuries, you might say, solemnly handed down from mother to daughter, time out of mind.

And so when that girl asked me whether I had a recipe for a happy marriage I didn't give the receipt a thought. Besides, I'm sure she didn't mean an actual recipe, but some kind of formula like let the husband know he's boss, or some such foolishness.

Anyway, there I was feeling penitent about not giving Ray the attention he should have had so that he was bored enough by me to go out and risk his life at the hands of Marjorie Brown's jealous husband.

So I thought, well, it's the hardest receipt I've ever studied and has more ingredients than I've ever heard of, but it's the least I can

do for Ray. So I went here and there to the grocery stores, to drug-
stores, to apothecaries, to people who said, good Lord, no, we
don't carry that but if you've got to have it try so-and-so, who
turned out to be somebody way out in the country that looked at
me as if I asked for the element that would turn base metal into
gold and finally came back with a little packet and a foolish question as to what on earth I needed that for.

Then I came on back home and began grinding and pounding
and mixing and baking and sitting in the kitchen waiting for the
mixture to rise. When it was done it was the prettiest thing I had
ever baked.

I served it for dessert that night.

Ray began to eat the cake and to savor it and to say extravagant
things to me, and when he finished the first slice he said, Lucyhon,
may I have another piece, a big one, please.

Why, Ray, it's all yours to eat as you like, I said.

After a while he pushed the plate away and looked at me with
a wonderful expression of gratitude on his face and he said, Oh,
Lucyhoney, I could die happy. And as far as I know he did.

When I tapped on his door the next morning to give him his
first cup of coffee and open the shutters and turn on his bathwater
he was dead, and there was the sweetest smile on his face.

But that young woman was still looking at me while I had been
reminiscing, and she was fluttering her notes and wetting her lips
with her tongue like a speaker with lots of things to say. And she
sort of bawled out at me as if I were an entire audience whose
attention had strayed: Do you think that the way to a man's heart is
through his stomach?

Excuse me, young lady, I wanted to say, but I never heard of
Cleopatra saying to Mark Antony or any of the others she favored,
Here, won't you taste some of my potato salad, and I may be wrong
because my reading of history is skimpy, but it sounds a little
unlikely that Madame de Pompadour ever whispered into the ear
of Louis XV, I've baked the nicest casserole for you.

My not answering put the girl off, and I felt that I ought to apologize, yet I couldn't bring myself around to it.

She glanced at her notes to the next question and was almost
beet-red from embarrassment when she asked: Did the financial
situation of your husbands ever have anything to do with your
marrying them?

I didn't even open my mouth. I was as silent as the tomb. Her questions kept getting more and more irrelevant. And I was getting more stupefied as her eyes kept running up and down her list of questions.

She tried another one: What do you think is the best way to get a husband?

Now that's a question I have never asked myself and about which I have nothing to offer anybody in a Saint Valentine's Day article or elsewhere. I have never gone out to *get* a husband. I haven't ever, as that old-fashioned expression has it, set my cap for anybody.

Take Lewis, who is this minute in the kitchen giggling with Eliza McIntyre. I certainly did not set out to get him. It was some months after Alton—no, Edward—had died, and people were trying to cheer me up, not that I needed any cheering up. I mean, after all the losses I've sustained, I've become philosophical. But my cousin Wanda's grandson had an exhibition of paintings. The poor deluded boy isn't talented, not a bit. All the same I bought two of his paintings, which are downstairs in the hall closet, shut off from all eyes.

Anyway, at the opening of the exhibition there was Lewis, looking all forlorn. He had come because the boy was a distant cousin of his dead wife. Lewis leaped up from a bench when he got a glimpse of me and said, Why, Lucy, I haven't seen you in donkey's years, and we stood there talking while everybody was going ooh and aah over the boy's paintings, and Lewis said he was hungry and I asked him to come on home with me and have a bite to eat.

I fixed a quick supper and Lewis ate like a starving man, and then we sat in the back parlor and talked about this and that, and about midnight he said, Lucy, I don't want to leave. This is the nicest feeling I've ever had, being here with you. I don't mean to be disrespectful to the dead, but there wasn't any love lost between Ramona and me. I'd like to stay on here forever.

Well, after that—after a man's revealed his innermost thoughts to you—you can't just show him the door. Besides, I couldn't put him out because it was beginning to snow, and in a little while the snow turned to sleet. He might have fallen and broken his neck going down the front steps, and I'd have had that on my conscience the rest of my life.

Lewis, I said, it seems foolish at this stage of the game for me to worry about my reputation, but thank heaven Cousin Alice came down from Washington for the exhibition and is staying with me, and she can chaperon us until we can make things perfectly legal and aboveboard.

That's how it happened.

You don't plan things like that, I wanted to tell the girl. They happen in spite of you. So it's silly of you to ask me what the best way is to get a husband.

My silence hadn't bothered her a bit. She sort of closed one eye like somebody about to take aim with a rifle and asked: Exactly how many times have you been married?

Well, she had backed up. She was repeating herself. That was practically the same question she had asked me earlier. It had been put a little differently this time, that was all.

I certainly had no intention of telling her the truth, which was that I wasn't exactly sure myself. Sometimes my husbands become a little blurred and blended. Sometimes I have to sit down with pencil and paper and figure it out.

Anyhow, that's certainly no way to look at husbands—the exact number or the exact sequence.

My husbands were an exceptional bunch of men, if I do say so. And fine-looking, too. Even Art, who had a harelip. And they were all good providers. Rich and didn't mind spending their money— not like some rich people. Not that I needed money. Because Aunt Sallie Mae, for all Mama's suspicions, left me hers, and there was nothing spiteful about her stipulations. I could have the money when, as, and how I wanted it.

Anyway, I never have cared about money or what it could buy for me.

There's nothing much I can spend it on for myself. Jewelry doesn't suit me. My fingers are short and stubby and my hands are square—no need to call attention to them by wearing rings. Besides, rings bother me. I like to cook and rings get in the way. Necklaces choke me and earrings pinch. As for fur coats, mink or chinchilla or just plain squirrel—well, I don't like the idea of anything that has lived ending up draped around me.

So money personally means little to me. But it's nice to pass along. Nothing gives me greater pleasure, and there's not a husband of mine who hasn't ended up without having a clinic or a college library or a hospital wing or a research laboratory or something of the sort founded in his honor and named after him.

Sometimes I've had to rob Peter to pay Paul. I mean, some of them have left more than others, and once in a while I've had to take some of what one left me to pay on the endowment for another. But it all evened itself out.

Except for Buster. There was certainly a nice surplus where Buster was concerned. He lived the shortest time and left me the most money of any of my husbands. For every month I lived with him I inherited a million dollars. Five.

My silent reminiscing like that wasn't helping the girl with her Saint Valentine's Day article. If I had been in anybody's house and the hostess was as taciturn as I was, I'd have excused myself and reached for the knob of the front door.

But, if anything, that young lady became even more impertinent.

Have you had a favorite among your husbands? she asked, and her tongue flicked out like a snake's.

I was silent even when my husbands asked that question. Sometimes they would show a little jealousy for their predecessors and make unkind remarks. But naturally I did everything in my power to reassure whoever made a disparaging remark about another.

All my husbands have been fine men, I would say in such a case, but I do believe you're the finest of the lot. I said it whether I really thought so or not.

But I had nothing at all to say to that girl on the subject.

Yet if I ever got to the point of being forced to rank my husbands, I guess Luther would be very nearly at the bottom of the list. He was the only teetotaler in the bunch. I hadn't noticed how he felt about drink until after we were married—that's when things you've overlooked during courtship can confront you like a slap in the face. Luther would squirm when wine was served to guests during a meal, and his eyes looked up prayerfully toward heaven when anybody took a second glass. At least he restrained himself to the extent of not saying any word of reproach to a guest, but Mama said she always expected him to hand around some of those tracts that warn against the pitfalls that lie in wait for drunkards.

Poor man. He was run over by a beer truck.

The irony of it, Mama said. There's a lesson in it for us all. And it was broad daylight, she said, shaking her head, not even dark, so that we can't comfort ourselves that Luther didn't know what hit him.

Not long after Luther's unfortunate accident Matthew appeared—on tiptoe, you might say. He was awfully short and always stretched himself to look taller. He was terribly apologetic about his height. I'd ask you to marry me, Lucy, he said, but all your husbands have been over six feet tall. Height didn't enter into it, I told him, and it wasn't very long before Matthew and I were married.

He seemed to walk on tiptoe and I scrunched down, and still there was an awful gap between us, and he would go on about Napoleon almost conquering the world in spite of being short. I started wearing low-heeled shoes and walking hunched over, and Mama said, For God's sake, Baby, you can push tact too far. You never were beautiful but you had an air about you and no reigning queen ever had a more elegant walk, and here you are slumping. Your aunt Francine was married to a midget, as you well know, but there wasn't any of this bending down and hunching over. She let him be his height and he let her be hers. So stop this foolishness.

But I couldn't. I still tried literally to meet Matthew more than halfway. And I had this feeling—well, why shouldn't I have it, seeing as how they had all died on me—that Matthew wasn't long for this world, and it was my duty to make him feel as important and as tall as I possibly could during the little time that was left to him.

Matthew died happy. I have every reason to believe it. But then, as Mama said, they all died happy.

Never again, Mama, I said. Never again. I feel like Typhoid Mary or somebody who brings doom on men's heads.

Never is a long time, Mama said.

And she was right. I married Hugh.

I think it was Hugh.

Two things I was proud of and am proud of. I never spoke a harsh word to any one of my husbands, and I never did call one of them by another's name, and that took a lot of doing because after a while they just all sort of melted together in my mind.

After every loss, Homer was the greatest solace and comfort to me. Until he retired last year, Homer was the medical examiner, and he was a childhood friend, though I never saw him except in his line of duty, you might say. It's the law here, and perhaps elsewhere, that if anyone dies unattended or from causes that aren't obvious, the medical examiner must be informed.

The first few times I had to call Homer I was chagrined. I felt apologetic, a little like calling the doctor up in the middle of the night when, however much the pain may be troubling you, you're afraid it's a false alarm and the doctor will hold it against you for disturbing his sleep.

But Homer always was jovial when I called him. I guess that's not the right word. Homer was reassuring, not jovial. Anytime, Lucy, anytime at all, he would say when I began to apologize for having to call him.

I think it was right after Sam died. Or was it Carl? It could have been George. Anyway, Homer was there reassuring me as always, and then this look of sorrow or regret clouded his features. It's a damned pity, Lucy, he said, you can't work me in somewhere or other. You weren't the prettiest little girl in the third grade, or the smartest, but damned if from the beginning there hasn't been something about you. I remember, he said, that when we were in the fourth grade, I got so worked up over you that I didn't pass a single subject but arithmetic and had to take the whole term over. Of course you were promoted, so for the rest of my life you've been just out of my reach.

Why, Homer, I said, that's the sweetest thing anybody has ever said to me.

I had it in the back of my mind once the funeral was over and everything was on an even keel again that I'd ask Homer over for supper one night. But it seemed so calculating, as if I was taking him up on that sweet remark he had made about wishing I had worked him in somewhere among my husbands. So I decided against it.

Instead I married Beau Green.

There they go laughing again—Eliza and Lewis down in the kitchen. My kitchen.

It's funny that Eliza has turned up in my kitchen, acting very much at home, when she's the one and only person in this town I never have felt very friendly toward—at least, not since word got to me that she had said I snatched Beau Green right from under her nose.

That wasn't a nice thing for her to say. Besides, there wasn't a word of truth in it. I'd like to see the man that can be snatched from under anybody's nose unless he wanted to be.

Eliza was surely welcome to Beau Green if she had wanted him and if he had wanted her.

Why, I'd planned to take a trip around the world, already had my tickets and reservations, and had to put it off for good because Beau wouldn't budge any farther away from home than to go to Green River—named for his family—to fish. I really wanted to take that cruise—had my heart especially set on seeing the Taj Mahal by moonlight—but Beau kept on saying if I didn't marry him he would do something desperate, which I took to mean he'd kill himself or take to drink. So I canceled all those reservations and turned in all those tickets and married him.

Well, Eliza would certainly have been welcome to Beau.

I've already emphasized that I don't like to rank my husbands, but in many ways Beau was the least satisfactory one I ever had. It was his nature to be a killjoy—he had no sense of the joy of living, and once he set his mind on something he went ahead with it, no matter if it pleased anybody else or not.

He knew good and well I didn't care for jewelry. But my preference didn't matter to Beau Green, not one bit. Here he came with this package and I opened it. I tried to muster all my politeness when I saw that it was a diamond. Darling, I said, you're sweet to give me a present, but this is a little bit big, isn't it?

It's thirty-seven carats, he said.

I felt like I ought to take it around on a sofa pillow instead of wearing it, but I did wear it twice and felt as conspicuous and as much of a show-off as if I'd been waving a peacock fan around and about.

It was and is my habit when I get upset with someone to go to my room and write my grievances down and get myself back in a good humor, just as I'm doing now because of that girl's questions; but sometimes it seemed like there wasn't enough paper in the world on which to write down my complaints against Beau.

Then I would blame myself. Beau was just being Beau. Like all God's creatures he was behaving the way he was made, and I felt so guilty that I decided I ought to do something for him to show I really loved and respected him, as deep in my heart I did.

So I decided to make him a cake by that elaborate recipe that had been in our family nobody is sure for how long. I took all one day to do the shopping for it. The next day I got up at five and stayed in the kitchen until late afternoon.

Well, Beau was a bit peckish when it came to eating the cake. Yet he had the sweetest tooth of any of my husbands.

Listen, darling, I said when he was mulish about eating it, I
made this special for you—it's taken the best part of two days. I
smiled at him and asked wouldn't he please at least taste it to
please me. Really, I was put out when I thought of all the work that
had gone into it. For one terrible second I wished it were a custard
pie and I could throw it right in his face, like in one of those old
Keystone comedies; and then I remembered that we were sworn to
cherish each other, so I just put one arm around his shoulder and
with my free hand I pushed the cake a little closer and said, Belle
wants Beau to eat at least one small bite. Belle was a foolish pet
name he sometimes called me because he thought it was clever for
him to be Beau and for me to be Belle.

He looked sheepish and picked up his fork and I knew he was
trying to please me: the way I had tried to please him by wearing
that thirty-seven-carat diamond twice.

Goodness, Belle, he said, when he swallowed his first mouthful,
this is delicious.

Now, darling, you be careful, I said. That cake is rich.

Best thing I ever ate, he said, and groped around on the plate
for the crumbs, and I said, Darling, wouldn't you like a little coffee
to wash it down?

He didn't answer, just sat there smiling. Then after a little while
he said he was feeling numb. I can't feel a thing in my feet, he said.
I ran for the rubbing alcohol and pulled off his shoes and socks
and started rubbing his feet, and there was a sort of spasm and his
toes curled under, but nothing affected that smile on his face.

Homer, I said a little later—because of course I had to telephone him about Beau's death—what on earth is it? Could it be
something he's eaten? And Homer said, What do you mean,
something he's eaten? Of course not. You set the best table in the
county. You're famous for your cooking. It couldn't be anything
he's eaten. Don't be foolish, Lucy. He began to pat me on the
shoulder and he said, I read a book about guilt and loss and it
said the bereaved often hold themselves responsible for the
deaths of their beloved ones. But I thought you had better sense
than that, Lucy.

Homer was a little bit harsh with me that time.

Julius Babb settled Beau's estate. Beau left you a tidy sum, all
right, he said, and I wanted to say right back at him but didn't: not
as tidy as most of the others left me.

Right then that young woman from the *Bulletin* repeated her last question.

Have you had a favorite among your husbands? Her tone was that of a prosecuting attorney and had nothing to do with a reporter interested in writing about love for Saint Valentine's Day.

I had had enough of her and her questions. I dragged myself up to a sitting position in the bed. Listen here, young lady, I said. It looks as if I've gotten off on the wrong foot with you—and then we both laughed at the pun I had made.

The laughter put us both in a good humor and then I tried to explain that I had an unexpected caller downstairs who needed some attention, and that I really was willing to cooperate on the Saint Valentine's Day article, but all those questions at first hearing had sort of stunned me. It was like taking an examination and finding all the questions a surprise. I told her if she would leave her list with me I'd mull over it, and she could come back tomorrow and I'd be prepared with my answers and be a little more presentable than I was now, wearing a rumpled wrapper and with my hair uncombed.

Well, she was as sweet as apple pie and handed over the list of questions and said she hoped that ten o'clock tomorrow morning would be fine; and I said, Yes, it would.

There goes Eliza's laugh again. It's more of a caw than a laugh. I shouldn't think that. But it's been such a strange day, with that young reporter being here and Eliza showing up so early.

Come to think of it, Eliza has done very well for herself, as far as marrying goes. That reporter should ask Eliza some of those questions.

Mama was a charitable woman all her life and she lived to be eighty-nine, but Eliza always rubbed Mama's skin the wrong way. To tell the truth, Eliza rubbed the skin of all the women in this town the wrong way. It's not right, Baby, Mama said, when other women have skimped and saved and cut corners all their lives and then when they're in their last sickness here comes Eliza getting her foot in the door just because she's a trained nurse. Then the next thing you hear, Eliza has married the widower and gets in one fell swoop what it took the dead wife a lifetime to accumulate.

That wasn't the most generous way in the world for Mama to put it, but I've heard it put much harsher by others. Mrs. Perkerson across the street, for one. Eliza is like a vulture, Mrs. Perkerson said. First she watches the wives die, then she marries, and then she watches the husbands die. Pretty soon it's widow's weeds for Eliza and a nice-sized bank account, not to mention some of the most valuable real estate in town.

Why, Mrs. Perkerson said the last time I saw her, I know that Lois Eubanks McIntyre is turning in her grave thinking of Eliza inheriting that big estate, with gardens copied after the Villa d'Este. And they tell you nursing is hard work.

I hadn't seen Eliza in some time. We were friendly enough, but not real friends, never had been, and I was especially hurt after hearing what she said about me taking Beau Green away from her. But we would stop and chat when we bumped into each other downtown, and then back off smiling and saying we must get together. But nothing ever came of it.

And then three weeks ago Eliza telephoned and I thought for sure somebody was dead. But, no, she was as sweet as magnolia blossoms and cooing as if we saw each other every day, and she invited me to come by that afternoon for a cup of tea or a glass of sherry. I asked her if there was anything special, and she said she didn't think there had to be any special reason for old friends to meet, but, yes, there was something special. She wanted me to see her gardens—of course they weren't her gardens, except by default, they were Lois Eubanks McIntyre's gardens, which she had opened for the Church Guild Benefit Tour and I hadn't come. So she wanted me to see them that afternoon.

It was all so sudden that she caught me off guard. I didn't want to go and there wasn't any reason for me to go, but for the life of me I couldn't think of an excuse not to go. And so I went.

The gardens really were beautiful, and I'm crazy about flowers.

Eliza gave me a personally guided tour. There were lots of paths and steep steps and unexpected turnings, and I was so delighted by the flowers that I foolishly didn't pay attention to my footing. I wasn't used to walking on so much gravel or going up and down uneven stone steps and Eliza didn't give me any warning.

Then all of a sudden, it was the strangest feeling, not as if I'd fallen but as if I'd been pushed, and there Eliza was leaning over me saying she could never forgive herself for not telling me about the broken step, and I was to lie right there and not move until the doctor could come, and what a pity it was that what she had wanted to be a treat for me had turned into a tragedy. Which was making a whole lot more out of it than need be because it was only a broken foot—not that it hasn't been inconvenient.

But Eliza has been fluttering around for three weeks saying that I should sue her as she carried liability insurance, and anyway it was lucky she was a nurse and could see that I got devoted attention. I don't need a nurse, but she has insisted on coming every day, and on some days several times; she seems to be popping in and out of the house like a cuckoo clock.

I had better get on with that reporter's questions.

Do you have a recipe for a happy marriage?

I've already told her I don't, and of course there's no such thing as a recipe for a happy marriage; but I could tell her this practice I have of working through my grievances and dissatisfactions by writing down what bothers me and then tearing up what I've written. For all I know it might work for somebody else, too.

I didn't hear Eliza coming up the stairs. It startled me when I looked up and saw her at my bedside. What if she discovered I was writing about her? What if she grabbed the notebook out of my hands and started to read it? There isn't a thing I could do to stop her.

But she just smiled and asked if I was ready for lunch, and she hoped I'd worked up a good appetite. How on earth she thinks I could have worked up an appetite by lying in bed I don't know, but that's Eliza for you, and all she had fixed was canned soup and it wasn't hot.

All I wanted was just to blot everything out—that girl's questions, Eliza's presence in my home, my broken foot.

I would have thought that I couldn't have gone to sleep in a thousand years. But I was so drowsy that I couldn't even close the notebook, much less hide it under the covers.

I don't know what woke me up. It was pitch-dark, but dark comes so soon these winter days you can't tell whether it's early dark or midnight.

I felt refreshed after my long nap and equal to anything. I was ready to answer any question on that girl's list.

The notebook was still open beside me and I thought that if Eliza had been in here and had seen what I had written about her it served her right.

Then from the kitchen rose a wonderful smell and there was a lot of noise downstairs. Suddenly, the back stairway and hall were flooded with light, and then Eliza and Lewis were at my door and they were grinning and saying they had a surprise for me. Then Lewis turned and picked up something from a table in the hall and brought it proudly toward me. I couldn't tell what it was. It was red and heartshaped and had something white on top. At first I thought it might be a hat, and then I groped for my distance glasses, but even with them on I still couldn't tell what Lewis was carrying.

Lewis held out the tray. It's a Saint Valentine's Day cake, he said, and Eliza said, we iced it and decorated it for you; then Lewis tilted it gently and I saw *L U C Y* in wobbly letters spread all across the top.

I don't usually eat sweets. So their labor of love was lost on me. Then I thought how kind it was that they had gone to all that trouble, and I forgave them for messing up my kitchen and meddling with my recipes—or maybe they had just used a mix. Anyway, I felt I had to show my appreciation, and it certainly wouldn't kill me to eat some of their cake.

They watched me with such pride and delight as I ate the cake that I took a second piece. When I had finished they said it would be best for me to rest, and I asked them to take the cake and eat what they wanted, then wrap it in foil.

And now the whole house is quiet.

I never felt better in my life. I'm smiling a great big contented smile. It must look exactly like that last sweet smile on all my husbands' faces—except Luther, who was run over by a beer truck.

I feel wonderful and so relaxed.

But I can hardly hold this pencil.

Goodness, it's

f

  a

   l

    l

     l

      i

       n

        g

Valentine's Day Cake

2½ cups sugar
1 cup butter
6 eggs
3 cups cake flour
½ tsp. baking soda
½ tsp. salt
1 cup sour cream
½ tsp. orange extract
½ tsp. lemon extract
1 tsp. vanilla extract
1 Tbsp. fresh orange rind, finely chopped
3 pints fresh strawberries, washed, hulled, and sliced
  in half
1 cup whipping cream
3 Tbsp. confectioner's sugar
½ tsp. vanilla extract
½ cup chocolate syrup
mint sprigs to garnish (optional)

PREHEAT OVEN TO 350 degrees F.

GREASE AND FLOUR 10-inch tube pan. Set aside.

CREAM SUGAR AND butter until light and fluffy. Add eggs one at a time, beating well after each addition. Sift flour, soda, and salt together. Add dry ingredients in three additions to the creamed butter and sugar, alternating with the sour cream. Add extracts and orange rind, beat well for two minutes. Pour into prepared tube pan. Bake for roughly one hour and 20 minutes, until done (cake top springs back when gently pressed).

MAKE WHIPPING CREAM. Whip cream until soft peaks form. Stir in sugar and vanilla. Place in refrigerator until cake is cool enough to eat.

SERVE EACH SLICE of cake topped with strawberries and whipped cream, drizzled with chocolate sauce, and garnished with a sprig of mint.

Death Cup

Joyce Carol Oates

*A*manita *phalloides* he began to hear in no voice he could
recognize.

Murmurous, only just audible—*Amanita phalloides.*

More distinctly that morning, a rain-chilled Saturday morning
in June, at his uncle's funeral. In the austere old Congregationalist
church he only entered, as an adult, for such ceremonies as wed-
dings and funerals. As, seated beside his brother Alastor of whom
he disapproved strongly, he leaned far forward in the cramped
hardwood pew, framing his face with his fingers so that he was
spared seeing his brother's profile in the corner of his eye. Feeling
an almost physical repugnance for the man who was his brother. He
tried to concentrate on the white-haired minister's solemn words
yet was nervously distracted by *Amanita phalloides.* As if, beneath the
man's familiar words of Christian forbearance and uplift, another
voice, a contrary voice, strange, incantatory, was struggling to
emerge. And during the interlude of organ music. The Bach Toc-
cata and Fugue in D Minor which his uncle, an amateur musician
and philanthropist, had requested be played at his funeral. Lyle was
one who, though he claimed to love music, was often distracted
during it; his mind drifting; his thoughts like flotsam, or froth; now
hearing the whispered words, only just audible in his ears *Amanita
phalloides, Amanita phalloides.* He realized he'd first heard these mysterious words the night before, in a dream. A sort of fever-dream.
Brought on by his brother's sudden, unexpected return.

He did not hate his brother Alastor. Not here, in this sacred place. *Amanita phalloides. Amanita phalloides.*

How beautiful, the Bach organ music! Filling the spartan plain, dazzling white interior of the church with fierce cascades of sound pure and flashing as a waterfall. Such music argued for the essential dignity of the human spirit. The transcendence of physical pain, suffering, loss. All that's petty, ignoble. *The world is a beautiful place if you have the eyes to see it and the ears to hear it,* Lyle's uncle had often said, and had seemed to believe through his long life, apparently never dissuaded from the early idealism of his youth; yet how was such idealism possible, Lyle couldn't help but wonder, Lyle who wished to believe well of others yet had no wish to be a fool, how was such idealism possible after the evidence of catastrophic world wars, the unspeakable evil of the Holocaust, equally mad, barbaric mass slaughters in Stalin's Russia, Mao's China? Somehow, his uncle Gardner King had remained a vigorous, good-natured, and generous man despite such facts of history; there'd been in him, well into his seventies, a childlike simplicity which Lyle, his nephew, younger than he by decades, seemed never to have had. Lyle had loved his uncle, who'd been his father's eldest brother. Fatherless himself since the age of eleven, he'd been saddened by his uncle's gradual descent into death from cancer of the larynx, and had not wanted to think that he would probably be remembered, to some degree, in his uncle's will. The bulk of the King estate, many millions of dollars, would go into the King Foundation, which was nominally directed by his wife, now widow, Alida King; the rest of it would be divided among numerous relatives. Lyle was troubled by the anticipation of any bequest, however modest. The mere thought filled him with anxiety, almost a kind of dread. *I would not wish to benefit in any way from Uncle Gardner's death, I could not bear it.*

To which his brother Alastor would have replied in his glib, jocular way, as, when they were boys, he'd laughed at Lyle's over-scrupulous conscience: *What good's that attitude? Our uncle is dead and he isn't coming back, is he?*

Unfortunate that Alastor had returned home to Contracoeur on the very eve of their uncle's death, after an absence of six years.

Still, it could only have been coincidence. So Alastor claimed. He'd been in communication with none of the relatives, including his twin brother Lyle.

How murmurous, teasing in Lyle's ears—*Amanita phalloides.*

Intimate as a lover's caressing whisper, and mysterious— *Amanita phalloides.*

Lyle was baffled at the meaning of these words. Why, at such a time, his thoughts distracted by grief, they should assail him.

In the hardwood pew, unpleasantly crowded by Alastor on his left, not wanting to crowd himself against an elderly aunt on his right, Lyle felt his lean, angular body quiver with tension. His neck was beginning to ache from the strain of leaning forward. It annoyed him to realize that, in his unstylish matte-black gabardine suit that fitted him too tightly across the shoulders and too loosely elsewhere, with his ash-colored hair straggling past his collar, his face furrowed as if with pain, and the peculiar way he held his outstretched fingers against his face, he was making himself conspicuous among the rows of mourners in the King family pews. Staring at the gleaming ebony casket so prominently placed in the center aisle in front of the communion rail, that looked so forbidding; so gigantic; far larger than his uncle Gardner's earthly remains, diminutive at the end, would seem to require. *But of course death is larger than life. Death envelops life: the emptiness that precedes our brief span of time, the emptiness that follows.*

A shudder ran through him. Tears stung his cheeks like acid. How shaky, how emotional he'd become!

A nudge in his side—his brother Alastor pressed a handkerchief, white, cotton, freshly laundered, into his hand, which Lyle blindly took.

Managing, even then, not to glance at his brother. Not to upset himself seeing yet again his brother's mock-pious mock-grieving face. His watery eyes, in mimicry of Lyle's.

Now the organ interlude was over. The funeral service was ending so soon! Lyle felt a childish stab of dismay, that his uncle would be hurried out of the sanctuary of the church, out of the circle of the community, into the impersonal, final earth. Yet the white-haired minister was leading the congregation in a familiar litany of words beginning, "Our heavenly father . . ." Lyle wiped tears from his eyelashes, shut his eyes tightly in prayer. He hadn't been a practicing Christian since adolescence, he was impatient with unquestioned piety and superstition, yet there was solace in such a ritual, seemingly shared by an entire community. Beside him, his aunt Agnes prayed with timid urgency, as if God were in this church and needed only to be beseeched by the right formula of words, and in the right tone of voice. On his other side, his brother Alastor intoned the prayer, not ostentatiously but distinctly enough to be heard for several pews; Alastor's voice was a deep, rich baritone, the voice of a trained singer you might think, or an actor. A roaring in Lyle's ears like a waterfall—*Amanita phalloides! Amanita phalloides!* and suddenly he remembered what *Amanita phalloides* was: the death-cup mushroom. He'd been reading a pictorial article on edible and inedible fungi in one of his science magazines and the death-cup mushroom, more accurately a "toadstool," had been imprinted on his memory.

His month had gone dry, his heart was hammering against his ribs. With the congregation, he murmured, "Amen." All volition seemed to have drained from him. Calmly he thought, *I will kill my brother Alastor after all. After all these years.*

OF COURSE, THIS WOULD never happen. Alastor King was a hateful person who surely deserved to die, but Lyle, his twin brother, was not one to commit any act of violence; not even one to fantasize any act of violence. *Not me! Not me! Never.*

IN THE CEMETERY BEHIND the First Congregationalist Church of Contracoeur, the remainder of the melancholy funeral rite was enacted. There stood Lyle King, the dead man's nephew, in a daze in wet grass beneath a glaring opalescent sky, awakened by strong fingers gripping his elbow. "All right if I ride with you to Aunt Alida's, Lyle?" Alastor asked. There was an edge of impatience to his lowered voice, as if he'd had to repeat his question. And Lyle's twin brother had not been one, since the age of eighteen months, to wish to repeat questions. He was leaning close to Lyle as if hoping to read his thoughts; his eyes were steely blue, narrowed. His breath smelled of something sweetly chemical, mouthwash probably, to disguise the alcohol on his breath; Lyle knew he was carrying a pocket flask in an inside pocket. His handsome ruddy face showed near-invisible broken capillaries like exposed nerves. Lyle murmured, "Of course, Alastor. Come with me." His thoughts flew ahead swiftly—there was Cemetery Hill that was treacherously steep, and the High Street Bridge—opportunities for accidents? Somehow Lyle's car might swerve out of control, skid on the wet pavement, Alastor, who scorned to wear a seat belt, might be thrown against the windshield, might be injured, might die, while he, Lyle, buckled in safely, might escape with but minor injuries. And blameless. Was that possible? Would God watch over him?

Not possible. For Lyle would have to drive other relatives in his car, too. He couldn't risk their lives. And there was no vigilant God.

A SIMPLE SELF-EVIDENT FACT, though a secret to most of the credulous world: Alastor King, attractive, intelligent, and deathly "charming" as he surely was, was as purely hateful, vicious, and worthless an individual as ever lived. His brother Lyle had grown to contemplate him with horror the way a martyr of ancient times might have contemplated the engine of pain and destruction rushing at him. *How can so evil a person deserve to live?* Lyle had wondered, sick with loathing of him. (This was years ago when the brothers were twenty. Alastor had secretly seduced their seventeen-year-old cousin Susan, and within a week or two lost interest in her, causing the girl to attempt suicide and to suffer a breakdown from which she would never fully recover.) Yet, maddening, Alastor had continued to live, and live. Nothing in the normal course of events would stop him.

Except Lyle. His twin. Who alone of the earth's billions of inhabitants understood Alastor's heart.

And so how shocked Lyle had been, how sickened, having hurried to the hospital when word came that his uncle Gardner was dying, only to discover, like the materialization of one of his nightmares, his brother Alastor already there! Strikingly dressed as usual, with all expression of care, concern, solicitude, clasping their aunt Alida's frail hand and speaking softly and reassuringly to her, and to the others, most of them female relatives, in the visitors' waiting room outside the intensive care unit. As if Alastor had been mysteriously absent from Contracoeur for six years, not

having returned even for their mother's funeral; as if he hadn't
disappeared abruptly when he'd left, having been involved in a
dubious business venture and owing certain of the relatives
money, including Uncle Gardner (an undisclosed sum—Lyle
didn't doubt it was many thousands of dollars) and Lyle himself
(thirty-five hundred dollars).

Lyle had stood in the doorway, staring in disbelief. He had not
seen his twin brother in so long, he'd come to imagine that Alastor
no longer existed in any way hurtful to him.

Alastor cried, "Lyle, Brother, hello! Good to see you!—except
this is such a tragic occasion."

Swiftly, Alastor came to Lyle, seizing his forearm, shaking his
hand vigorously as if to disarm him. He was smiling broadly, with
his old bad-boyish air, staring Lyle boldly in the face and daring
him to wrench away. Lyle stammered a greeting, feeling his face
burn. *He has come back like a bird of prey, now that Uncle Gardner is
dying.* Alastor nudged Lyle in the ribs, saying in a chiding voice
that he'd returned to Contracoeur just by chance, to learn the sad
news about their uncle—"I'd have thought, Lyle, that you might
have kept your own brother better informed. As when Mother
died, too, so suddenly, and I didn't learn about it for months."

Lyle protested, "But you were traveling—in Europe, you said—
out of communication with everyone. You—"

But Alastor was performing for Aunt Alida and the others, and
so interrupted Lyle to cry, with a pretense of great affection, "How
unchanged you are, Lyle! How happy I am to see you." It wasn't
enough for Alastor to have gripped Lyle's hand so hard he'd
nearly broken the fingers, now he had to embrace him; a rough
bearlike hug that nearly cracked Lyle's ribs, calculated to suggest
to those who looked on, *See how natural I am, how spontaneous and
loving, and how stiff and unnatural my brother is, and has always been,
though we're supposed to be twins.* Lyle had endured this performance
in the past and had no stomach for it now, pushing Alastor away
and saying in an angry undertone, "You! What are you doing here?
I'd think you'd be damned ashamed, coming back like this." Not
missing a beat, Alastor laughed and said, winking, one actor to
another in a play performed for a credulous, foolish audience,
"But why, Brother? When you can be ashamed for both of us?" And
he squeezed Lyle's arm with deliberate force, making him wince;
as he'd done repeatedly when they were boys, daring Lyle to

protest to their parents. *Daring me to respond with equal violence.* Then slinging a heavy arm around Lyle's shoulders, and walking him back to the women, as if Lyle were the reluctant visitor, and he, Alastor, the self-appointed host. Lyle quickly grasped, to his disgust, that Alastor had already overcome their aunt Alida's distrust of him and had made an excellent impression on everyone, brilliantly playing the role of the misunderstood prodigal son, tenderhearted, grieved by his uncle's imminent death, and eager—so eager—to give comfort to his well-to-do aunt.

How desperately Lyle wanted to take Aunt Alida aside, for she was an intelligent woman, and warn her, *Take care! My brother is after Uncle Gardner's fortune!* But of course he didn't dare; it wasn't in Lyle King's nature to be manipulative.

IN THIS WAY, ALASTOR KING returned to Contracoeur.

And within a few days, to Lyle's disgust, he'd reestablished himself with most of the relatives and certain of his old friends and acquaintances; probably, Lyle didn't doubt, with former women friends. He'd overcome Alida King's distrust and this had set the tone for the others. Though invited to stay with relatives, he'd graciously declined and had taken up residence at the Black River Inn; Lyle knew that his brother wanted privacy, no one spying on him, but others interpreted this gesture as a wish not to intrude, or impinge upon family generosity. How thoughtful Alastor had become, how kind, how *mature.* So Lyle was hearing on all sides. It was put to him repeatedly, maddeningly: "You must be so happy, Lyle, that your brother has returned. You must have missed him terribly."

And Lyle would smile warily, politely, and say, "Yes. Terribly."

The worst of it was, apart from the threat Alastor posed to Alida King, that Lyle, who'd succeeded in pushing his brother out of his thoughts for years, was forced to think of him again; to think obsessively of him again; to recall the myriad hurts, insults, outrages he'd suffered from Alastor; and the numerous cruel and even criminal acts Alastor had perpetrated, with seeming impunity. And of course he was always being thrown into Alastor's company: always the fraudulent, happy cry, "Lyle! Brother"—always the exuberant, rib-crushing embrace, a mockery of brotherly affection.

On one occasion, when he'd gone to pick up Alastor at the hotel, Lyle had staved Alastor off with an elbow, grimacing. "Damn you, Alastor, stop. We're not on stage, no one's watching." Alastor said, laughing, with a contemptuous glance around, "What do you mean, Brother? Someone is always watching."

It was true. Even on neutral ground, in the foyer of the Black River Inn, for instance, people often glanced at Alastor King. In particular, women were drawn to his energetic, boyish good looks and bearing.

As if they saw not the man himself but the incandescent, seductive image of the man's desire: his wish to deceive.

While, seeing Lyle, they saw merely—Lyle.

What particularly disgusted Lyle was that his brother's hypocrisy was so transparent. Yet so convincing. And he, the less demonstrative brother, was made to appear hesitant, shy, anemic by comparison. Lacking, somehow, manliness itself. Alastor was such a dazzling sight: his hair that should have been Lyle's identical shade of faded ashy-brown was a brassy russet-brown, lifting from his forehead in waves that appeared crimped, while Lyle's thinning hair was limp, straight. Alastor's sharply blue eyes were alert and watchful and flirtatious while Lyle's duller blue eyes were gently myopic and vague behind glasses that were invariably finger-smudged. Apart from a genial flush to his skin, from an excess of food and drink, Alastor radiated an exuberant sort of masculine health; if you didn't look closely, his face appeared youthful, animated, while Lyle's was beginning to show the inroads of time, small worried dents and creases, particularly at the corners of his eyes. Alastor was at least twenty pounds heavier than Lyle, thick in the torso, as if he'd been building up muscles, while Lyle, lean, rangy, with all unconscious tendency to slouch, looked by comparison wan and uncoordinated. (In fact, Lyle was a capable swimmer and an enthusiastic tennis player.) Since early adolescence Alastor had dressed with verve: At the hospital, he'd worn what appeared to be a suit of suede, honey-colored, with an elegantly cut jacket and a black silk shirt worn without a tie; after their uncle's death, he'd switched to theatrical mourning, in muted-gray fashionable clothes, a linen coat with exaggerated padded shoulders, trousers with prominent creases, shirts so pale a blue they appeared a grieving white, and a midnight-blue neck-tie of some beautiful glossy fabric. And he wore expensive black leather shoes with soles that gave him an extra inch of height—so that Lyle, who had always been Alastor's height exactly, was vexed by being forced *to look up at him.* Lyle, who had no vanity, and some might say not enough pride, wore the identical matte-black gabardine suit in an outdated style he'd worn for years on special occasions; often he shaved without really looking at himself in the mirror, his mind turned inward; sometimes he rushed out of the house without combing his hair. He was a sweet-natured, vague-minded young-old man with the look of a perennial bachelor, held in affectionate if bemused regard by those who knew him well, largely ignored by others. After graduating summa cum laude from Williams College—while Alastor had dropped out, under suspicious circumstances, from Amherst—Lyle had returned to Contracoeur to lead a quiet, civilized life: He lived in an attractively converted carriage house on what had been his parents' property, gave private music lessons, and designed books for a small New England press specializing in limited editions distinguished within the trade, but little known elsewhere. He'd had several moderately serious romances that had come to nothing yet he harbored, still, a vague hope of marriage; friends were always trying to match him with eligible young women, as in a stubborn parlor game no one wished to give up. (In fact, Lyle had secretly adored his cousin Susan, whom Alastor had seduced; after that sorry episode, and Susan's subsequent marriage and move to Boston, Lyle seemed to himself to have lost heart for the game.) It amused Lyle to think that Alastor was considered a "world traveler"—an "explorer"—for he was certain that his brother had spent time in prison, in the United States; in Europe, in his late twenties, he'd traveled with a rich older woman who'd conveniently died and left him some money.

It wasn't possible to ask Alastor a direct question, and Lyle had long since given up trying. He'd given up, in fact, making much effort to communicate with Alastor at all. For Alastor only lied to him, with a maddening habit of smiling and winking and sometimes nudging him in the ribs as if to say *I know you despise me, Brother. And so what? You're too cowardly to do anything about it.*

AT THE FUNERAL LUNCHEON, Lyle noted glumly that Alastor was seated beside their aunt Alida and that the poor woman, her mind clearly weakened from the strain of her husband's death, was gazing up at Alastor as once she'd gazed at her husband Gardner: with infinite trust. Aunt Alida was one of those women who'd taken a special interest in Lyle from time to time, hoping to match him with a potential bride, and now, it seemed, she'd forgotten Lyle entirely. But then she was paying little attention to anyone except Alastor. Through the buzz and murmur of voices—Lyle winced to hear how frequently Alastor was spoken of, in the most laudatory way—he could make out fragments of their conversation; primarily Alastor's grave, unctuous voice. "And were Uncle Gardner's last days peaceful?—did he look back upon his life with joy?—that's all that matters." Seeing Lyle's glare of indignation, Alastor raised his glass of wine in a subtly mocking toast, smiling, just perceptibly winking, so that no one among the relatives could guess the message he was sending to his twin, as frequently he'd done when they were boys, in the company of their parents. *See? How clever I am? And what gullible fools these others are, to take me seriously?*

Lyle flushed angrily, so distracted he nearly overturned his water goblet.

Afterward, questioned about his travels, Alastor was intriguingly vague. Yet all his tales revolved around himself; always, Alastor King was the hero. Saving a young girl from drowning when a Greek steamer struck another boat, in the Mediterranean; establishing a medical trust fund for beggars, in Cairo; giving aid to a young black heroin addict, adrift in Amsterdam . . . Lyle listened with mounting disgust as the relatives plied Alastor with more questions, believing everything he said no matter how absurd; having forgotten, or wishing to forget, how he'd disappeared from Contracoeur owing some of them money. Alastor was, it seemed, now involved in the importing into the United States of "masterworks of European culture"; elliptically, he suggested that his business would flourish, and pay off investors handsomely, if only it might be infused with a little more capital. He was in partnership with a distinguished Italian artist of an "impoverished noble family." . . . As Alastor sipped wine, it seemed to Lyle that his features grew more vivid, as if he were an actor in a film, magnified many times. His artfully dyed brassy-brown hair framed his thuggish fox-face in crimped waves so that he looked like an animated doll. Lyle would have asked him skeptically who the distinguished artist was, what was the name of their business, but he knew that Alastor would give glib, convincing answers. Except for Lyle, everyone at the table was gazing at Alastor with interest, admiration, and, among the older women, yearning; you could imagine these aging women, shaken by the death of one of their contemporaries, looking upon Alastor as if he were a fairy prince, promising them their youth again, their lost innocence. They had only to believe in him unstintingly, to "invest" in his latest business scheme. "Life is a ceaseless pilgrimage up a mountain," Alastor was saying. "As long as you're in motion, your perspective is obscured. Only when you reach the summit and turn to look back, can you be at peace."

There was a hushed moment at the table, as if Alastor had uttered holy words. Aunt Alida had begun to weep, quietly. Yet there was a strange sort of elation in her weeping. Lyle, who rarely drank, and never during the day, found himself draining his second glass of white wine. *Amanita phalloides. Amanita . . .* he recalled how, years ago, when they were young children, Alastor had so tormented him that he'd lost control suddenly and screamed, flailing at his brother with his fists, knocking Alastor backward, astonished. Their mother had quickly intervened. But Lyle remembered vividly. *I wasn't a coward, once.*

Lyle drove Alastor back to the Black River Inn in silence. And Alastor himself was subdued, as if his performance had exhausted him. He said, musing aloud, "Aunt Alida has aged so, I was shocked. They all have. I don't see why you hadn't kept in closer touch with me, Lyle; you could have reached me care of American Express anytime you'd wanted in Rome, in Paris, in Amsterdam . . . Who will be overseeing the King Foundation now? Aunt Alida will need help. And that enormous English Tudor house. And all that property: thirty acres. Uncle Gardner refused even to consider selling to a developer, but it's futile to hold out much longer. All of the north section of Contracoeur is being developed; if Aunt Alida doesn't sell, she'll be surrounded by tract homes in a few years. It's the way of the future, obviously." Alastor paused, sighing with satisfaction. It seemed clear that the future was a warm beneficent breeze blowing in his direction. He gave Lyle, who was hunched behind the steering wheel of his nondescript automobile, a sly, sidelong glance. "And that magnificent Rolls Royce. I suppose, Brother, you have your eye on *that*?" Alastor laughed, as if nothing was more amusing than the association of Lyle with a Rolls Royce. He was dabbing at his flushed face, overheated from numerous glasses of wine.

Quietly, Lyle said, "I think you should leave the family alone, Alastor. You've already done enough damage to innocent people in your life."

"But—by what measure is 'enough'?" Alastor said, with mock seriousness. "By your measure, Brother, or mine?"

"There is only one measure—that of common decency."

"Oh well, then, if you're going to lapse into 'common' decency," Alistor said genially, "it's hopeless to try to talk to you."

At the Black River Inn, Alastor invited Lyle inside so that they could discuss "family matters" in more detail. Lyle, trembling with indignation, coolly declined. He had work to do, he said; he was in the midst of designing a book, a new limited edition with hand-sewn pages and letterpress printing, of Edgar Allan Poe's short story "William Wilson." Alastor shrugged, as if he thought little of this; not once had he shown the slightest interest in his brother's beautifully designed books, any more than he'd shown interest in his brother's life. "You'd be better off meeting a woman," he said. "I could introduce you to one."

Lyle said, startled, "But you've only just arrived back in Contracoeur."

Alastor laughed, laying a heavy hand on Lyle's arm, and squeezing him with what seemed like affection. "God, Lyle! Are you serious? Women are everywhere. And any time."

Lyle said disdainfully, "A certain kind of woman, you mean."

Alastor said, with equal disdain, "No. There is only one kind of woman."

Lyle turned his car into the drive of the Black River Inn, his heart pounding with loathing of his brother. He knew that Alastor spoke carelessly, meaning only to provoke; it was pointless to try to speak seriously with him, let alone reason with him. He had no conscience in small matters as in large. *What of our cousin Susan? Do you ever think of her, do you feel remorse for what you did to her?*—Lyle didn't dare ask. He would only be answered by a crude, flippant remark which would only upset him further.

The Black River Inn was a handsome "historic" hotel recently renovated, at considerable cost, now rather more a resort motel than an inn, with landscaped grounds, a luxurious swimming pool, tennis courts. It seemed appropriate that Alastor would be staying in such a place; though surely deep in debt, he was accustomed to first-rate accommodations. Lyle sat in his car watching his brother stride purposefully away without a backward glance. Already he'd forgotten his chauffeur.

Two attractive young women were emerging from the front entrance of the inn as Alastor approached. Their expressions when they saw him—alert, enlivened—the swift exchange of smiles, as if in a secret code—cut Lyle to the quick. *Don't you know that man is evil? How can you be so easily deceived by looks?* Lyle opened his car door, jumped from the car, stood breathless and staring at the young women as they continued on the walk in his direction; they were laughing together, one of them glancing over her shoulder after Alastor (who was glancing over his shoulder at her, as he pushed into the hotel's revolving door) but their smiles faded when they saw Lyle. He wanted to stammer—what? Words of warning, or apology? Apology for his own odd behavior? But without slowing their stride the women were past, their glances sliding over Lyle; taking him in, assessing him, and sliding over him. They seemed not to register that Alastor, who'd so caught their eye, and Lyle were twins; they seemed not to have seen Lyle at all.

RECALLING HOW YEARS AGO in circumstances long since forgotten he'd had the opportunity to observe his brother flirting with a cocktail waitress, a heavily made-up woman in her late thirties, still a glamorous woman yet no longer young, and Alastor had drawn her out, asking her name, teasing her, shamelessly flattering her, making her blush with pleasure; then drawing back with a look of offended surprise when the waitress asked him his name, saying, "Excuse me? I don't believe that's any of your business, miss." The hurt, baffled look on the woman's face! Lyle saw how, for a beat, she continued to smile, if only with her mouth; wanting to believe that this was part of Alastor's sophisticated banter. Alastor said, witheringly, "You don't seem to take your job seriously. I think I must have a conversation with the manager." Alastor was on his feet, incensed; the waitress immediately apologized, "Oh no, sir, please—I'm so sorry—I misunderstood—" Like an actor secure in his role since he has played it numberless times, Alastor walked away without a backward glance. It was left to Lyle (afterward, Lyle would realize how deliberately it had been left to him) to pay for his brother's drinks, and to apologize to the stunned waitress, who was still staring after Alastor. "My brother is only joking, he has a cruel sense of humor. Don't be upset, please!" But the woman seemed scarcely to hear Lyle, her eyes swimming with tears; nor did she do more than glance at him. There she stood, clutching her hands at her breasts as if she'd been stabbed, staring after Alastor, waiting for him to return.

It would be cream of *Amanita phalloides* soup that Lyle served to his brother Alastor when, at last, Alastor found time to come to lunch.

An unpracticed cook, Lyle spent much of the morning preparing the elaborate meal. The soft, rather slimy, strangely cool pale-gray-pulpy fungi chopped with onions and moderately ground in a blender. Cooked slowly in a double boiler in chicken stock, seasoned with salt and pepper and grated nutmeg; just before Alastor was scheduled to arrive, laced with heavy cream and two egg yolks slightly beaten, and the heat on the stove turned down. How delicious the soup smelled! Lyle's mouth watered, even as a vein pounded dangerously in his forehead. When Alastor arrived in a taxi, a half-hour late, swaggering into Lyle's house without knocking, he drew a deep startled breath, savoring the rich cooking aroma, and rubbed his hands together in anticipation. "Lyle, wonderful! I didn't know you were a serious cook. I'm famished."

Nervously, Lyle said, "But you'll have a drink first, Alastor? And—relax?"

Of course Alastor would have a drink. Or two. Already he'd discovered, chilling in Lyle's refrigerator, the two bottles of good Italian chardonnay Lyle had purchased for this occasion. "May I help myself? You're busy."

Lyle had found the recipe for cream of mushroom soup in a battered Fanny Farmer cookbook in a secondhand bookshop in town. In the same shop he'd found an amateur's guide to fungi, edible and inedible, with pages of illustrations. Shabby mane, chanterelles, beefsteak mushrooms—these were famously edible. But there amid the inedible, the sinister lookalike toadstools, was *Amanita phalloides*. The death cup. A white-spored fungi, as the caption explained, with the volva separate from the cap. Highly poisonous. And strangely beautiful, like a vision from the deepest recesses of one's dreams brought suddenly into the light.

The "phallic" nature of the fungi was painfully self-evident. How ironic, Lyle thought, and appropriate. For a man like Alastor who sexually misused women.

It had taken Lyle several days of frantic searching in the woods back beyond his house before he located what appeared to be *Amanita phalloides*. He'd drawn in his breath at the sight—a malevolent little crop of toadstools luminous in the mist, amid the snaky gnarled roots of a gigantic beech tree. Almost, as Lyle quickly gathered them with his gloved hands, dropping them into a bag, the fungi exuded an air of sentient life. Lyle imagined he could hear faint cries of anguish as he plucked at them, in haste; he had an unreasonable fear of someone discovering him. *But those aren't edible mushrooms, those are death cups, why are you gathering those?*

Alastor was seated at the plain wooden table in Lyle's spartan dining room. Lyle brought his soup bowl in from the kitchen and set it, steaming, before him. At once Alastor picked up his soup spoon and began noisily to eat. He said he hadn't eaten yet that day; he'd had an arduous night—"well into the morning." He laughed, mysteriously. He sighed. "Brother, this *is* good. I think I can discern—chanterelles? My favorites."

Lyle served crusty French bread, butter, a chunk of goat's cheese, and set a second bottle of chardonnay close by Alastor's place. He watched, mesmerized, as Alastor lifted spoonfuls of soup to his mouth and sipped and swallowed hungrily, making sounds of satisfaction. How flattered Lyle felt, who could not recall ever having been praised by his twin brother before in his life. Lyle sat tentatively at his place, fumbling with icy fingers to pick up his soup spoon. He'd prepared for himself soup that closely resembled Alastor's but was in fact Campbell's cream of mushroom slightly altered. This had never been a favorite of Lyle's and he ate it now slowly, his eyes on his brother; he would have wished to match Alastor spoon for spoon, but Alastor as always ate too swiftly. The tiny, near-invisible capillaries in his cheeks glowed like incandescent wires; his steely blue eyes shone with pleasure. *A man who enjoys life, where's the harm in that?*

Within minutes Alastor finished his large deep bowl of streaming hot creamy soup, licking his lips. Lyle promptly served him another. "You have more talent, Brother, than you know," Alastor said with a wink. "We might open a restaurant together: I, the keeper of the books; you, the master of the kitchen." Lyle almost spilled a spoonful of soup as he lifted it tremendously to his lips. He was waiting for *Amanita phalloides* to take effect. He'd had the idea that the poison was nearly instantaneous, like cyanide. Evidently not. Or had—the possibility filled him with horror—boiling the chopped-up toadstool diluted its toxin? He was eating sloppily, continually wiping at his chin with a napkin. Fortunately, Alastor didn't notice. Alastor was absorbed in recounting, as he sipped soup, swallowed large mouthfuls of bread, butter, and cheese, and the tart white wine, a lengthy lewd tale of the woman, or women, with whom he'd spent his arduous night at the Black River Inn. He'd considered calling Lyle to insist that Lyle come join him—"As you'd done that other time, eh? To celebrate our twenty-first birthday?" Lyle blinked at him as if not comprehending his words, let alone his meaning. Alastor went on to speak of women generally. "They'll devour you alive if you allow it. They're vampires." Lyle said, fumblingly, "Yes, Alastor, I suppose so. If you say so." "Like Mother, who sucked life out of poor Father. To give birth to *us*—imagine!" Alastor shook his head, laughing. Lyle nodded gravely, numbly; yes, he would try to imagine. Alastor said, with an air almost of bitterness, though he was eating and drinking with as much appetite as before, "Yes, Brother, a man has to be vigilant. Has to make the first strike." He brooded, as if recalling more than one sorry episode. Lyle had a sudden unexpected sense of his brother with a history of true feeling, regret. Remorse? It was mildly astonishing, like seeing a figure on a playing card stir into life.

Lyle said, "But what of—Susan?"

"Susan?—who?" The steely blue eyes, lightly threaded with red, were fixed innocently upon Lyle.

"Our cousin Susan."

"Her? But I thought—" Alastor broke off in mid-sentence. His words simply ended. He was busying himself swiping at the inside of his soup bowl with a piece of crusty bread. A tinge of apparent pain made his jowls quiver and he pressed the heel of a hand against his midriff. A gas pain, perhaps.

Lyle said ironically, "Did you think Susan was dead, Alastor? Is that how you remember her?"

"I don't in fact remember her at all." Alastor spoke blithely, indifferently. A mottled flush had risen from his throat into his cheeks. "The girl was your friend, Brother. Not mine."

"No. Susan was never my friend again," Lyle said bitterly. "She never spoke to me, or answered any call or letter of mine, again. After . . . what happened."

Alistor snorted in derision. "Typical!"

" 'Typical'—?"

"Female fickleness. It's congenital."

"Our cousin Susan was not a fickle woman. You must know that, Alastor, damn you!"

"Why damn *me*? What have I to do with it? I was a boy then, hardly more than a boy, and you—so were *you*." Alastor spoke with his usual rapid ease, smiling, gesturing, as if what he said made perfect sense; he was accustomed to the company of uncritical admirers. Yet he'd begun to breathe audibly; perspiration had broken out on his unlined forehead in an oily glisten. His artfully dyed and crimped hair that looked so striking in other settings looked here, to Lyle's eye, like a wig set upon a mannequin's head. And there was an undertone of impatience, even anger, in Alastor's speech. "Look, she did get married and move away—didn't she? She did—I mean didn't—have a baby?"

Lyle stared at Alastor for a long somber moment.

"So far as I know, she did not. Have a baby."

"Well, then!" Alastor made an airy gesture of dismissal, and dabbed at his forehead with a napkin.

Seeing that Alastor's soup bowl was again empty, Lyle rose silently and carried it back into the kitchen and a third time ladled soup into it, nearly to the brim: This was the end of the cream of *Amanita phalloides* soup. Surely, now, within the next few minutes, the powerful poison would begin to act! When Lyle returned to the dining room with the bowl, he saw Alastor draining his second or third glass of the tart white wine and replenishing it without waiting for his host's invitation. His expression had turned mean, grim; as soon as Lyle reappeared, however, Alastor smiled up at him, and winked. "Thanks, Brother!" Yet there was an air of absolute complacency in Alastor as in one accustomed to being served by others.

Incredibly, considering all he'd already eaten, Alastor again picked up his spoon and enthusiastically ate.

So the luncheon, planned so obsessively by Lyle, passed in a blur, a confused dream. Lyle stared at his handsome, ruddy-faced twin, who spoke with patronizing affection of their aunt Alida—"A befuddled old woman who clearly needs guidance"; and of the King Foundation—"An anachronism that needs total restructuring, top to bottom"; and the thirty acres of prime real estate—"The strategy must be to pit developers against one another, I've tried to explain"; and of the vagaries of the international art market—"All that's required for 1,000-percent profits is a strong capital base to withstand dips in the economy." Lyle could scarcely hear for the roaring in his ears. What had gone wrong? He had mistaken an ordinary, harmless, edible mushroom for *Amanita phalloides*, the death cup? He'd been so eager and agitated out there in the woods, he hadn't been absolutely certain of the identification.

Numbed, in a trance, Lyle drove Alastor back to the Black River Inn. It was a brilliant summer day. A sky of blank blue, the scales of the dark river glittering. Alastor invited Lyle to visit him at the inn sometime soon, they could go swimming in the pool—"You meet extremely interesting people, sometimes, in such places." Lyle asked Alastor how long he intended to stay there and Alastor smiled enigmatically and said, "As long as required, Brother. You know me!"

At the inn, Alastor shook Lyle's hand vigorously, and, on all impulse, or with the pretense of acting on impulse, leaned over to kiss his cheek! Lyle was as startled as if he'd been slapped.

Driving away he felt mortified, yet in a way relieved. *It hasn't happened yet. I am not a fratricide, yet.*

GARDNER KING'S WILL WAS read. It was a massive document enumerating over one hundred beneficiaries, individuals and organizations.

Lyle, who hadn't wished to be present at the reading, heard of the bequest made to him from his brother Alastor, who had apparently escorted Aunt Alida to the attorney's office. Lyle was to receive several thousand dollars, plus a number of his uncle's rare first-edition books. With forced ebullience Alastor said, "Congratulations, Brother! You must have played your cards right, for once." Lyle wiped at his eyes; he'd genuinely loved their uncle Gardner, and was touched to be remembered by him in his will; even as he'd expected to be remembered, to about that degree. *Yes, and there's greater pleasure in the news, if Alastor has received nothing.* At the other end of the line Alastor waited, breathing into the receiver. Waiting for—what? For Lyle to ask him how he'd fared? For Lyle to offer to share the bequest with him? Alastor was saying dryly, "Uncle Gardner left me just a legal form, 'forgiving' me my debts." He went on to complain that he hadn't even remembered he owed their uncle money; you would think, wouldn't you, with his staff of financial advisors, Gardner King could have reminded him; it should have been his responsibility, to remind him; Alastor swore he'd never been reminded—not once in six years. Vividly, Lyle could imagine his brother's blue glaring eyes, his coarse, flushed face, and the clenched self-righteous set of his jaws. Alastor said, hurt, "I suppose I should be grateful for being 'forgiven,' Lyle, eh? It's so wonderfully Christian."

Lyle said coolly, "Yes. It is Christian. I would be grateful, in your place."

"In my place, Brother, how would you know what you would be? You're 'Lyle' not 'Alastor.' Don't give yourself airs."

Rudely, Alastor hung up. Lyle winced as if his brother had poked him in the chest as so frequently he'd done when they were growing up together, as a kind of exclamation mark to a belligerent statement of his.

Only afterward did Lyle realize, with a sick stab of resentment, that, in erasing Alastor's debt to him, which was surely beyond $10,000, their uncle had in fact given Alastor the money; and it was roughly the equivalent of the amount he'd left Lyle in his will. *As if, in his uncle's mind, Alastor and he were of equal merit after all.*

SHE CAME TO HIM when he summoned her. Knocking stealthily at his door in the still, private hour beyond midnight. And hearing him murmur *Come in!* and inside in the shadows he stood watching. How she trembled, how excited and flattered she was. Her girlish face, her rather too large hands and feet, a braid of golden-red hair wrapped around her head. In her uniform that fitted her young shapely body so becomingly. In a patch of caressing moonlight. Noiselessly, he came behind her to secure the door, lock and double-lock it. He made her shiver kissing her hand, and the soft flesh at the inside of her elbow. So she laughed, startled. He was European, she'd been led to believe. A European gentleman. Accepting the first drink from him, a toast to mutual happiness. Accepting the second drink, her head giddy. How flattered by his praise *Beautiful girl! Lovely girl!* And: *Remove your clothes please.* Fumbling with the tiny buttons of the violet rayon uniform. Wide lace collar, lace cuffs. He kissed her throat, a vein in her throat. Kissed the warm cleft between her breasts. *Lee Ann is it? Lynette?* In their loveplay on the king-sized bed he twisted her wrist just slightly. Just enough for her to laugh, startled; to register discomfort; yet not so emphatically she would realize he meant anything by it. *Here, Lynette. Give me a real kiss.* Boldly pressing her fleshy mouth against his and her heavy breasts against his chest and he bit her lips, hard; she recoiled from him, and still his teeth were clamped over her lips that were livid now with pain. When at last he released her she was sobbing and her lips were bleeding and he, the European gentleman, with genuine regret crying *Oh what did I do!—Forgive me, I was carried away by passion, my darling.* She cringed before him on her hands and knees, her breasts swinging. Her enormous eyes. Shining like a beast's. And wanting still to believe, how desperate to believe, so within a few minutes she allowed herself to be persuaded it had been an accident, an accident of passion, an accident for which she was herself to blame, being so lovely, so desirable she'd made him crazed. Kissing her hands, pleading for forgiveness, and at last forgiven and tenderly he arranged her arms and legs, her head at the edge of the bed, her long, wavy, somewhat coarse golden-red hair undone from its braid hanging over onto the carpet. She would have screamed except he provided a rag to shove into her mouth, one in fact used for previous visitors in Suite 181 of the Black River Inn.

"How can you be so cruel, Alastor!"

Laughing, Alastor had recounted this lurid story for his brother Lyle as the two sat beside the hotel pool in the balmy dusk of an evening, in late June. Lyle had listened with mounting dismay and disgust and at last cried out.

Alastor said carelessly, " 'Cruel'?—why am I 'cruel'? The women love it, Brother. Believe me."

Lyle felt ill. Not knowing whether to believe Alastor or not—wondering if perhaps the entire story had been fabricated, to shock.

Yet there was something matter-of-fact in Alastor's tone that made Lyle think, yes, it's true. He wished he'd never dropped by the Black River Inn to visit with Alastor, as Alastor had insisted. And he would not have wished to acknowledge even to himself that Alastor's crude story had stirred him sexually.

I am falling into pieces, shreds. Like something brittle that has been cracked.

The day after the luncheon, Lyle had returned to the woods behind his house to look for the mysterious fungi; but he had no luck retracing his steps, and failed even to locate the gigantic beech tree with the snaky exposed roots. In a rage he'd thrown away *The Amateur's Guide to Fungi Edible & Inedible*. He'd thrown away *The Fanny Farmer Cookbook*.

Since the failure of the *Amanita phalloides* soup, Lyle found himself thinking obsessively of his brother. As soon as he woke in the morning he began to think of Alastor, and through the long day he thought of Alastor; at night his dreams were mocking, jeering, turbulent with emotion that left him enervated and depressed. It was no longer possible for him to work even on projects, like the book design for Poe's "William Wilson," that challenged his imagination. Though he loved his hometown, and his life here, he wondered despairingly if perhaps he should move away from Contracoeur, for hadn't Contracoeur been poisoned for him by Alastor's presence? Living here, with Alastor less than ten minutes away by car, Lyle had no freedom from thinking of his evil brother. For rumors circulated that Alastor was meeting with local real estate developers though Gardner King's widow was still insisting that her property would remain intact as her husband had wished; that Alastor was to be the next director of the King Foundation, though the present director was a highly capable man who'd had his position for years and was universally respected; that Alastor and his aunt Alida were to travel to Europe in the fall on an art-purchasing expedition, though Alida King had always expressed a nervous dislike, even a terror, of travel, and had grown frail since her husband's death. It had been recounted to Lyle by a cousin that poor Alida had said, wringing her hands, "Oh, I do hope I won't be traveling to Europe this fall, I know I won't survive away from Contracoeur!" and when the cousin asked why on earth she might be traveling to Europe if she didn't wish to, Alida had said, starting to cry, "But I may decide that I do wish to travel, that's what frightens me. I know I will never return alive."

Cocktail service at poolside had ended at 9:00 P.M.; the pool was officially closed, though its glimmering synthetic-aqua water was still illuminated from below; only boastful Alastor and his somber brother Lyle remained in deck chairs, as an eroded-looking but glaring bright moon rose in the night sky. Alastor, in swim trunks and a terry cloth shirt, trotted off barefoot for another drink, and Lyle, looking after him, felt a childish impulse to flee while his brother was in the cocktail lounge. He was sickened by the story he'd been told; knowing himself sullied as if he'd been present in Alastor's suite the previous night. As if, merely hearing such obscenities, he was an accomplice of Alastor's. *And perhaps somehow in fact he'd been there, helping to hold the struggling girl down, helping to thrust the gag into her mouth.*

Alastor returned with a fresh drink. He was eyeing Lyle with a look of bemusement as he'd done so often when they were boys, gauging to what extent he'd shocked Lyle or embarrassed him. After their father's death, for instance, when the brothers were eight years old, Lyle had wept for days; Alastor had ridiculed his grief, saying that if you believed in God (and weren't they all supposed to believe in God?) you believed that everything was ordained; if you were a good Christian, you believed that their father was safe and happy in heaven—"So why bawl like a baby?"

Why, indeed?

Alastor was drunker than Lyle had known. He said commandingly, his voice slurred, "Midnight swim. Brother, c'mon!"

Lyle merely laughed uneasily. He was fully dressed; hadn't brought swim trunks; couldn't imagine swimming companionably with his brother, even as adults; he who'd been so tormented by

Alastor when they were children, tugged and pummeled in the water, his head held under until he gasped and sputtered in panic. *Your brother's only playing, Lyle. Don't cry. Alastor, be good!*

Enlivened by drink, Alastor threw off his shirt and announced that he was going swimming, and no one could stop him. Lyle said, "But the pool is closed, Alastor"—as if that would make any difference. Alastor laughed, swaggering to the edge of the pool to dive. Lyle saw with reluctant admiration and a tinge of jealousy that his brother's body, unlike his own, was solid, hard-packed; though there was a loose bunch of flesh at his waist, and his stomach had begun to protrude, his shoulders and thighs were taut with muscle. A pelt of fine glistening hairs covered much of his body and curled across his chest; the nipples of his breasts were purply-dark, distinct as small staring eyes. Alastor's head, held high with exaggerated bravado as he flexed his knees, positioning himself to dive, was an undeniably handsome head; Alastor looked like a film star of another era, a man accustomed to the uncritical adoration of women and the envy of men. The thought flashed through Lyle like a knifeblade *It's my moral obligation to destroy this man, because he is evil; and because there is no one else to destroy him but me.*

With the showy ebullience of a twelve-year-old boy, Alastor dived into the pool at the deep end; a less-than-perfect dive that must have embarrassed him, with Lyle as a witness; Lyle who winced feeling the harsh slap of the water, like a retributive hand, against his own chest and stomach. Like a deranged seal, Alastor surfaced noisily, blowing water out of his nose, snorting; as he began to swim in short, choppy, angry-looking strokes, not nearly so coordinated as Lyle would have expected, Lyle felt his own arm and leg muscles strain in involuntary sympathy. How alone they were, Lyle and his twin brother Alastor! Overhead the marred moon glared like a light in an examination room.

Lyle thought *I could strike him on the head with—what?* One of the deck chairs, a small wrought-iron table caught his eye. And even as this thought struck Lyle, Alastor in the pool began to flail about; began coughing, choking; he must have inhaled water and swallowed it; drunker than he knew, in no condition to be swimming in water over his head. As Lyle stood at the edge of the pool staring he saw his brother begin to sink. And there was no one near! No witness save Lyle himself! Inside the inn, at a distance of perhaps one hundred feet, there was a murmur and buzz of voices, laughter, music; every hotel window facing the open courtyard and the pool area was veiled by a drape or a blind; most of the windows were probably shut tight, and the room air conditioners on. No one would hear Alastor cry for help even if Alastor could cry for help. Excited, clenching his fists, Lyle ran to the other side of the pool to more closely observe his brother, now a helpless, thrashing body sunk beneath the surface of the water like a weighted sack. A trail of bubbles lifted from his distorted mouth; his dyed hair too lifted, like seaweed. How silent was Alastor's deathly struggle, and how lurid the bright aqua water with its theatrical lights from beneath. Lyle was panting like a dog, crouched at the edge of the pool, muttering, "Die! Drown! Damn your soul to hell! You don't deserve to live!"

The next moment, Lyle had kicked off his shoes, torn his shirt off over his head, and dived into the water to save Alastor. With no time to think, he grabbed at the struggling man, overpowered him, hauled him to the surface; he managed to get Alastor's head in a hammerlock and swim with him into the shallow end of the pool; managed to lift him, a near-dead weight, a dense body streaming water, onto the tile. Alastor thrashed about like a beached seal, gasping for breath; he vomited, coughed, and choked, spitting up water and clots of food. Lyle crouched over him, panting, as Alastor rolled onto his back, his hair in absurd strings about his face and his face now bloated and puffy, no longer a handsome face, as if in fact he'd drowned. His breath was erratic, heaving. His eyes rolled in his head. Yet he saw Lyle, and must have recognized him. "Oh, God, Lyle, w-what happened?" he managed to say.

"You were drunk, drowning. I pulled you out."

Lyle spoke bitterly. He too was streaming water; his clothes were soaked; he felt like a fool, a dupe. Never, never would he comprehend what he'd done. Alastor, deathly pale, weak and stricken still with the terror of death, not hearing the tone of Lyle's voice or seeing the expression of impotent fury on Lyle's face, reached out with childlike pleading to clutch at Lyle's hand.

"Brother, thank you!"

THE WORLD IS A beautiful place if you have the eyes to see it and the ears to hear it.

Was this so? Could it be so? Lyle would have to live as if it were, for his brother Alastor could not be killed. Evidently. Or in any case, Lyle was not the man to kill him.

A WEEK AFTER HE'D saved Alastor from drowning, on a radiantly sunny July morning when Lyle was seated disconsolately at his workbench, a dozen rejected drawings for "William Wilson" scattered and crumpled before him, the telephone rang and it was Alastor announcing that he'd decided to move after all to Aunt Alida's house—"She insists. Poor woman, she's frightened of 'ghosts'—needs a man's presence in that enormous house. Brother, will you help me move? I have only a few things." Alastor's voice was buoyant and easy; the voice of a man perfectly at peace with himself. Lyle seemed to understand that his brother had forgotten about the near-drowning. His pride would not allow him to recall it, nor would Lyle ever bring up the subject. Lyle drew breath to say sharply, "No! Move yourself, damn you," but instead he said, "Oh, I suppose so. When?" Alastor said, "Within the hour, if possible. And, by the way, I have a surprise for you—it's for both of us, actually. A memento from our late beloved Uncle Gardner." Lyle was too demoralized to ask what the memento was.

When he arrived at the Black River Inn, there was Alastor proudly awaiting him at the front entrance, drawing a good deal of admiring attention. A tanned, good-looking, youthful man with a beaming smile, in a pale pinstriped seersucker suit, collarless white shirt, and straw hat, a dozen or more suitcases and valises on the sidewalk; and, in the drive beneath the canopy, a gleaming-black, chrome-glittering Rolls Royce. Alastor laughed heartily at the look on Lyle's face. "Some memento, eh, Brother? Aunt Alida was so sweet, she told me, 'Your uncle would want both you boys to have it. He loved you so—his favorite nephews.'"

Lyle stared at the Rolls Royce. The elegant car, vintage 1971, was as much a work of art, and culture, as a motor vehicle. Lyle had ridden in it numerous times, in his uncle's company, but he'd never driven it. Nor even fantasized driving it. "How—did it get here? How is this possible?" Lyle stammered. Alastor explained that their aunt's driver had brought the car over that morning and that Lyle should simply leave his car (so ordinary, dull, and plebeian a car—a compact American model Alastor merely glanced at, with a disdainful look) in the parking lot, for the time being. "Unfortunately, I lack a valid driving license in the United States at the present time," Alastor said, "or I would drive myself. But you know how scrupulous I am about obeying the law—technically." He laughed, rubbing his hands briskly together. Still Lyle was staring at the Rolls Royce. How like the hearse that had borne his uncle's body from the funeral home to the church it was; how magnificently black, and the flawless chrome and windows so glittering, polished to perfection. Alastor poked Lyle in the ribs to wake him from his trance and passed to him, with a wink, a silver pocket flask. Pure scotch whiskey at 11:00 A.M. of a weekday morning? Lyle raised his hand to shove the flask aside but instead took it from his brother's fingers, lifted it to his lips, and drank.

And a second time, drank. Flames darted in his throat and mouth, his eyes stung with tears.

"Oh! God."

"Good, eh? Just the cure for your ridiculous anemia, Brother," Alastor said teasingly.

While Alastor settled accounts in the Black River Inn, using their aunt's credit, Lyle and an awed, smiling doorman loaded the trunk and plush rear seat of the Rolls with Alastor's belongings. The sun was vertiginously warm and the scotch whiskey had gone to Lyle's head and he was perspiring inside his clothes, murmuring to himself and laughing. *The world is a beautiful place. Is a beautiful place. A beautiful place.* Among Alastor's belongings were several handsome new garment bags crammed, apparently, with clothing. There were suitcases of unusual heaviness that might have been crammed with—what? Statuary? There were several small canvases (oil paintings?) wrapped hastily in canvas and secured with adhesive tape; there was a heavy sports valise with a broken lock, inside which Lyle discovered, carelessly wrapped in what appeared to be women's silk underwear, loose jewelry of all kinds—gold chains, strings of pearls jumbled together, a silver pendant with a sparkling red ruby, bracelets and earrings and a single brass candlestick holder and even a woman's high-heeled slipper, stained (bloodstained?) white satin with a carved mother-of-pearl ornament. Lyle stared, breathless. What a treasure trove! Once, he would have been morbidly suspicious of his brother, suspecting him of theft—and worse. Now he merely smiled, and shrugged.

By the time Lyle and the doorman had loaded the Rolls, Alastor emerged from the inn, slipping on a pair of dark glasses. By chance—it must have been chance—a striking blond woman was walking with him, smiling, chatting, clearly quite impressed by him—a beautiful woman of about forty with a lynx face, a bold red mouth, and diamond earrings, who paused to scribble something (telephone number? address?) on a card and slip it into a pocket of Alastor's seersucker coat.

Exuberantly, Alastor cried, "Brother, let's go! Across the river and to Aunt Alida's—to our destiny."

Like a man in a dream Lyle took his place behind the wheel of the Rolls; Alastor climbed in beside him. Lyle's heart was beating painfully, with an almost erotic excitement. Neither brother troubled to fasten his seat belt; Lyle, who'd perhaps never once driven any vehicle without fastening his seat belt first, seemed not to think of doing so now as if, simply by sliding into this magnificent car, he'd entered a dimension in which old, tedious rules no longer applied. Lyle was grateful for Alastor passing him the silver flask, for he needed a spurt of strength and courage. He drank thirstily, in small choking swallows: how the whiskey burned, warmly glowed, going down! Lyle switched on the ignition, startled at how readily, how quietly, the engine turned over. Yes, this was magic. He was driving his uncle Gardner King's Rolls Royce is if it were his own; as he turned out of the hotel drive, he saw the driver of an incoming vehicle staring at the car, and at him, with frank envy.

And now on the road. In brilliant sunshine, and not much traffic. The Rolls resembled a small, perfect yacht; a yacht moving without evident exertion along a smooth, swiftly running stream. What a thrill, to be entrusted with this remarkable car; what sensuous delight in the sight, touch, smell of the Rolls! Why had he, Lyle King, been a puritan all of his life? What a blind, smug fool to be living in a world of luxury items and taking no interest in them; as if there were virtue in asceticism; in mere ignorance. Driving the Rolls on the highway in the direction of the High Street Bridge, where they would cross the Black River into the northern, affluent area of Contracoeur in which their aunt lived, Lyle felt intoxicated as one singled out for a special destiny. He wanted to shout out the car window *Look! Look, at me! This is the first morning of the first day of my new life.*

Not once since Alastor's call that morning had Lyle thought of—what? What had it been? The death-cup mushroom, what was its Latin name? At last, to Lyle's relief, he'd forgotten.

Alastor sipped from the pocket flask as he reminisced, tenderly, of the old Contracoeur world of their childhood. That world, that had seemed so stable, so permanent, was rapidly passing now, vanishing into a newer America. Soon, all of the older generation of Kings would be deceased. "Remember when we were boys, Lyle? What happy times we had? I admit, I was a bit of a bastard, sometimes—I apologize. Truly. It's just that I resented you, you know. My twin brother." His voice was caressing yet lightly ironic.

"Resented me? Why?" Lyle laughed, the possibility seemed so far-fetched.

"Because you were born on my birthday, of course. Obviously, I was cheated of presents."

Driving the daunting, unfamiliar car, that seemed to him higher built than he'd recalled, Lyle was sitting stiffly forward, gripping the elegant mahogany steering wheel and squinting through the windshield as if he were having difficulty seeing. The car's powerful engine vibrated almost imperceptibly, like the coursing of his own heated blood. Laughing, though slightly anxious, he said, "But, Alastor, you wouldn't have wished me not to have been born, would you? For the sake of some presents?"

An awkward silence ensued. Alastor was contemplating how to reply when the accident occurred.

Approaching the steep ramp of the High Street Bridge, Lyle seemed for a moment to lose the focus of his vision, and jammed down hard on the brake pedal; except it wasn't the brake pedal but the accelerator. A diesel truck crossing the bridge, belching smoke, seemed then to emerge out of nowhere as out of a tunnel. Lyle hadn't seen the truck until, with terrifying speed, the Rolls careened up the ramp and into the truck's oncoming grille. There was a sound of brakes, shouts, a scream, and as truck and car collided, a sickening wrenching of metal and a shattering of glass. Together the vehicles tumbled from the ramp, through a low guardrail, and onto an embankment; there was an explosion, flames; the last thing Lyle knew, he and his shrieking brother were being flung forward into a fiery-black oblivion.

THOUGH BADLY INJURED, THE driver of the diesel truck managed to crawl free of the flaming wreckage; the occupants of the Rolls Royce were trapped inside their smashed vehicle, and may have been killed on impact. After the fire was extinguished, emergency medical workers would discover in the wreckage the charred remains of two Caucasian males of approximately the same height and age; so badly mangled, crushed, burned, they were never to be precisely identified. As if the bodies had been flung together from a great height, or at a great speed, they seemed to be but a single body, hideously conjoined. It was known that the remains were those of the King brothers, Alastor and Lyle, fraternal twins who would have been thirty-eight years old on the following Sunday. But which body was which, whose charred organs, bones, blood had belonged to which brother, no forensic specialist would ever determine.

Cream of Mushroom Soup

¼ cup butter (divided use)
1 small onion, finely chopped
8 oz. fresh mushrooms, sliced
Two 14.5-oz. cans chicken stock (or 4 cups home-
    made)
2 Tbsp. flour or cornstarch
¾ tsp. salt (or to taste)
1 cup cream
¼ cup white wine or 2 Tbsp. light sherry
Fresh chives, finely chopped, to garnish (optional)

MELT TWO TABLESPOONS butter in large skillet. Add onion, sauté until clear and soft. Add mushrooms and sauté for about two minutes, until mushrooms are brown and limp. Add chicken stock and simmer on medium heat for 15 minutes, stirring occasionally. While the stock is simmering, melt remaining butter in a large saucepan. Slowly add flour or cornstarch, stirring constantly, and cook until thick and bubbly to make a roux. Add salt. Add chicken stock very slowly, stirring constantly, until liquid is smoothly incorporated into the mixture. Add cream slowly, stirring constantly. Add white wine or sherry, stir. Serve soup warm, topped with fresh chives.

Poison Peach

Gillian Linscott

". . . care must be taken not to bruise any part of the shoot; the wounds made by the knife heal quickly, but a bruise often proves incurable."
                    —*The Gardener's Monthly Volume*: "The Peach."
        George W. Johnson and R. Errington. October 1847.

J anuary was the time for pruning. In the peach house the journeyman gardeners untied the branches from their wires on the whitewashed wall and spread them out as delicately as spiders spinning webs. The fruit-house foreman stepped among them with his bone-handled knife, trimming off the dead wood that had carried last year's fruit, choosing the shoots for this year's. Behind him an apprentice moved like an altar boy with a small basket, picking up every piece of branch as it fell. Few words were said, or needed to be said.

In the eighty years since the peach houses had been built by the grandfather of the present owner, this same ritual had gone on, winter after winter. Victoria ruled an empire and died, apprentices took root and grew into head gardeners, the nineteenth century turned the corner into the twentieth, and always, just after the turn of the year, with the solstice past but the days not yet perceptibly lengthening, the trees were pruned in the peach house at Briarley.

From the door between the peach house and the grape house, Henry Valance watched as his father and his grandfather had watched before him, all of them decent, careful men, accepting their role of guarding, cautiously improving, passing on to sons. What was different this January was that Henry's wife, Edwina, stood beside him, staring out through the sloping glass at the brassicas and bare soil of the kitchen garden. In the five years they'd been married, Edwina hadn't taken a great interest in the garden, being more concerned with the house and the duties of a hostess—although not yet of a mother. She didn't seem very interested now, but in the last few months had accepted her husband's timid suggestions on how to spend her time as if they were commands, following him dutifully but without the animation that had once sparked in her every word or movement. Her hair under the turban hat was still as glossy as the shoulder of a chestnut horse, her tall figure graceful in the long astrakhan coat she wore because it was cold, even inside the glass houses. But her hands, smoothly gloved in silver-gray kid, were clasped tightly together and her face was as blank as the winter sky.

HER HUSBAND MOVED CLOSER to her so that the men working on the peaches couldn't hear them.

"I've had a letter from Stephen."

Over the past few months they'd fallen into the habit of talking about the things that mattered in almost public places, with the servants not far away. It limited the scope for damage. She moved her head a little, still looking out at the vegetable garden, as if the stiff rows of brussels sprouts might creep away if not watched.

"It seems he's written a book."

"What kind of book?"

"A novel."

"Why would he do that?"

Her voice had always been low. Now it was scarcely alive.

"He says he needs to make a career for himself." She said nothing. He glanced at her face, then away at the peach pruning. "I've written offering to pay him. I've told him I'll double whatever he's expecting to make from it, if he'll agree not to publish."

"He won't accept."

She said it with flat certainty. They stood for a while, then he gave her his arm and they walked away through the glass galleries of the grape house and the empty melon house scrubbed clean for winter, their feet echoing on the iron gratings. In the peach house, the foreman watched as two journeymen used strips of cloth to tie to the wall, fan-shaped, the tree he'd pruned back. He signaled them to stop, stepped forward with his pruning knife, hesitated over a fruiting spur, and then, without cutting, nodded to them to carry on. The shape was right after all and the shoot should live to carry its peach. Behind the fruit houses men were cleaning and riddling the great boiler that fed hot water into the pipes under the floor gratings. Soon, when the pruning was finished and the stopcock turned to start the artificial indoor spring, the sap would begin to rise up the narrow trunks, along the spread branches, and into that spur, along with the rest. For a day or two longer the peach trees could rest.

BY APRIL THE PEACH house was warm and full of pink blossoms, although the air outside hadn't lost the edge of winter. Amongst the petals, the gardeners fought their campaign against small pests that might threaten the setting of the fruit. An apprentice with a brass syringe walked the aisles between the trees, spraying the leaves with tobacco water to control the aphids. A journeyman with a paintbrush worked a mixture of sulfur and soft soap into every joint and crevice to kill off the eggs of red spiders and kept an eye on the apprentice at the same time.

"Careful with that bloody thing. You nearly knocked that spur clean off."

In fact, the apprentice's momentary carelessness had scarcely dislodged a petal, and the journeyman's attention was not wholly on the killing of spider eggs and aphids. Things were happening that even the apprentices knew about and the waves that had started in the family rooms of the house had spread out through the upper staff down to the kitchens, out through the scullery door to the gardeners who carried up baskets of vegetables every day. A collection had been organized among the journeyman gardeners and a discreet order placed at the bookshop in the nearest town. The groom was to collect the result of it when he went down to the station, along with the other copies ordered by the upstairs staff, the kitchen staff, and the stables. The butler, who had connections in London, was believed to have got his hands on a copy already but wasn't showing anybody. At lunchtime the journeyman gardeners gathered in their bothy behind the wall at the back of the fruit houses, made themselves as comfortable as possible on sacks and buckets, and elected a reader. His attempts to make an orderly start at the beginning of chapter 1 were immediately voted down.

"That's not what all the trouble's about. Start at the business between him and her, and we'll go back to the beginning later."

"If we want to."

Laughter, but muted. They were allowed half an hour in the bothy for their bread and cheese, but what they were doing was no part of their duties and could lead to trouble, and even dismissal for impudence, if discovered. The door had been firmly shut in the noses of the apprentices but was no protection against foreman or head gardener. The reader asked, plaintively, how he was supposed to know where the business was.

"They don't put it in the margins like they do with the Bible."

"I heard it was chapter 10."

The reader rustled pages, scanned silently, then whistled between his teeth.

Several voices told him to get on with it and not keep it to himself.

"It's where she calls him in to give him a piece of her mind because he's been getting too friendly with one of the maids."

"Is that how they put it—too friendly?"

"Oh, get on with it."

Now it had come to it, they were all a little embarrassed. The man trusted with the book read it in a fast mutter so that they had to crane forward to hear him. The lady calls the gentleman into her boudoir. She is stern. She does not usually listen to servants' gossip, but he must realize that the young housemaids are in her care and as employer she has a moral duty to them and to their parents. If the gentleman can assure her that these rumors are baseless then she will take severe action against the people spreading them. A sound outside. The men froze, but it was only two apprentices trying to listen and they were seen off, nursing cuffed ears.

"Go on."

The gentleman cannot give her that assurance. He compliments her instead on her good taste in employing such very attractive housemaids. She is unbelieving at first, then furious. He remains calm then asks her if she is not, perhaps, jealous, She loses control and actually tries to hit him. He grabs her by the wrist and she falls back across the sofa, her furious black eyes gazing up at him. He stands looking down at her, smiling a little inward smile.

"Well, what happens after that?"

"Nothing. It's the end of the chapter."

He turned the book toward them to show the blank half page.

"Well, go on to the next one then."

He turned the page.

"It doesn't go on. Not with that, anyway. It goes back to the husband at his club."

"Well, what does he—"

The bothy door opened suddenly. In the doorway was the square, bowler-hatted figure of the head gardener himself, who could dismiss all of them with a snap of his fingers, quick as pulling an earwig in half.

"What do you men think you're doing? You've been nearly an hour in here."

Then he saw the book and snatched it out of the reader's hand.

"I'm ashamed of you all. You should know where this filth belongs."

With the journeymen trailing shamefaced after him and the apprentices peering from behind the pot shed, he marched across the yard to the barrel that held liquid fertilizer, pats of cow dung seething in rainwater. He nodded to one of the men to remove the lid, tossed the book into it, and waited while it globbed into the viscous depths. Another nod, and the lid went back.

"If I catch anybody in my gardens dirtying his hands with that again, if I catch anybody even mentioning it or looking as if he's thinking about it, he'll be applying for a new post without a character. Now get back to your work, all of you."

Dispiritedly they went, two of them toward the fruit houses.

"Tell you what, though, he got one thing wrong."

"What's that?"

"Her eyes aren't black—they're brown."

They laughed at that but sobered up when they found Hobbes, the fruit foreman, waiting for them, and couldn't meet his eyes.

". . . neither peaches nor nectarines acquire perfection, either in richness or flavor, unless they be exposed to the full influence of the sun during their last swelling."

—*An Encyclopaedia of Gardening*
J. C. Loudon, 1835.

BY LATE JUNE THE peaches were close to perfection. Cosseted and watched over from the time the first green knobs formed behind the blossom, scrutinized and selected until there was just one fruit to every spur, all they waited for now was their final ripening. In case the midsummer sun should be too strong and scorch them through the glass, early every morning Hobbes would stand among the orderly rows of leaves, looking up, then say a few words, quietly as in church, to his assistant. The assistant would operate a wheel to open rows of ventilating panes, inch by inch, until they were at the exact angle to give a gentle circulation of air, and the process would be repeated every few hours as the sun climbed. Once the ventilators were open the peach house was tidied as carefully as a drawing room, every fragment of loam swept off the path, every tree checked for the slightest sign of insect damage, because by this time the season was at its height and the peaches were out in society. Briarley was famous for its fruit houses, and a stroll between breakfast and lunch past the swelling grapes, under green and golden melons hanging among their heavy leaves, was almost a social duty for guests. In fact, there'd not been many guests at Briarley that season, but the fruit houses were always kept ready for them, as they always had been. Today Henry Valance came on his morning visit alone. Alone, that is, apart from the train that followed at a respectful distance, first the head gardener, then Hobbes the foreman, then the two journeymen with particular responsibility for fruit.

Occasionally, he'd pause, palpate and sniff a melon, finger a grape. When this happened the head gardener would catch up with him and a few serious words would be exchanged. The procession made its slow way to the peach house and stopped between the rows of trees.

"Nearly ripe then, are they?"

A nod from the head gardener signaled to Hobbes to come closer. It was a sign of the respect he had for Hobbes as a master in his own field that he allowed the foreman to answer the employer's question directly. Hobbes stood there in his dark suit and hat in the green-dappled shade, gardening apron discarded for this formal visit, watch chain gleaming.

"The Hale's Early should be ripe by next Monday, sir, and the Early Beatrice not long after. Then the Rivers and the Mignonnes are coming on very nicely."

"Excellent. We'll look forward to that."

Henry's father and grandfather had stood in the same place and used much the same words. The difference was in the flatness of his voice that said everything he might have looked forward to was already in the past. Then, with an effort:

"You'll make sure we have plenty ripe for the second weekend in July, won't you? We have a lot of people coming, house quite full."

The two journeymen exchanged glances. It would be the first house party since it happened. The staff had been speculating that there wouldn't be any this year.

"We'll make sure, sir."

His question had not been necessary. It was the work of them all to see that there were ripe peaches all through the summer, whether there were guests to eat them or not. Still, there was no resentment that he'd asked it. He was, on the whole, liked by the gardening staff—and pitied.

"Nets . . . are perfectly useless in keeping off wasps and other insects, as they will alight on the outside and, folding their wings, pass through those of the smallest meshes."

—*An Encyclopaedia of Gardening*

THERE WAS THE SOUND of footsteps coming through the glass galleries from the direction of the house, too light and quick for a gardener's, too confident for a maid's. Hurrying steps. The man went tense.

"Henry."

His wife's voice with scarcely controlled panic in it. He met her in the doorway.

"A letter for you. It's just arrived."

She held it out to him. At first he'd looked simply puzzled. Dozens of letters arrived every day, and it was no part of Edwina's duties to chase him round the estate with them. Then he saw the handwriting. Took it from her and read.

"He's heard about the house party. He's inviting himself."

"No!"

The gardeners were in an impossible position. To eavesdrop on employers' private conversation was unthinkable. On the other hand, it was equally unthinkable to melt away through the door into the kitchen garden, since they'd been given no sign to go. They made a great business of scrutinizing the peach leaves, which they already knew were perfect.

"Write to him. Tell him he can't come."

"I can't do that. He is my brother, after all."

"He can't come if you don't let him."

"He'd come in any case, and what could I do then? Call the police to bring a van and drag him away? Tell the men to throw him in the lake, with the house full of visitors? It would mean that people would go on talking about it for years."

"That's what he wants."

"Yes, and the only way we can prevent him from getting it is facing it out, letting him come here."

"No."

But it was a different word now, numb and dispirited. He put out a hand to her, but she moved away and her slow steps back toward the house seemed to go on for a long time.

THE HEAD GARDENER SAID kindly: "The figs are doing very nicely, sir. Would you care to look at them?"

"Figs. Yes, certainly, figs."

As they were moving off, the head gardener stopped suddenly.

"Excuse me, sir, but look at that."

He pointed at one of the peaches. An intake of breath from the gardeners.

"A wasp. Early for them, isn't it?"

The insect was sitting, wings folded, on the down of a peach. Hobbes stepped forward, mortified.

"I'm sorry, sir."

One of the journeymen ventured, unasked: "The lad was saying he'd seen a nest of them at the back of the pot shed."

The head gardener glared at him.

"Well, why didn't you do something about it? See to it, will you, Hobbes." His instruction to the foreman was less brusque than it might have been, considering the shame of the wasp's invasion. Hobbes nodded and the party moved on.

"A gentle squeeze at the point where the stalk joins the fruit will soon determine whether it be ripe enough."
—*The Gardener's Monthly Volume.* "The Peach"

JULY, AND THE SCENT of ripe peaches hung on the air like a benignant gas. Every morning the foreman would pick the ripest and lay them gently onto a padded tray held by the apprentice, ready for the house party at lunch. All but a few. It was a custom at Briarley that some of the best fruit should be left on the trees for the look of it when the visitors walked round, glowing through green like the eyes of a sleepy animal. But the party hadn't reached the peach house yet, lingering on the way to admire the ripe purple clusters on the grapevine. Murmurs of admiration and white-gloved hands reaching out, almost touching but stopping just before making contact, unwilling to smudge a bloom on the fruit like the first morning in Eden. But one pair of hands, male and gloveless, kept moving, breached the invisible barrier, picked a grape. A little shiver, half shocked, half pleased, ran through the party. Relishing the attention, the picker put the grape in his mouth. His lips were full, for a man's, and as he munched he let the underside of his lower lip show, slick and smooth.

"Is it good?"

The woman guest who asked the question had dark piled hair and wide eyes. She smelt of carnations, and her dressmaker had been perhaps a shade too attentive in cutting her dress so exactly to the curve of her full breasts. Instead of answering in words, the man picked another grape and held it a half inch from her lips. Her eyes flickered sideways to where her host and hostess were standing, then she opened her lips in a little round pout just wide enough to let the grape in, dipped her head, and took it from his fingers like a bird.

"Yes, very good."

A silence, then from the side of the group, their host's voice: "Shall we go and look at the peaches?" But he couldn't stop himself adding: "If you've had enough, Stephen."

"Oh, enough for now, don't you think?"

The party moved on in silence.

"It is common practice to lay littery material beneath the trees to save from bruising the fruit which falls, and sometimes those which fall are extremely luscious."

—*The Gardener's Monthly Volume: "The Peach"*

ON SUNDAY MORNING THE day started later. Only a few guests came to the fruit houses between breakfast and lunch. Host and hostess went to church as usual. A few of the house party went with them, but it was a hot day and most preferred to stroll by the lake or in the lime avenue. After lunch, with the weekend drawing to its close, the strolls became lazier and polite slow-motion competition developed for places on rustic benches under the trees. Afterward, nobody knew who had proposed another tour of the fruit houses. It might have been a suggestion from the host—certainly not one from Edwina, because she had a headache and had retired to the drawing room after lunch, with an old friend in attendance. The suggestion might have come from Stephen, as he'd been the focus of the younger set in the part for most of the weekend. A stranger might have taken him for the host instead of his brother, although his behavior toward Henry and Edwina had been entirely correct throughout. He'd let it be known that he enjoyed being back at the old place so much that he thought he might stay for the week. Whoever suggested it, the proposal collected a little following and about a dozen people joined the tour, including the woman who smelt of carnations. Some of the older guests felt that for a woman whose husband was working abroad she'd been a little too eager for Stephen's company over the weekend. Late at night, among some of the men lingering in the billiard room after too much port, there'd been jokes about Stephen doing research for his next novel, only not in Henry's hearing. Only one more night to go and she'd be leaving on Monday morning. The men in the billiard room had even been placing bets.

SUN, FOOD, AND WINE swept away the touch of solemnity that usually went with the fruit house tour. Stephen was triumphant, unstoppable. He ranged along the fruit-smelling avenues like a big child, greedy to see, touch, taste. The younger element in the party had caught his mood. The woman who'd eaten the grape had competition now as they all fingered, dared, ate. A melon was parted from its stem and thrown from hand to hand until golden flesh and pips splattered on the red-tiled floor. Henry watched, impassive. Farther back, not part of the party, the head gardener watched, equally impassive. He stayed ten yards behind them as they laughed and pattered through the grape house, leaving the bunches blemished with bare stems and torn tongues of purple skin.

WHEN THEY GOT TO the green-dappled shade of the peach house, Hobbes was at work there, and it looked for a moment as if he were going to commit the sackable sin of rudeness to his employer's guests in defense of his cherished peaches. He actually stood for a moment in the path of the party until the head gardener caught his eye, and he stood reluctantly aside. This little stutter of opposition seemed to increase Stephen's pleasure. He challenged one of the women to eat a peach without picking it. She moved her lips toward a red and golden fruit that trembled on its stem with ripeness. Hobbes started toward her, perhaps intending to hand it to her with proper respect for lady and peach. The head gardener looked alarmed at the impending breach of etiquette and might have stopped him, but at the last minute the woman drew her face away from the peach, giggling.

"You can't. It would fall. Nobody could."

"Yes, you can. All you need is a soft mouth. Look."

In silence, with them all watching him, Stephen advanced on the largest peach in sight. It hung conveniently on a level with his chin, standing out from the leaves on its spur. He bent a little at the knees and turned his head back so that the fruit was almost resting on his mouth. His teeth closed on it. Juice ran down his chin, dribbled onto the lapel of his white jacket. A little gasp from one of the women, hushed at once. The peach shifted a little, rotating on its stem, but still didn't fall. His neck muscles tensed and he took another, larger bite. Then there was a little cracking sound and he was falling, falling backward with the peach clenched in his jaws. This time the gasps weren't hushed but turned to screams. Because of the way he'd been standing, the back of his head hit the iron grating with a crash that sent every leaf in the place quivering. Then voices.

"Choking. For heaven's sake, get it out of his mouth."

"Air. Get some air in here."

"Get the ladies out."

"Isn't there a doctor?"

Henry was at the front of the group, along with the head gardener and the foreman. They turned Stephen over, wrenched the peach from his teeth. From the look of his contorted face it seemed likely that he'd choked on the fruit before his head hit the grating, but since he couldn't be dead twice over, that didn't seem to matter. Henry got to his feet coughing, staggered backward against the wall, then was violently sick.

"Get him outside. Get him into the air."

"Everybody, outside."

"A piece of cloth fastened to a stick, soaked in a saturated solution of cyanide of potassium, is immediate death to all wasps within or returning to the nest."

—*The Fruit Grower's Guide*
John Wright. 1892.

IT TOOK SOME TIME for the doctor to reach Briarley, and while they waited for him doubts were already setting in, mainly because of the smell. Several of the men besides Henry were coughing as they came out of the peach house, and a woman collapsed and had to be revived. When Henry and most of the party were on their way back to the house, the head gardener, Hobbes, and a few of the male guests covered the body with clean sacks. Then they shut the door firmly and waited on the other side of it in the grape house, the guests smoking, the two gardeners standing a little apart from them. When the doctor arrived at last they followed him in but stood at a safe distance although most of the smell had worn off by then. He peeled back the sack from the face.

"What did you say happened?"

"He was eating a peach and he choked."

He examined the body briefly, then told them they should cover it up again but not do anything else until the police arrived. He was a comparatively new doctor in the village, Scottish and conscientious. The old doctor might have managed things more tactfully.

THE VERDICT WAS NEVER in doubt: Stephen Valance had deserved what he got. If you seduce your brother's maidservant, then his wife, and—and for a profit—tell the world about it, you can't complain if your peach turns out to contain cyanide. Even those who had quite liked Stephen and watched his career with interest felt a kind of satisfaction that there was a limit after all, although there had been some sporting interest in seeing how far and fast a man could go before he hit it. Stephen had chosen to ride his course that way and by the natural law of things he was heading for a fall. No more needed to be done and very little said, except in private when the servants were out of the room.

THAT, AT ANY RATE, was the immediate verdict of society. The verdict of the country's system of justice was another matter and at first seemed likely to throw up more difficulties. That Stephen had died by cyanide poisoning and that the carrier of the poison had been the peach was never seriously in doubt. The hopeful theory of suicide in a moment of well-earned remorse was abandoned instantly by anybody who had the slightest acquaintance with Stephen or his reputation. Which left . . .

"Well, I suppose if it comes right down to it, it has to be murder."

The discussion was going on very late at night in the billiard room. Not that anybody had actually tried to play billiards, which would have been totally inappropriate on a Sunday, with the hostess prostrate upstairs, the host at her bedside, and the host's younger brother in the mortuary. The men who had influence had naturally congregated there—not the giddier sort who had followed Stephen but the more sober ones who had known Henry's father, who sat as magistrates and chose men to stand for Parliament.

"You can't blame him. I'd have done the same thing myself."

"Not very nice, poison."

"Quick, though. Practically painless, I'd have thought. Anyway, what can you do? I mean, you can't challenge a man to a duel in this day and age."

"I suppose the next thing's the inquest. They can bring in murder by person or persons unknown . . ."

"Or they can even name the person they think did it, if they think there's enough evidence."

Silence, while they considered it.

"Of course, there's always accidental death."

"There was a glass vial of cyanide in that peach. How does that get in there accidentally?"

"They use cyanide to kill wasp nests in glass houses. At any rate, my gardener does, and I don't suppose Henry's are any different. You get a lot of wasps after peaches."

More silence, finally broken by the oldest man amongst them.

"I think I'd better have a word with his head gardener in the morning."

"Only professional men can use it safely."
—*The Fruit Grower's Guide*

HOBBES STOOD IN A shaft of sunlight in the coroner's court, dark-suited in his Sunday best, new bowler hat on the table in front of him, and gave his evidence. By that point the court had already heard from the brother of the deceased, from two doctors, from a police officer, and from the head gardener, who clearly remembered telling the fruit foreman to do something about the wasps in the peach house. The coroner had been respectful to the brother's grief, businesslike with the doctors and the head gardener. To the fruit foreman his tone was colder, and Hobbes answered respectfully. He had been in Mr. Valance's employment for twenty years. Yes, he had used potassium cyanide on a wasp's nest; they kept a drum of it for the purpose in the pot shed. No, he did not know how it had come to contaminate a peach. Yes, he had been warned to be careful with it and knew that it was poisonous. If any of it had somehow come onto the fruit, from his gardening gloves or some tool, then that was very great carelessness. Could he think of any other way that the cyanide might have come onto the peach? No sir, he could think of no other way. There was a rustling and sighing in the court, like heavy leaves in a breeze. The coroner paused to let the answer sink in, then turned to another aspect of the matter. The doctor who had certified death and the police officer had noticed small fragments of glass in the peach.

"It was put on the floor, sir, by one of the gentlemen, when they took it out of his mouth."

"You're suggesting that was when the glass became attached to it?"

"Yes, sir."

"Are you accustomed to leaving glass fragments lying on the floor of your employer's fruit houses?"

"Not accustomed, no sir."

"And yet glass fragments were there?"

"Yes, sir."

"Should we assume that this was another example of carelessness?"

It took Hobbes some time to realize that an answer was required. When he did he said "Yes, sir" again in the same respectful voice. At last he was permitted to stand down. The head gardener—who would hardly allow a petal to settle on the floor of the glass houses for more than a second or two—looked straight ahead throughout the foreman's evidence, face expressionless. In his summing-up the coroner had some hard things to say about carelessness by men who should know better. Hobbes took them all, head bent over the bowler hat that rested on his knees. The verdict was accidental death.

OUTSIDE THE COURT, ONE of Henry Valance's friends went up to Hobbes as he stood on his own among departing cars and carriages.

"Well, Hobbes, always best to own up to things."

"Yes, sir."

"I gather Mr. Valance is letting you keep your position."

"Yes, sir."

"A very generous man, Mr. Valance. I'm sure you're grateful."

"Yes, sir."

And although he'd been one of the chief movers in arranging things so satisfactorily, the friend really did feel that Henry was acting generously. The coroner's rebuke had wrapped itself around Hobbes and his deplorable carelessness with cyanide was now a fact of history, officially recorded.

"Anyway, I don't suppose it will happen again."

"No, sir."

Both men took their hats off as the Valances' motor car drove slowly past, with Edwina sitting very upright beside her husband, pale under her heavy veil.

By October the peach season was almost over. A few Prince of Wales and Lady Palmerstons still gleamed among the leaves, but there hadn't been much call for peaches from the household, or many tours of the glass houses. Henry made his dutiful rounds from time to time and exchanged a few words with Hobbes about indifferent things, but that was all. One morning when there was already a frosty feel to the air outside, the head gardener came in while Hobbes was retying labels on wires. There was nobody else within hearing.

"All well, Hobbes?"

"Yes."

The head gardener looked out through the panes to where the men were digging over a potato plot.

"Some people are saying you got left with the dirty end of the stick. Still, you said your piece very well and you didn't lose by it."

No response. The head gardener's attention seemed to be all on the men outside, then he said: "Funny, the things you find when you dig."

The wire under Hobbes's hand suddenly tightened and began vibrating. He kept his head down.

"What are you thinking of?"

"End of July, I was in the herb garden and I noticed this little freshly dug patch right at the back of the angelica. Now, I hadn't told anyone to dig there. I went and got a spade from the shed and turned it over to have a look. What do you suppose I found there?"

Hobbes's grip on the wire was now so tight that the tree branch it supported was quivering too.

"Peaches, that's what I found. I backed off quickly, I can tell you. There's a paving slab over them now, in case of any more accidents."

The tree branch was near to breaking when Hobbes released his grip of the wire and straightened up. The head gardener took his arm, not roughly.

"Of course, you couldn't be sure he'd take that one peach so you'd have to do a few of them. And you were going to stop the lady when she looked like biting into one of them instead."

Hobbes nodded. "How did you know?"

"That it was you? Well, Mr. Valance might have done the one of them, but to do more than one like that you needed to be neat-fingered and you needed to have time. Nobody has more time in

the peach house than you do, and nobody's got neater fingers.
I've watched you grafting fruit trees."

Hobbes took the compliment with another nod.

"And another thing I know—I know why you did it, and I don't
blame you."

The foreman looked at the head gardener's face, then the
words surged out of him.

"They were all talking about what he'd done to her, to
Mrs. Valance, as if my girl didn't matter. All this about the book,
everybody reading about what he'd done to the housemaid, to my
girl, and the lady calling him in to talk about it and then he . . .
When I knew he had the face to come back here, laughing at us, I
started thinking—supposing I did so and so. And, well, I did it."

The head gardener's hand stayed on his arm. Anybody looking
into the peach house from outside would have seen nothing but
two men enjoying the autumn sunshine on their employer's time.

"How is your girl?"

"Gone to her aunt in Wales. They've put it about that the
father's a sailor lost at sea. She won't be coming back here."

Silence. They were two men used to patience, but Hobbes gave
way first.

"Let's be going and get it over with."

"It *is* over. You've been careless. The coroner said so."

"But—"

"Be quiet. I'm thinking."

"I thought you'd already done the thinking."

"That space over there. Do you think another couple of Rivers
or maybe Lord Napiers instead?"

Hobbes stared first at the blank white wall, then at him.

"You're asking me that—now?"

"Why not? None too soon for you to start planning for next
year, is it?"

"For next year . . ."

It took him some time to understand. When he did he said
thank you and turned back to the fruit trees. A spur, fruitless now,
snagged at his cuff, but he freed it with a hand still shaking a little
and went on with his work.

Perfect Peach Pie

CRUST FOR A 9-inch double-crust pie, either homemade or purchased (for the time-crunched cook, Pillsbury refrigerated piecrusts are excellent). In peach season, 2 pounds fresh peaches, blanched, peeled, pitted, and sliced. Out of season, two 12-oz. bags frozen unsweetened peach slices (prepared fruit should be about 4 to 5 cups)

> **2 Tbsp. lemon juice**
> **¾ cup sugar**
> **2 Tbsp. flour**
> **½ tsp. cinnamon**
> **½ tsp. salt**
> **3 Tbsp. chilled butter, cut into small cubes**
> **1 Tbsp. sugar**
> **½ tsp. cinnamon**

SET AN EMPTY cookie sheet on the bottom rack of your oven. This will save the oven bottom if the pie boils over and will keep the bottom crust from burning. Preheat oven to 400 degrees F.

PLACE PEACH SLICES in a large mixing bowl. Add lemon juice, toss to coat. In a smaller bowl, mix together ¾ cup sugar, flour, ½ teaspoon cinnamon, and salt. Pour dry mixture over peach slices, toss to coat. Put coated peach slices into bottom crust. Arrange them in a nice rounded pile. Sprinkle butter cubes on top of filling. Cover with top crust, and crimp and prick the top crust. Sprinkle one tablespoon sugar and ¼ teaspoon cinnamon over the top crust. Set the pie in the preheated oven on the middle rack. Bake the pie at 400 degrees F. for 15 minutes. Without opening the oven, reduce the heat to 300 degrees F. Bake about 50 more minutes, until crust is browned and flaky, and the filling is thick and bubbly. Serve warm or cold.

Of Course You Know That Chocolate Is a Vegetable

Barbara D'Amato

Of course you know that chocolate is a vegetable," I said.
"Lovely! That means I can eat all I want," Ivor Sutcliffe
burbled, reaching his fork toward the flourless double-
fudge cake.

Eat more *than you want, you great tub of guts,* I thought. The tub-of-
guts part was rather unfair of me; I could stand to lose a pound or two
myself. What I said aloud was, "Of course it's a vegetable. Has to be.
It's not animal or mineral, surely. It grows on a tree—a large bush,
actually, I suppose. It's as much a vegetable as pecans or tomatoes.
And aren't we told to have several servings of vegetables every day?"

We were seated at a round table covered with a crisp white cloth
at Just Desserts, a scrumptious eatery in central Manhattan that
specializes in chocolate desserts, handmade chocolate candy, and
excellent coffees. Just Desserts was willing to serve salads and a few
select entrees to keep themselves honest, but if you could eat
chocolate, why would you order anything else?

"I must say, Ms. Grenfield, it's very handsome of you to invite me
after my review of your last book," Ivor said, dropping a capsule on

his tongue, which then took the medication inside, his mouth closing like a file drawer. He washed the medication down with coffee.

I said, "No hard feelings. Reviewing books is your job."

"I may have been just a bit harsh."

Harsh? Like scrubbing your eyeball with a wire brush is harsh?
I said, "Well, of course an author's feelings get hurt for a day or
two. But we can't hold it against the critic. Not only is it his job,
but, to be frank, it's in our best interests as writers to keep on
pleasant terms. There are always future reviews to come, aren't
there?"

"Very true."

Ivor's review had begun:

> In *Snuffed,* the victim, Rufus Crown, is dispatched with a gaseous
> fire extinguisher designed for use on fires in rooms with com-
> puter equipment and other such unpleasant hardware, though
> neither the reader nor the fictional detectives know this at the
> start when his dead but mysteriously unblemished body is found.
> The reader is treated to long efforts—quite incompatible with
> character development—on the part of the lab and medical
> examiner to establish what killed him.

"That's right; give away the ending," I had snarled to myself
when I read this.

Snuffed had been universally praised by the critics and I
thought I was a shoo-in for an award until the Ivor Sutcliffe review
came out.

At the awards banquet, where I was not a nominee, fortune had
seated me next to Sutcliffe. Just when the sorbet arrived, and I had
happily pictured him, facedown, drowning in strawberry goo, he
began to wheeze. My mind had quickly changed to picturing him
suffocating. But he had popped a capsule in his greedy pink mouth
and after a few minutes he quit wheezing.

Since one has to be moderately cordial at these events, or at
least appear to be, I asked courteously, "Do you have a cold?"

"Asthma," he said.

"Sorry to hear that. My son had asthma. Seems to have out-
grown it."

"Lucky for him. What did he take for it?"

I said, "Theophylline."

"Ah, yes. That's what my doctor gave me. So proud of his big words, just like you. Standard treatment, I believe. I have been taking it for several weeks." He said this as if conferring a great benediction upon the drug.

I was about to relate an anecdote about the time my husband, son, and I were on a camping trip, without the theophylline. We'd left it at home, since it had been many months since Teddy's last attack, and we weren't expecting trouble. Then Teddy had developed a wheeze. As evening came on, it got worse. And worse. There's nothing scarier than hearing your child struggle for breath. We were two hours away from civilization, and my husband and I panicked. We packed Teddy into the car, ready to race for the nearest country hospital; then I had called Teddy's doctor on my cell phone.

"Do you have any coffee?" he said. Well, of course we had. Who went camping without coffee?

"Give him some. Caffeine is chemically similar to theophylline. Then drive to the hospital."

All this I was about to tell Sutcliffe when something stopped me. It was not more than the faint aroma of an idea, a distant stirring of excitement. So—theophylline and caffeine were similar. Hmm.

Teddy had been warned to take his theophylline as directed, but never to overdose.

Then and there I invited Sutcliffe out to a "good will" snack the following week. He accepted. Well, my will was going to feel the better for it.

Sutcliffe's review had gone on:

> I deplore the substitution of technical detail for real plotting. One could amplify the question "Who cares who killed Roger Ackroyd?" by asking, "Who cares how Roger Ackroyd was killed?" No one cares what crime labs and pathologists really do.

"Agatha Christie cared," I had whispered as I read it, trying not to gnash my teeth. "And Dorothy Sayers and just about everybody then and just about everybody now on any best-seller list—Crichton, Clark, Cornwell, Grisham." In the first place, readers like to learn things. Second, technology is real and it's *now*. Third, it's exacting. Keeps a writer honest. You can't fake technical detail; it has to be right. You can't use the untraceable exotic poison these days. It has to be something people know about or even use every day. Or know they *should* know about. Then it's tantalizing.

But Ivor Sutcliffe wasn't scientific-minded. A know-it-all who knew nothing. A gross, hideous, undisciplined individual with bad table manners. I had once seen him, at a banquet, eat his own dinner and the dinners of three other guests who had failed to show.

So after the banquet I went home to my shelf of reference books, looking for something I almost knew about, or knew I should know about—just like a reader of fiction. I keep a large shelf of reference books. Having them at hand saves time, effort, and parking fees.

What would an overdose of theophylline do to a human being?

I turned first to the *Physician's Desk Reference.* This is a huge volume, twenty-eight hundred pages of medications, with their manufacturers, their brand names, their appearance shown in color pictures, their uses, their dosages, their effects, their adverse effects, and—overdosage.

An overdosage of theophylline was serious business. It said, "Contact a poison-control center." That was good. One didn't issue that kind of warning for minor side effects. I read on. One had to monitor the dose carefully. Apparently, the useful dose and dangerous dose were not far apart. I read on. Overdosage could produce restlessness, circulatory failure, convulsion, collapse, and coma. Or death.

Theophylline in normal use, it said, relaxed the smooth muscles of the bronchial airways and pulmonary blood vessels, acting as a bronchodilator and smooth-muscle relaxant. That was why it helped an asthma attack.

And then the punch line: "Theophylline should not be administered concurrently with other xanthines." And what were xanthines?

I turned to my unabridged dictionary. Why, xanthines included theophylline, caffeine (given Teddy's experience, this was no surprise), and the active ingredient of chocolate, theobromine. Aha!

Hmmm. Being similar, they would have an additive effect, wouldn't they? Synergistic, maybe? I turned to the *Merck Manual,* also huge, a twenty-seven-hundred-page volume, a bible of illnesses, their causes and treatments. In its section on poisons, caffeine poisoning was in the same sentence with theophylline poisoning. Among the symptoms of both were restlessness, circulatory-system collapse, and convulsions.

A medical text told me that 50 percent of theophylline convulsions result in death.

Isn't this fun? Research is so rewarding.

Well, I knew that theophylline was potentially deadly. Now, what about the caffeine?

My book on coffees from around the world told me that a cup of coffee, depending on how it's brewed, contains 70 to 150 milligrams of caffeine. Drip coffee is strongest. Well, what about the extra-thick specialty coffees at Just Desserts? Could I assume they might have 200 milligrams?

What the book didn't tell me was how much caffeine would kill.

I pulled out the *Merck Index,* a different publication from the *Merck Manual,* the *Index* being an encyclopedia of chemicals. Here I found that if you had a hundred mice and gave them all 137 milligrams of caffeine per kilogram of body weight, half would die. This was cheerfully called LD 50, or lethal dose for 50 percent. My dictionary said a kilogram is 2.2 pounds. So if a man reacted like a mouse (although to me Ivor was more like a rat), that would work out to 13.7 grams of caffeine per 220 pounds. Of course, getting 13 grams of caffeine into the 220-plus-pound Ivor was not going to happen, but then caffeine was not the only xanthine that was going to be going into Ivor.

A volume for the crime writer on poisons told me that one gram of caffeine could cause toxic symptoms, but it didn't tell me how much would kill. Well, if one gram was toxic, two grams ought to cause real trouble.

Now, what about theobromine, the xanthine in chocolate? The *Merck Index* informed me that theobromine, "the principal alkaloid of the cacao bean," was a smooth-muscle relaxant, diuretic, cardiac stimulant, and vasodilator. My, my! Sounded a lot like theophylline and caffeine. It said chocolate also contained some caffeine. That couldn't hurt.

How could I find out how much chocolate was dangerous? Certainly, people eat large amounts with no ill effects. But at some point, with the other two xanthines . . ?

I turned on my computer, thinking to get on the Net and ask how much theobromine there was in an average piece of dark bittersweet chocolate. But I held my hand back. This could be dangerous. I could be traced. Somewhere I had heard of people receiving catalogues from companies that sold items they had queried the Net about. Like travel brochures when they'd asked about tourist destinations or smoked salmon when they'd asked about where to get good fish. Webmasters could learn everything about you. I certainly didn't want anybody to know I was the person making queries about theobromine in chocolate. Could I ask anonymously? No. How could I be sure the query couldn't be traced?

Then I remembered the library at the local law school. If you looked like you belonged there, you could query databases at no charge, although there was a time limit. And there was a per-page charge if you wanted to print out what you found, but why should I want it in black and white? Now, if they just didn't ask for names. I grabbed my coat and ran out the door.

Two hours later I left the library highly pleased. I'd asked two databases to find articles that used "chocolate" within ten words of "theobromine" and got all kinds of good stuff. Chocolate, it seemed, frequently killed dogs. Dogs and cats didn't excrete the theobromine as well as humans. The poisoned animals would suffer rapid heart rates, muscle tremors, rapid respiration, convulsions, and even death.

Dark chocolate, I learned, contains ten times as much theobromine as milk chocolate. Bitter cooking chocolate contains four hundred milligrams in an ounce! And—oh, yes!—the amount in a moderate amount of chocolate is about the same as the amount of caffeine in a moderate amount of coffee.

In humans, theobromine is a heart stimulant, smooth-muscle relaxant, and dilates coronary arteries. So what if we eliminate it faster than Rover would? It still had to have an additive effect with the other two.

All three of my drugs caused low blood pressure, irregular heart rhythm, sweating, convulsions, and, potentially, cardiac arrest. What's not to like? Ha! *Take that!* I thought. Hoist with your own petard.

The *PDR* had said that oral theophylline acted almost as swiftly as intravenous theophylline. But I knew I would need time to get a lot of coffee and chocolate into Ivor. He'd better not feel sick right away and just stop eating. Well, the desserts themselves should slow the absorption.

At this point in my research I phoned Sutcliffe and suggested we hold our rendezvous at Just Desserts.

When the day came and we sat down like two friends at Just Desserts, I encouraged Ivor to try the dense "flourless chocolate cake" first.

"It's excellent," I said. "Like a huge slice of dark chocolate. I'll have a piece myself." The waiter brought the cake promptly and filled our coffee cups with mocha-java.

We tasted, nodded in appreciation, ate in companionable silence for a few minutes. Then I suggested he try the Turkish coffee, just for comparison, along with an almond-chocolate confection, for the blend of flavors. He agreed readily.

Now, since he was eating at my expense, he found the need to be borderline pleasant. "You know, I did say in the review that I've liked much of your past work."

Actually, no, you clot. His review of my first book, graven on my heart, said, "This novel is obviously the work of a beginner." And his review of my second book, also etched somewhere in my guts, said, "Ms. Grenfield has not yet got her sea legs for the mystery genre." The most recent review had, in fact, damned with faint praise: *This effort,* Snuffed, *is not up to her former standard.*

"Thank you," I said mildly.

"I suppose I should be frightened of eating with you, Ms. Grenfield. I've read so many novels where the central character, feeling wronged, invites his nemesis to dinner and poisons him."

"Well, Ivor, I was actually aware you might worry about that. I had thought of inviting you to my home. But it occurred to me that you might find it intimidating to be at the mercy of my cooking. Hence—Just Desserts."

Disarmed and possibly a little abashed, Sutcliffe said, "Well—you could hardly have found a more competent kitchen than this."

I nodded agreeably as Ivor finished his third cup of coffee—one regular, two Turkish so far—and pushed his cup within reach of the waiter. The calculator in my brain said that was six hundred milligrams of caffeine now, give or take, and another two hundred on the way as the hot brew filled the cup.

Let's see. Add the capsule of theophylline just half an hour ago when he arrived. Didn't dare ask him the dosage, but it had to be either the standard 300 or the 400-milligram dose. Plus he had taken his morning dose, I supposed.

Ha! Well, me fine beauty, we'll just see how inartistic technology is. And we'll give you every chance to save yourself. Just a little paying of attention, Ivor. A morsel of humility.

Lord! That man could eat! *Schokoladenpudding*, which was a German chocolate-coffee-almond pudding served warm with whipped cream. *Rigo Jancsi* squares, dense Viennese cake that was more like frosting, which the waiter explained was named after a Gypsy violinist. And a slice of Sacher torte, a Viennese chocolate cake glazed with dark chocolate. *Shokoladno mindalnyi tort*, a Russian chocolate-almond torte made with rum, cinnamon, and, of all things, potato. Then just to be fair to the United States, he agreed to a simple fudge brownie with chocolate frosting, à la mode, as he put it, with coffee ice cream on the side. I had cherry strudel.

With each dessert he tried a different coffee. Ethiopian *sidamo*, Kenyan *brune*, a Ugandan dark roast. In my coffee reading I had noted that the *robusta* coffees have more than twice as much caffeine as the *arabica* species, and smiled indulgently as he drank some.

Two grams of caffeine by now, minimum. Clever of me to suggest he switch to the demitasses of various strong coffees. Just as strong and less filling. He could drink more of them.

Plus two to maybe four or five grams of theobromine from the chocolate.

"What are you working on these days, Ms. Grenfield?" Ivor said in his plummy voice. Could I detect a slight restless, hyper edge in his tone now?

"A mystery with historical elements," I answered, and almost giddy with delight, lobbed him a clue. "About Balzac, and the discovery of some unknown, unpublished, very valuable manuscript." Balzac, of course, an avid, indeed compulsive coffee drinker, died of caffeine poisoning. Let's see if this self-important arbiter, this poseur, was any better at literature than he was at science.

"Oh, interesting," he drawled in boredom. "You know, I *could* just manage another dessert."

"Of course!" I caroled in glee. "How about a chocolate mousse? And another Turkish coffee to go with it." The waiter appeared, beaming. "And I'll have a vanilla cream horn."

"This is very pleasant," he said, chuckling as be plunged a spoon into his new dessert and gobbled the glob. "Actually, I'm rather surprised."

"Why?"

He became distracted, watching as another waiter passed with a silver tray of various chocolate candies on a lace doily—the house specialty, glossy dark bittersweet chocolates with various fillings, handmade in their own kitchens. I raised a finger, said, "One of each for the gentleman," and pointed at Ivor. The waiter tenderly lifted the little beauties from the tray with silver tongs and placed them on a white china dish near Ivor's hand.

"Why surprised?" I reminded him.

He said, "I'd always thought of you as lacking in appreciation of the finer things."

"Oh, surely not."

"All those bloody and explicit murders, or poisons with their effects lovingly detailed. Hardly the work of a subtle mind."

"*Au contraire*, Ivor. I am very subtle."

"Well, I suppose it does require a certain amount of delicacy to keep the knowledge of whodunit from a reader until the end." He fidgeted as if nervous.

"Yes. Until the end."

Ivor began to cram the candies into his chunky, piggy cheeks. The pitch of his voice was rising, not louder but more shrill. Satiated, he pushed the dish away.

"Come on. Have another chocolate."

"I shouldn't."

"Oh, you only live once."

"Well, maybe just a taste or two." His fat hand, as he reached for the morsels, showed a faint tremor. He shifted his bulk. Restlessness.

Time for another clue, Ivor. Last chance, Ivor.

"Did you know that the botanical name for the cacao tree is Greek and that it translates to 'food of the gods'? *Theobroma*," I said, trying not to chortle. Last chance, Ivor, you who know so much.

"Nope. Didn't know that. Rather apt, actually," he said without interest. He didn't care about this detail, either, didn't care how close to theophylline it sounded. His flushed face was a bit sweaty, seen in the subdued restaurant light. In fact, he looked as if he had been lightly buttered. He cleared his throat, took another swallow of coffee, and said, "Odd. I'm feeling a little short of breath."

"Your asthma?"

"Could be."

"That's too bad. Well, you know how to deal with it, anyhow."

"Ah—whew." Puff. "Yes."

"Well, shouldn't you do something? Don't you think you should take one of your pills?"

"I already did when I got here. The doc says don't exceed two per day."

"But that's a preventative dose, isn't it? If you have an attack coming on—?"

"Probably right." He groaned as he leaned his heavy bulk sideways to claw in his pocket for the pill vial. Wheezing harder, he drew it out. He tipped a capsule into his hand.

"Here," I said helpfully, and I pushed his cup of *robusta* coffee toward him. The waiter topped it up again.

"Hmmmp," was all the thanks he managed as he popped the pill and swallowed the java.

For another minute or so, Ivor sat still, catching his breath or whatever. His face was flushed, and he moved his head back and forth as if confused.

"Are you feeling all right, Ivor?"

"I may have eaten just a tad too much."

"Well, let's just sit awhile, then."

"Yes. Yes, we'll do that."

Ivor sat, but his hands twitched, then his fingers started to pleat and smooth the tablecloth. He took in deep breaths and let them out. His face was pinker still, almost the color of rare roast beef.

"I'm not sure about that tie you're wearing, Ivor," I said. "It's not up to your former standard."

Ivor goggled at me, but his bulging eyes were unfocused. He blew his cheeks out, let them sag back, then blew them out again. His head began to bob up and down in a kind of tremor.

"And that suit," I said. "A fine, well-bred wool. Quite incompatible with your character."

No answer. I said, "But perhaps that's a bit harsh."

He leaned forward, holding onto the table. Very slowly he drifted sideways, then faster and faster, until he fell off his chair, pulling the snowy white tablecloth, silver forks and spoons, a china cup, the remains of brownie à la mode, and the dregs of *robusta* coffee with him.

"Oh, my goodness!" I shouted.

The waiter came running. I fanned Ivor with a menu. "Stand back. Give him air," I said. The waiter stepped back obediently.

The manager came running also. He tried the Heimlich maneuver. No luck. Several diners stood up and gawked. Ivor was making bubbling, gasping sounds.

"That's not a fainting fit," the manager said, obviously a more analytical chap than the waiter.

"I guess not," I said.

The manager wrung his hands. "What should we do? What should we do?"

"Maybe it's an asthma attack. He carries some pills for it. They're in his pocket, I think."

The manager felt in Ivor's pocket. He read the label. A genuine doctor's prescription in a real pharmacy container. "Yes. Here they are. At least they can't hurt."

"This coffee is cool enough," I said. "Wash it down with this." He did, even though Ivor choked a lot and showed no awareness of what was going on.

"Call the paramedics," the manager told the waiter, who bustled away. The manager slapped Ivor's cheek. I envied the man this role, but had to stand by. Ivor produced no reaction to being slapped, now well and truly in a coma.

The paramedics arrived with reasonable promptness. The one with the box of medical supplies knelt by Ivor to take vital signs. The second said, "What can you tell us about this? What happened?"

I shook my head. "I can't imagine. He was just eating a perfectly delicious chocolate dessert."

Ivor gasped, but did not rouse. His cheeks were taking on a purplish hue, the color of a fine old burgundy.

I thought of the last line of Ivor Sutcliffe's review:

In Snuffed, *the only thing deader than Rufus Crown is Ms. Grenfield's plot.*

French Silk Pie

Prepared crust for single-crust 9-inch pie, either homemade or purchased

3 oz. dark chocolate, broken into small pieces

2 sticks butter, slightly softened

1 cup sugar

1 cup egg substitute (4 whole eggs can be used, but since the filling isn't cooked, be absolutely sure they are Pasteurized)

2 cups sweetened whipped cream, or 1 small container whipped topping, thawed

1 oz. dark chocolate, shredded into curls to garnish (optional)

PREHEAT OVEN TO 450 degrees F. Prick and weight piecrust (pie weights work best, but lining the piecrust with heavy-duty foil and filling the foil with either dried beans or coins will do the job, too.) Bake piecrust for 9 to 11 minutes, until brown and flaky. Remove from oven and remove pie weights as soon as they are cool enough to handle. Set piecrust aside to cool completely (usually about an hour from the time it was removed from the oven).

MELT CHOCOLATE OVER very low heat in a small saucepan. Set aside to cool. (Chocolate can also be melted in a microwave with 10-second bursts at medium power, stirring after each burst until the chocolate is smooth and fully melted, if preferred, but this is riskier. Be very careful not to burn or scorch the chocolate. It takes longer on the stove, but the risk of destroying the chocolate is much lower than in the microwave.)

CREAM (MIX UNTIL light and fluffy, and sugar grains can't be felt) butter and sugar in mixing bowl. Add melted chocolate and blend. Add vanilla, blend. Slowly add egg substitute, beating until mixture is light, smooth, and fluffy. Pour mixture into cooked piecrust. Refrigerate for at least three hours.

TO SERVE, TOP with whipped cream or whipped topping and garnish with chocolate curls.

Poison à la Carte

Rex Stout

I slanted my eyes down to meet her big brown ones, which were slanted up. "No," I said, "I'm neither a producer nor an agent. My name's Archie Goodwin, and I'm here because I'm a friend of the cook. My reason for wanting it is purely personal."

"I know," she said, "it's my dimples. Men often swoon."

I shook my head. "It's your earrings. They remind me of a girl I once loved in vain. Perhaps if I get to know you well enough—who can tell?"

"Not me," she declared. "Let me alone. I'm nervous, and I don't want to spill the soup. The name is Nora Jaret, without an *H*, and the number is Stanhope five, six-six-two-one. The earrings were a present from Sir Laurence Olivier. I was sitting on his knee."

I wrote the number down in my notebook, thanked her, and looked around. Most of the collection of attractive young females were gathered in an alcove between two cupboards, but one was over by a table watching Felix stir something in a bowl. Her profile was fine and her hair was the color of corn silk just before it starts to turn. I crossed to her, and when she turned her head I spoke. "Good evening, Miss—Miss?"

"Annis," she said. "Carol Annis."

I wrote it down, and told her my name. "I am not blunt by nature," I said, "but you're busy, or soon will be, and there isn't time to talk up to it. I was standing watching you and all of a sudden I had an impulse to ask you for your phone number, and

277

I'm no good at fighting impulses. Now that you're closed up it's even stronger, and I guess we'll have to humor it."

But I may be giving a wrong impression. Actually, I had no special hankering that Tuesday evening for new telephone numbers; I was doing it for Fritz. But that could give a wrong impression too, so I'll have to explain.

One day in February, Lewis Hewitt, the millionaire orchid fancier for whom Nero Wolfe had once handled a tough problem, had told Wolfe that the Ten for Aristology wanted Fritz Brenner to cook their annual dinner, to be given as usual on April 1, Brillat-Savarin's birthday. When Wolfe said he had never heard of the Ten for Aristology, Hewitt explained that it was a group of ten men pursuing the ideal of perfection in food and drink, and he was one of them. Wolfe had swiveled to the dictionary on its stand at a corner of his desk, and after consulting it had declared that "aristology" meant the science of dining, and therefore the Ten were witlings, since dining was not a science but an art. After a long argument Hewitt had admitted he was licked and had agreed that the name should be changed, and Wolfe had given him permission to ask Fritz to cook the dinner.

In fact, Wolfe was pleased, though of course he wouldn't say so. It took a big slice of his income as a private detective to pay Fritz Brenner, chef and housekeeper in the old brownstone on West 35th Street—about the same as the slice that came to me as his assistant detective and man Friday, Saturday, Sunday, Monday, Tuesday, Wednesday, and Thursday—not to mention what it took to supply the kitchen with the raw materials of Fritz's productions. Since I am also the bookkeeper, I can certify that for the year 1957 the kitchen and Fritz cost only slightly less than the plant rooms on the roof bulging with orchids.

So when Hewitt made it clear that the Ten, though they might be dubs at picking names, were true and trustworthy gourmets, that the dinner would be at the home of Benjamin Schriver, the shipping magnate, who wrote a letter to *The Times* every year on September 1 denouncing the use of horseradish on oysters, and that the cook would have a free hand on the menu and the Ten would furnish whatever he desired, Wolfe pushed a button to summon Fritz. There was a little hitch when Fritz refused to commit himself until he had seen the Schriver kitchen, but Hewitt settled that by escorting him out front to his Heron town car and driving him down to Eleventh Street to inspect the kitchen.

That's where I was that Tuesday evening, April 1, collecting phone numbers—in the kitchen of the four-story Schriver house on Eleventh Street west of Fifth Avenue. Wolfe and I had been invited by Schriver, and though Wolfe dislikes eating with strangers and thinks that more than six at table spoils a meal, he knew Fritz's feelings would be hurt if he didn't go; and besides, if he stayed home who would cook his dinner? Even so, he would probably have balked if he had learned of one detail which Fritz and I knew about but had carefully kept from him: that the table was to be served by twelve young women, one for each guest.

When Hewitt had told me that, I had protested that I wouldn't be responsible for Wolfe's conduct when the orgy got under way, that he would certainly stamp out of the house when the girls started to squeal. Good Lord, Hewitt said, nothing like that; that wasn't the idea at all. It was merely that the Ten had gone to ancient Greece not only for their name but also for other precedents. Hebe, the goddess of youth, had been cupbearer to the gods, so it was the custom of the Ten for Aristology to be waited on by maidens in appropriate dress. When I asked where they got the maidens he said through a theatrical agency, and added that at that time of year there were always hundreds of young actresses out of a job glad to grab at a chance to make fifty bucks, with a good meal thrown in, by spending an evening carrying food, one plate at a time. Originally, they had hired experienced waitresses from an agency, but they had tripped on their stolas.

Wolfe and I had arrived at seven on the dot, and after we had met our host and the rest of the Ten, and had sampled oysters and our choice of five white wines, I had made my way to the kitchen to see how Fritz was making out. He was tasting from a pot on the range, with no more sign of fluster than if he had been at home getting dinner for Wolfe and me. Felix and Zoltan, from Rusterman's, were there to help, so I didn't ask if I was needed.

And there were the Hebes, cupbearers to the gods, twelve of them, in their stolas, deep rich purple, flowing garments to their ankles. Very nice. It gave me an idea. Fritz likes to pretend that he has reason to believe that no damsel is safe within a mile of me, which doesn't make sense since you can't tell much about them a mile off, and I thought it would do him good to see me operate at

close quarters. Also, it was a challenge and an interesting sociolog-
ical experiment. The first two had been a cinch: one named Fern
Faber, so she said, a tall blonde with a wide lazy mouth, and Nora
Jaret with the big brown eyes and dimples. Now I was after this
Carol Annis with hair like corn silk.

"I have no sense of humor," she said and turned back to watch
Felix.

I stuck. "That's a different kind of humor and an impulse like
mine isn't funny. It hurts. Maybe I can guess it. Is it Hebe one, oh-
oh-oh-oh?"

No reply.

"Apparently not. Plato two, three-four-five-six?"

She said, without turning her head, "It's listed. Gorham eight,
three-two-one-seven." Her head jerked to me. "Please?" It jerked
back again.

It rather sounded as if she meant please go away, not please
ring her as soon as possible, but I wrote it down anyway, for the
record, and moved off. The rest of them were still grouped in the
alcove, and I crossed over. The deep purple of the stolas was a
good contrast for their pretty young faces topped by nine different
colors and styles of hairdos. As I came up the chatter stopped and
the faces turned to me.

"At ease," I told them. "I have no official standing. I am merely
one of the guests, invited because I'm a friend of the cook, and I
have a personal problem. I would prefer to discuss it with each of
you separately and privately, but since there isn't time for that—"

"I know who you are," one declared. "You're a detective and
you work for Nero Wolfe. You're Archie Goodwin."

She was a redhead with milky skin. "I don't deny it," I told her,
"but I'm not here professionally. I don't ask if I've met you because
if I had I wouldn't have forgot—"

"You haven't met me. I've seen you and I've seen your picture.
You like yourself. Don't you?"

"Certainly. I string along with the majority. We'll take a vote.
How many of you like yourselves? Raise your hands."

A hand went up with a bare arm shooting out of the purple
folds, then two more, then the rest of them, including the redhead.

"Okay," I said, "that's settled. Unanimous. My problem is that I
decided to look you over and ask the most absolutely, irresistibly

beautiful and fascinating one of the bunch for her phone number, and I'm stalled. You are all it. In beauty and fascination you are all far beyond the wildest dreams of any poet, and I'm not a poet. So obviously I'm in a fix. How can I possibly pick on one of you, any one, when—"

"Nuts." It was the redhead. "Me, of course. Peggy Choate. Argyle two, three-three-four-eight. Don't call before noon."

"That's not fair," a throaty voice objected. It came from one who looked a little too old for Hebe, and just a shade too plump. It went on, "Do I call you Archie?"

"Sure, that's my name."

"All right, Archie, have your eyes examined." She lifted an arm, baring it, to touch the shoulder of one beside her. "We admit we're all beautiful, but we're not in the same class as Helen Iacono. Look at her!"

I was doing so, and I must say that the throaty voice had a point. Helen Iacono, with deep dark eyes, dark velvet skin, and wavy, silky hair darker than either skin or eyes, was unquestionably rare and special. Her lips were parted enough to show the gleam of white teeth, but she wasn't laughing. She wasn't reacting at all, which was remarkable for an actress.

"It may be," I conceded, "that I am so dazzled by the collective radiance that I am blind to the glory of any single star. Perhaps I'm a poet after all, I sound like one. My feeling that I must have the phone numbers of *all* of you is certainly no reflection on Helen Iacono. I admit that that will not completely solve the problem, for tomorrow I must face the question which one to call first. If I feel as I do right now I would have to dial all the numbers simultaneously, and that's impossible. I hope to heaven it doesn't end in a stalemate. What if I can never decide which one to call first? What if it drives me mad? Or what if I gradually sink—"

I turned to see who was tugging at my sleeve. It was Benjamin Schriver, the host, with a grin on his ruddy round face. He said, "I hate to interrupt your speech, but perhaps you can finish it later. We're ready to sit. Will you join us?"

THE DINING ROOM, ON the same floor as the kitchen, three feet or so below street level, would have been too gloomy for my taste if most of the darkwood paneling hadn't been covered with pictures of geese, pheasants, fish, fruit, vegetables, and other assorted edible objects; and also it helped that the tablecloth was white as snow, the wineglasses, seven of them at each place, glistened in the soft light from above, and the polished silver shone. In the center was a low gilt bowl, or maybe gold, two feet long, filled with clusters of Phalaenopsis Aphrodite, donated by Wolfe, cut by him that afternoon from some of his most treasured plants.

As he sat he was scowling at them, but the scowl was not for the orchids; it was for the chair, which, though a little fancy, was perfectly okay for you or me but not for his seventh of a ton. His fundament lapped over at both sides. He erased the scowl when Schriver, at the end of the table, complimented him on the flowers, and Hewitt, across from him, said he had never seen Phalaenopsis better grown, and the others joined in the chorus, all but the aristologist who sat between Wolfe and me. He was a Wall Street character and a well-known theatrical angel named Vincent Pyle, and was living up to his reputation as an original by wearing a dinner jacket, with tie to match, which looked black until you had the light at a certain slant and then you saw that it was green. He eyed the orchids with his head cocked and his mouth puckered, and said, "I don't care for flowers with spots and streaks. They're messy."

I thought, but didn't say, *Okay, drop dead.* If I had known that that was what he was going to do in about three hours I might not even have thought it. He got a rise, not from Wolfe and me, or Schriver or Hewitt, but from three others who thought flowers with spots and streaks were wonderful: Adrian Dart, the actor who had turned down an offer of a million a week, more or less, from Hollywood; Emil Kreis, chairman of the board of Codex Press, book publishers; and Harvey M. Leacraft, corporation lawyer.

Actually, cupbearers was what the Hebes were not. The wines, beginning with the Montrachet with the first course, were poured by Felix; but the girls delivered the food, with different routines for different items. The first course, put on individual plates in the kitchen, with each girl bringing in a plate for her aristologist, was small blinis sprinkled with chopped chives, piled with caviar, and topped with sour cream—the point, as far as Fritz was concerned, being that he had made the blinis, starting on them at eleven that morning, and also the sour cream, starting on that Sunday evening. Fritz's sour cream is very special, but Vincent Pyle had to get in a crack. After he had downed all his blinis he remarked loud enough to carry around the table, "A new idea, putting sand in. Clever. Good for chickens, since they need grit."

The man on my left, Emil Kreis, the publisher, muttered at my ear, "Ignore him. He backed three flops this season."

The girls, who had been coached by Fritz and Felix that afternoon, handled the green turtle soup without a splash. When they had brought in the soup plates Felix brought the bowl, and each girl ladled from it as Felix held it by the plate. I asked Pyle cordially, "Any sand?" but he said no, it was delicious, and cleaned it up.

I was relieved when I saw that the girls wouldn't dish the fish— flounders poached in dry white wine, with a mussel-and-mushroom sauce that was one of Fritz's specialties. Felix did the dishing at a side table, and the girls merely carried. With the first taste of the sauce there were murmurs of appreciation, and Adrian Dart, the actor, across from Wolfe, sang out, "Superb!" They were making various noises of satisfaction, and Leacraft, the lawyer, was asking Wolfe if Fritz would be willing to give him the recipe, when Pyle, on my right, made a face and dropped his fork on his plate with a clatter.

I thought he was putting on an act, and still thought so when his head drooped and I heard him gnash his teeth, but then his shoulders sagged and he clapped a hand to his mouth, and that seemed to be overdoing it. Two or three of them said something, and he pushed his chair back, got to his feet, said, "You must excuse me, I'm sorry," and headed for the door to the hall. Schriver arose and followed him out. The others exchanged words and glances.

Hewitt said, "A damn shame, but I'm going to finish this," and used his fork. Someone asked if Pyle had a bad heart, and someone else said no. They all resumed with the flounder and the conversation, but the spirit wasn't the same.

When, at a signal from Felix, the maidens started removing the plates, Lewis Hewitt got up and left the room, came back in a couple of minutes, sat, and raised his voice. "Vincent is in considerable pain. There is nothing we can do, and Ben wishes us to proceed. He will rejoin us when—when he can."

"What is it?" someone asked.

Hewitt said the doctor didn't know. Zoltan entered bearing an enormous covered platter, and the Hebes gathered at the side table, and Felix lifted the cover and began serving the roast pheasant, which had been larded with strips of pork soaked for twenty hours in Tokay, and then—but no. What's the use? The annual dinner of the Ten for Aristology was a flop. Since for years I have been eating three meals a day cooked by Fritz Brenner I would like to show my appreciation by getting in print some idea of what he can do in the way of victuals, but it won't do here. Sure, the pheasant was good enough for gods if there had been any around, and so was the suckling pig, and the salad, with a dressing which Fritz calls Devil's Rain, and the chestnut croquettes, and the cheese—only the one kind, made in New Jersey by a man named Bill Thompson under Fritz's supervision; and they were all eaten, more or less. But Hewitt left the room three more times and the last time was gone a good ten minutes, and Schriver didn't rejoin the party at all, and while the salad was being served Emil Kreis went out and didn't come back.

When, as coffee and brandy were being poured and cigars and cigarettes passed, Hewitt left his chair for the fifth time, Nero Wolfe got up and followed him out. I lit a cigar just to be doing something, and tried to be sociable by giving an ear to a story Adrian Dart was telling, but by the time I finished my coffee I was getting fidgety. By the glower that had been deepening on Wolfe's face for the past hour I knew he was boiling, and when he's like that, especially away from home, there's no telling about him. He might even have had the idea of aiming the glower at Vincent Pyle for ruining Fritz's meal. So I put what was left of the cigar in a tray, arose, and headed for the door, and was halfway to it when here he came, still glowering.

"Come with me," he snapped, and kept going.

The way to the kitchen from the dining room was through a pantry, twenty feet long, with counters and shelves and cupboards on both sides. Wolfe marched through with me behind. In the kitchen the twelve maidens were scattered around on chairs and stools at tables and counters, eating. A woman was busy at a sink. Zoltan was busy at a refrigerator. Fritz, who was pouring a glass of wine, presumably for himself, turned as Wolfe entered and put the bottle down.

Wolfe went to him, stood, and spoke. "Fritz. I offer my apologies. I permitted Mr. Hewitt to cajole you. I should have known better. I beg your pardon."

Fritz gestured with his free hand, the wineglass steady in the other. "But it is not to pardon, only to regret. The man got sick, that's a pity, only not from my cooking. I assure you."

"You don't need to. Not from your cooking as it left you, but as it reached him. I repeat that I am culpable, but I won't dwell on that now; it can wait. There is an aspect that is exigent." Wolfe turned. "Archie. Are those women all here?"

I had to cover more than half a circle to count them, scattered as they were. "Yes, sir, all present. Twelve."

"Collect them. They can stand"—he pointed to the alcove—"over there. And bring Felix."

It was hard to believe. They were eating; and for him to interrupt a man, or even a woman, at a meal, was unheard of. Not even me. Only in an extreme emergency had he ever asked me to quit food before I was through. Boiling was no name for it. Without even bothering to raise a brow, I turned and called out, "I'm sorry, ladies, but if Mr. Wolfe says it's urgent that settles it. Over there, please? All of you."

Then I went through the pantry corridor, pushed the two-way door, caught Felix's eye, and wiggled a beckoning finger at him, and he came. By the time we got to the kitchen, the girls had left the chairs and stools and were gathering at the alcove, but not with enthusiasm. There were mutterings, and some dirty looks for me as I approached with Felix. Wolfe came with Zoltan and stood, tight-lipped, surveying them.

"I remind you," he said, "that the first course you brought to the table was caviar on blinis topped with sour cream. The portion served to Mr. Vincent Pyle, and eaten by him, contained arsenic. Mr. Pyle is in bed upstairs, attended by three doctors, and will probably die within an hour. I am speaking—"

He stopped to glare at them. They were reacting, or acting, no matter which. There were gasps and exclamations, and one of them clutched her throat, and another, baring her arms, clapped her palms to her ears. When the glare had restored order, Wolfe went on, "You will please keep quiet and listen. I am speaking of conclusions formed by me. My conclusion that Mr. Pyle ate arsenic is based on the symptoms—burning throat, faintness, intense burning pain in the stomach, dry mouth, cool skin, vomiting. My conclusion that the arsenic was in the first course is based, first, on the amount of time it takes arsenic to act; second, on the fact that it is highly unlikely it could have been put in the soup or the fish; and third, that Mr. Pyle complained of sand in the cream or caviar. I admit the possibility that one or both of my conclusions will be proven wrong, but I regard it as remote and I am acting on them." His head turned. "Fritz. Tell me about the caviar from the moment it was put on the individual plates. Who did that?"

I had once told Fritz that I could imagine no circumstances in which he would look really unhappy, but now I wouldn't have to try. He was biting his lips, first the lower and then the upper. He began, "I must assure you—"

"I need no assurance from you, Fritz. Who put it on the plates?"

"Zoltan and I did." He pointed. "At that table."

"And left them there? They were taken from that table by the women?"

"Yes, sir."

"Each woman took one plate?"

"Yes, sir. I mean, they were told to. I was at the range."

Zoltan spoke up. "I watched them, Mr. Wolfe. They each took one plate. And believe me, nobody put any arsenic—"

"Please, Zoltan. I add another conclusion: that no one put arsenic in one of the portions and then left to chance which one of the guests would get it. Surely the poisoner intended it to reach a certain one—either Mr. Pyle, or, as an alternative, some other one and it went to Mr. Pyle by mishap. In any case, it was the portion Pyle ate that was poisoned, and whether he got it by design or by mischance is for the moment irrelevant." His eyes were at the girls. "Which one of you took that plate to Mr. Pyle?"

No reply. No sound, no movement.

Wolfe grunted. "Pfui. If you didn't know his name, you do now. The man who left during the fish course and who is now dying. Who served him?"

No reply; and I had to hand it to them that no pair of eyes left Wolfe to fasten on Peggy Choate, the redhead. Mine did. "What the heck," I said. "Speak up, Miss Choate."

"I didn't!" she cried.

"That's silly. Of course you did. Twenty people can swear to it. I looked right at you while you were dishing his soup. And when you brought the fish—"

"But I didn't take him that first thing! He already had some!"

Wolfe took over. "Your name is Choate?"

"Yes." Her chin was up. "Peggy Choate."

"You deny that you served the plate of caviar, the first course, to Mr. Pyle?"

"I certainly do."

"But you were supposed to? You were assigned to him?"

"Yes. I took the plate from the table there and went in with it, and started to him, and then I saw that he had some, and I thought I had made a mistake. We hadn't seen the guests. That man"—she pointed to Felix—"had shown us which chair our guest would sit in, and mine was the second from the right on this side as I went in, but that one had already been served, and I thought someone else had made a mistake or I was mixed up. Anyway, I saw that the man next to him, on his right, hadn't been served, and I gave it to him. That was you. I gave it to you."

"Indeed." Wolfe was frowning at her. "Who was assigned to me?"

That wasn't put on. He actually didn't know. He had never looked at her. He had been irritated that females were serving, and besides, he hates to twist his neck. Of course, I could have told him, but Helen Iacono said, "I was."

"Your name, please?"

"Helen Iacono." She had a rich contralto that went fine with the deep dark eyes and dark velvet skin and wavy silk hair.

"Did you bring me the first course?"

"No. When I went in I saw Peggy serving you, and a man on the left next to the end didn't have any, so I gave it to him."

"Do you know his name?"

"I do," Nora Jaret said. "From the card. He was mine." Her big brown eyes were straight at Wolfe. "His name is Kreis. He had his when I got there. I was going to take it back to the kitchen, but then I thought, someone had stage fright but I haven't, and I gave it to the man at the end."

"Which end?"

"The left end. Mr. Schriver. He came and spoke to us this afternoon."

She was corroborated by Carol Annis, the one with hair like corn silk who had no sense of humor. "That's right," she said. "I saw her. I was going to stop her, but she had already put the plate down, so I went around to the other side of the table with it when I saw that Adrian Dart didn't have any. I didn't mind because it was him."

"You were assigned to Mr. Schriver?"

"Yes. I served him the other courses, until he left."

It was turning into a ring-around-a-rosy, but the squat was bound to come. All Wolfe had to do was get to one who couldn't claim a delivery, and that would tag her. I was rather hoping it wouldn't be the next one, for the girl with the throaty voice had been Adrian Dart's, and she had called me Archie and had given Helen Iacono a nice tribute. Would she claim she had served Dart herself?

No. She answered without being asked. "My name is Lucy Morgan," she said, "and I had Adrian Dart, and Carol got to him before I did. There was only one place that didn't have one, on Dart's left, the next but one, and I took it there. I don't know his name."

I supplied it. "Hewitt. Mr. Lewis Hewitt." A better name for it than ring-around-a-rosy would have been passing-the-buck. I looked at Fern Faber, the tall blonde with a wide lazy mouth who had been my first stop on my phone-number tour. "It's your turn, Miss Faber," I told her. "You had Mr. Hewitt. Yes?"

"I sure did." Her voice was pitched so high it threatened to squeak.

"But you didn't take him his caviar?"

"I sure didn't."

"Then who did you take it to?"

"Nobody."

I looked at Wolfe. His eyes were narrowed at her. "What did you do with it, Miss Faber?"

"I didn't do anything with it. There wasn't any."

"Nonsense. There are twelve of you, and there were twelve at the table, and each got a portion. How can you say there wasn't any?"

"Because there wasn't. I was in the john fixing my hair, and when I came back in she was taking the last one from the table, and when I asked where mine was he said he didn't know, and I went to the dining room and they all had some."

"Who was taking the last one from the table?"

She pointed to Lucy Morgan.

"Whom did you ask where yours was?"

She pointed to Zoltan. "Him."

Wolfe turned. "Zoltan?"

"Yes, sir. I mean, yes, sir, she asked where hers was. I had turned away when the last one was taken. I don't mean I know where she had been, just that she asked me that. I asked Fritz if I should go in and see if they were one short and he said no, Felix was there and would see to it."

Wolfe went back to Fern Faber. "Where is that room where you were fixing your hair?"

She pointed toward the pantry. "In there."

"The door's around the corner," Felix said.

"How long were you in there?"

"My God, I don't know, do you think I timed it? When Archie Goodwin was talking to us, and Mr. Schriver came and said they were going to start, I went pretty soon after that."

Wolfe's head jerked to me. "So that's where you were. I might have known there were young women around. Supposing that Miss Faber went to fix her hair shortly after you left—say three minutes—how long was she at it, if the last plate had been taken from the table when she returned to the kitchen?"

I gave it a thought. "Fifteen to twenty minutes."

He growled at her, "What was wrong with your hair?"

"I didn't say anything was wrong with it." She was getting riled. "Look, Mister, do you want all the details?"

"No." Wolfe surveyed them for a moment, not amiably, took in enough air to fill all his middle—say two bushels—let it out again, turned his back on them, saw the glass of wine Fritz had left on a table, went and picked it up, smelled it, and stood to make noises, and, hearing them, he put the glass down and came back.

"You're in a pickle," he said. "So am I. You heard me apologize to Mr. Brenner and avow my responsibility for his undertaking to cook that meal. When, upstairs, I saw that Mr. Pyle would die, and reached the conclusions I told you of, I felt myself under compulsion to expose the culprit. I am committed. When I came down here I thought it would be a simple matter to learn who had served poisoned food to Mr. Pyle, but I was wrong.

"It's obvious now that I have to deal with one who is not only resourceful and ingenious, but also quick-witted and audacious. While I was closing in on her just now, as I thought, inexorably approaching the point where she would either have to contradict one of you or deny that she had served the first course to anyone, she was fleering at me inwardly, and with reason, for her coup had worked. She had slipped through my fingers, and—"

"But she didn't!" It came from one of them whose name I didn't have. "She said she didn't serve anybody!"

Wolfe shook his head. "No. Not Miss Faber. She is the only one who is eliminated. She says she was absent from this room during the entire period when the plates were being taken from the table and she wouldn't dare to say that if she had in fact been here and taken a plate and carried it in to Mr. Pyle. She would certainly have been seen by some of you."

He shook his head again. "Not her. But it could have been any other one of you. You—I speak now to that one, still to be identified—you must have extraordinary faith in your attendant godling, even allowing for your craft. For you took great risks. You took a plate from the table—not the first probably, but one of the first—and on your way to the dining room you put arsenic in the cream. That wasn't difficult; you might even have done it without stopping if you had the arsenic in a paper spill. You could get rid of the spill later, perhaps in the room which Miss Faber calls a john. You took the plate to Mr. Pyle, came back here immediately, got another plate, took it to the dining room, and gave it to one who had not been served. I am not guessing; it had to be like that. It was a remarkably adroit stratagem, but you can't possibly be impregnable."

He turned to Zoltan. "You say you watched as the plates were taken, and each of them took only one. Did one of them come back and take another?"

Zoltan looked fully as unhappy as Fritz. "I'm thinking, Mr. Wolfe. I can try to think, but I'm afraid it won't help. I didn't look at their faces, and they're all dressed alike. I guess I didn't watch very close."

"Fritz?"

"No, sir. I was at the range."

"Then try this, Zoltan. Who were the first ones to take plates—the first three or four?"

Zoltan slowly shook his head. "I'm afraid it's no good, Mr. Wolfe. I could try to think, but I couldn't be sure." He moved his eyes right to left and back again, at the girls. "I tell you, I wasn't looking at their faces." He extended his hands, palms up. "You will consider, Mr. Wolfe, I was not thinking of poison. I was only seeing that the plates were carried properly. Was I thinking which one has got arsenic? No."

"I took the first plate," a girl blurted—another whose name I didn't know. "I took it in and gave it to the man in my chair, the one at the left corner at the other side of the table, and I stayed there. I never left the dining room."

"Your name, please?"

"Marjorie Quinn."

"Thank you. Now, the second plate. Who took it?"

Apparently, nobody. Wolfe gave them ten seconds, his eyes moving to take them all in, his lips tight. "I advise you," he said, "to jog your memories, in case it becomes necessary to establish the order in which you took the plates by dragging it out of you. I hope it won't come to that." His head turned. "Felix, I have neglected you purposely, to give you time to reflect. You were in the dining room. My expectation was that after I had learned who had served the first course to Mr. Pyle you would corroborate it, but now that there is nothing for you to corroborate I must look to you for the fact itself. I must ask you to point her out."

In a way Wolfe was Felix's boss. When Wolfe's oldest and dearest friend, Marko Vukcic, who had owned Rusterman's restaurant, had died, his will had left the restaurant to members of the staff in trust, with Wolfe as the trustee, and Felix was the *maître d'hôtel.* With that job at the best restaurant in New York, naturally Felix was both bland and commanding, but now he was neither. If he felt the way he looked, he was miserable.

"I can't," he said.

"Pfui! You, trained as you are to see everything?"

"That is true, Mr. Wolfe. I knew you would ask me this, but I can't. I can only explain. The young woman who just spoke, Marjorie Quinn, was the first one in with a plate, as she said. She did not say that as she served it one of the blinis slid off onto the table, but it did. As I sprang toward her she was actually about to pick it up with her fingers, and I jerked her away and put it back on the plate with a fork, and I gave her a look. Anyway, I was not myself.

Having women as waiters was bad enough, and not only that, they were without experience. When I recovered command of myself I saw the redheaded one, Choate, standing back of Mr. Pyle, to whom she had been assigned, with a plate in her hand, and I saw that he had already been served. As I moved forward she stepped to the right and served the plate to you. The operation was completely upset, and I was helpless. The dark-skinned one, Iacono, who was assigned to you, served Mr. Kreis, and the—"

"If you please." Wolfe was curt. "I have heard them, and so have you. I have always found you worthy of trust, but it's possible that in your exalted position, *maître d'hôtel* at Rusterman's, you would rather dodge than get involved in a poisoning. Are you dodging, Felix?"

"Good God, Mr. Wolfe, I *am* involved!"

"Very well. I saw that woman spill the blini and start her fingers for it, and I saw you retrieve it. Yes, you're involved, but not as I am." He turned to me. "Archie. You are commonly my first resort, but now you are my last. You sat next to Mr. Pyle. Who put that plate before him?"

Of course I knew that was coming, but I hadn't been beating my brain because there was no use. I said merely but positively, "No." He glared at me and I added, "That's all, just no, but like Felix I can explain. First, I would have had to turn around to see her face, and that's bad table manners. Second, I was watching Felix rescue the blini. Third, there was an argument going on about flowers with spots and streaks, and I was listening to it and so were you. I didn't even see her arm."

Wolfe stood and breathed. He shut his eyes and opened them again, and breathed some more. "Incredible," he muttered. "The wretch had incredible luck."

"I'm going home," Fern Faber said. "I'm tired."

"So am I," another one said, and was moving, but Wolfe's eyes pinned her. "I advise you not to," he said. "It is true that Miss Faber is eliminated as the culprit, and also Miss Quinn, since she was under surveillance by Felix while Mr. Pyle was being served, but I advise even them to stay. When Mr. Pyle dies, the doctors will certainly summon the police, and it would be well for all of you to be here when they arrive. I had hoped to be able to present them with an exposed murderer. Confound it! There is still a chance. Archie, come with me. Fritz, Felix, Zoltan, remain with these women. If one or more of them insist on leaving do not detain them by force, but have the names and the times of departure. If they want to eat, feed them. I'll be—"

"I'm going home," Fern Faber said stubbornly.

"Very well, go. You'll be got out of bed by a policeman before the night's out. I'll be in the dining room, Fritz. Come, Archie."

He went and I followed, along the pantry corridor and through the two-way door. On the way I glanced at my wristwatch: ten past eleven. I rather expected to find the dining room empty, but it wasn't. Eight of them were still there, the only ones missing being Schriver and Hewitt, who were probably upstairs. The air was heavy with cigar smoke. All of them but Adrian Dart were at the table with their chairs pushed back at various angles, with brandy glasses and cigars. Dart was standing with his back to a picture of honkers on the wing, holding forth. As we entered he stopped and heads turned.

Emil Kreis spoke. "Oh, there you are. I was coming to the kitchen but didn't want to butt in. Schriver asked me to apologize to Fritz Brenner. Our custom is to ask the chef to join us with champagne, which is barbarous but gay, but of course in the circumstances . . ." He let it hang, and added, "Shall I explain to him? Or will you?"

"I will." Wolfe went to the end of the table and sat. He had been on his feet for nearly two hours—all very well for his twice-a-day sessions in the plant rooms, but not elsewhere. He looked around. "Mr. Pyle is still alive?"

"We hope so," one said. "We sincerely hope so."

"I ought to be home in bed," another one said. "I have a hard day tomorrow. But it doesn't seem . . ." He took a puff on his cigar.

Emil Kreis reached for the brandy bottle. "There's been no word since I came down." He looked at his wrist. "Nearly an hour ago. I suppose I should go up. It's so damned unpleasant." He poured brandy.

"Terrible," one said. "Absolutely terrible. I understand you were asking which one of the girls brought him the caviar. Kreis says you asked him."

Wolfe nodded. "I also asked Mr. Schriver and Mr. Hewitt. And Mr. Goodwin and Mr. Brenner, and the two men who came to help at my request. And the women themselves. After more than an hour with them I am still at fault. I have discovered the artifice the culprit used, but not her identity."

"Aren't you a bit premature?" Leacraft, the lawyer, asked. "There may be no culprit. An acute and severe gastric disturbance may be caused—"

"Nonsense. I am too provoked for civility, Mr. Leacraft. The symptoms are typical of arsenic, and you heard Mr. Pyle complain of sand, but that's not all. I said I have discovered the artifice. None of them will admit serving him the first course. The one assigned to him found he had already been served and served me instead. There is indeed a culprit. She put arsenic in the cream *en passant*, served it to Mr. Pyle, returned to the kitchen for another portion, and came and served it to someone else. That is established."

"But then," the lawyer objected, "one of them served no one. How could that be?"

"I am not a tyro at inquiry, Mr. Leacraft. I'll ravel it for you later if you want, but now I want to get on. It is no conjecture that poison was given to Mr. Pyle by the woman who brought him the caviar; it is a fact. By a remarkable combination of cunning and luck she has so far eluded identification, and I am appealing to you. All of you. I ask you to close your eyes and recall the scene. We are here at table, discussing the orchids—the spots and streaks. The woman serving that place"—he pointed—"lets a blini slip from the plate and Felix retrieves it. It helps to close your eyes. Just about then a woman enters with a plate, goes to Mr. Pyle, and puts it before him. I appeal to you: which one?"

Emil Kreis shook his head. "I told you upstairs, I don't know. I didn't see her. Or if I did, it didn't register."

Adrian Dart, the actor, stood with his eyes closed, his chin up, and his arms folded, a fine pose for concentration. The others, even Leacraft, had their eyes closed, too, but of course they couldn't hold a candle to Dart. After a long moment the eyes began to open and heads to shake.

"It's gone," Dart said in his rich musical baritone. "I must have seen it, since I sat across from him, but it's gone. Utterly."

"I didn't see it," another said. "I simply didn't see it."

"I have a vague feeling," another said, "but it's too damn vague. No."

They made it unanimous.

Wolfe put his palms on the table. "Then I'm in for it," he said grimly. "I am your guest, gentlemen, and would not be offensive, but I am to blame that Fritz Brenner was enticed to this deplorable fiasco. If Mr. Pyle dies, as he surely will—"

The door opened and Benjamin Schriver entered. Then Lewis Hewitt, and then the familiar burly frame of Sergeant Purley Stebbins of Manhattan Homicide West.

Schriver crossed to the table and spoke. "Vincent is dead. Half an hour ago. Doctor Jameson called the police. He thinks that it is practically certain—"

"Hold it," Purley growled at his elbow. "I'll handle it if you don't mind."

"My God," Adrian Dart groaned, and shuddered magnificently.

That was the last I heard of the affair from an aristologist.

"I DID NOT!" INSPECTOR Cramer roared. "Quit twisting my words around! I didn't charge you with complicity! I merely said you're concealing something, and what the hell is that to scrape your neck? You always do!"

It was a quarter to two Wednesday afternoon. We were in the office on the first floor of the old brownstone on West 35th Street—Wolfe in his oversized chair. The daily schedule was messed beyond repair. When we had finally got home, at five o'clock in the morning, Wolfe had told Fritz to forget about breakfast until further notice, and had sent me up to the plant rooms to leave a note for Theodore saying that he would not appear at nine in the morning and perhaps not at all. It had been not at all. At half-past eleven he had buzzed on the house phone to tell Fritz to bring up the breakfast tray with four eggs and ten slices of bacon instead of two and five, and it was past one o'clock when the sounds came of his elevator and then his footsteps in the hall, heading for the office.

If you think a problem child is rough, try handling a problem elephant. He is plenty knotty even when he is himself, and that day he was really special. After looking through the mail, glancing at his desk calendar, and signing three checks I had put on his desk, he snapped at me, "A fine prospect. Dealing with them singly would be interminable. Will you have them all here at six o'clock?"

I kept calm. I merely asked, "All of whom?"

"You know quite well. Those women."

I still kept calm. "I should think ten of them would be enough. You said yourself that two of them can be crossed off."

"I need them all. Those two can help establish the order in which the plates were taken."

I held on. I too was short on sleep, shorter even than he, and I didn't feel up to a fracas. "I have a suggestion," I said. "I suggest that you postpone operations until your wires are connected again. Counting up to five hundred might help. You know damn well that all twelve of them will spend the afternoon either at the District Attorney's office or receiving official callers at their homes—probably most of them at the DA's office. And probably they'll spend the evening there too. Do you want some aspirin?"

"I want *them*," he growled.

I could have left him to grope back to normal on his own and gone up to my room for a nap, but after all he pays my salary. So I picked up a sheet of paper I had typed and got up and handed it to him. It read:

	Assigned to	*Served*
Peggy Choate	Pyle	Wolfe
Helen Iacono	Wolfe	Kreis
Nora Jaret	Kreis	Schriver
Carol Annis	Schriver	Dart
Lucy Morgan	Dart	Hewitt
Fern Faber	Hewitt	No one

"Fern Faber's out," I said, "and I realize it doesn't have to be one of those five, even though Lucy Morgan took the last plate. Possibly one or two others took plates after Peggy Choate did, and served the men they were assigned to. But it seems—"

I stopped because he had crumpled it and dropped it in the wastebasket. "I heard them," he growled. "My faculties, including my memory, are not impaired. I am merely ruffled beyond the bounds of tolerance."

For him that was an abject apology, and a sign that he was beginning to regain control. But a few minutes later, when the bell rang, and after a look through the one-way glass panel of the front door I told him it was Cramer, and he said to admit him, and Cramer marched in and planted his fanny on the red leather chair and opened up with an impolite remark about concealing facts connected with a murder, Wolfe had cut loose; and Cramer asked him what the hell was that to scrape his neck, which was a new one to me but sounded somewhat vulgar for an inspector. He had probably picked it up from some hoodlum.

Ruffling Cramer beyond the bounds of tolerance did Wolfe good. He leaned back in his chair. "Everyone conceals something," he said placidly. "Or at least omits something, if only because to include everything is impossible. During those wearisome hours, nearly six of them, I answered all questions, and so did Mr. Goodwin. Indeed, I thought we were helpful. I thought we had cleared away some rubble."

"Yeah." Cramer wasn't grateful. His big pink face was always a little pinker than normal, not with pleasure, when he was tackling Wolfe. "You had witnessed the commission of a murder, and you didn't notify—"

"It wasn't a murder until he died."

"All right, a felony. You not only failed to report it, you—"

"That a felony had been committed was my conclusion. Others present disagreed with me. Only a few minutes before Mr. Stebbins entered the room, Mr. Leacraft, a member of the bar himself an officer of the law, challenged my conclusion."

"You should have reported it. You're a licensed detective. Also you started an investigation, questioning the suspects—"

"Only to test my conclusion. I would have been a ninny to report it before learning—"

"Damn it," Cramer barked, "will you let me finish a sentence? Just one?"

Wolfe's shoulders went up an eighth of an inch and down again. "Certainly, if it has import. I am not baiting you, Mr. Cramer. But I have already replied to these imputations, to you and Mr. Stebbins and an assistant district attorney. I did not wrongly delay reporting a crime, and I did not usurp the function of the police. Very well, finish a sentence."

"You knew Pyle was dying. You said so."

"Also my own conclusion. The doctors were trying to save him."

Cramer took a breath. He looked at me, saw nothing inspiring, and returned to Wolfe. "I'll tell you why I'm here. Those three men—the cook, the man that helped him, and the man in the dining room—Fritz Brenner, Felix Courbet, and Zoltan Mahany, were all supplied by you. All close to you. I want to know about them, or at least two of them. I might as well leave Fritz out of it. In the first place, it's hard to believe that Zoltan doesn't know who took the first two or three plates or whether one of them came back for a second one, and it's also hard to believe that Felix doesn't know who served Pyle."

"It is indeed," Wolfe agreed. "They are highly trained men. But they have been questioned."

"They sure have. It's also hard to believe that Goodwin didn't see who served Pyle. He sees everything."

"Mr. Goodwin is present. Discuss it with him."

"I have. Now, I want to ask your opinion of a theory. I know yours, and I don't reject it, but there are alternatives. First, a fact. In a metal trash container in the kitchen—not a garbage pail—we found a small roll of paper, ordinary white paper that had been rolled into a tube, held with tape, smaller at one end. The laboratory has found particles of arsenic inside. The only two fingerprints on it that are any good are Zoltan's. He says he saw it on the kitchen floor under a table some time after the meal had started, he can't say exactly when, and he picked it up and dropped it in the container, and his prints are on it because he pinched it to see if there was anything in it."

Wolfe nodded. "As I surmised. A paper spill."

"Yeah. I don't say it kills your theory. She could have shaken it into the cream without leaving prints, and she certainly wouldn't have dropped it on the floor if there was any chance it had her prints. But it *has* got Zoltan's. What's wrong with the theory that Zoltan poisoned one of the portions and saw that it was taken by a certain one? I'll answer that myself. There are two things wrong with it. First, Zoltan claims he didn't know which guest any of the girls were assigned to. But Felix knew, and they could have been in collusion. Second, the girls all deny that Zoltan indicated which plate they were to take, but you know how that is. He could have done it without her knowing it. What else is wrong with it?"

"It's not only untenable, it's egregious," Wolfe declared. "Why, in that case, did one of them come back for another plate?"

"She was confused. Nervous. Dumb."

"Bosh. Why doesn't she admit it?"

"Scared."

"I don't believe it. I questioned them before you did." Wolfe waved it away. "Tommyrot, and you know it. My theory is not a theory; it is a reasoned conviction. I hope it is being acted on. I suggested to Mr. Stebbins that he examine their garments to see if some kind of pocket had been made in one of them. She had to have it readily available."

"He did. They all had pockets. The laboratory has found no trace of arsenic." Cramer uncrossed his legs. "But I wanted to ask you about those men. You know them."

"I do, yes. But I do not answer for them. They may have a dozen murders on their souls, but they had nothing to do with the death of Mr. Pyle. If you are following up my theory—my conviction, rather—I suppose you have learned the order in which the women took the plates."

Cramer shook his head. "We have not, and I doubt if we will. All we have is a bunch of contradictions. You had them good and scared before we got to them. We do have the last five, starting with Peggy Choate, who found that Pyle had been served and gave it to you, and then—but you got that yourself."

"No. I got those five, but not that they were the last. There might have been others in between."

"There weren't. It's pretty well settled that these five were the last. After Peggy Choate the last four plates were taken by Helen Iacono, Nora Jaret, Carol Annis, and Lucy Morgan. Then that Fern Faber, who had been in the can, but there was no plate for her. It's the order in which they took them before that, the first seven, that we can't pry out of them—except the first one, that Marjorie Quinn. You couldn't either."

Wolfe turned a palm up. "I was interrupted."

"You were not. You left them there in a huddle, scared stiff, and went to the dining room to start in on the men. Your own private murder investigation, and to hell with the law. I was surprised to see Goodwin here when I rang the bell just now. I supposed you'd have him out running errands like calling at the agency they got the girls from. Or getting a line on Pyle to find a connection between him and one of them. Unless you're no longer interested?"

"I'm interested willy-nilly," Wolfe declared. "As I told the assistant district attorney, it is on my score that a man was poisoned in food prepared by Fritz Brenner. But I do not send Mr. Goodwin on fruitless errands. He is one and you have dozens, and if anything is to be learned at the agency or by inquiry into Mr. Pyle's associations your army will dig it up. They're already at it, of course, but if they had started a trail you wouldn't be here. If I send Mr. Goodwin—"

The doorbell rang and I got up and went to the hall. At the rear the door to the kitchen swung open part way and Fritz poked his head through, saw me, and withdrew. Turning to the front for a look through the panel, I saw that I had exaggerated when I told Wolfe that all twelve of them would be otherwise engaged. At least one wasn't. There on the stoop was Helen Iacono.

It had sounded to me as if Cramer had about said his say and would soon be moving along, and if he bumped into Helen Iacono in the hall she might be too embarrassed to give me her phone number, if that was what she had come for; so as I opened the door I pressed a finger to my lips and *sshhe*d at her, and then crooked the finger to motion her in. Her deep dark eyes looked a little startled, but she stepped across the sill, and I shut the door, turned, opened the first door on the left, to the front room, motioned to her to enter, followed, and closed the door.

"What's the matter?" she whispered.

"Nothing now," I told her. "This is soundproofed. There's a police inspector in the office with Mr. Wolfe and I thought you might have had enough of cops for now. But if you want to meet him—"

"I don't. I want to see Nero Wolfe."

"Okay, I'll tell him as soon as the cop goes. Have a seat. It shouldn't be long."

There is a connecting door between the front room and the office, but I went around through the hall, and here came Cramer. He was marching by without even the courtesy of a grunt, but I stepped to the front to let him out, and then went to the office and told Wolfe, "I've got one of them in the front room. Helen Iacono, the tawny-skinned Hebe who had you but gave her caviar to Kreis. Shall I keep her while I get the rest of them?"

He made a face. "What does she want?"

"To see you."

He took a breath. "Confound it. Bring her in."

I went and opened the connecting door, told her to come, and escorted her across to the red leather chair. She was more ornamental in it than Cramer, but not nearly as impressive as she had been at first sight. She was puffy around the eyes and her skin had lost some glow. She told Wolfe she hadn't had any sleep. She said she had just left the district attorney's office, and if she went home her mother would be at her again, and her brothers and sister would come home from school and make noise, and anyway she had decided she had to see Wolfe. Her mother was old-fashioned and didn't want her to be an actress. It was beginning to sound as if what she was after was a place to take a nap, but then Wolfe got a word in.

He said dryly, "I didn't suppose, Miss Iacono, you came to consult me about your career."

"Oh, no. I came because you're a detective and you're very clever and I'm afraid. I'm afraid they'll find out something I did, and if they do I won't have any career. My parents won't let me even if I'm still alive. I nearly gave it away already when they were asking me questions. So I decided to tell you about it and then if you'd help me I'll help you. If you promise to keep my secret."

"I can't promise to keep a secret if it is a guilty one—if it is a confession of a crime or knowledge of one."

"It isn't."

"Then you have my promise, and Mr. Goodwin's. We have kept many secrets."

"All right. I stabbed Vincent Pyle with a knife and got blood on me."

I stared. For half a second I thought she meant that he hadn't died of poison at all, that she had sneaked upstairs and stuck a knife in him, which seemed unlikely since the doctors would probably have found the hole.

Apparently, she wasn't going on, and Wolfe spoke. "Ordinarily, Miss Iacono, stabbing a man is considered a crime. When and where did this happen?"

"It wasn't a crime because it was in self-defense." Her rich contralto was as composed as if she had been telling us the multiplication tables. Evidently, she saved the inflections for her career. She was continuing. "It happened in January, about three months ago. Of course, I knew about him—everybody in show business does. I don't know if it's true that he backs shows just so he can get girls, but it might as well be. There's a lot of talk about the girls he gets, but nobody really knows because he was always very careful about it. Some of the girls have talked but he never did. I don't mean just taking them out, I mean the last ditch. We say that on Broadway. You know what I mean?"

"I can surmise."

"Sometimes we say the last stitch, but it means the same thing. Early last winter he began on me. Of course, I knew about his reputation, but he was backing *Jack in the Pulpit* and they were about to start casting, and I didn't know it was going to be a flop, and if a girl expects to have a career she has to be sociable. I went out with him a few times, dinner and dancing and so forth, and then he asked me to his apartment, and I went. He cooked the dinner himself—I said he was very careful. Didn't I?"

"Yes."

"Well, he was. It's a penthouse on Madison Avenue, but no one else was there. I let him kiss me. I figured it like this, an actress gets kissed all the time on the stage and the screen and TV, and what's the difference? I went to his apartment three times and there was no real trouble, but the fourth time—that was in January—he turned into a beast right before my eyes, and I had to do something, and I grabbed a knife from the table and stabbed him with it. I got blood on my dress, and when I got home I tried to get it out but it left a stain. It cost forty-six dollars."

"But Mr. Pyle recovered."

"Oh, yes. I saw him a few times after that, I mean just by accident, but he barely spoke and so did I. I don't think he ever told anyone about it, but what if he did? What if the police find out about it?"

Wolfe grunted. "That would be regrettable, certainly. You would be pestered even more than you were now. But if you have been candid with me you are not in mortal jeopardy. The police are not simpletons. You wouldn't be arrested for murdering Mr. Pyle last night, let alone convicted, merely because you stabbed him in self-defense last January."

"Of course I wouldn't," she agreed. "That's not it. It's my mother and father. They'd find out about it because they would ask them questions, and if I'm going to have a career I would have to leave home and my family, and I don't want to. Don't you see?" She came forward in the chair. "But if they find out right away who did it, who poisoned him, that would end it and I'd be all right. Only I'm afraid they won't find out right away, but I think you could if I help you, and you said last night that you're committed. I can't offer to help the police because they'd wonder why."

"I see." Wolfe's eyes were narrowed at her. "How do you propose to help me?"

"Well, I figure it like this." She was on the edge of the chair. "The way you explained it last night, one of the girls poisoned him. She was one of the first ones to take a plate in, and then she came back and got another one. I don't quite understand why she did that, but you do, so all right. But if she came back for another plate that took a little time, and she must have been one of the last ones, and the police have got it worked out who were the last five. I know that because of the questions they asked this last time. So it was Peggy Choate or Nora Jaret or Carol Annis or Lucy Morgan."

"Or you."

"No, it wasn't me." Just matter-of-fact. "So it was one of them. And she didn't poison him just for nothing, did she? You'd have to have a very good reason to poison a man, I know I would. So all we have to do is find out which one had a good reason, and that's where I can help. I don't know Lucy Morgan, but I know Carol a little, and I know Nora and Peggy even better. And now we're in this together, and I can pretend to them I want to talk about it. I can talk about him because I had to tell the police I went out with him a few times, because I was seen with him and they'd find out, so I thought I'd better tell them. Dozens of girls went out with him, but he was so careful that nobody knows which ones went to the last ditch except the ones that talked. And I can find out which one of those four girls had a reason, and tell you, and that will end it."

I was congratulating myself that I hadn't got her phone number; and if I had got it, I would have crossed it off without a pang. I don't say that a girl must have true nobility of character before I'll buy her a lunch, but you have to draw the line some- where. Thinking that Wolfe might be disgusted enough to put into words the way I felt, I horned in. "I have a suggestion, Miss Iacono.

You could bring them here, all four of them, and let Mr. Wolfe talk it over with them. As you say, he's very clever."

She looked doubtful. "I don't believe that's a good idea. I think they'd be more apt to say things to me, just one at a time. Don't you think so, Mr. Wolfe?"

"You know them better than I do," he muttered. He was controlling himself.

"And then," she said, "when we find out which one had a reason, and we tell the police, I can say that I saw her going back to the kitchen for another plate. Of course, just where I saw her, where she was and where I was, that will depend on who she is. I saw you, Mr. Wolfe, when I said you could if I helped you, I saw the look on your face. You didn't think a twenty-year-old girl could help, did you?"

He had my sympathy. Of course, what he would have liked to say was that it might well be that a twenty-year-old hellcat could help, but that wouldn't have been tactful.

"I may have been a little skeptical," he conceded. "And it's possible that you're oversimplifying the problem. We have to consider all the factors. Take one: her plan must have been not only premeditated but also thoroughly rigged, since she had the poison ready. So she must have known that Mr. Pyle would be one of the guests. Did she?"

"Oh, yes. We all did. Mr. Buchman at the agency showed us a list of them and told us who they were, only of course he didn't have to tell us who Vincent Pyle was. That was about a month ago, so she had plenty of time to get the poison. Is arsenic very hard to get?"

"Not at all. It is in common use for many purposes. That is, of course, one of the police lines of inquiry, but she knew it would be and she is no bungler. Another point: when Mr. Pyle saw her there, serving food, wouldn't he have been on his guard?"

"But he didn't see her. They didn't see any of us before. She came up behind him and gave him that plate. Of course, he saw her afterward, but he had already eaten it."

Wolfe persisted. "But then? He was in agony, but he was conscious and could speak. Why didn't he denounce her?"

She gestured impatiently. "I guess you're not as clever as you're supposed to be. He didn't know she had done it. When he saw her she was serving another man, and—"

"What other man?"

"How do I know? Only it wasn't you, because I served you. And anyway, maybe he didn't know she wanted to kill him. Of course, she had a good reason, I know that, but maybe he didn't know she felt like that. A man doesn't know how a girl feels—anyhow, some girls. Look at me. He didn't know I would never dream of going to the last ditch. He thought I would give up my honor and my virtue just to get a part in that play he was backing, and anyhow it was a flop." She gestured again. "I thought you wanted to get her. All you do is make objections."

Wolfe rubbed the side of his nose. "I do want to get her, Miss Iacono. I intend to. But like Mr. Pyle, though from a different motive, I am very careful. I can't afford to botch it. I fully appreciate your offer to help. You didn't like Mr. Goodwin's suggestion that you get them here in a body for discussion with me, and you may be right. But I don't like your plan, for you to approach them singly and try to pump them. Our quarry is a malign and crafty harpy, and I will not be a party to your peril. I propose an alternative. Arrange for Mr. Goodwin to see them, together with you. Being a trained investigator, he knows how to beguile, and the peril, if any, will be his. If they are not available at the moment, arrange it for this evening—but not here. Perhaps one of them has a suitable apartment, or if not, a private room at some restaurant would do. At my expense, of course. Will you?"

It was her turn to make objections, and she had several. But when Wolfe met them, and made it plain that he would accept her as a colleague only if she accepted his alternative, she finally gave in. She would phone to let me know how she was making out with the arrangements. From her manner, when she got up to go, you might have thought she had been shopping for some little item, say a handbag, and had graciously deferred to the opinion of the clerk. After I graciously escorted her out and saw her descend the seven steps to the sidewalk, I returned to the office and found Wolfe sitting with his eyes closed and his fists planted on the chair arms.

"Even money," I said.

"On what?" he growled.

"On her against the field. She knows damn well who had a good reason and exactly what it was. It was getting too hot for comfort and she decided that the best way to duck was to wish it on some dear friend."

His eyes opened. "She would, certainly. A woman whose conscience has no sting will stop at nothing. But why come to me? Why didn't she cook her own stew and serve it to the police?"

"I don't know, but for a guess she was afraid the cops would get too curious and find out how she had saved her honor and her virtue and tell her mother and father, and Father would spank her. Shall I also guess why you proposed your alternative instead of having her bring them here for you?"

"She wouldn't. She said so."

"Of course she would, if you had insisted. That's your guess. Mine is that you're not desperate enough yet to take on five females in a bunch. When you told me to bring the whole dozen you knew darned well it couldn't be done, not even by me. Okay, I want instructions."

"Later," he muttered, and closed his eyes.

IT WAS ON THE fourth floor of an old walk-up in the West Nineties near Amsterdam Avenue. I don't know what it had in the way of a kitchen or bedroom—or bedrooms—because the only room I saw was the one we were sitting in. It was medium-sized, and the couch and chairs and rugs had a homey look, the kind of homeyness that furniture gets by being used by a lot of different people for fifty or sixty years. The chair I was on had a wobbly leg, but that's no problem if you keep it in mind and make no sudden shifts. I was more concerned about the spidery little stand at my elbow on which my glass of milk was perched. I can always drink milk and had preferred it to Bubble-Pagne, registered trademark, a dime a bottle, which they were having. It was ten o'clock Wednesday evening.

The hostesses were the redhead with milky skin, Peggy Choate, and the one with big brown eyes and dimples, Nora Jaret, who shared the apartment. Carol Annis, with the fine profile and the corn-silk hair, had been there when Helen Iacono and I arrived, bringing Lucy Morgan and her throaty voice after detouring our taxi to pick her up at a street corner. They were a very attractive collection, though of course not as decorative as they had been in their ankle-length purple stolas. Girls always look better in uniforms or costumes. Take nurses or elevator girls or Miss Honeydew at a melon festival.

I was now calling her Helen, not that I felt like it, but in the detective business you have to be sociable, of course preserving your honor and virtue. In the taxi, before picking up Lucy Morgan, she told me she had been thinking it over and she doubted if it would be possible to find out which one of them had a good reason to kill Pyle, or thought she had, because Pyle had been so very careful when he had a girl come to his penthouse. The only way would be to get one of them to open up, and Helen doubted if she could get her to, since she would be practically confessing murder. So the best way would be for Helen and me, after spending an evening with them, to talk it over and decide which one was the most likely, and then she would tell Wolfe she had seen her going back to the kitchen and bringing another plate, and Wolfe would tell the police, and that would do it.

No, I didn't feel like calling her Helen. I would just as soon have been too far away from her to call her at all.

Helen's declared object in arranging the party—declared to them—was to find out from me what Nero Wolfe and the cops had done and were doing, so they would know where they stood. Helen was sure I would loosen up, she had told them, because she had been to see me and found me very nice and sympathetic. So the hostesses were making it sort of festive and intimate by serving Bubble-Pagne, though I preferred milk. I had a suspicion that at least one of them, Lucy Morgan, would have preferred whiskey or gin or rum or vodka, and maybe they all would, but that might have made me suspect that they were not just a bunch of wholesome, hardworking artists.

They didn't look festive. I wouldn't say they were haggard, but much of the bloom was off. And they hadn't bought Helen's plug for me that I was nice and sympathetic. They were absolutely skeptical, sizing me up with sidewise looks, especially Carol Annis, who sat cross-legged on the couch with her head cocked. It was she who asked me, after a few remarks had been made about how awful it had been and still was, how well I knew the chef and the other man in the kitchen. I told her she could forget Fritz. He was completely above suspicion, and anyway he had been at the range while the plates were taken. As for Zoltan, I said that though I had

known him a long while we were not intimate, but that was irrelevant because, granting that he had known which guest each girl
would serve, if he poisoned one of the portions and saw that a certain girl got it, why did she or some other girl come back for
another plate?

"There's no proof that she did," Carol declared. "Nobody saw
her."

"Nobody *noticed* her." I wasn't aggressive; I was supposed to be
nice and sympathetic. "She wouldn't have been noticed leaving
the dining room because the attention of the girls who were in
there was on Felix and Marjorie Quinn, who had spilled a blini,
and the men wouldn't notice her. The only place she would have
been noticed was in the corridor through the pantry, and if she
met another girl there she could have stopped and been patting
her hair or something. Anyhow, one of you must have gone back
for a second plate, because when Fern Faber went for hers there
wasn't any."

"Why do you say one of us?" Nora demanded. "If you mean one
of us here. There were twelve."

"I do mean one of you here, but I'm not saying it, I'm just quoting the police. They think it was one of you here because you were
the last five."

"How do you know what they think?"

"I'm not at liberty to say. But I do."

"I know what I think," Carol asserted. She had uncrossed her
legs and slid forward on the couch to get her toes on the floor. "I
think it was Zoltan. I read in the *Gazette* that he's a chef at Rusterman's, and Nero Wolfe is the trustee and so he's the boss there,
and I think Zoltan hated him for some reason and tried to poison
him, but he gave the poisoned plate to the wrong girl. Nero Wolfe
sat right next to Pyle."

There was no point in telling her that she was simply ignoring
the fact that one of them had gone back for a second helping, so I
just said, "Nobody can stop you thinking. But I doubt very much if
the police would buy that."

"What would they buy?" Peggy asked.

My personal feelings about Peggy were mixed. For: she had recognized me and named me. Against: she had accused me of liking
myself. "Anything that would fit," I told her. "As I said, they think it

was one of you five that went back for more, and therefore they have to think that one of you gave the poison to Pyle, because what other possible reason could you have had for serving another portion? They wouldn't buy anything that didn't fit into that. That's what rules out everybody else, including Zoltan." I looked at Carol. "I'm sorry, Miss Annis, but that's how it is."

"They're a bunch of dopes," Lucy Morgan stated. "They get an idea and then they haven't got room for another one." She was on the floor with her legs stretched out, her back against the couch. "I agree with Carol, there's no proof that any of us went back for another plate. That Zoltan said he didn't see anyone come back. Didn't he?"

"He did. He still does."

"Then he's a dope, too. And he said no one took two plates. Didn't he?"

"Right. He still does."

"Then how do they know which one he's wrong about? We were all nervous, you know that. Maybe one of us took two plates instead of one, and when she got to the dining room there she was with an extra, and she got rid of it by giving it to some guest that didn't have any."

"Then why didn't she say so?" I asked.

"Because she was scared. The way Nero Wolfe came at us was enough to scare anybody. And now she won't say so because she has signed a statement and she's even more scared."

I shook my head. "I'm sorry, but if you analyze that you'll see that it won't do. It's very tricky. You can do it the way I did this afternoon. Take twenty-four little pieces of paper, on twelve of them write the names of the guests, and arrange them as they sat at the table. On the other twelve pieces write the names of the twelve girls Then try to manipulate the twelve girl pieces so that one of them either took in two plates at once, and did not give either of them to Pyle, or went back for a second plate, and did not give either the first one or the second one to Pyle. It can't be done. For if either of those things happened there wouldn't have been one mix-up, there would have been two. Since there was only one mix-up, Pyle couldn't possibly have been served by a girl who either brought in two plates at once or went back for a second one. So the idea that a girl *innocently* brought in two plates is out."

"I don't believe it," Nora said flatly.

"It's not a question of believing." I was still sympathetic. "You might as well say you don't believe two plus two is four. I'll show you. May I have some paper? Any old kind."

She went to a table and brought some, and I took my pen and wrote the twenty-four names, spacing them, and tore the paper into twenty-four pieces. Then I knelt on a rug and arranged the twelve guest pieces in a rectangle as they had sat at table—not that that mattered, since they could have been in a straight line or a circle, but it was plainer that way. The girls gathered around.

"Okay," I said, "show me." I took *Quinn* and put it back of *Leacraft.* "There's no argument about that, Marjorie Quinn brought the first plate and gave it to Leacraft. Remember there was just one mix-up, started by Peggy when she saw Pyle had been served and gave hers to Nero Wolfe. Try having any girl bring in a second plate—or bring in two at once if you still think that might have happened without either serving Pyle or starting a second mix-up."

My memory has had a long stiff training under the strains and pressure Wolfe has put on it, but I wouldn't undertake to report all the combinations they tried, huddled around me on the floor. They stuck to it for half an hour or more. The most persistent was Peggy Choate, the redhead. After the others had given up she stayed with it, frowning and biting her lip, propped first on one hand and then the other. Finally, she said, "Nuts," stretched an arm to make a jumble of all the pieces of paper, guests and girls, got up, and returned to her chair.

"It's just a trick," said Carol Annis, perched on the couch again.

"I still don't believe it," Nora Jaret declared. "I do not believe that one of us deliberately poisoned a man—one of us sitting here." Her big brown eyes were at me. "Good Lord, look at us! Point at her! Point her out! I dare you to!"

That, of course, was what I was there for—not exactly to point her out, but at least to get a hint. I had had a vague idea that one might come from watching them maneuver the pieces of paper, but it hadn't. Nor from anything any of them had said. I had been expecting Helen Iacono to introduce the subject of Vincent Pyle's *modus operandi* with girls, but apparently she had decided it was up to me. She hadn't spoken more than twenty words since we arrived.

"If I could point her out," I said, "I wouldn't be bothering the rest of you. Neither would the cops if *they* could point her out. Sooner or later, of course, they will, but it begins to look as if they'll have to get at it from the other end. Motive. They'll have to find out which one of you had a motive, and they will—sooner or later—and on that maybe I can help. I don't mean help them, I mean help you—not the one who killed him, the rest of you. That thought occurred to me after I learned that Helen Iacono had admitted that she had gone out with Pyle a few times last winter. What if she had said she hadn't? When the police found out she had lied, and they would have, she would have been in for it. It wouldn't have proved she had killed him, but the going would have been mighty rough. I understand that the rest of you have all denied that you ever had anything to do with Pyle. Is that right? Miss Annis?"

"Certainly." Her chin was up. "Of course, I had met him. Everybody in show business has. Once when he came backstage at the Coronet, and once at a party somewhere, and one other time but I don't remember where."

"Miss Morgan?"

She was smiling at me, a crooked smile. "Do you call this helping us?" she demanded.

"It might lead to that after I know how you stand. After all, the cops have your statement."

She shrugged. "I've been around longer than Carol, so I had seen him to speak to more than she had. Once I danced with him at the Flamingo, two years ago. That was the closest I had ever been to him."

"Miss Choate?"

"I never had the honor. I only came to New York last fall. From Montana. He had been pointed out to me from a distance, but he never chased me."

"Miss Jaret?"

"He was Broadway," she said. "I'm TV."

"Don't the twain ever meet?"

"Oh, sure. All the time at Sardi's. That's the only place I ever saw the great Pyle, and I wasn't with him."

"So there you are," I said, "you're all committed. If one of you poisoned him, and though I hate to say it I don't see any way out of that, that one is lying. But if any of the others are lying, if you saw more of him than you admit, you had better get from under quick. If you don't want to tell the cops tell me, tell me now, and I'll pass it on and say I wormed it out of you. Believe me, you'll regret it if you don't."

"Archie Goodwin, a girl's best friend," Lucy said. "My bosom pal."

No one else said anything.

"Actually," I asserted, "I *am* your friend, all of you but one. I have a friendly feeling for all pretty girls, especially those who work, and I admire and respect you for being willing to make an honest fifty bucks by coming there yesterday to carry plates of grub to a bunch of finickers. I *am* your friend, Lucy, if you're not the murderer."

I leaned forward, forgetting the wobbly chair leg, but it didn't object. It was about time to put a crimp in Helen's personal project. "Another thing. It's quite possible that one of you *did* see her returning to the kitchen for another plate, and you haven't said so because you don't want to squeal on her. If so, spill it now. The longer this hangs on, the hotter it will get. When it gets so the pressure is too much for you and you decide you have got to tell it, it will be too late. Tomorrow may be too late. If you go to the cops with it tomorrow they probably won't believe you; they'll figure that you did it yourself and you're trying to squirm out. If you don't want to tell me here and now, in front of her, come with me down to Nero Wolfe's office and we'll talk it over."

They were exchanging glances, and they were not friendly glances. When I had arrived probably not one of them, excluding the murderer, had believed that a poisoner was present, but now they all did, or at least they thought she might be; and when that feeling takes hold it's good-bye to friendliness. It would have been convenient if I could have detected fear in one of the glances, but fear and suspicion and uneasiness are too much alike on faces to tell them apart.

"You *are* a help," Carol Annis said bitterly. "Now you've got us hating each other. Now everybody suspects everybody."

I had quit being nice and sympathetic. "It's about time," I told her. I glanced at my wrist. "It's not midnight yet. If I've made you all realize that this is no Broadway production, or TV either, and the longer the payoff is postponed the tougher it will be for everybody, I *have* helped." I stood up. "Let's go. I don't say Mr. Wolfe can do it by just snapping his fingers, but he might surprise you. He has often surprised me."

"All right," Nora said. She arose. "Come on. This is getting too damn painful. Come on."

I don't pretend that that was what I had been heading for. I admit that I had just been carried along by my tongue. If I arrived with the gang at midnight and Wolfe had gone to bed, he would almost certainly refuse to play. Even if he were still up, he might refuse to work, just to teach me a lesson, since I had not stuck to my instructions. Those thoughts were at me as Peggy Choate bounced up and Carol Annis started to leave the couch.

But they were wasted. That tussle with Wolfe never came off. A door at the end of the room which had been standing ajar suddenly swung open, and there in its frame was a two-legged figure with shoulders almost as broad as the doorway, and I was squinting at Sergeant Purley Stebbins of Manhattan Homicide West. He moved forward, croaking, "I'm surprised at you, Goodwin. These ladies ought to get some sleep."

OF COURSE I WAS a monkey. If it had been Stebbins who had made a monkey of me I suppose I would have leaped for a window and dived through. Hitting the pavement from a fourth-story window should be enough to finish a monkey, and life wouldn't be worth living if I had been bamboozled by Purley Stebbins. But obviously it hadn't been him; it had been Peggy Choate or Nora Jaret, or both; Purley had merely accepted an invitation to come and listen in.

So I kept my face. To say I was jaunty would be stretching it, but I didn't scream or tear my hair. "Greetings," I said heartily. "And welcome. I've been wondering why you didn't join us instead of skulking in there in the dark."

"I'll bet you have." He had come to arm's length and stopped. He turned. "You can relax, ladies." Back to me: "You're under arrest for obstructing justice. Come along."

"In a minute. You've got all night." I moved my head. "Of course, Peggy and Nora knew this hero was in there, but I'd—"

"I said come along!" he barked.

"And I said in a minute, I intend to ask a couple of questions. I wouldn't dream of resisting arrest, but I've got leg cramp from kneeling too long and if you're in a hurry you'll have to carry me." I moved my eyes. "I'd like to know if you all knew. Did you, Miss Iacono?"

"Of course not."

"Miss Morgan?"

"No."

"Miss Annis?"

"No, I didn't, but I think you did." She tossed her head and the corn silk fluttered. "That was contemptible. Saying you wanted to help us, so we would talk, with a policeman listening."

"And then he arrests me?"

"That's just an act."

"I wish it were. Ask your friends Peggy and Nora if I knew—only I suppose you wouldn't believe them. *They* knew, and they didn't tell you. You'd better all think over everything you said. Okay, Sergeant, the leg cramp's gone."

He actually started a hand for my elbow, but I was moving and it wasn't there. I opened the door to the hall. Of course, he had me go first down the three flights; no cop in his senses would descend stairs in front of a dangerous criminal in custody. When we emerged to the sidewalk and he told me to turn left I asked him, "Why not cuffs?"

"Clown if you want to," he croaked.

He flagged a taxi on Amsterdam Avenue, and when we were in and rolling I spoke. "I've been thinking, about laws and liberties and so on. Take false arrest, for instance. And take obstructing justice. If a man is arrested for obstructing justice and it turns out that he didn't obstruct any justice, does that make the arrest false? I wish I knew more about law. I guess I'll have to ask a lawyer. Nathaniel Parker would know."

It was the mention of Parker, the lawyer Wolfe uses when the occasion calls for one, that got him. He had seen Parker in action.

"They heard you," he said, "and I heard you, and I took some notes. You interfered in a homicide investigation. You quoted the police to them. You told them what the police think, and what they're doing and are going to do. You played a game with them with those pieces of paper to show them exactly how it figures. You tried to get them to tell you things instead of telling the police, and you were going to take them to Nero Wolfe so he could pry it out of them. And you haven't even got the excuse that Wolfe is representing a client. He hasn't got a client."

"Wrong. He has."

"Like hell he has. Name her."

"Not her, him. Fritz Brenner. He is seeing red because food cooked by him was poisoned and killed a man. It's convenient to have the client living right in the house. You admit that a licensed detective has a right to investigate on behalf of a client."

"I admit nothing."

"That's sensible," I said approvingly. "You shouldn't. When you're on the stand being sued for false arrest, it would be bad to have it thrown up to you, and it would be two against one because the hackie could testify. Can you hear us, driver?"

"Sure I can hear you," he sang out. "It's very interesting."

"So watch your tongue," I told Purley. "You could get hooked for a year's pay. As for quoting the police, I merely said that they think it was one of those five, and when Cramer told Mr. Wolfe that he didn't say it was confidential. As for telling them what the police think, same comment. As for playing that game with them, why not? As for trying to get them to tell me things, I won't comment on that at all because I don't want to be rude. That must have been a slip of the tongue. If you ask me why I didn't balk there at the apartment and bring up these points then and there, what was the use? You had spoiled the party. They wouldn't have come downtown with me. Also I am saving a buck of Mr. Wolfe's money, since you had arrested me and therefore the taxi fare is on the city of New York. Am I still under arrest?"

"You're damn right you are."

"That may be ill-advised. You heard him, driver."

"Sure I heard him."

"Good. Try to remember it."

We were on Ninth Avenue, stopped at Forty-second Street for a light. When the light changed and we moved, Purley told the hackie to pull over to the curb, and he obeyed. At that time of night there were plenty of gaps. Purley took something from a pocket and showed it to the hackie, and said, "Go get yourself a Coke and come back in ten minutes," and he climbed out and went. Purley turned his head to glare at me.

"I'll pay for the Coke," I offered.

He ignored it. "Lieutenant Rowcliff," he said, "is expecting us at Twentieth Street."

"Fine. Even under arrest, one will get you five that I can make him start stuttering in ten minutes."

"You're not under arrest."

I leaned forward to look at the meter. "Ninety cents. From here on we'll split it."

"Damn it, quit clowning! If you think I'm crawling, you're wrong. I just don't see any percentage in it. If I deliver you in custody I know damn well what you'll do. You'll clam up. We won't get a peep out of you, and in the morning you'll make a phone call and Parker will come. What will that get us?"

I could have said, "A suit for false arrest," but I made it, "Only the pleasure of my company."

There was one point of resemblance between Purley and Carol Annis, just one: no sense of humor. "But," he said, "Lieutenant Rowcliff is expecting you, and you're a material witness in a homicide case, and you were up there working on the suspects."

"You could arrest me as a material witness," I suggested.

He uttered a word that I was glad the hackie wasn't there to hear, and added, "You'd clam up and in the morning you'd be out on bail. I know it's after midnight, but the lieutenant is expecting you."

He's a proud man, Purley is, and I wouldn't go so far as to say that he has nothing to be proud of. He's not a bad cop, as cops go. It was a temptation to keep him dangling for a while, to see how long it would take him to bring himself to the point of coming right out and asking for it, but it was late and I needed some sleep.

"You realize," I said, "that's it's a waste of time and energy. You can tell him everything we said, and if he tried to go into other aspects with me I'll only start making cracks and he'll start stuttering. It's perfectly useless."

"Yeah, I know, but—"

"But the lieutenant expects me."

He nodded. "It was him Nora Jaret told about it, and he sent me. The inspector wasn't around."

"Okay. In the interest of justice, I'll give him an hour. That's understood? Exactly one hour."

"It's not understood with me." He was empathic. "When we get there you're his and he's welcome to you. I don't know if he can stand you for an hour."

AT NOON THE NEXT day, Thursday, Fritz stood at the end of Wolfe's desk, consulting with him on a major point of policy: whether to switch to another source of supply for watercress. The quality had been below par, which for them means perfection, for nearly a week. I was at my desk, yawning. It had been after two o'clock when I got home from my chat with Lieutenant Rowcliff, and with nine hours' sleep in two nights I was way behind.

The hour since Wolfe had come down at eleven o'clock from his morning session with the orchids had been spent, most of it, by me reporting and Wolfe listening. My visit with Rowcliff needed only a couple of sentences, since the only detail of any importance was that it had taken me eight minutes to get him stuttering, but Wolfe wanted my conversation with the girls verbatim, and also my impressions and conclusions. I told him my basic conclusion was that the only way she could be nailed, barring a stroke of luck, would be by a few dozen men sticking to the routine—her getting the poison and her connection with Pyle.

"And," I added, "her connection with Pyle may be hopeless. In fact, it probably is. If it's Helen Iacono, what she told us is no help. If what she told us is true she had no reason to kill him, and if it isn't true how are you going to prove it? If it's one of the others she is certainly no half-wit, and there may be absolutely nothing to link her up. Being very careful with visitors to your penthouse is fine as long as you're alive, but it has its drawbacks if one of them feeds you arsenic. It may save her neck."

He was regarding me without enthusiasm. "You are saying in effect that it must be left to the police. I don't have a few dozen men. I can expose her only by a stroke of luck."

"Right. Or a stroke of genius. That's your department. I make no conclusions about genius."

"Then why the devil were you going to bring them to me at midnight? Don't answer. I know. To badger me."

"No, sir. I told you. I had got nowhere with them. I had got them looking at each other out of the corners of their eyes, but that was all. I kept on talking, and suddenly I heard myself inviting them to come home with me. I was giving them the excuse that I wanted them to discuss it with you, but that may have been just a cover for certain instincts that a man is entitled to. They are very attractive girls—all but one."

"Which one?"

"That's what we're working on."

He probably would have harped on it if Fritz hadn't entered to present the watercress problem. As they wrestled with it, dealing with it from all angles, I swiveled my back to them so I could do my yawning in private. Finally, they got it settled, deciding to give the present source one more week and then switch if the quality didn't improve; and then I heard Fritz say, "There's another matter, sir. Felix phoned me this morning. He and Zoltan would like an appointment with you after lunch, and I would like to be present. They suggested half-past two, if that will suit your convenience."

"What is it?" Wolfe demanded. "Something wrong at the restaurant?"

"No, sir. Concerning the misfortune of Tuesday evening."

"What about it?"

"It would be better for them to tell you. It is their concern."

I swiveled for a view of Fritz's face. Had Felix and Zoltan been holding out on us? Fritz's expression didn't tell me, but it did tell Wolfe something: that it would be unwise for him to insist on knowing the nature of Felix's and Zoltan's concern because Fritz had said all he intended to. There is no one more obliging than Fritz, but also there is no one more immovable when he has taken a stand. So Wolfe merely said that half-past two would be convenient. When Fritz had left I offered to go to the kitchen and see if I could pry it out of him, but Wolfe said no, apparently it wasn't urgent.

As it turned out, it wasn't. Wolfe and I were still in the dining room, with coffee, when the doorbell rang at 2:25 and Fritz answered it, and when we crossed the hall to the office Felix was in the red leather chair, Zoltan was in one of the yellow ones, and Fritz was standing. Fritz had removed his apron and put on a jacket, which was quite proper. People do not attend business conferences in aprons.

When we had exchanged greetings, and Fritz had been told to sit down and had done so, and Wolfe and I had gone to our desks, Felix spoke. "You won't mind, Mr. Wolfe, if I ask a question? Before I say why we requested an appointment?"

Wolfe told him no, go ahead.

"Because," Felix said, "we would like to know this first. We are under the impression that the police are making no progress. They haven't said so, they tell us nothing, but we have the impression. Is it true?"

"It was true at two o'clock this morning, twelve hours ago. They may have learned something by now, but I doubt it."

"Do you think they will soon make progress? That they will soon be successful?"

"I don't know. I can only conjecture. Archie thinks that unless they have a stroke of luck the inquiry will be long and laborious, and even then may fail. I'm inclined to agree with him."

Felix nodded. "That is what we fear—Zoltan and I and others at the restaurant. It is causing a most regrettable atmosphere. A few of our most desirable patrons make jokes, but most of them do not, and some of them do not come. We do not blame them. For the *maître d'hôtel* and one of our chefs to assist at a dinner where a guest is served poison—that is not pleasant. If the—"

"Confound it, Felix! I have avowed my responsibility. I have apologized. Are you here for the gloomy satisfaction of reproaching me?"

"No, sir." He was shocked. "Of course not. We came to say that if the poisoner is not soon discovered, and then the affair will be forgotten, the effect on the restaurant may be serious. And if the police are making no progress that may happen, so we appeal to you. We wish to engage your professional services. We know that with you there would be no question. You would solve it quickly and completely. We know it wouldn't be proper to pay you from restaurant funds, since you are the trustee, so we'll pay you with our own money. There was a meeting of the staff last night, and all will contribute, in a proper ration. We appeal to you."

Zoltan stretched out a hand, arm's length. "We appeal to you," he said.

"Pfui," Wolfe grunted.

He had my sympathy. Not only was their matter-of-fact confidence in his prowess highly flattering, but also their appealing instead of demanding, since he had got them into it, was extremely touching. But a man with a long-standing reputation for being hard and blunt simply can't afford the softer feelings, no matter what the provocation. It called for great self-control.

Felix and Zoltan exchanged looks. "He said 'pfui,' " Zoltan told Felix.

"I heard him," Felix snapped, "I have ears."

Fritz spoke. "I wished to be present," he said, "so I could add my appeal to theirs. I offered to contribute, but they said no."

Wolfe took them in, his eyes going right to left and back again. "This is preposterous," he declared. "I said 'pfui' not in disgust but in astonishment. I am solely to blame for this mess, but you offer to pay me to clean it up. Preposterous! You should know that I have already bestirred myself. Archie?"

"Yes, sir. At least you have bestirred me."

He skipped it. "And," he told them, "your coming is opportune. Before lunch I was sitting here considering the situation, and I concluded that the only way to manage the affair with dispatch is to get the wretch to betray herself; and I conceived a plan. For it I need your cooperation. Yours, Zoltan. Your help is essential. Will you give it? I appeal to you."

Zoltan upturned his palms and raised his shoulders. "But yes! But how?"

"It is complicated. Also it will require great dexterity and aplomb. How are you on the telephone? Some people are not themselves, not entirely at ease, when they are phoning. A few are even discomfited. Are you?"

"No." He reflected. "I don't think so. No."

"If you are it won't work. The plan requires that you telephone five of those women this afternoon. You will first call Miss Iacono, tell her who you are, and ask her to meet you somewhere—in some obscure restaurant. You will say that on Tuesday evening, when you told me that you had not seen one of them return for a second plate, you were upset and flustered by what had happened, and later, when the police questioned you, you were afraid to contradict yourself and tell the truth. But now that the notoriety is harming the restaurant you feel that you may have to reveal the fact that you did see her return for a second plate, but that before—"

"But I didn't!" Zoltan cried. "I told—"

"*Tais-toi!*" Felix snapped at him.

Wolfe resumed. "—but that before you do so you wish to discuss it with her. You will say that one reason you have kept silent is that you have been unable to believe that anyone as attractive and charming as she is could be guilty of such a crime. A parenthesis. I should have said at the beginning that you must not try to parrot my words. I am giving you only the substance; the words must be your own, those you would naturally use. You understand that?"

"Yes, sir." Zoltan's hands were clasped tight.

"So don't try to memorize my words. Your purpose is to get her to agree to meet you. She will of course assume that you intend to blackmail her, but you will not say so. You will try to give her the impression, in everything you say and in your tone of voice, that you will not demand money from her, but expect her favors. In short, that you desire her. I can't tell you how to convey that impression; I must leave that to you. The only requisite is that she must be convinced that if she refuses to meet you, you will go at once to the police and tell them the truth."

"Then you know," Zoltan said. "Then she is guilty."

"Not at all. I haven't the slightest idea who is guilty. When you have finished with her you will phone the other four and repeat the performance—Miss Choate, Miss Annis, Miss—"

"My God, Mr. Wolfe! That's impossible!"

"Not impossible, merely difficult. You alone can do it, for they know your voice. I considered having Archie do it, imitating your voice, but it would be too risky. You said you would help, but there's no use trying it if the bare idea appalls you. Will you undertake it?"

"I don't . . . I would . . ."

"He will," Felix said. "He is like that. He only needs to swallow it. He will do it well. But I must ask, can he be expected to get them all to agree to meet him? The guilty one, yes, but the others?"

"Certainly not. There is much to discuss and arrange. The innocent ones will react variously according to their tempers. One or more of them will probably inform the police, and I must provide for that contingency with Mr. Cramer." To Zoltan: "Since it is possible that one of the innocent ones will agree to meet you, for some unimaginable reason, you will have to give them different hours for the appointments. There are many details to settle, but that is mere routine. The key is you. You must, of course, rehearse, and into a telephone transmitter. There are several stations on the house phone. You will go to Archie's room and speak from there. We will listen at the other stations: Archie in the plant rooms, I in my room, Fritz in the kitchen, and Felix here. Archie will handle the other end of the conversation; he is much better qualified than I to improvise the responses of young women.

"Do you want me to repeat the substance of what you are to say before rehearsal?"

Zoltan opened his mouth and closed it again.

"Yes," he said.

SERGEANT PURLEY STEBBINS SHIFTED his fanny for the nth time in two hours. "She's not coming," he muttered. "It's nearly eight o'clock." His chair was about half big enough for his personal dimensions.

We were squeezed in a corner of the kitchen of John Piotti's little restaurant on 14th Street between Second and Third Avenues. On the midget table between us were two notebooks, his and mine, and a small metal case. Of the three cords extending from the case, the two in front went to the earphones we had on, and the one at the back ran down the wall, through the floor, along the basement ceiling toward the front, back up through the floor, and on through a tabletop, where it was connected to a microphone hidden in a bowl of artificial flowers. The installation, a rush order, had cost Wolfe $191.67. Permission to have it made had cost him nothing because he had once got John Piotti out of a difficulty and hadn't soaked him beyond reason.

"We'll have to hang on," I said. "You never can tell with a red-head."

The exposed page of my notebook was blank, but Purley had written on his. As follows:

Helen Iacono	6:00 P.M.
Peggy Choate	7:30 P.M.
Carol Annis	9:00 P.M.
Lucy Morgan	10:30 P.M.
Nora Jaret	12:00 P.M.

It was in my head. If I had had to write it down I would certainly have made 1:00 "P.M." do, but policemen are trained to do things right.

"Anyhow," Purley said, "we know damn well who it is."

"Don't count your poisoners," I said, "before they're hatched." It was pretty feeble, but I was tired and still short on sleep.

I hoped to heaven he was right, since otherwise the operation was a flop. So far everything had been fine. After half an hour of rehearsing, Zoltan had been wonderful. He had made the five calls from the extension in my room, and when he was through I told him his name should be in lights on a Broadway marquee. The toughest job had been getting Inspector Cramer to agree to Wolfe's terms, but he had no good answer to Wolfe's argument that if he insisted on changing the rules Zoltan wouldn't play. So Purley was in the kitchen with me, Cramer was with Wolfe in the office, prepared to stay for dinner, Zoltan was at the restaurant table with the hidden mike, and two homicide dicks, one male and one female, were at another table twenty feet away. One of the most elaborate charades Nero Wolfe had ever staged.

Purley was right when he said we knew who it was, but I was right too—she hadn't been hatched yet. The reactions to Zoltan's calls had settled it. Helen Iacono had been indignant and after a couple of minutes had hung up on him, and had immediately phoned the district attorney's office. Peggy Choate had let him finish his spiel and then called him a liar, but she had not said definitely that she wouldn't meet him, and the DA or police hadn't heard from her. Carol Annis, after he had spoken his lines, had used only ten words: "Where can I meet you?" and, after he had told her where and when: "All right, I'll be there." Lucy Morgan had coaxed him along, trying to get him to fill it all in on the phone, had finally said she would keep the appointment, and then had rushed downtown and rung our doorbell, told me her tale, demanded that I accompany her to the rendezvous, and insisted on seeing Wolfe. I had to promise to go to get rid of her. Nora Jaret had called him assorted names, from liar on up, or on down, and had told him she had a friend listening in on an extension, which was almost certainly a lie. Neither we nor the law had had a peep from her.

So it was Carol Annis with the corn-silk hair, that was plain enough, but there was no salt on her tail. If she was really smart and really tough she might decide to sit tight and not come, figuring that when they came at her with Zoltan's story she would say he was either mistaken or lying, and we would be up a stump. If she was dumb and only fairly tough she might scram. Of course, they would find her and haul her back, but if she said Zoltan was lying and she had run because she thought she was being framed, again we would be up a stump. But if she was both smart and tough but not quite enough of either, she would turn up at nine o'clock and join Zoltan. From there on it would be up to him, but that had been rehearsed too, and after his performance on the phone, I thought he would deliver.

At half-past eight Purley said, "She's not coming," and removed his earphone.

"I never thought she would," I said. The "she" was of course Peggy Choate, whose hour had been 7:30. "I said you never can tell with a redhead merely to make conversation."

Purley signaled to Piotti, who had been hovering around most of the time, and he brought us a pot of coffee and two fresh cups. The minutes were snails, barely moving. When we had emptied the cups I poured more. At 8:48 Purley put his earphone back on. At 8:56 I asked, "Shall I do a countdown?"

"You'd clown in the hot seat," he muttered, so hoarse that it was barely words. He always gets hoarser as the tension grows; that's the only sign.

It was four minutes past nine when the phone brought me the sound of a chair scraping, then faintly Zoltan's voice saying good evening, and then a female voice, but I couldn't get the words.

"Not loud enough," Purley whispered hoarsely.

"Shut up." I had my pen out. "They're standing up."

There came the sound of chairs scraping, and other little sounds, and then:

Zoltan: Will you have a drink?

Carol: No. I don't want anything.

Zoltan: Won't you eat something?

Carol: I don't feel . . . maybe I will.

Purley and I exchanged glances. That was promising. That sounded as if we might get more than conversation.

Another female voice, belonging to Mrs. Piotti: We have good Osso Buco, madame. Very good. A specialty.

Carol: No, not meat.

Zoltan: A sweet perhaps?

Carol: No.

Zoltan: It is more friendly if we eat. The spaghetti with anchovy sauce is excellent. I had some.

Carol: You had some?

I bit my lip, but he handled it fine.

Zoltan: I've been here half an hour, I wanted so much to see you. I thought I should order something, and I tried that. I might even eat another portion.

Carol: You should know good food. All right.

Mrs. Piotti: Two spaghetti anchovy. Wine? A very good Chianti?

Carol: No. Coffee.

Pause.

Zoltan: You are more lovely without a veil, but the veil is good, too. It makes me want to see behind it. Of course I—

Carol: You have seen behind it, Mr. Mahany.

Zoltan: Ah! You know my name?

Carol: It was in the paper.

Zoltan: I am not sorry that you know it, I want you to know my name, but it will be nicer if you call me Zoltan.

Carol: I might some day. It will depend. I certainly won't call you Zoltan if you go on thinking what you said on the phone. You're mistaken, Mr. Mahany. You didn't see me go back for another plate, because I didn't. I can't believe you would tell a vicious lie about me, so I just think you're mistaken.

Mrs. Piotti, in the kitchen for the spaghetti, came to the corner to stoop and whisper into my free ear, "She's wearing a veil."

Zoltan: I am not mistaken, my dear. That is useless. I know. How could I be mistaken when the first moment I saw you I felt . . . but I will not try to tell you how I felt. If any of the others had come and taken another plate I would have stopped her, but not you. Before you I was dumb. So it is useless.

Needing only one hand for my pen, I used the free one to blow a kiss to Purley.

Carol: I see. So you're sure.

Zoltan: I am, my dear. Very sure.

Carol: But you haven't told the police.

Zoltan: Of course not.

Carol: Have you told Nero Wolfe or Archie Goodwin?

Zoltan: I have told no one. How could I tell anyone? Mr. Wolfe is sure that the one who returned for another plate is the one who killed that man, gave him poison, and Mr. Wolfe is always right. So it is terrible for me. Could I tell anyone that I know you killed a man? You? How could I? That is why I had to see you, to talk with you. If you weren't wearing that veil I could look into your beautiful eyes. I think I know what I would see there. I would see suffering and sorrow. I saw that in your eyes Tuesday evening. I know he made you suffer. I know you wouldn't kill a man unless you had to. That is why—

The voice stopped. That was understandable, since Mrs. Piotti had gone through the door with the spaghetti and coffee and had had time to reach their table. Assorted sounds came as she served them.

Purley muttered, "He's overdoing it," and I muttered back, "No. He's perfect." Mrs. Piotti came over and stood looking down at my notebook. It wasn't until after Mrs. Piotti was back in the kitchen that Carol's voice came.

Carol: That's why I am wearing the veil, Zoltan, because I know it's in my eyes. You're right. I had to. He did make me suffer. He ruined my life.

Zoltan: No, my dear. Your life is not ruined. No! No matter what he did. Was he . . . did he . . .

I was biting my lip again. Why didn't he give them the signal?

The food had been served and presumably they were eating. He had been told that it would be pointless to try to get her to give him any details of her relations with Pyle, since they would almost certainly be lies. Why didn't he give the signal? Her voice was coming:

Carol: He promised to marry me. I'm only twenty-two years old, Zoltan. I didn't think I would ever let a man touch me again, but the way you . . . I don't know. I'm glad you know I killed him because it will be better now, to know that somebody knows. To know that *you* know. Yes, I had to kill him, I *had* to, because if I didn't I would have had to kill myself. Some day I may tell you what a fool I was, how I—Oh!

Zoltan: What? What's the matter?

Carol: My bag. I left it in my car. Out front. And I didn't lock the car. A blue Plymouth hardtop. Would you . . . I'll go . . .

Zoltan: I'll get it.

The sound came of his chair scraping, then faintly his footsteps, and then silence. But the silence was broken in ten seconds, whereas it would have taken him much longer to go for the purse and return. What broke it was a male voice saying, "I'm an officer of the law, Miss Annis" and a noise from Carol. Purley, shedding his earphone, jumped up and went, and I followed, notebook in hand.

It was quite a tableau. The male dick stood with a hand on Carol's shoulder. Carol sat stiff, her chin up, staring straight ahead. The female dick, not much older than Carol, stood facing her from across the table, holding with both hands, at breast level, a plate of spaghetti. She spoke to Purley. "She put something in it and then stuck something in her dress. I saw her in my mirror."

I moved in. After all, I was in charge, under the terms Cramer had agreed to. "Thank you, Miss Annis," I said. "You were a help. On a signal from Zoltan they were going to start a commotion to give him an excuse to leave the table, but you saved them the trouble. I thought you'd like to know. Come on, Zoltan. All over. According to plan."

He had entered and stopped three paces off, a blue handbag under his arm. As he moved toward us, Purley put out a hand. "I'll take that."

CRAMER WAS IN THE red leather chair. Carol Annis was in a yellow one facing Wolfe's desk, with Purley on one side of her and his female colleague on the other. The male colleague had been sent to the laboratory with the plate of spaghetti and a small roll of paper that had been fished from inside Carol's dress. Fritz, Felix, and Zoltan were on the couch near the end of my desk.

"I will not pretend, Miss Annis," Wolfe was saying. "One reason that I persuaded Mr. Cramer to have you brought here first on your way to limbo was that I needed to appease my rancor. You had injured and humiliated not only me, but also one of my most valued friends, Fritz Brenner, and two other men whom I esteem, and I had arranged the situation that gave you your opportunity; and I wished them to witness your own humiliation, contrived by me in my presence."

"That's enough of that," Cramer growled.

Wolfe ignored him. "I admit the puerility of that reason, Miss Annis, but in candor I wanted to acknowledge it. A better reason was that I wished to ask you a few questions. You took such prodigious risks that it is hard to believe in your sanity, and it would give me no satisfaction to work vengeance on a madwoman. What would you have done if Felix's eyes had been on you when you entered with the plate of poison and went to Mr. Pyle? Or if, when you returned to the kitchen for a second plate, Zoltan had challenged you? What would you have done?"

No answer. Apparently, she was holding her gaze straight at Wolfe, but from my angle it was hard to tell because she still had the veil on. Asked by Cramer to remove it, she had refused. When the female dick had extracted the roll of paper from inside Carol's dress she had asked Cramer if she should pull the veil off and Cramer had said no. No rough stuff.

There was no question about Wolfe's gaze at her. He was forward in his chair, his palms flat on his desk. He persisted. "Will you answer me, Miss Annis?"

She wouldn't.

"Are you a lunatic, Miss Annis?"

She wasn't saying.

Wolfe's head jerked to me. "Is she deranged, Archie?"

That was unnecessary. When we're alone I don't particularly mind his insinuations that I presume to be an authority on women, but there was company present. I gave him a look and snapped, "No comment."

He returned to her. "Then that must wait. I leave to the police such matters as your procurement of the poison and your relations with Mr. Pyle, mentioning only that you cannot now deny possession of arsenic, since you used it a second time this evening. It will unquestionably be found in the spaghetti and in the roll of paper you concealed in your dress; and so, manifestly, if you are mad you are also ruthless and malevolent. You may have been intolerably provoked by Mr. Pyle, but not by Zoltan. He presented himself not as a nemesis, but as a bewitched champion. He offered his homage, making no demands, and your counteroffer was death."

"You lie," Carol said. "And he lied. He was going to lie about me. He didn't see me go back for a second plate, but he was going to say he did. And you lie. He did make demands. He threatened me."

Wolfe's brows went up. "Then you haven't been told?"

"Told what?"

"That you were overheard. That is the other question I had for you. I have no apology for contriving the trap, but you deserve to know you are in its jaws. All that you and Zoltan said was heard by two men at the other end of a wire in another room, and they recorded it—Mr. Stebbins of the police, now at your left, and Mr. Goodwin."

"You lie," she said.

"No, Miss Annis. This isn't the trap; it has already been sprung. You have it, Mr. Stebbins?"

Purley nodded. He hates to answer questions from Wolfe.

"Archie?"

"Yes, sir."

"Did Zoltan threaten her or make demands?"

"No, sir. He followed instructions."

He returned to Carol. "Now you know. I wanted to make sure of that. To finish, since you may have had a just and weighty grievance against Mr. Pyle, I would myself prefer to see you made to account for your attempt to kill Zoltan, but that is not in my discretion. In any case, my rancor is appeased, and I hold—"

"That's enough," Cramer blurted, leaving his chair. "I didn't agree to let you preach at her all night. Bring her along, Sergeant."

As Purley arose a voice came. "May I say something?" It was Fritz. Heads turned as he left the couch and moved, detouring around Zoltan's feet and Purley's bulk to get to Carol, and turning to stand looking down at her.

"On account of what Mr. Wolfe said," he told her. "He said you injured me, and that is true. It is also true that I wanted him to find you. I can't speak for Felix, and you tried to kill Zoltan and I can't speak for him, but I can speak for myself. I forgive you."

"You lie," Carol said.

Cheese Blinis

Blini:
   1 cup flour
   ½ tsp. salt
   1 tsp. baking soda
   2 Tbsp. sugar
   2 eggs at room temperature, beaten until light yellow
   ⅔ cup milk
   ⅓ cup water
   1 tsp. vanilla

Filling:
   1½ cups smooth-curd cottage cheese
   ¼ cup egg substitute
   1 Tbsp. butter, softened
   1 Tbsp. vanilla
   Butter-flavored Pam
   Sour cream to garnish
   Confectioner's sugar to garnish
   Cinnamon to garnish

MAKE FILLING:

Mix cottage cheese, egg substitute, butter, and vanilla together. Beat until smooth.

MAKE BLINI:

Sift flour, salt, baking powder, and sugar together. Mix eggs, milk, water, and vanilla together in a bowl. Add dry ingredients all at once. Mix just until blended. (Over-beating makes them tough.) Batter will be thin.

SPRAY A SKILLET with Pam. Heat until drops of water dance on the surface. Pour batter onto skillet two tablespoonfuls at a time and spread thinly across the pan by tipping it or by spreading batter quickly about with the back of the spoon. Cook on one side only.

Slide each cake off the grill to a damp tea towel when it is done— top will no longer be glossy. Cook until batter is gone, respraying grill with Pam as needed.

ASSEMBLE BLINI:

Place two tablespoons of filling in the center of each pancake. Fold over sides of cake to make burrito-like shape with filling inside. Place filled cakes seam-side down on a serving plate. Garnish each cake with a dollop of sour cream, a shake of cinnamon, and a shake of confectioner's sugar.

Authors' Biographies

Stanley Ellin (1916–1986) stood the mystery genre on its head with his evocatively written crime fiction. His style, as pithy and poignant as any literary writer's; his ideas, the equal of such great idea-men as Roald Dahl and Saki; and his worldview, which was every bit as complex as some of his darker protagonists, all combined to create a paradigm that was a breath of fresh air from the delicate cozies and hard-boiled noir that until then had been staples of the genre. For all this, though, he also had a sense of everyday life and everyday people that few in the genre ever came close to matching. Perhaps this was because, early in his life, he was a steelworker, a dairy farmer, and a teacher. While he is primarily thought of as a short-story writer, he wrote a number of excellent novels, among them *The Eighth Circle* and *Mirror, Mirror on the Wall.*

Joyce Christmas is the creator of two mystery series, one featuring a retired office manager named Betty Trenka, the other centered on an English noblewoman, Lady Margaret Priam, who lives and sleuths in New York City. A former book and magazine editor, she has also written three other novels and several children's plays. Recent novels include *Mood to Murder* and *Dying Well.*

Ruth Rendell's stories of psychological suspense always reveal a new twist in the human psyche that seemed to be just waiting for an author like her to reveal it. The author of more than twenty novels and innumerable short stories, she explores the dark recesses of the mind that make men and women do inexplicable things. Her short fiction has regularly appeared in the year's best anthologies, as well as *The Best British Mysteries of the 20th Century*. Recent novels include *Bloodlines, Keys to the Street, The Reason Why*, and *Road Rage*.

Walter Satterthwaite is adept at all facets of the mystery genre, as his nominations for the Agatha and Shamus Awards indicate. His two series are as different as night and day. In his historical series, Harry Houdini and Sir Arthur Conan Doyle team up to solve a baffling crime in the novel *Escapade*, which won the French Prix du Roman d'Aventures Award. His second series is contemporary, featuring Santa Fe sleuth Joshua Croft and his partner Rota Mondragon. A former encyclopedia salesman, proofreader, bartender, and restaurant manager, Satterthwaite lives in Santa Fe, New Mexico.

M. D. Lake's fiction has appeared in anthologies such as *The Mysterious West* and *Funny Bones*. His most recent novel is *Death Calls the Tune*. A writer with a gift for dialogue and a natural talent for description, here he is at his best in this rather one-sided conversation over a nice cup of tea where several not-so-nice discoveries are made.

Linda Grant is the pseudonym of Linda V. Williams and the author of a detective series featuring private investigator Catherine Saylor and her partner, Jesse. Her short fiction has appeared in *The Mysterious West, The First Lady Murders*, and *Women on the Case*. Twice nominated for the Anthony Award, she lives and works in Berkeley, California. Recent novels include *Vampire Bytes* and *Remind Me Who I Am, Again*.

Bill Pronzini is one of those writers whose long career shows steady and remarkable progress. While he was always an above-average professional, the fourth decade of his career saw him produce novels of true distinction, *Blue Lonesome* and *A Wasteland of Strangers* among them. His "Nameless" novels, popular now for three full decades, are really chapters in the life of a working-class private investigator who lives in the spiritual epicenter of modern-day San Francisco. Students of history as well as crime fiction will be reading his fiction a hundred years from now.

Bill Crider won the Anthony Award for his first novel in the Sheriff Dan Rhodes series. His first novel in the Truman Smith series was nominated for a Shamus Award, and a third series features college English professor Carl Burns. His short stories have appeared in numerous anthologies, including past *Cat Crimes II* and *III*, *Celebrity Vampires*, *Once Upon a Crime*, and *Werewolves*. His recent work includes collaborating on a series of cozy mysteries with television personality Willard Scott. The first novel, *Death under Blue Skies*, was published in 1997, and the second, *Murder in the Mist*, was recently released.

When you write about **Ed Hoch**, the temptation is to dwell on his prolific writing career. Probably the most abundant short-story writer in the history of mystery, with a story in every issue of *Ellery Queen's Mystery Magazine* for more than twenty years, what is often overlooked is the sheer quality of his work. Whether he's working on a locked-room setup featuring his police detective Captain Leopold, or going rustic with one of his more laid-back series characters, or even getting tough (his collection of hard-boiled stories will be published soon), he is always totally in charge of his material. And what wonderful material it is. His stories are classic treatises on the proper execution of the mystery story.

Caroline Benton was born in Somerset, England, in 1947. She now lives in France and is currently working on a full-length mystery. This is the first time her work has been published in book form.

Peter Crowther is the editor or coeditor of nine anthologies and the coauthor (with James Lovegrove) of the novel *Escardy Gap*.

Since the early 1990s, he has sold some seventy short stories and poems to a wide variety of magazines and chapbooks on both sides of the Atlantic. He has also recently added two chapbooks, *Forest Plains* and *Fugue on a G-String*, and a single-author collection, *The Longest Single Note*, to his credits. His review columns and critical essays on the fields of fantasy, horror, and science fiction appear regularly in *Interzone* and *Hellnotes* Internet magazine. He has also served on the board of trustees of the Horror Writer's Association. He lives in Harrogate, England, with his wife and two sons.

Janwillem van de Wetering, born in Rotterdam, the Netherlands, is a former policeman and businessman now living in rural Maine. In 1971, when he was forty-one, he launched his writing career by publishing *The Empty Mirror*, an autobiographical account of his experiences in a Buddhist monastery. Inspired by the mystery fiction of George Simenon, he tapped into his experience in the Amsterdam Special Constabulary, which he joined in lieu of being drafted into the military. He has written more than thirteen novels featuring Adjutant Grijpstra and Sergeant de Gier, as well as non-fiction and children's books.

Barbara Collins's other short fiction can be found in *Marilyn: Shades of Blonde, Till Death Do Us Part*, and *The Year's 25 Finest Crime and Mystery Stories, Third Edition*. Adept at many forms of mystery fiction, she lives in Muscatine, Iowa, with her husband, novelist Max Allan Collins, and their son Nathan.

Nedra Tyre is a prolific contributor to the mystery magazines, especially *Alfred Hitchcock's Mystery Magazine* and *Ellery Queen's Mystery Magazine*. She has also written several mystery novels, notably *Hall of Death* and *Twice So Fair*.

Joyce Carol Oates, a master of psychological fiction in both novel length and short form, is arguably among the top authors in the United States. She examines the usually fragile bonds that hold people together, whether it be by marriage or blood, then introduces the catalyst that more often than not tears that relationship apart, all the while imbuing her characters with a fully realized life of their own that practically makes them walk off the page. Her most recent novel is *My Heart Laid Bare*, and she recently edited the anthology *Telling Stories: An Anthology for Writers*. Her most recent book is *Blonde*, an exploration of the life of Marilyn Monroe.

Gillian Linscott is known for her series of Edwardian novels featuring radical suffragette Nell Bray, which now includes five books. A former Parliamentary reporter for the BBC, she has also written a historical mystery set in Alaska as well as a contemporary mystery series featuring ex-policeman-turned-physical-trainer Birdie Linnett. Her short fiction appears in such anthologies as *Murder, They Wrote* and *Murder Most Medieval*. She lives with her husband, nonfiction author Tony Geraghty, in England.

Barbara D'Amato is an accomplished writer whose short fiction has appeared in *I, P.I.*, *Cat Crimes*, and *Malice Domestic V*. The main protagonists of her short fiction, Chicago police officers Suzanne Figueroa and Norm Bennis, made their first novel-length appearance in *Killer.app*. Her other series features Catherine "Cat" Marsala, an investigative reporter in Chicago. Her mystery tales range from poignant to parsimonious, cozy to chilling, and always leave a reader wanting more.

While **Rex Stout** (1886–1975) will be fondly remembered for his creation of the corpulent detective and gourmet Nero Wolfe, during his writing career of more than forty years he produced mainstream and science fiction novels and also founded his own publishing house, Vanguard Press. After serving as a U.S. Navy yeoman on President Theodore Roosevelt's yacht, he worked as a bookkeeper and hotel manager before turning to writing in 1927. During his lifetime, he was active in many authors' organizations, including the Author's League of America, the Author's Guild, and the Mystery Writers of America.

Copyrights and Permissions

11/07
HO